Mike Cutler.

Gina tried to roll over and push herself up, but she couldn't seem to get her arm beneath her. The snow and clouds and black running shoes all swirled together inside her head.

"Easy, Gina. I need you to lie still. An ambulance is on its way. You've injured your shoulder. I don't want you to aggravate it. And if that bullet is still inside you, I don't want it traveling anywhere." His warm hand cupped her face and she realized just how cold she was. She wished she could wrap her whole body up in that kind of heat. She looked up into his stern expression. "Stay with me."

"Catnip."

"What?"

Her eyelids drifted shut.

"Gina!"

The last thing she saw was her blood seeping into the snow. The last thing she felt was the man's strong hands pressing against her breast and shoulder. The last thing she heard was his voice on her radio.

"Officer down. I repeat, officer down!"

CLAIMING
HER GROUND

USA TODAY BESTSELLING AUTHOR
Julie Miller &
Janie Crouch

Previously published as *Kansas City Cop* and
Armed Response

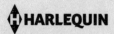

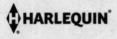

Recycling programs
for this product may
not exist in your area.

ISBN-13: 978-1-335-42472-3
Claiming Her Ground
Copyright © 2021 by Harlequin Books S.A.

Kansas City Cop
First published in 2018. This edition published in 2021.
Copyright © 2018 by Julie Miller

Armed Response
First published in 2018. This edition published in 2021.
Copyright © 2018 by Janie Crouch

This edition published by arrangement with Harlequin Books S.A.

For questions and comments about the quality of this book,
please contact us at CustomerService@Harlequin.com.

Harlequin Enterprises ULC
22 Adelaide St. West, 40th Floor
Toronto, Ontario M5H 4E3, Canada
www.Harlequin.com

Printed in U.S.A.

CONTENTS

Julie Miller is an award-winning *USA TODAY* bestselling author of breathtaking romantic suspense—with a National Readers' Choice Award and a Daphne du Maurier Award, among other prizes. She has also earned an *RT Book Reviews* Career Achievement Award. For a complete list of her books, monthly newsletter and more, go to juliemiller.org.

Books by Julie Miller

Harlequin Intrigue

Personal Protection
Target on Her Back
K-9 Protector

The Precinct

Beauty and the Badge
Takedown
KCPD Protector
Crossfire Christmas
Military Grade Mistletoe
Kansas City Cop

The Precinct: Bachelors in Blue

APB: Baby
Kansas City Countdown
Necessary Action
Protection Detail

Visit the Author Profile page at Harlequin.com for more titles.

KANSAS CITY COP

Julie Miller

To Edna Castillo, reader and bookseller extraordinaire.
A fellow *The Wizard of Oz* fan, too!
Thanks for your help with the Spanish.
Any mistakes are my own.

Chapter 1

The bright sunlight glaring off the fresh February snow through the police cruiser's windshield was as blinding as the headache forming behind Officer Gina Galvan's dark brown eyes.

"No, Tia Mami, I can't." She glanced across the front seat to her partner, Derek Johnson, and silently mouthed an apology for yet another family crisis infringing on their shift time with KCPD. "I don't get off until seven. And that's if our paperwork's done. That's why I left my car at home and took the bus this morning—so Sylvie could drive you and Tio Papi to his doctor's appointment."

"Sylvie no come home from school," her great-aunt Lupe replied quietly, as though apologizing for the news.

"What? Where is she?"

"Javi said he saw her riding with that boyfriend of hers we don't like."

"Seriously?" Anger and concern flooded Gina's cheeks with heat. The boyfriend they didn't like had too much money to have gotten it in the old neighborhood by any legal means. But Bobby Estes's flashy cars and devilish good looks were too much for Gina's dreamy, dissatisfied baby sister to resist. And if Bobby was a teenager, as he claimed, then Gina was Santa Claus. Clearly, her last conversation with Sylvie, about the definition of statutory rape and learning to act like an adult if she wanted to be treated like one, had not made a memorable impact. "I'm going to have to ground her. That's all there is to it."

But dealing with her sister's rash choices didn't get Tio Papi to the doctor's office. Gina slipped her fingers beneath the base of her wavy brunette ponytail to massage the tension gathering at the nape of her neck.

Derek nudged her with his elbow. "Need a ride home tonight?"

Missing the point! Although, in his defense, Derek was only hearing half the conversation. Gina summoned a smile for the friend she'd been riding a squad car with for almost two years now. "It's okay. Just a miscommunication at home."

"Gotta love our families, right?" Derek teased. She knew he had a strained relationship with his father. And there was no love lost for Derek's mother, who'd divorced his father and moved away, leaving her teenage son behind to be raised by an aging hippie who had trouble keeping a job and staying out of jail.

A difficult upbringing was part of the common ground they shared, and had helped solidify their working relationship and understanding of each other. Gina gave the sarcasm right back, whispering so her great-aunt couldn't hear. "Do we really have to?"

Derek grinned and directed her back to her phone. "Tell Aunt Lupe hi for me, okay?"

"I will. Tia Mami, Derek says hi."

"You teach that young man to say *hola*, and bring him to dinner sometime."

"I'm working on it." Gina continued the conversation with appropriate responses while her great-aunt rattled on about other concerns she'd have to deal with once she got home. While Lupe talked, Gina concentrated on the scenery as they drove past, partly because it was her job to observe the neighborhood and take note of anything that looked suspicious or unsafe, and partly because she'd already heard the same worried speech too many times before about fast cars and traffic accidents, young men who didn't come to the door to pick up a date and Uncle Rollo's deteriorating health.

Now *there* was something different. Gina lifted her chin for a better look. A tall man in silver and black running gear came around the corner off Pennsylvania Avenue and ran down the narrow side street. A jogger in this neighborhood was unusual. Maybe he was one of those yuppie business owners who'd opened an office in this part of town for a song, or he'd bought a loft in one of the area's abandoned warehouses, thinking he could revitalize a little part of Kansas City. Not for the first time, she considered the irony of people with money moving into this part of the city, while the natives like her were doing all they could to raise enough money to move out.

But irony quickly gave way to other thoughts. The

runner was tall, lean and muscular. Although the stocking cap and wraparound sunglasses he wore masked the top half of his head, the well-trimmed scruff of brown beard on his golden skin was like catnip to her. Plus, she could tell he was fit by the rhythmic clouds of his breath in the cold air. He wasn't struggling to maintain that pace and, for a woman who worked hard to stay physically fit, she appreciated his athleticism.

As they passed each other, he offered her a polite wave, and Gina nodded in return. Since he already knew she'd been staring, she shifted her gaze to the side mirror to watch him run another block. Long legs and a tight butt. Gina's lips curved into a smile. They probably had a lot of scenery like that in the suburbs. A relationship was one thing she didn't have time for at this point in her life. And no way did she want to tie herself to anyone from the neighborhood who might want her to stay. But there was no harm in looking and getting her blood circulating a little faster. After all, it was only twenty-two degrees out, and a woman had to do whatever was necessary to stay warm.

Gina glanced over at her partner. Derek was handsome in his own way. He, too, had brown hair, but his smooth baby face was doing nary a thing for her circulation.

"Do we need to take a detour to your house and have a conversation with your sister? I'd be happy to um, have a word, with that boyfriend of hers." He took his hands off the steering wheel to make air quotes around *have a word*, as if he had ideas about roughing up Bobby on her behalf. As if she couldn't take care of her family's issues herself.

Since the car was moving, Gina guided one hand back to the steering wheel and changed the subject.

She covered the speaker on her phone and whispered, "Hey, since things are quiet right now, why don't you swing by a coffee shop and get us something hot to drink. I haven't been able to shake this chill since that first snow back in October."

Although the remembered impression of Sexy Jogger Guy made that last sentence a lie, her request had the desired effect of diverting Derek's interest in her family problems.

"That I can do. One skinny mocha latte coming up."

Distracted with his new mission, Derek turned the squad car onto a cross street, plowing through a dip filled with dirty slush as they continued their daily patrol through the aging neighborhood. With houses and duplexes so close together that a person could barely walk between them, vehicles parked bumper-to-bumper against the curb and junk piling on porches and spilling into yards, this was a part of the city she knew far too well. Add in the branches of tall, denuded maple trees heavy with three months' worth of snow arching over the yards and narrow streets, and Gina felt claustrophobic. As much as she loved Kansas City and her job as a police officer, she secretly wondered if she was the reincarnation of some Central American ancestor and was meant for living on the high, arid plains of her people with plenty of blue sky and wide-open space, without a single snowflake in sight.

Setting aside her own restless need to escape, Gina turned toward the passenger door to find some privacy for this personal conversation. "Did you call Sylvie?" she asked her great-aunt, once the older woman's need to vent had subsided.

"She don't answer."

"What about Javi?" Her brother, Javier, was twenty-one, although that didn't necessarily mean he was making better choices than Sylvie. She kept hoping for the day when he would step up as the man of the family and allow their great-uncle to truly enjoy his retirement. "Can he drive you?"

"He's already gone. He's picking up some extra hours at work."

Well, that was one plus in the ongoing drama that was Gina's life. Maybe so long as Javi was intent on saving up to buy a truck, he would focus on this job and avoid the influence of his former friends who'd made some less productive choices with their lives, like stealing cars, selling drugs and running with gangs. "Good."

"Papi says he can drive," Lupe Molina offered in a hushed, uncertain tone.

Gina sat up as straight as her seat belt and protective vest allowed. "No. Absolutely not. The whole reason he's going for these checkups is because he passed out the last time his blood pressure spiked. He can't be behind the wheel."

"What do I do?" Lupe asked quietly.

As much as she loved her great-aunt and -uncle who'd taken in the three Galvan siblings and raised them after their mother had died, Lupe and Rollo Molina were now both close to eighty and didn't need the hassle of dealing with an attention-craving teenager. Especially not with Rollo's health issues. "I'll call Sylvie. See if I can get her home to help like she promised. If you don't hear from her or me in ten minutes, call the doctor's office and reschedule the appointment for tomorrow. I'll be off except for practicing for my next SWAT test on the shooting range. I'll make sure you get there."

"All right. I can do that. You see? This is where having a young man to help you would be a good thing."

Gina rolled her eyes at the not-so-subtle hint. There was more than one path to success besides getting married and making babies. "I love you, Tia Mami. *Adios.*"

"*Te amo*, Gina. You're always my good girl."

By the time she disconnected the call, Derek had pulled the black-and-white into the coffee shop's tiny parking lot but was making no effort to get out and let her deal with her family on her own. Instead, he rested the long black sleeve of his uniform on the steering wheel and grinned at her. "Sylvie off on another one of her escapades?"

Gina might as well fill in the blanks for him. "She's supposed to be driving my uncle to the doctor. Instead, she's cruising around the city with a young man who's too old for her."

Derek shook his head. "She does look older than seventeen when she puts on all her makeup." He dropped his green-eyed gaze to her black laced-up work boots. "She's got the family legs, too."

Ignoring the gibe at her five-foot-three-inch height, Gina punched in Sylvie's number. Then she punched Derek's shoulder, giving back the teasing camaraderie they shared. "You're eyeballing my little sister?"

"Hey, when you decorate the Christmas tree, you're supposed to celebrate it."

"Well, you don't get to hang any ornaments on my sister, understand? She's seventeen. You could get into all kinds of trouble with the department. And me."

Derek raised his hands in surrender. "Forget the department. You're the one who scares me. You're about to become one of SWAT's finest. I'm not messing with anyone in your family."

The call went straight to Sylvie's voice mail. "Damn it." Gina tucked her phone back into her vest and held her hand out for Derek's. "Could I borrow yours? Maybe if she doesn't recognize the number, she'll pick up."

"That means I'll have her number in my phone, you know. And Sylvie *is* a hottie."

"Seven. Teen." Gina repeated the warning with a smile and typed in her wayward sister's number.

She'd barely been a teenager herself when her mother had passed away and their long-absent father had willingly signed away his parental rights, leaving the three Galvans orphans in No-Man's Land, one of the toughest neighborhoods in downtown Kansas City. They'd moved out of their cramped apartment into a slightly less cramped house. Instead of prostitutes, drug dealers and gangbangers doing business beneath Gina's bedroom window, they'd graduated to the vicinity of a meth lab, which KCPD had eventually closed down, at the end of the block. Naturalized citizens who were proud to call themselves Americans, her great-aunt and -uncle had stressed the values of education and hard work, and they'd grown up proud but poor. With her diminutive stature, Gina had quickly learned how to handle herself in a fight and project an attitude so that no one would mess with her family or take advantage of her. That hardwired drive to protect her loved ones had morphed into a desire to protect any innocent who needed her help, including this neighborhood and her entire city. But she couldn't forget which side of the tracks the Galvans and Molinas had come from—and just how far she had to go to secure something better for them.

"Hey, don't jinx the SWAT thing for me, okay?" A little bit of her great-aunt and -uncle's superstitious nature buzzed through her thoughts like an annoying gnat she thought she'd gotten rid of. If she made Special Weapons and Tactics, the rise in status with the department and subsequent raise in pay would finally allow her to move her whole family into a house with a real yard in a safer suburb. She wasn't afraid of setting goals and working hard to achieve them, but it was rare that she allowed anything so personal as wanting some open space to plant a proper garden or get a dog or owning a bathroom she didn't have to share with four other people to motivate her. "I'm not the only recruit on Captain Cutler's list of candidates for the new SWAT team he's forming. There are ten people on a list for five spots. Including you."

"Yeah, but you're the toughest."

"Jinxing, remember?" Gina crossed her fingers and kissed her knuckles before touching them to her heart, a throwback from her childhood to cootie shots and negating bad karma. "We all have our talents."

"I'm just repeating what Cutler said at the last training meeting. McBride scored the highest at the shooting range. And you, my kickass little partner, are the one he said he'd least like to face one-on-one in a fight. Take the compliment."

It was on the tip of her tongue to remind Derek that she wasn't his *little* anything, but she was dealing with enough conflict already today. "You're doing well, too, or you'd have been eliminated already. Captain Cutler announces things like that so we stay competitive."

"Hey, I'm not quittin' anything until those new promotions are posted. I only have to be fifth best and I'll still make the team."

"Fifth best?" Gina laughed. "Way to aim high, Johnson."

"It's too bad about Cho, though. He's been acing all the written tests and procedure evaluations."

Gina agreed. Colin Cho was a fellow SWAT candidate who'd suffered three cracked ribs when he'd been shot twice while directing traffic around a stalled car on the North Broadway Freeway in the middle of the night two weeks ago. Only his body armor had prevented the incident from becoming a fatality. "Any idea how he's doing?"

"I heard he's up and around, but he won't be running any races soon. He's restricted to desk duty for the time being. I wonder if they'll replace him on the candidate list or just shorten it to nine potential SWAT officers."

"Cho's too good an officer to remove from contention," Gina reasoned, hitting the phone icon on the screen to connect the call.

"But there *is* a deadline," Derek reminded her. "If he can't pass the physical…"

The number rang several times before her sister finally picked up. "Sylvie Galvan's phone," a man answered.

Not her sister but that slimy lothario who struck Gina as a mobster wannabe—if he wasn't already running errands and doing small jobs for some of the bigger criminals in town. Gina swallowed the curse on her tongue. She needed to keep this civil if she wanted to get her great-aunt and -uncle the help they needed. "Bobby, put Sylvie on."

"It's your wicked big sister," he announced. The sounds of horns honking and traffic moving in the background told her they were in his car. Hopefully, in the front seat and not stretched out together in the back. "What will you give me to hand you this phone?"

That teasing request was for her sister.

Gina cringed at the high-pitched sound of her sister's giggles. She groaned at the wet, smacking sound of a kiss. Or two. So much for keeping it civil. "Bobby Estes, you keep your hands off my sister or I will—"

"Blah, blah, blah." Sylvie was on the line now. Finally. She could live without the breathless gasps and giggles and the picture the noises created of a practically grown man making out with her innocent sister. "What do you want?"

"You forgot Tio Papi's doctor's appointment." Better to stick to the purpose of the phone call than to get into another lecture about the bad choices Sylvie was making. "You promised me you would drive him today."

"Javi can do it."

"He's at work. Besides, it was your responsibility." Her fingers curled into a fist at the sound of her sister's gasp. Really? Bobby couldn't keep his hands to himself for the ten seconds it would take to finish this call? "Do you want me to treat you like a grown-up or not?"

"I just got home from school."

"A half hour ago. I was counting on you. This isn't about me. It's about helping Rollo and Lupe. Do you want to explain to them why you've forgotten them?"

Bobby purred against her sister's mouth, and the offensive noise crawled over Gina's skin. "Is big sis being a downer again? You know she's jealous of us. Hang up, baby."

"Bobby, stop." Sylvie sounded a little irritated with her boyfriend. For once. The shuffling noises and protests made her think Sylvie was pushing him away. Gina suppressed a cheer. "When is the appointment?"

"Four forty-five. Can you do it?"

"Yeah. I can help." Thank goodness Sylvie still had enough little girl in her to idolize her pseudo grandparents. She'd do for them what she wouldn't do for Gina. Or herself, unfortunately. Her tone shifted to Bobby. "I need to go home."

"I said I was taking you out to dinner. I was gonna show you my friend's club," he whined. "Just because Gina's a cop, she doesn't make the rules. She sure as hell isn't in charge of what I do."

"Don't get mad, Bobby. Just drive me home." Sylvie was doing some purring of her own. "I'll make it up to you later."

"Promise?"

"Promise."

"Ooh, I like it when you do that, baby."

Gina wished she could reach through the phone and yank her sister out of Bobby's car before she got into the kind of trouble that even a big sister with a badge couldn't help her with. "Sylvie?"

"I'll call Tia Mami and tell her we're on our way."

"Bobby doesn't need to go with you." A powerful car engine revved in the background. "Seeing him will only upset—"

"Bye."

Bobby shouted an unwanted goodbye. "Bye-bye, big sis."

She groaned when her sister's phone went silent. Gina cursed. "Have I ever mentioned how much I want to use Bobby Estes as one of the dummies in our fight-training classes?"

Derek laughed as he put away his phone. "Once or twice." He opened his door, and Gina shivered at the blast of wintry wind. "I keep telling you that I'd be happy to help run him in."

At least the chill helped some of her temper dissipate, as did Derek's unflinching support. "Bobby's too squeaky clean for that. He does just enough to annoy me, but not enough that I can prove he's committing any kind of crime. And Sylvie isn't about to rat him out."

"Just say the word, and I'm there for you, G." He turned to climb out. "I'll leave the car running so you stay warm."

But the dispatch radio beeped, and he settled back behind the wheel to listen to the details of the all-call. "So much for coffee."

Derek closed the door as the dispatch repeated. "Attention all units in the Westport area. We have a 10-52 reported. Repeat, domestic dispute report. Approach with caution. Suspect believed to be armed with a knife."

"That's the Bismarck place." Derek frowned as he shifted the cruiser into Drive and pulled out onto the street. "I thought Vicki Bismarck took out a restraining order against her ex."

"She did." This wasn't the first time they'd answered a call at the Bismarcks' home. The address was just a couple of blocks from their location. Gina picked up the radio while Derek flipped on the siren and raced through the beginnings of rush-hour traffic. "Unit 4-13 responding."

Her family troubles were forgotten as she pulled up the suspect's name on the laptop mounted on the dashboard. Domestic-disturbance calls were her least favorite kind of call. The situations were unpredictable, and there were usually innocent parties involved. This one was no different.

"Gordon Bismarck. I don't think he's handling the divorce very well." Gina let out a low whistle. "He's got so many D&Ds and domestic-violence calls the list goes on to a second page. No outstanding warrants, though, so we can't just run him in." She glanced over at Derek as they careened around a corner. "Looks like he's not afraid to hurt somebody. You ready for this?"

"I know you've got my back. And I've got yours."

She hoped he meant it because when they pulled up in front of the Bismarck house, they weren't alone. And the men belonging to a trio of motorcycles and a beat-up van didn't look like curiosity seekers who'd gathered to see what all the shouting coming from inside the bungalow was about.

Derek turned off the engine and swore. "How many thugs does it take to terrorize one woman? I hope Vicki's okay. Should I call for reinforcements?"

"Not yet." Gina tracked the men as they put out cigarettes and split up to block the end of the driveway and the sidewalk leading to the front door. Middle-aged. A couple with potbellies. One had prison tats on his neck. Another took a leisurely drink from a flask before tucking it inside the sheepskin-lined jacket he wore. Their bikes were in better shape than they were. But any one of them could be armed. And she could guess that the guy with the flask wasn't the only one who'd been drinking. Judging by what she'd read on the cruiser's computer screen, these were friends, if not former cell mates, of Gordon Bismarck's. Gina's blood boiled in her veins at the lopsided odds. She reached for the door handle. "But keep your radio at the ready."

Gina pushed open the cruiser door and climbed out. "Gentlemen." She rested her hand on the butt of her holstered Glock. "I need you to disperse."

"You *need* us, *querida*?" Flask Man's leer and air kisses weren't even close to intimidating, and she certainly wasn't his *darling* anything.

Derek circled the cruiser, positioning himself closer to the two in the driveway while she faced off against the two on the sidewalk. "In case you don't understand the big word, you need to get on your bikes and ride away."

"We gave Gordy a ride home," Potbelly #1 said, thumbing over his shoulder just as something made of glass shattered inside the house.

A woman's voice cried out, "Gordon, stop it!"

"I paid for this damn house. And I'll—"

Gina needed to get inside to help Vicki Bismarck. But she wasn't going to leave these four aging gang-bangers out here where they could surround the house or lie in wait for her and Derek to come back outside. "We're not interested in you boys today," she articulated in a sharp, authoritative tone. "But if you make me check the registrations on your bikes or van, or I get close enough to think any of you need a Breathalyzer test, then it *will* be about you."

Prison Tat Guy was the first to head toward his bike. "Hey, I can't have my parole officer gettin' wind of this."

Potbelly #2 quickly followed suit. "I'm out of here, man. Gordy doesn't need us to handle Vic. My old lady's already ticked that I stayed out all night."

Potbelly #1 clomped the snow off his boots before climbing inside the van. But he sat with the door open, looking toward the man with the flask. "What do you want me to do, Denny? I told Gordy I'd give him a ride back to his place."

Flask Man's watery brown eyes never left Gina's. "We ain't doin' nothing illegal here, *querida*. We're just a bunch of pals hangin' out at a friend's place."

"It's *Officer Galvan* to you." She had to bite down on the urge to tell him in two languages exactly what kind of man he was. But she wasn't about to give this patronizing lowlife the satisfaction of losing her temper. She was a cop. Proud of it. And this guy was about to get a lesson in understanding exactly who was in charge here. "Mr. Bismarck isn't going to need a ride." Potbelly #1 slammed his door and started the van's engine. Gina smiled at Flask Man and pulled out her handcuffs. "Denny, is it? I've got plenty of room in the backseat for both you and good ol' Gordy." She moved toward him, dangling the cuffs in a taunt to emphasize her words. "How do impeding an officer in the performance of her duty, aiding and abetting a known criminal, public intoxication and operating a vehicle under the influence sound to you?"

"You can't arrest me for all that."

"I wouldn't test that theory if I were you." Derek stepped out of the way of the van as it backed out of the driveway and sped after the two men on motorcycles. "Not with her."

Gina was close enough to see Flask Man's nostrils flaring with rage. "Handcuffs or goodbye?"

"I don't like a woman telling me what to do," he muttered, striding toward his bike. "Especially one like you." Once he was astraddle, he revved the engine, yelling something at Derek that sounded a lot like a warning to keep his woman in check. The roar of the bike's motor drowned out his last parting threat as he raced down the street, but Gina was pretty sure it had something to do with her parentage and how their next meeting would have a very different ending.

"Make sure they stay gone," Gina said, hooking her cuffs back onto her belt and running to the front door. She opened the glass storm door and knocked against the inside door. "KCPD!" she announced. The woman screamed, and the man yelled all kinds of vile curses. "Vicki Bismarck, are you all right? This is the police, answering a call to this address. I'm coming inside."

Twenty minutes later, Gina and Derek had Gordon Bismarck and his former wife, Vicki, separated into two rooms of their tiny, trashed home. Gina had bagged the box cutter Gordon had dropped when she'd pulled her gun and blinked her watery eyes at the stench of alcohol, vomit and sweat coming off Gordon's body. Either Gordy and his buddies had been beefing up their courage for this confrontation or they'd partied hard and gotten stupid enough to think violating a restraining order was a good idea.

Although the slurred epithets were still flying from the living room where Derek had taken Gordon to put a winter coat on over his undershirt, and Vicki was bawling in the kitchen while Gina tried to assess the woman's injuries, Gina was already wrapping up this case in her head. Even if Vicki refused to press charges, she could book Gordon on breaking and entering, violating his restraining order and public intoxication—all of which should keep him out of Vicki's life long enough for her to get the help she needed. If she'd ask for it. Clearly, this wasn't the Bismarcks' first rodeo with KCPD. That probably explained why Gordon had brought his friends.

Although she hadn't noted any stab wounds on Vicki, the woman was cradling her left arm as if it had been yanked or twisted hard enough to do some internal damage. Gina glanced around at the slashed curtains and overturned chairs in the kitchen, her gaze landing on the shattered cell phone in the corner that had been crushed beneath a boot or hurled across the room. Clearly, there'd been a substantial altercation here.

Gina righted one of the chairs and urged the skinny woman to sit. "Will you let me look at that arm?" Gina asked, tearing off a fresh paper towel for the woman to dab at her tears. When Vicki nodded, Gina knelt beside her. Bruise marks that fit the span of a man's hand were already turning purple around her elbow. But there didn't seem to be any apparent deformity suggesting a broken bone. Didn't mean it hadn't been twisted savagely, spraining muscles and tendons. Gina pushed to her feet and headed toward the refrigerator-freezer. "An ice pack should help with the swelling."

She heard a crash from the living room and spun around as Derek cursed. "Gina—heads up!"

"Are you turnin' me in, you bitch? My boys are gonna kill you!"

"Gordy!" Vicki screamed as Gordon charged into the kitchen.

Chapter 2

Gina simply reacted, putting herself between the frightened woman and the red-faced man. There was no time to wonder how the drunk had gotten away from Derek. She ducked beneath the attacker's fist, kicked out with her leg, tripped the big brute, then caught his arm and twisted it behind his back, following him down to the floor. Before his chin smacked the linoleum, she had her knee in his back, pinning him in place.

"He's too big for the damn cuffs," Derek shouted, running in behind the perp. He knelt on the opposite side, catching the loose chain that was only connected to one wrist.

Gordon Bismarck writhed beneath her, trying to wrestle himself free. His curses switched from Vicki to Gina to women in general. Locking her own hand-cuffs around his free arm, Gina twisted his wrist and arm another notch until he yelped. "Don't make me mad, Mr. Bismarck. Your buddies outside already put me in a mood."

The mention of his friends sparked a new protest. "Denny! Al! Jim! I need—"

"Uh-uh." She pushed his cheek back to the floor. "They went bye-bye. Now you be a good boy while my partner walks you out to the squad car so you can sober up and chill that temper."

"My boys left?"

"That's right, Gordy." Derek wiped a dribble of blood from beneath his nose while Gina locked the ends of both cuffs together, securing him. "You're on your own."

"I don't want him touchin' me," Gordy protested. "I don't want him in my house."

"Not your choice." Gina stayed on top of the captive, her muscles straining to subdue him until he gave up the fight. She glanced up at Derek, assessing his injury. Other than the carpet lint clinging to his dark uniform from a tussle of some kind, he wasn't seriously hurt. Still, she kept her voice calm and firm, trying to reassure Vicki that they could keep her safe. "You got him okay?"

"I got him. Thanks for the save. I didn't realize the cuff wasn't completely closed around his fat wrist, and I ended up with an elbow in my face." Derek pulled the man to his feet, his bruised ego making him a little rough as he shoved Bismarck toward the front door. "Forget the coat. Now we can add assaulting a police officer to your charges. Come on, you lousy son of a…"

The door banged shut as Derek muscled Bismarck outside. Gina inhaled several deep breaths, cooling her own adrenaline rush. She watched from the foyer until she saw her partner open the cruiser and unceremoniously dump the perp into the backseat. Only after Derek had closed the door and turned to lean his hip against the fender did she breathe a sigh of relief. The situation was finally secure.

When he pulled out a cigarette and started to light it, Gina muttered a curse beneath her breath. She immediately thumbed the radio clipped to the shoulder of her uniform. "Derek," she chided, wanting to warn him it was too soon to let down his guard. "Call the sitrep in to Dispatch, and tell them we'll be bringing in the suspect. I'll finish getting the victim's statement."

"Chill, G. Let a man catch his breath." He lit the cigarette and exhaled a puff before answering. "Roger that."

Gina shook her head. She supposed that losing control of the perp had not only dinged his ego but also rattled him. Maybe she should have a low-key chat with her partner. Aiming for fifth place wasn't going to get the job done. If he didn't light a fire under his butt and start showing all the ways he could excel at being a cop, Captain Cutler might cut him from the SWAT candidate list altogether.

But she had more pressing responsibilities to attend to right now than to play the bossy big sister role with her partner and nudge Derek toward success. After softly closing the front door on the cold and the visual of Gordon Bismarck spewing vitriol in the backseat of the cruiser while Derek smacked the window and warned him to be quiet, Gina pulled out her phone again and returned to the kitchen. She found Vicki making a token effort to clean up some of the mess.

"Is he gone?" the woman asked in a tired voice. Although the tears had stopped, her eyes were an unnaturally bright shade of green from all her crying.

"He's locked in the back of the police cruiser, and I sent his friends away. He won't get to you again. Not today. Not while I'm here."

"Thank you." Vicki dropped a broken plate into the trash. "And Derek's okay?"

"'Derek'?"

"Officer Johnson." A blush tinted Vicki's pale cheeks. "I thought maybe Gordy thought…having another man in the house…" She shrugged off the rambling explanation. "I remember you two from the last time you were here. So does Gordy."

"I'm sure Officer Johnson will be fine. May I?" Gina held up her phone and, at Vicki's nod, snapped a couple of photos of the woman's injuries and sent them to her computer at work. "I'll need them to file my report."

"What if I refuse to press charges?" Vicki asked. "Gordy's friends might come back, even if he's not here. Denny's his big brother. He looks out for him."

Reminding herself that she hadn't lived Vicki Bismarck's life, and that the other woman probably had had the skills and confidence to cope with a situation like this beaten and terrorized out of her by now, Gina took a towel and filled it with some ice from the freezer. "I still have to take Mr. Bismarck in because he resisted arrest and assaulted an officer. And he's clearly violated his restraining order." She pressed the ice pack to Vicki's elbow and nodded toward the abrasion on her cheek. "You should get those injuries checked out by a doctor. Would you like me to call an ambulance?"

Vicki shook her head. "I can't afford that."

"How about I call another officer to take you to the ER? Or I can come back once we get your husband processed."

"No. No more cops, please." Vicki sank into a chair and rested her elbow on the table. "It just makes Gordy mad."

"What set him off this time?" Not that it mattered. Violence like this was never acceptable. But if Gina could get the victim talking, she might get some useful information to help get the repeat offender off the street and out of his wife's life. "I could smell the alcohol on him."

"He's been sleeping at Denny's house." Gina pulled out her notepad and jotted the name and information. "Gordy's been out of work for a while. Got laid off at the fertilizer plant. And I haven't been working long enough to get paid yet. I asked him if he'd picked up his unemployment check. He said he'd help me with groceries."

"And that set him off?"

"He doesn't like to talk about money. But no, as soon as I opened the door, he started yelling at me. Denny had said he saw me talking to another man." Vicki shrugged, then winced at the movement. "I just started a job at the convenience store a couple blocks from here. Guys come in, you know. I have to talk to them when I ring them up. I guess Denny told Gordy I was flirting."

Gina bit back her opinion of Gordy's obsession and maintained a cool facade. "When was the last time you ate?" If the woman needed money for groceries, Gina guessed it had been a while. She unzipped another pocket in her vest and pulled out an energy bar, pushing it into the woman's hand. "Here." She pulled out a business card for the local women's shelter as well, and handed it to Vicky. "You get hungry again, you go here, not to Gordy. They'll help you get groceries at the food pantry. Mention my name and they'll even sneak you an extra chocolate bar."

Finally, that coaxed a smile from the frightened woman. "I haven't eaten real chocolate in months. Sounds heavenly."

After getting a few more details about Vicki's relationship with Gordon and her injuries, Gina wrapped up the interview. "You need to be checked out by a doctor," she reiterated. "Sooner rather than later. Do you have a friend who can take you to the hospital or your regular doctor?"

"I can call my sister. She keeps nagging me to move in with her and her husband."

"Good." Gina handed Vicki her phone. "Why don't you go ahead and do that while I'm here?"

Vicki hesitated. "Will Gordy be back when I get home?"

"I can keep him locked up for up to forty-eight hours—longer if he doesn't make bail." Gina had a feeling Vicki's husband would be locked up for considerably longer than that but didn't want to guarantee anything she couldn't back up. "We can send a car through the neighborhood periodically to watch if his brother and friends come back. See a doctor. Go to your sister's, and get a good night's sleep. Call the shelter, and get the help you need."

"Thank you." Vicki punched in her sister's phone number and smiled again. "That was sweet to see you take Gordy down—and you aren't any bigger than I am. Maybe I should learn some of those moves."

Gina smiled back and pulled out her own business card. "It's all about attitude. Here. Call me when you're feeling up to it. A few other officers and I teach free self-defense training sessions."

Although Vicki didn't look entirely convinced that she could learn to stand up for herself, at least she had made arrangements with her sister and brother-in-law to stay with them for a few nights by the time Gina was closing the front door behind her and heading down the front walk toward the street. What passed for sunshine on the wintry day was fading behind the evening clouds that rolled across the sky and promised another dusting of snow. Despite the layers of the sweater, flak vest and long-sleeved uniform she wore, Gina shivered at the prospect of spring feeling so far out of reach.

Ignoring the glare of blurry-eyed contempt aimed at her from the backseat of the cruiser, Gina arched a questioning eyebrow at Derek. "Bismarck didn't hurt you, did he?"

Derek massaged the bridge of his nose that was already bruising and circled around the car as she approached. "Just my pride. I don't even know if the guy meant to clock me. But I was on the floor, and he was on his way to the kitchen before my eyes stopped watering."

"Ouch."

"Just don't tell anybody that a drunk got the upper hand on me and you had to save my ass. I don't imagine that would impress Captain Cutler."

"We're a team, Derek. We help each other out."

"And keep each other's secrets?"

"Something like that."

His laughter obscured his face with a cloud of warm breath in the chilly air. "Now I really owe you that cup of coffee." Her aversion to the cold weather was hardly a secret compared to his possible incompetence in handling the suspect. Maybe her partner wasn't ready for the demands of the promotion. He pulled open his door. "Come on. Let's get you warmed up—"

The sharp crack of gunfire exploded in the cold air.

Derek's green eyes widened with shock for a split second before he crumpled to the pavement. "Derek!"

A second bullet thwacked against the shatterproof glass of the windshield. A third whizzed past her ear and shattered the glass in Vicki Bismarck's storm door. Gina pulled the Glock at her hip and dove the last few feet toward the relative shelter of the car. A stinging shot of lead or shrapnel burned through her calf, and she stumbled into the snow beside the curb.

Where were the damn shots coming from? Who was shooting? Had Denny Bismarck come back? She hadn't heard a motorcycle on the street. But then, he hadn't been alone, either.

"Derek? I need you to talk to me." There was still no answer. Bullets hit the cruiser and a tree trunk in the front yard. Several more shots scuffed through the snow with such rapidity that she knew the shooter either had an automatic weapon or several weapons that he could drop and keep firing. Gina crouched beside the wheel well, listening for the source of the ambush, praying there were no innocent bystanders in the line of fire. The bullets were coming from across the street. But from a house? An alley? A car?

"Derek?" The amount of blood seeping down her leg into her shoe told her the shooter was using something large caliber, meant to inflict maximum damage. But her wound was just a graze. She could still do her job. Before she sidled around the car to pull her partner to safety, Gina got on her radio and called it in. "This is Officer Galvan. Unit 4-13. Officers need assistance. Shots fired." She gave the street address and approximation of where she thought the shooter might be before repeating the urgent request, "Officers need assistance."

Gina stilled her breath and heard Gordon Bismarck cussing up a blue streak inside the cruiser. She'd heard Vicki screaming inside the house. What she didn't hear was her partner. Guilt and fear punched her in the stomach. She hadn't done job one and kept him safe. She hadn't had his back when he needed her most.

"Derek?" she called out one more time before cradling the gun in her hands. When she heard the unexpected pause between gunshots, she crept around the trunk of the car, aiming her weapon toward the vague target of the shooter. "Police! Throw down your weapon!" she warned.

A quick scan revealed empty house, empty alley, empty house…bingo! Driver in a rusty old SUV parked half a block down. Gina straightened. "Throw down your weapon, and get out of the vehicle!"

The man's face was obscured by the barrel of the rifle pointed at her.

There was no mistaking his intent.

Gina squeezed off a shot and dove for cover, but it was too late.

A bullet struck her in the arm, tearing through her right shoulder, piercing the narrow gap between her arm and her protective vest. She hit the ground, and her gun skittered from her grip. Unlike the graze along the back of her leg, she knew this wound was a bad one. The path of the bullet burned through her shoulder.

She clawed her fingers into the hardened layers of snow and crawled back into the yard, away from the shooter. It was hard to catch her breath, hard to orient herself in a sea of clouds and snow. She rolled onto her back, praying she wasn't imagining the sound of sirens in the distance, hating that she was certain of the grinding noise of the SUV's engine turning over.

She saw Vicki Bismarck hovering at her broken front door. When Gina turned her head the other direction, she looked beneath the car and saw Derek on the ground, unmoving. Was he even alive? "Derek?"

Did someone have a grudge against him? Against her? Against cops? She hadn't made any friends among Denny Bismarck and his crew. Was this payback for arresting his brother? For being bested by a woman?

Her shoulder ached, and her right arm was numb. Her chest felt like a boulder sat on it. Still, she managed to reach her radio with her other hand and tug it off her vest. The shooter's car was speeding away. She couldn't see much from her vantage point, couldn't read the license plate or confirm a make of vehicle. The leg wound stung like a hot poker through her calf, but the wound to her shoulder—the injury she could no longer feel—worried her even more. Finding that one spot beneath her armor was either one hell of a lucky shot or the work of a sharpshooter. Gina's vision blurred as a chill pervaded her body.

"Stay inside the house!" a man yelled. "Away from the windows."

She saw silver running pants and black shoes stomping through the snow toward her. Gina tried to find her gun.

"Officer?" The tall jogger with the sexy beard scruff came into view as he knelt in the snow beside her. "It's okay, ma'am." His eyes were hidden behind reflective sunglasses, and he clutched a cell phone to his ear, allowing her few details as to what he looked like. He picked up her Glock from the snow where it had landed and showed it to her before tucking it into the back of his waistband. "Your weapon is secure."

She slapped her left hand against his knee and pulled at the insulated material there. "You have to stay down. Shooter—"

"He's driving away," the man said. She wasn't exactly following the conversation, but then he was talking on his cell phone as he leaned over her, running his free hand up and down her arms and legs. "No, I couldn't read the license. It was covered with mud and slush. Yes, just the driver. Look, I'll answer your questions later. Just get an ambulance here. Now!" He disconnected the call and stuffed the phone inside his pocket. He tossed aside his sunglasses and looked down into her eyes. Wow. He was just as good-looking up close as he'd been from a distance. "You hit twice?"

Gina nodded, thinking more about her observation than her answer. She reached up and touched her shaking fingertips to the sandpapery stubble that shadowed his jaw. "I know you." Before her jellified brain could place why he looked so familiar to her, he grabbed her keys off her belt and bolted to his feet. She turned her head to watch him unlock the trunk to get the med kit. How did he know it was stored there? He was acting like a cop—he'd provided the squad car number and street address on that phone call. He knew KCPD lingo and where her gear was stowed. "Captain Cutler?" That wasn't right. But the blue eyes and chiseled features were the same. But she'd never seen the SWAT captain with that scruffy catnip on his face.

She wasn't any closer to understanding what she was seeing when he knelt beside her again, opening the kit and pulling out a compress. She winced as he slipped the pad beneath her vest and pressed his hand against her wound to stanch the bleeding. The deep, sure tone of voice was a little like catnip to her groggy senses, too. "I'm Mike Cutler. I've had para-medic training. Lie still."

Why were her hormones involved in any of this con-versation? She squeezed her eyes shut to concentrate. She was a KCPD police officer. She'd been shot. The perp had gotten away. There was protocol to follow. She had a job to do. Gina opened her eyes, gritting her teeth against the pressure on her chest and the fog inside her head. "Check my partner. He's hit."

"You're losing blood too fast. I'm not going any-where until I slow the bleeding." The brief burst of clarity quickly waned. The Good Samaritan trying to save her life tugged on her vest the moment her eyes closed. "Officer Galvan? No, no, keep your eyes open. What's your first name?"

"Gina."

"Gina?" He was smiling when she blinked her eyes open. "That's better. Pretty brown eyes. Like a good cup of coffee. I want to keep seeing them, okay?" She nodded. His eyes were such a pretty color. No, not pretty. There wasn't anything *pretty* about the angles of his cheekbones and jaw. He certainly wasn't from this part of town. She'd have remembered a face like that. A face that was still talking. "Trust me. I'm on your side. If I look familiar, it's because you're a cop, and you probably know my dad."

Mike Cutler. My dad. Gina's foggy brain cleared with a moment of recognition. "Captain Cutler? Oh, God. I'm interviewing with him... Don't tell him I got shot, okay?" But he'd left her. Gina called out in a panic. "Cutler?"

"I'm here." Her instinct to exhale with relief ended up in a painful fit of coughing. "Easy. I was just checking your partner."

"How is he?"

"Unconscious. As far as I can tell, he has a gunshot wound to the arm. But he may have hit his head on the door frame or pavement. His nose is bruised."

"That was...before." She tried to point to the house.

"Before what?"

The words to explain the incident with Gordon Bismarck were lost in the fog of her thoughts. But her training was clear. Derek was shot. And she had a job to do.

"The prisoner?" Gina tried to roll over and push herself up, but she couldn't seem to get her arm beneath her. The snow and clouds and black running shoes all swirled together inside her head.

"Easy, Gina. I need you to lie still. An ambulance

is on its way. You've injured your shoulder, and I don't see an exit wound. If that bullet is still inside you, I don't want it traveling anywhere." He unzipped his jacket and shrugged out of it. He draped the thin, insulated material over her body, gently but securely tucking her in, surrounding her with the residual warmth from his body and the faint, musky scent of his workout. "The guy in the backseat is loud, but unharmed. The lady at the front door looks scared, but she isn't shot. Lie down. You're going into shock." He pulled her radio from beneath the jacket and pressed the call button. "Get that bus to…" Gina's vision blurred as he rattled off the address. "Stay with me. Gina?" His warm hand cupped her face, and she realized just how cold she was. She wished she could wrap her whole body up in that kind of heat. She looked up into his stern expression. "Stay with me."

"Catnip."

"What?" Her eyelids drifted shut. "Gina!"

The last thing she saw was her blood seeping into the snow. The last thing she felt was the man's strong hands pressing against her breast and shoulder. The last thing she heard was his voice on her radio.

"Officer down! I repeat: officer down!"

Chapter 3

Six weeks later

"He shoots! He scores!" The basketball sailed through the hoop, hitting nothing but net. Troy Anthony spun his wheelchair on the polished wood of the physical therapy center's minicourt. His ebony braids flew around the mocha skin of his bare, muscular shoulders, and one fist was raised in a triumphant gloat before he pointed to Mike. "You are buying the beers."

"How do you figure that?" Mike Cutler caught the ball as it bounced past him, dribbled it once and shoved a chest pass at his smirking competitor. It was impossible not to grin as his best friend and business partner, Troy, schooled him in the twenty-minute pickup game. "I thought we were playing to cheer *me* up."

Troy easily caught the basketball and shoved it right back. "I was playing to win, my friend. Your head's not in the game."

Mike's hands stung, forgetting to catch the pass with his fingertips instead of his palms. He *was* distracted. "Fine. Tonight at the Shamrock. Beers are on me."

He tucked the ball under his arm as he climbed out of the wheelchair he'd been using. Once his legs un-kinked and the electric jolts of random nerves firing across his hips and lower back subsided, he pushed the chair across the polished wood floor to stow the basketball in the PT center's equipment locker. At least he didn't have to wear those joint pinching leg braces or a body cast anymore.

But he wasn't about to complain. Twelve years ago, he hadn't been able to walk at all, following a car accident that had shattered his legs from the pelvis on down, so he never griped about the damaged nerves or aches in his mended bones or stiff muscles that protested the changing weather and an early morning workout. As teenagers, Mike and Troy had bonded over wheelchair basketball and months of physical rehabilitation therapy with the woman who had eventually become Mike's stepmother. Unlike Mike, because of a gunshot wound he'd sustained in a neighborhood shooting, Troy would never regain the use of his legs. But the friendship had stuck, and now, at age twenty-eight, they'd both earned college degrees and had opened their own physical therapy center near downtown Kansas City.

"C'mon, man. Don't make me feel like I'm beatin' up on ya. I said you didn't have to go back to the chair to play me. I could beat you standing on your two feet.

Today, at any rate." Troy pushed his wheels once and coasted over to the edge of the court beside Mike. His omnipresent smile and smart-ass attitude had disappeared. "Losing that funding really got to you, huh? Or is this mood about a woman?"

He hadn't put his heart on the line and gotten it stomped on by anyone of the female persuasion lately. Not since Caroline. "No. No woman."

Troy picked up a towel off the supply cart and handed one to Mike, grinning as he wiped the perspiration from his chest. "No woman? That would sure put *me* in a mood."

"You're a funny guy, you know that," Mike deadpanned, appreciating his friend's efforts to improve his disposition. But he couldn't quite shake the miasma of frustration that had plagued his thoughts since opening that rejection letter in the mail yesterday. "I had a brilliant idea, writing that grant proposal." Mike toweled the dampness from his skin before tossing Troy his gray uniform polo shirt. "We had enough money from the bank loan and our own savings to get this place built. But it's hardly going to sustain itself with the handful of patients we have coming in. If we were attached to a hospital—"

"We specifically decided against that." Troy didn't have to remind him of their determination to give back to the community. Mike opened the laundry compartment on the supply cart and Troy tossed both towels inside. "We wanted to be here in the city where the people who needed us most could have access to our services."

"I still believe in that." Mike stared at the CAPT logo for the Cutler-Anthony Physical Therapy Center embroidered on the chest of his own shirt before pulling it over his head and tugging the hem down to cover his long torso. "But those are the same people who don't always have insurance and can't always pay. I was certain that urban development grant for small businesses would help us."

"There'll be other grants." Troy donned his shirt and peeled off the fingerless gloves he wore when he played anything competitive in his wheelchair. "Caroline said she'd fund a grant for us. To thank you for being there when she needed you."

"And that would be right up until the night she turned down my proposal?" The fact that he could talk about it now told Mike that his ego had taken a bigger blow than his heart had. But that blow had been the third strike in the relationship game. He had no plans to step up to the plate and put his heart on the line anymore. If he couldn't tell the difference between a friends-with-benefits package and a connection that was leading to forever, he'd do well to steer clear of anything serious. He'd been the shoulder to cry on, the protective big brother and the best friend too many times to risk it. He could rely on his principles, his family and friends like Troy. But he wasn't about to rely on his heart again. "No. No asking Caroline. I didn't propose because I wanted her money, and I'm not going to take it now as a consolation prize."

Troy knew just how far he could push the relationship button before he made a joke. "Maybe you could hock the engagement ring. That'd keep us open another month."

Mike glared down at his friend for a moment before laughter shook through his chest. "More like a day and a half."

"Dude, no wonder she said no."

The shared laughter carried them through the rest of putting away the equipment they'd used and prepping for their first—and, as far as Mike knew, their only—appointment of the morning. But even Troy's mood had sobered by the time they headed toward the door leading into the entry area and hallway that led to a row of offices and locker rooms. "You're a smart guy, Mikey. You'll figure out a way to keep us solvent."

"Without losing your apartment or my house?"

"I'd be happy to go out and recruit us more female clientele. It's Ladies' Night at the Shamrock tonight. I can pour on some of that legendary Anthony charm."

"Creeper."

"You got a better plan?"

"Not at the moment."

"You're thinkin' too hard on this, Mike. We haven't even been open a year. We'll get more paying customers soon. I feel it in my bones." He held up a fist and waited for Mike to absorb some of his positive thinking.

Trusting his friend's outlook more than his own, Mike bumped his fist against Troy's. "I just have to be patient, right?"

"Nobody waits out trouble better than you."

Mike shook his head. "Is that supposed to be a compli—?" The door opened before they reached it, and the center's office manager, Frannie Mesner, stepped into the gym. "Good morning."

"Hey, Sun…shine." Troy's effusive greeting fell flat when they saw the puffy, red-rimmed eyes behind Frannie's glasses. He rolled his chair over to get a box of tissues off the supply cart and take them to her. She sniffed back a sob as she took the box.

Was she hurt? Had she gotten some bad news? Mike moved in beside her and dropped a comforting arm around her trembling shoulders. "Frannie?"

The flush of distress on Frannie's pale cheeks made her freckles disappear. She pulled out a handful of tissues and dabbed her eyes before blowing her nose. "Leo gets released on parole today."

Her ex. She wasn't hurt. But definitely bad news.

"Has he contacted you?" Mike asked.

"He's not supposed to."

"Has he contacted you?" he repeated, articulating the protective concern in his voice. Frannie shook her head, stirring short wisps of copper hair over her damp cheeks.

Troy set the tissue box in his lap. "Is the restraining order still in effect?"

Mike watched the confidence she'd built over the past few months disappear in the span of a few heartbeats.

When she didn't answer, Mike pulled away to face her. "Take a few minutes to call your attorney and make sure it is. If not, make an appointment to get it reinstated. Troy or I can go with you, if you want."

Troy slid Frannie a worried glance before spinning away from the conversation to return the box to its shelf. "Yeah. I can do that. We'd have to take my van, though. If you don't mind riding shotgun. And you trust my driving."

What happened to that legendary Anthony charm? The Troy he knew was all mouth and swagger 99 percent of the time. Except when it came to the office manager Mike had hired for their fledgling physical therapy center. Frannie had been their first client. But more than rebuilding her physical strength after a beat-down from her ex that had cost her the sight in one eye, she had needed a job, and Mike and Troy had provided it. He suspected she also appreciated the office's predictable routine and the haven of a well-built workplace run by the son of a cop and a paraplegic, whose friends were also cops.

Mike might not carry a gun but, because of his dad and friends at KCPD, he knew how to keep a woman safe. Avoiding dangerous situations in the first place was rule one. "You know we'll give you the time off for personal business like that. Make sure that protection order is in place. Beyond that, Troy or I will escort you to your car and follow you home. You notify the police if he calls or you see his face anywhere close to you."

"I can swing by your place and double check the locks on the windows and door," Troy offered.

Mike nodded. "Sounds like a plan."

"My building isn't handicapped accessible." Frannie sniffed away the last of her tears and dabbed at the pink tip of her nose. "I'm sorry."

Troy shrugged, then reached for her hand. There was definitely something going on with him where Frannie was concerned. "Don't you apologize for that."

Mike wasn't sure how to help his friend, other than alleviate his concern about Frannie. "I'll stop by after work, then."

At least she felt safe here at the clinic. She tucked the used tissues into the pocket of her khaki slacks and dredged up a shy smile. "You guys are the best bosses ever. Thank you." Although she'd started the job with no secretarial experience, Frannie had eventually found her feet and her own system of organization that worked—for her. And, when she wasn't afraid for her life like she was this morning, she was a friendly, quiet presence who made their patients feel welcome at the clinic. She wound her arm around Mike's waist and squeezed him in a shy hug. "Thanks." She turned toward Troy with her arms outstretched and leaned over to give him a hug, too. "Thank you."

Troy turned his nose into her hair, breathing deeply. "No sweat, Sunshine."

Either sensing Troy's interest or feeling a similar longing herself, Frannie quickly pulled away and tipped her face to Mike. "Your eight o'clock appointment is here. He's already changing in the locker room."

Chaz Kelly, a retired firefighter with a new knee, opened the door behind Frannie, startling her. "Hey, pretty lady. You weren't at your desk to greet me this morning when I checked in." Bald and blustery, his gaze darted over to Troy and Mike. "Morning, boys. Ready to put this fat old man through his paces?"

Frannie's body visibly contracted away from Chaz's pat on her shoulder. Uh-huh. So much for feeling safe. She scooted closer to Troy's chair and didn't look any more comfortable there. "Your dad is here, too, Mike."

"Here?" It was rarely a good thing for the supervisor of KCPD's SWAT teams to make a surprise visit. Mike's concern instantly went to his stepmother and much younger half brother. "Is everything okay? Jillian? Will?"

"He didn't say. But I think it's work related. He's in uniform. There's someone with him. I put them in your office. I'll go start a pot of coffee." Her hand went self-consciously to one tear-stained cheek. "And wash my face."

As Frannie left, Mike pulled his phone from his pocket, wondering if he'd missed a text or call during the basketball game. The lack of messages altered his concern into curiosity.

Troy tapped his fist against Mike's arm and pointed at the door. "I got this. Better not keep the captain waiting." Troy spun his chair around toward the door on the far side of the half gym that led to the equipment room and treatment tables. "Come on, Chaz. Let's get you on the treadmill and get you warmed up. Did you stick to that diet we gave you?"

Their conversation faded as Mike hurried down the outer hallway to his office. "Dad?" Michael Cutler Sr. was on his feet to greet him with a handshake and a hug when Mike rounded the corner into his office. "Hey. Everything okay?"

"Not to worry. I'm fine. The family's fine."

Both standing at six-four, father and son looked each other in the eye as Mike pulled away. "What's up?" His eyes widened when he saw the petite woman waiting behind his father. "Officer Galvan."

Her dark eyes shared his surprise. "Catnip…" Mike arched his brows at her stunned whisper. She blinked away the revelation of emotion. "It *was* you."

"Excuse me?"

Gina Galvan was shorter than he remembered. Of course, his perspective was a little different, standing upright versus kneeling over her supine body. Without the hazards of gunfire or a medical emergency to focus on, Mike stole a few seconds to take in details about his visitor. She'd changed her hair. Instead of a long ponytail spilling over the snow, short, loose waves danced against the smooth line of her jaw. She wore a black sling over her right shoulder, keeping her arm immobile against her stomach. And he shouldn't have noticed the athletic curves arcing beneath the narrow waist of her jeans. But he did.

"The day I got shot—you were the runner who stopped to help us." Her gaze shifted between Mike and his father. "You two look so much alike, I guess I convinced myself I'd hallucinated you."

Mike chuckled at her admission. Although there was a peppering of gray in his dad's dark brown hair and Mike didn't shave as closely as KCPD regulations required, it wasn't the first time he'd been mistaken for his father. "I don't think I've ever been anyone's hallucination before. Fantasy, maybe, but…"

She frowned as if she didn't get the joke. His father looked away, embarrassed at his lame attempt at humor. Right. Leave the jokes to Troy.

The proud tilt of her chin and intense study from her dark eyes warned him that Gina Galvan wasn't inclined to laugh at much of anything. Which was a pity because he suddenly wondered what those pink lips would look like softened with a smile.

Reel it in, Cutler. Clearly, this wasn't a social call. And he already had enough on his plate without letting his errant hormones steer him into another misguided relationship.

Starched and pressed and always in charge of the room, Michael Sr. turned to include them both. "I wasn't sure you two would remember each other after a meeting like that. I guess there's no need for introductions."

"No, sir." Off-duty and out of uniform, she still talked like a cop.

"Nah." Mike invited them both to sit in the guest chairs in front of his desk before circling around to pull out his own chair. "How's the recovery going?" Gina's gaze drilled into his. He interpreted that as a *Don't ask.* "Did they catch the guy who did it?"

"No."

He'd suspected that was the case, or else a detective or investigator from the DA's office would have been back to question him on his account of the incident. "Sorry to hear that. And I'm sorry I couldn't give KCPD a better description of the shooter's SUV or license plate. The whole back end was covered in frozen mud and slush."

She nodded. "He probably went straight to a car wash afterward so we couldn't even look for a dirty vehicle."

"Probably. How's your partner?"

"Back on active duty."

"That's good news." Or not, judging by the scowl that darkened her expression. Even with a frown like that, Mike had a hard time calling Gina Galvan anything but pretty. High cheekbones. Full lips. Dark, sensuous eyes. Hair the color of dark-roast coffee. "You cut your hair since I saw you last."

"I was bleeding in the snow when you saw me last." The subtle warmth of an accent made an intriguing contrast to the crisp snap of her words.

"I like it—the hair, not the blood. I didn't realize how wavy your hair was."

"Well, long hair is hardly practical with—" she gestured at her arm in the sling "—this. And I am not going to rely on my aunt or my sister to put my hair up every day."

"Sounds smart."

"Why are we talking about my hair?" The accent grew a little more pronounced as a hint of acid entered her tone. Was that anger? Frustration? A clear message that she wasn't interested in his compliments or flirtations—idle or otherwise. She froze for a moment before inhaling a deep breath. Then, oddly, she crossed her fingers and brushed them against her lips and heart before settling her hand back into her lap. He thought it must be some kind of calming ritual because her posture relaxed a fraction and the tension left her voice. "I owe you for saving my life, Mr. Cutler. Thank you."

He'd heard the gunshots on his morning run through the neighborhood just a mile or so from the clinic. What else was he supposed to do besides try to help? "It's just Mike. And you're welcome."

Was that what this visit was about? A proud woman wanting to thank him? But she'd indicated that she hadn't remembered him.

Mike's father clearly had a purpose for coming to the clinic. "Could you give us a few minutes, Galvan?"

Gina popped to her feet, eager to please the captain or simply eager to escape the uncomfortable conversation. "Yes, sir."

Mike stood, too, as Frannie stepped into the room carrying a tray of steaming coffee mugs with packets of sugar and creamer. He scooted aside a stack of bills for her to set the tray on his desk. "Thanks. Why don't you give Officer Galvan a tour of the facility while Dad and I talk."

"Okay." Frannie's eyes were still puffy behind her glasses, but the pale skin beneath her freckles and pixie haircut was back to normal. She smiled at Gina and led her into the hallway. "We can start with the women's locker room."

Mike closed the door and returned to his seat, looking across the desk as his father picked up a mug and blew the steam off the top. "How worried should I be about this impromptu visit?"

Chapter 4

His father pursed his lips and made a rare face before swallowing. "Um…"

Mike took a sip and spit the sour brew back into his mug. "Sorry about that. Frannie must have cleaned the coffeemaker out with vinegar again."

"Did she rinse it afterward?"

"I'll sneak in there and make a new pot later this morning while she's busy." Mike spun his chair and emptied his mug into the potted fern beside the door. "She's a little distracted. Her ex gets out on parole today."

"Leo Mesner?" Mike nodded, returning his mug to the tray. Michael Sr. followed his lead, dumping out his coffee. "I'll find out who Leo's parole officer will be so we can keep tabs on him for her."

"Thanks. After that last assault, he shouldn't have

any contact with her, but you never know if prison sobered him up and made him rethink hurting his ex-wife or just made him even angrier and bent on revenge. We'll do what we can to keep her safe from this end, too."

"I know you will, son. You're too kindhearted for your own good."

"You know it's not all kindness, Dad." His father's blue eyes pierced right into Mike's soul, understanding his need to atone for the damage he'd done in his youth—and wishing his older son would forgive himself already. Mike smiled a reassurance to ease his father's concern. "But you didn't come here to talk about my problems. I'm assuming this visit has to do with Officer Galvan?"

His dad nodded. "I'm bringing you a new client."

He pointed briefly to his own shoulder. "She had surgery?"

"Stitches in her leg to seal up the bullet graze there. Emergency surgery to repair a nicked lung. She's recovered from those without incident." His dad's expression turned grim. "But the second bullet went through her shoulder and tore it up. The doctors had to rebuild the joint. The PT is for muscle and nerve damage there."

"What kind of nerve damage?"

"You're the expert. But I know it has affected her hand. She can't hold a gun."

"Only six weeks after getting shot? She shouldn't be trying."

"You don't know Gina." His dad leaned forward, sharing a confidence. "She's nobody's pretty princess. Not the easiest person to get along with, especially since the shooting. She's already quit one therapist, and another refused to work with her after the first session."

"But I'm so desperate for patients, you think I'll take her on?"

"No." He leaned back, his features carved with an astute paternal smile. "I know how tough you are. All you've survived and been through. I know how resourceful you can be. If anybody can stand up to Gina, it's you."

There was a compliment in there somewhere, one that ranked right up there with Troy's claim that he could outlast trouble. Maybe his dad and friend were subtly trying to tell him that he was too hardheaded for his own good. "What was the issue with the other therapists? She wouldn't do the work?"

"Just the opposite. She pushed herself too hard."

Mike nodded. "Did more damage than helped her recovery. You think Troy and I want to risk that kind of liability?"

"She's an ambitious woman. Trying to do better for herself and her family. Other than her great-uncle's disability and social security, she's their sole support. But she's a good cop. Good instincts. Well trained. Gina can think on her feet. Once the bad guys realize they've underestimated her, they discover they don't want to mess with her. I was ready to put her on my new SWAT team until the shooting. I've still got a spot for her." His dad's shoulders lifted with a wry apology. "But if she can't handle the physical demands of the job, I can't use her."

"You want me to fix her so she can make the team?"

"I want you to fix her so we don't lose her to No-

Man's Land." Just a few city blocks north of the clinic. Poverty, gangs, drugs, prostitution, homelessness—it was a tough place to grow up. His dad's second wife, Jillian, had barely survived her time in one of Kansas City's most dangerous neighborhoods. Troy had almost lost his life there. Mike knew his father and his SWAT team had answered several calls there over the years. There was a lot to admire about a woman who held down a good job and took care of her family in the No-Man's Land neighborhood. In *this* neighborhood, where he and Troy were determined to make a difference. Michael Cutler Sr. was a professional hostage negotiator. He knew what buttons to push to ensure Mike's cooperation, and helping someone deserving in this part of the city was a big one. "Help her realize her potential. KCPD needs her. She needs the job, and I want her if she can do it."

Mike scrubbed his hand over the stubble shading his jaw before deciding to swallow a little pride. "Can she pay?"

"I'll cover whatever her department insurance doesn't."

"You believe in her that much?"

"I do."

"Then I will, too." Appreciating the faith his father had always had in him, Mike rolled his chair back and stood. "I'll get the job done for you, Dad."

"Thanks. I knew I could count on you." With their business completed, Michael Sr. stood as well, adjusting the gun at his hip and pulling the black SWAT cap from his back pocket. He tipped his head toward the unpaid bills that Mike had pushed aside earlier. "Did you get the grant?"

"No."

"I suppose applying to Caroline's foundation is out of the question."

"Yes."

He shook his head as he crossed to the door. "To be honest, I think you dodged a bullet there, son. Caroline was a nice girl. But Jillian and I were never so bored out of our minds that night we had dinner with her parents. And, of course, if she can't appreciate you for who you are and not who she wants you to be—"

"Yeah, yeah." Mike grinned, patting his dad's shoulder to stop that line of well-meaning conversation. "Nice Dad Speech."

"I'm really good at 'em, aren't I?" They shared a laugh until Michael Sr. paused with his hand on the door knob to ask, "Say, what was that 'catnip' thing about with Gina?"

"Beats me. She said it to me before she lost consciousness the day of the shooting. Maybe she was delirious and thinking about her pet."

They both suspected there was more to the story than that but Mike didn't have the answer. His dad paused before opening the door. "You'll give me regular reports on Gina's progress?"

"Does she know you're setting this up for her?"

"She knows I want her on my team and that I was happy to give her a ride this morning. She still can't drive for another two weeks."

"And she knows this is her last chance to get her recovery right in time for you to name the new SWAT team?"

"Very astute. You got your mother's brains." They stepped into the hallway and Michael Sr. pulled his

SWAT cap on. "See you at Will's science fair presentation Thursday night?"

"I already told the squirt I'd be there."

A small parade, led by a grinning Troy, stopped them before they reached the clinic's entrance. Troy held out his hand. "Hey, Captain C. I wanted to make sure I said hi before you left."

"Troy." The two men exchanged a solid handshake. "Good to see you."

"You, too, sir."

Frannie and Gina waited behind Troy's chair. The two women were a stark contrast in coloring and demeanor—pale and dark, subdued and vibrant.

"How's Dex doing in med school?" Unaware of Mike's distracted gaze, Michael Sr. asked about Troy's younger brother. Since Mike and Troy had practically grown up together, Dexter Anthony and their grandmother who'd raised the boys were like extended family.

"Long hours. But he's killin' it."

"I knew he would. Jillian wants to know when you're coming over for dinner. More for the games afterward than the food."

"Just give me a time, and I'll be there. And tell her I've been reading the dictionary every night. I'm not losing that word game to her again."

"Will do." The two men shook hands again before his dad nodded to Gina over the top of Troy's head. "You sure you don't want me to stay and give you a ride home?"

"No, sir. Thank you, but you need to get to work. Besides, I've been getting home all by myself for a lot of years now."

"I'll make sure she gets home, Dad."

"Son." Michael traded one last nod with Mike before he left.

There was an awkward moment between the four of them in the congested hallway before Mike stepped to one side. Gina politely followed suit, giving Troy room to spin his chair around and head back to his patient in the workout room. Frannie quietly excused herself and slipped into her office, leaving Mike and Gina standing side by side with their backs against the wall. The woman didn't even come up to his shoulder. But he appreciated the view of dark waves capping her head and the tight, round bump of her bottom farther down.

One by one, doors closed behind Frannie, Troy and Mike's dad. The second her potential boss had gone and they were alone, Gina turned on him. "I didn't ask you to be my chauffeur."

Forget the raw attraction simmering in his veins. Her hushed, chiding tone gave Mike an idea of what the next few weeks were going to be like, and it wasn't going to involve fun or easy. But he'd been rising to one challenge or another his entire life. Five feet and a few inches or so of attitude wasn't about to scare him off. She might as well get used to how he intended to run things with her. "You didn't ask me to be your physical therapist, either. But it looks like *that's* going to happen." He took her into his office and closed the door. "Have a seat. I need to do an informal assessment before we get started."

She eyed the chair where she'd sat earlier, and obstinately remained in place. "I've already had two evaluations, three if you count the orthopedist who sent me to PT in the first place."

"Well, none of them reported to me, and I've got no paperwork on you, so have a seat." Mike sat and pulled up a new intake file on his computer screen.

She poked a finger at the corner of his desk. "Listen, Choir Boy. Your father outranks me and can give me orders. But you can't."

Choir Boy? What happened to *Catnip?*

And why couldn't the woman just call him Mike? "Fine. Stand. I'm still asking questions."

He typed in her name as she snatched her hand away. "Are you making fun of me now? You don't know me. You don't know my life."

If he recalled correctly, he'd saved that life.

"Age? Address? Phone number? Surgeon?" He typed in the answers as she rattled them off. "What are your goals?"

She puffed up like a banty hen, swearing a couple of words in Spanish, before perching on the chair across from him. "My goals? Isn't it obvious? I want to be a cop again. And not just some face sitting behind a desk, either. I want to be able to pick up my gun and take down a perp and be the first Latina on one of your father's SWAT teams."

"You want me to put in a good word for you?" He met her gaze across the desk. "You're going to have to earn that. I warn you, Dad and I are close, but he doesn't let anybody tell him what to do when it comes to the job." Mike leaned back in his chair. "But I have a feeling you're familiar with that kind of attitude."

"Are you trying to make me angry?"

"Apparently I don't have to work very hard at it."

Her eyes widened and the tight lines around her mouth vanished. "Things have been a little tense…"

She parted her lips to continue, closed them again, processed a thought, then leaned forward to ask. "Can you make me whole again? If I can't be a cop, I don't know… My family is counting on me… I'm used to dealing with problems myself. But this…" She tilted her chin, as if the proud stance could erase the vulnerability that had softened everything about her for a few moments. "I need this to happen."

In other words, *Rescue me.* He'd just taken a hit to his Achilles' heel. Not that this woman looked like she wanted a knight in shining armor, but a woman in need had always been a problem for Mike. Caroline had needed him to build her confidence and stand up to her parents. Frannie had needed him to feel safe. They weren't the first, and he had a feeling they wouldn't be the last. Maybe it had something to do with atoning for the mistakes of his rebellious youth after his mother had died of cancer. Maybe it had something to do with finding a purpose for his life the day he helped rescue his stepmother, Jillian, and Troy from a bomber. Maybe it had something to do with that lonesome need to be needed—to be the one man that a woman had to have in her life.

And maybe he *was* too hardheaded to accept defeat because he heard himself saying, "I can help it happen if you let me. You're going to have to take orders from someone besides my dad. Can you do that? Do what I tell you? *Not* do more than I tell you?" he emphasized, suspecting that *slow* and *easy* weren't in Gina's vocabulary. "You can do as much damage by pushing too hard too soon as the original injury inflicted."

"I can do more than those other therapists were letting me. I can handle pain. And training is something

I've done in sports since middle school, and certainly at the police academy. I'll do my job if you do yours."

Not exactly the clear-cut agreement he'd been looking for. But he'd take it. If Gina saw this as a competition, he'd give her a run for her money—and then make sure she won. He reached across the desk with his right hand, purposely challenging her to respond with the hand that rested limply in the sling.

A light flashed in her eyes, like a sprinkling of sugar dissolving in rich, warm coffee. Not the sour kind Frannie made, either. Then she thrust her hand out of the end of the sling. Her thumb and forefinger latched on to his hand with a decent grip, but the last three fingers simply batted against the back of his knuckles. Mike stretched each limp finger back, checking the muscle tone, before he finished the informal assessment and gave her hand a reassuring squeeze. Then he pulled away and pushed to his feet. "You accept that I'm in charge of your recovery? That when it comes to your health, I'm the boss?"

He towered over her, but there wasn't any backing down to this woman. Gina stood as well, adjusting her arm in the sling. "You want to be the boss, Choir Boy? Let's do this."

An hour later, she had a sheen of perspiration dotting her forehead and neck, and her left arm was shaking with the extra exertion of compensating for her damaged right shoulder and weak arm. Mike had a pretty good idea of why Gina had run into issues with her previous physical therapists. The woman was as fit as any athlete he'd ever worked with, and her frustration with the limited use of her hand and arm was obvious. Her assessment session had been a battle of wills, with Gina determined to perform any task Mike asked of her, even when the purpose of the exercise was to give him a clear idea of her limitations.

His dad had been right. Gina's recovery was going to be a mental challenge as much as a physical one. He walked her to the door, suggesting she wear something besides jeans for the next session and giving her a list of dos and don'ts for her recovery.

Since he'd been raised to be a gentleman, he lifted the denim jacket hanging from her left wrist as she struggled to put it on and slipped it up her arm before tucking it securely around her healing shoulder. He wasn't sure if that grunt was a protest of independence or a flash of pain. It certainly wasn't a *thank you*. Still, he helped her pull the ends of her hair from beneath the collar, sifting the damp waves through his fingers and learning their silky texture before he leaned in to whisper, "You're welcome." She grunted a second time, and Mike chuckled as he reached around her to push open the door and follow her out into the sunshine that warmed the springtime air. "How are you going to get home?"

She eyed the scattering of cars in the parking lot, between the reclaimed warehouses that had been converted into various businesses and lofts, and the busy street beyond. "If there's no snow on the ground, I can walk."

Mike thumbed over his shoulder at his black pickup truck. "I'll give you a ride."

"You're going to leave work in the middle of the day to drive me home?"

The gusting breeze blew her hair across her cheek, and he curled his fingers into his palms against the urge to touch those dark waves again. "It's not that far. My next appointment isn't until after lunch. Troy can cover any emergencies that crop up."

"Therapist, not chauffeur," she reminded him.

"Suit yourself. I'll see you tomorrow?"

"I'll be here."

"No working out between now and then, understand? You can do the hand exercises, but no running and no lifting weights."

She smoothed the fluttering hair behind her ear and held it in place there. "What about the yoga stretches?"

"Lower half of your body? Sure. But nothing that could create a balance issue. If you fall and catch yourself with that arm, you'll set your recovery back another two weeks, if not permanently."

"Understood." She stepped off the sidewalk and headed across the parking lot.

"Really?" he challenged. Promising to obey his directives was different from hearing the words and understanding them.

Her sigh was audible as she turned back to face him. "Are you always this stubborn?"

"You bring it out in me."

"I won't apologize for being a strong woman."

"I wouldn't want you to." However, that acceptance and respect needed to go both ways. "I won't apologize for being a nice guy."

"Who says you're—?"

"'Choir Boy'?"

She snapped her lips shut on the next retort, perhaps conceding that he knew exactly what the reverse prejudice of that nickname meant to her. Nice guys didn't cut it in her world. Too bad she hadn't known him back in the day. Of course, teenage bad-boy reputation aside, if he hadn't gotten his act together, he might still be in a wheelchair or even dead. He sure wouldn't have sobriety, a college degree, his own business, nor would he be in a position to help her.

He watched the debate on what she should say next play over her features. *That's right, sweetheart. There's a difference between nice and naive.* "My apologies, Mr. Cutler."

Without so much as a smile, she turned and walked out to the street, where she changed direction to follow traffic along the sidewalk toward the lights and crosswalk at the corner. Fine. So friendship wasn't going to happen between them anytime soon. And those curious, lustful urges she triggered in him were never going to be assuaged. But maybe, just maybe, they could learn how to get along.

Mike tucked his hands into the pockets of his gray nylon running pants. He mentally calculated how many blocks she'd have to walk and how many busy streets she'd have to cross before she got home. He'd cover two or three times that distance on his morning runs. But he didn't have two recent gunshot wounds or the muscle fatigue of a therapy session to slow him down. She'd be on her feet for another thirty minutes before she got the chance to rest.

Maybe he should have insisted on driving her home. He fingered the keys in his pocket, wondering how much Gina would protest if he pulled up beside her and…

That was weird.

Mike's eyes narrowed as Gina's steps stuttered and she suddenly darted toward the curb. She pulled up sharply, swiveling her gaze, looking everywhere except straight back at him. Mike's balance shifted to the balls of his feet. Had she seen or heard something that had alarmed her? Maybe she'd simply recognized a familiar face driving past.

Gina dodged a pair of businesswomen hurrying by in their suits and walking shoes, clearly unaware of whatever had caught her attention. Three more pedestrians passed her before she shook her head, as if dismissing what she'd seen or heard, and turned toward the intersection again.

By that time, Mike was already across the parking lot, jogging toward her. He fell into step about a half block behind her, following her through the intersection before the traffic light changed. Although the number of pedestrians heading to work or running to the periodic transit stops to catch the next city bus filled the sidewalk between them, he had no problem keeping Gina in sight, simply because of his height.

Her posture had subtly changed after that original reaction. There was less of the defiance she'd shown him at the clinic and more of a wary alertness. Judging by the occasional glimpses of either cheekbone, he could see she was scanning from side to side as she walked. Who was she looking for? What had she seen or heard that put her on guard like that?

She pulled out her cell phone, glancing over her left shoulder at the traffic as she placed a call, before Mike noticed what might have gotten her attention. A tan luxury sedan zipped across two lanes before it slowed dramatically, pulling even with Gina and matching her pace. He moved toward the curb, trying to read the license plate of the car. Other vehicles ran up behind the car, then swerved around it. He quick-ened his own pace to see the silhouette of a ball cap above the driver's seat headrest. That wasn't any little old lady driving it, poking along at her own pace. Was that car following Gina?

And then Mike saw something that hastened his feet into a dead run. The driver raised his arm over the passenger seat, his fingers holding a gun. "Gina!"

She spun around. The instant he shouted her name, the driver floored it, swinging into the next lane, dart-ing around a bus and speeding through a yellow light. Horns honked, brakes screeched.

Mike snaked his arm around Gina's waist, lifting her off her feet and hauling her away from the car. At the last second, he could see the driver hadn't held a weapon, after all, but had made that crass gesture with two outstretched fingers and a flick of his thumb, imi-tating firing a gun.

"What the hell, Choir Boy?" Gina's phone flew from her grasp, skittering across the sidewalk and get-ting kicked once before a helpful soul picked it up.

Mike set her down in front of the yellow brick fa-cade of a bail bondsman's office, keeping his body be-tween her and the street. The other man handed Gina her cell phone, pausing to eye Mike suspiciously, as if the guy thought he was assaulting her. Mike's hand was still at Gina's waist, the adrenaline of taking in-stinctive action to protect her still vibrating through his grip. He nearly bit out a warning for the other guy to move on when Gina smiled and waved him on his way.

Interesting how she managed a polite thank you and a reassurance that she was all right for the young man, but she'd cursed at Mike. Even more interesting how quickly the mix of concern and the remembered sensation of her body snugged against his made him vividly aware of every tight curve of her petite frame. He was so not thinking of her as a patient right now. But the sexual awareness burned through him as quickly as the shove against his chest separated them again. "Let go of me."

"Are you okay?"

"Are you following me?" Her question overlapped his.

"Somebody is." Mike splayed his fingers apart, releasing his grip without giving her space to move away from the wall. Those fractious nerves from his teenage injury tingled through his hips and the small of his back, protesting the abrupt movements and tension running through him. But he ignored the familiar shards of pain. "What the hell is going on?"

Although the casing on her phone was scratched, he could see on the screen between them that her call was still connected. Her focus was there instead of answering his questions. "I'm fine. Just let me do my job." She put the phone back to her ear, reporting a license plate number. "I didn't get the last two digits."

"Thirty-six," Mike answered, reciting the number he'd seen.

Her dark eyes tilted up to his. "Tan Mercedes?" He nodded. "Three six, Derek," she reported into the phone, holding Mike's gaze while she talked. "Yeah, it circled around the block. Let me know what you find out. Thanks." She disconnected the call and tucked the phone into the back pocket of her jeans. "What are you doing here? And don't you ever pick me up like that again."

"I want to know why that guy threatened you."

Her dark eyes narrowed as she studied his face. "Are you hurt?"

Yeah, a sharp twist of a pinched nerve had just made his left thigh go numb, so she must have noticed the tight clench of his jaw. But that injury was old news. He needed to understand what was going on now. "Answer the question."

Dismissing her concern because he had dismissed it, she glanced around him at the next stream of pedestrians getting off the bus and dropped her voice to a terse whisper. "I'm a cop."

Shifting to the side, Mike braced one hand on the bricks beside her head and created a barrier between Gina and anyone who might accidently bump into her shoulder. "You're not in uniform. Either we have some random whack-job roaming the streets of Kansas City or that was personal. Did you recognize him? Is he the man who shot you?"

She put her hand in the middle of his chest to hush him when a couple of people turned their heads and slowed, catching wind of the conversation. "You saw it. The driver was acting suspiciously. I was doing my duty by calling it in." When she tried to dismiss the conversation and move around him, Mike dropped his hand back to the cinch of her waist, refusing to budge. She muttered something in Spanish, then tipped her face up to his. "I was probably staring at him too long, and he mimicked shooting me instead of flipping me off. Thought he was being funny."

Mike wasn't laughing. "Okay, so you're a tough chick. I get that. Didn't anybody ever teach you how to answer a polite question? I grew up around cops—

I know the signs of somebody going into alert mode. You're not armed. You're injured. You don't have backup. I'm not going to think any less of you if you tell me that guy spooked you."

Her pinpoint gaze dodged his for an instant, revealing a chink in her armor. Mike summoned every bit of his patience to wait her out before she finally told him something that wasn't a flippant excuse, meant to dismiss his concern. "I've seen that car before—driving by my house at night the past couple of weeks. And now…" She curled her fingers into his shirt, pulling him half a step closer as a group of pedestrians strolled behind him. Sure, she was avoiding foot traffic, but she'd also moved him closer to whisper, "Do you remember the vehicle from the shooting?"

"Yeah, but it wasn't a car. Certainly not anything top-of-the-line like that. Did you recognize the driver? He could have ditched the truck I saw." Although he doubted the man who owned that piece of junk would also own a Mercedes.

"The man who shot me—I never saw his face." Mike dipped his head to hear her over the noise of the crowd and traffic. "I thought it might be someone else I'd recognize."

"Like who?"

"My sister's boyfriend. He doesn't like me, and the feeling's mutual. Or one of a group of bikers I ticked off a few weeks back…the day I got shot. That can't be a coincidence, can it?" One thing he had to give Gina credit for—whether she was venting her temper, discussing a case or admitting her fear—she looked him straight in the eye. He had to admire a woman with that kind of confidence. But it also gave Mike a chance to read the real emotions behind her words. "I couldn't see this guy's face, either. He had dark glasses on and a ball cap pulled low over his forehead. I couldn't even give you a hair color or age. I don't suppose you got a description of him?"

She was afraid, and it didn't take a rocket scientist to guess that fear wasn't an emotion she was used to feeling. Mike moved his fingers from her waist to stroke the sleek muscles of her arm, wanting to reassure her somehow. But he had an idea she wasn't used to accepting comfort, either. "No. But you think that car has been following you? Is that why you're running the plate number?"

"My partner is. Technically, I'm on medical leave. He's doing me a favor."

Knowing the shooter was still out there, and that she wouldn't be able to identify the man if he came back to finish the job until she saw a gun pointed at her would rattle anybody. Even an experienced cop like Gina. "Come back to the clinic. I'll drive you home."

"No." She started to push him away, but the tips of her fingers curled into the cotton knit of his polo, lightly clinging to the skin and muscle underneath. "No, thank you," she added, apologizing for the abruptness of her answer. "It's probably someone who lives or works in the neighborhood. There are gangbangers in my part of town. They know I'm a cop. Maybe one of them recognized me. And maybe it was nothing. After the shooting, I'm overly suspicious of any vehicle that slows down or stops when it shouldn't."

He was surprised to feel her reaching out to him, even more surprised to realize how every cell leaped beneath her touch, even one as casual as her hold on him now. This wild attraction he was feeling was un-expected—and most likely unreciprocated, if his track record for following his hormones and heart was any indication. Gina had had her entire life turned up-side down, and she was learning how to cope with the changes. All she needed from him right now was a steady presence she could hold on to for a few sec-onds while she regrouped. He could give her that. "I wouldn't rationalize away your suspicions, Gina. Sounds to me like survival skills, not paranoia."

Her gaze finally dropped from his to study the line of his jaw. She smiled when she murmured, "Physical therapist, not counselor. *Not* bodyguard."

"How about friend?" he offered. Because this pseudo embrace against the brick wall was starting to feel a lot like something more than a therapist–pa-tient relationship was happening between them.

"Maybe it *is* a little far to walk." But she wasn't ask-ing for a ride. Another bus pulled up behind him, her phone rang and she pulled away to take out her cell and join the line waiting to board the bus. "I'll see you tomorrow morning… Mike."

She paused before his name, as if it was hard to pronounce.

Maybe it was just hard to accept his offer. "Do you need me to pick you up?"

"*Not* my chauffeur." She raised her voice to be heard above the bus's idling engine.

He raised his, too. "I'm not being nice. I'm being practical."

But she was already climbing on, taking her call. Mike backed away as the bus door closed and the big vehicle hissed and growled, spewing fumes that blocked out the spicy scent he was learning to identify as Gina's.

Mike watched the bus chug up to speed and sail through the intersection before he turned back toward the PT clinic. He scanned the traffic as he walked, trying to spot the car again. Maybe the driver had circled around the block a third time. Maybe the tan sedan was long gone. Maybe it had nothing to do with Gina or the shooting.

Erring on the side of caution, he pulled out his own phone and texted himself the license plate number before he forgot it. He'd ask his dad or one of his buddies at the police department to see what they could find out about the car and its owner.

He hadn't gotten a look at the shooter who'd sped away that day, either. He'd been too focused on helping the cops who'd been wounded. Had the car triggered a memory in Gina's subconscious mind, reminding her of something she'd seen? Or was all that bravado she spouted the protective armor of a woman who'd had her confidence ripped out from under her feet?

Mike wasn't a cop. But he was thinking like one, and he needed answers.

Was the shooter tracking her down, learning her routine so he could come back and finish the job? If so, did that mean the shooting was personal? Not a random attack on cops?

Was Gina still in danger?

What kind of backup did a cop on medical leave have? Maybe she didn't need Mike to protect her. But, injured as she was, without the ability to use her gun, how would the woman protect herself?

Chapter 5

"Not my chauffeur, Choir Boy," Gina insisted, catching the towel Mike tossed her way with her left hand. Slightly breathless after a duel on side-by-side treadmills that she suspected he'd let her win, she dabbed at the perspiration at her neck and at the cleavage of the gray tank top she wore. "I can get to KCPD headquarters on my own."

After a week of physical therapy sessions with Mike Cutler, she had to give him grief, or else he might begin to think his jokes amused her—and that his efforts to be a gentleman and push her toward recovery with the same mix of authority and restraint his dad used at KCPD might result in her actually liking the guy.

At least he had the sense to respect her fitness level. He allowed her to push hard with her legs and left arm, in addition to the far gentler stretches and coordination exercises he did with her right hand and arm. "I suspect your legs are like jelly, so you're not walking. And I can't wait for you to get there by bus. How much time do you think I can spare for you out of my busy day?" he teased. He picked up his own towel to wipe his face. "I'm driving."

Busy day? Gina picked up the sling he'd let her remove before that last running challenge and swung her gaze over to where Troy was working with a retired firefighter with knee issues. She hadn't seen many other patients. And she'd overheard a conversation between Mike and Frannie on Monday about moving money from his personal account to make a payment on an expensive piece of equipment.

They might come from two different worlds, but growing up in suburbia hadn't guaranteed that a person could make ends meet. Still, the fact that he drove into this part of the city from somewhere else and probably lived in a house big enough to stretch out those long, muscular legs of his made her a little jealous. Heck, he no doubt had more bathrooms in that house than any one man could use, while she intended to take a quick shower here so that she wouldn't have to let her workout scent marinate while she waited in line to use the bathtub at home.

His tone grew serious as he sat down on the bench, facing her. "Are you worried about going back to Precinct headquarters? I'd rather evaluate the status of your grip at the shooting range than bring a gun here."

"No. That's fine. While we're there I can check in with my partner—see if there are any developments in the shooting investigation. Not that I can do anything about it officially, but…" Maybe she should take Mike up on his offer of a ride, in case being back in the building where she could no longer work stirred up her frustrations again—or embarrassment if she discovered she was no better at handling a firearm today than she'd been seven weeks ago. She'd hate to be waiting for the bus if she wanted to make a quick escape.

Those piercing blue eyes studied every nuance of her expression, trying to read her thoughts. "But you want to regain a little control over what you're going through?"

Funny how she'd lost control of everything during those few seconds in the street outside Vicki Bismarck's house.

Not funny how well this man could read her fears and insecurities. But she wasn't about to admit those vulnerabilities to Mike or anyone else. Better a chauffeur than a therapist. "All right, then. You can drive me."

He arced an eyebrow, looking as surprised by the one-time concession as she'd meant him to be. But her plan to catch him off guard and stop him from analyzing her emotions backfired when Mike pushed to his feet. Suddenly, she was nose-to-chest with Mike's lanky frame. His broad shoulders blocked her peripheral vision and she could feel the heat coming off his body. "Give me fifteen minutes to shower and change, and we'll go."

Catnip. She retreated a step when she realized she was inhaling the earthy smells of sweat and soap and man, and savoring the elemental response his scent triggered inside her. "Make it ten," she challenged, denying her body's feminine reaction. "How much time do you think I can spare for you out of my busy day?"

Mike laughed at her mimicking comeback, and she smiled for a moment before mumbling one of her great-uncle's curses and spinning away to march toward the women's locker room. When had his silly sense of humor started rubbing off on her? She wasn't supposed to like a man like Mike Cutler. At least, she wasn't supposed to like him as anything other than a physical therapist and maybe a friend. Besides, she already had enough responsibilities demanding her time and energy. When did she think she was going to squeeze in dating?

Mike was right about one thing. She needed to be in control of her life, in control of her future, again. She'd be smart to ignore any fluttering of her pulse, any urge to laugh at their banter, and that relentless pull to the heat of his body.

"Ten minutes, Choir Boy."

Gina had learned long ago how to get in and out of the bathroom quickly and came out of the shower five minutes later, her skin cooled and fresh, her libido firmly in check. She towel-dried her hair and finger-combed the chin-length waves into place before she started to dress. After the shooting, she'd switched to a front hook bra and button-up blouses so she could dress herself. But, though she'd taken Mike's advice and worn her KCPD sweats for their therapy sessions, she wasn't about to show up at Precinct headquarters looking like she'd just come from the gym. It would be hard enough to be there out of uniform, sending the obvious message to her coworkers and superior officers that this was just a visit. Looking like a bum might also give them the impression that she wasn't coming back.

But the fitted jeans she took from her bag were a little tricky when she had to pull them up, especially when her skin was still dewy from the shower. The twinge in her shoulder and resulting tingling in her fingers when she gave them a tug warned her she needed to swallow her pride and ask someone to help her. When she heard a woman's voice out in the locker area, Gina gave a mental prayer of thanks that she wouldn't have to leave the locker room with her jeans hanging on her hips to go get Mike.

"Hey, could you help...?" Gina's question died when she saw Frannie dabbing at her red-tipped nose as she folded towels from a laundry basket and stacked them on a shelf. The woman with hair the color of a penny kept muttering something that sounded like *stupid ninny*. Gina cleared her throat to announce her presence. "Are you okay?"

Frannie spun around, hugging a fluffy towel to her chest. "I'm sorry. Did you need something?"

Gina pointed to her jeans. "I'm stuck."

"Oh, right." Frannie dropped the towel into the basket and hurried over to give the black pants a final tug. "Mike said you needed to be careful with that arm."

"Thanks." Gina took over buttoning the waistband and pulling up the zipper. "I guess I need to stick to sweats." But Frannie had gone back to folding. Maybe this wasn't any of her business, but the woman had just helped her pull up her pants, so there was a bit of a connection there. Moving closer, Gina plucked a hand towel from the basket and held it out to the taller woman. "What happened? And don't say *nothing* because you've been crying for a while."

Frannie took the towel and pulled off her glasses to dry her eyes. "I got a phone call."

"From your ex?" Even the eye that didn't seem to focus looked startled. When the other woman backed away, Gina reached for her hand. "I eavesdrop. I'm a cop. I like to know who the people around me are. You and Troy were arguing about a restraining order for your ex yesterday."

Frannie put her glasses back on and sort of smiled. "We were arguing about Troy's van. He drove me to the judge's office to reinstate the order. Troy can't use his legs, you know, so he has this special van where he uses a hand brake and accelerator to drive. I mentioned one thing about how fast he was going before a jerky stop at a red light, and he started yelling about the van falling apart, and that he hadn't had a chance to clean it up before I rode in it. I thought he was mad at me. I don't deal with confrontation very well."

"Have you ridden with Troy before?"

Frannie shook her head.

Sounded like wounded male pride. She thought she'd detected a few stolen glances between the two coworkers. Maybe Troy wasn't keen on Frannie seeing the extent of his handicap. "Not everyone who argues with you is going to hurt you."

"I know. Troy's usually really sweet and funny. I probably caught him on a bad day." That sounded like a woman who'd been victimized making excuses for a man who'd yelled at her or hurt her.

This whole conversation—and all the other interactions she'd had with the skittish Frannie—reminded her of Vicki Bismarck. She wondered if that last call she'd been working on before the shooting had been resolved. Was Gordon Bismarck still in jail? Had his big brother, Denny, and his friends retaliated against Vicki in any way? Had Vicki gotten the medical treatment she'd needed? Moved in with her sister? Pressed charges against Gordon?

Or were Denny and his biker boys more interested in retaliating against the police officers who'd arrested Gordon? Had he been the man in the rusty SUV the day she'd been shot? Gina's fingers drifted to her right shoulder—not feeling a physical or even phantom pain, but remembering with vivid detail the bullet tearing through her body, the multiple gunshots exploding all around her and the snow soaking up her blood and body heat.

Gina realized she was shivering before she pulled herself from the memories. The Bismarcks weren't her case anymore. And everyone at KCPD was working on finding out who'd shot one of their own. Everyone but her, that is. She wasn't used to being the victim. She didn't like being out of the investigative loop or being taken off the front line of protecting her city, her family and herself.

But the situation right in front of her was one she could handle. Gina sat and patted the bench beside her. She had a feeling Frannie's tears weren't really about the argument with Troy. "Tell me about the phone call."

"From Leo?" Frannie hesitated for a moment before sitting. "I was getting ready for work this morning. I didn't pick up. As soon as I heard his voice, I let it go straight to my machine. He said he missed me. That he still loved me. That he always would." She paused a moment before adding, "He wants to see me."

"Is he supposed to have any contact with you?" When Frannie shook her head, Gina's first instinct was to pull out her own phone and file a report. But she wasn't a cop right now. She couldn't take action, but she could give advice. "Polite or not—even if Leo pulled at your heartstrings—you need to call the police and report it." The jerk had probably just been served with the restraining order and thought he could talk her out of it. "Keep a record of any contact he makes with you—by phone, email, certainly in person. Do you know his parole officer's name? He needs to know about the call, too."

The other woman straightened her shoulders and nodded. "I know that's what I'm supposed to do. I can ask Mike to help. He said his dad was looking into it." Frannie offered Gina a smile that quickly faded. "I'm such a ninny. Have you ever been so scared of a person that you can't even think when he's around?" She stood abruptly and carried the hand towel to the clothes hamper near the shower room. "Look who I'm talking to. You're not scared of anything."

Gina was thinking that never regaining the full use of her hand and arm was a pretty terrifying thing to contemplate. Losing her job. Letting her family down. Never getting the life she wanted for all of them. "Maybe not people," she confessed.

Although there was one faceless shooter who'd put her on guard from the moment she'd regained consciousness in the hospital. Like nearly every other waking moment, Gina wondered if there'd ever be an arrest of the man who'd targeted her and her partner.

They weren't on Gordon Bismarck's good side after arresting him. There'd certainly been plenty of time for Denny to switch vehicles and come back to the house to shoot her and Derek. According to Mike, the SUV's plates had been unreadable. A citywide search for a rusted SUV matching the description he'd given the police had turned up nothing useful. Even the license number on the tan sedan she and Mike had seen wasn't any help. The plates were stolen, according to Derek. The car they'd been registered to belonged to an elderly man who rarely drove it and didn't even know the plates were missing.

Could the Bismarck brothers and their friends be running a stolen-car ring? Or even have legitimate access to a variety of vehicles? In her mind, Bobby Estes was a viable suspect, too. She wouldn't put it past Bobby to try something like that. From what she knew of her sister's smarmy boyfriend, his driving a stolen car, or one with a falsified registration and plates like the Mercedes she'd seen following her, wouldn't surprise her. Shooting the woman who stood in the way of getting what he wanted wouldn't surprise her, either.

Surely someone at KCPD had looked into the background of the prime suspects who'd been at the scene right before the shooting or lived in the same neighborhood. She certainly would. If she was on the case. But she wasn't. And until someone else found the answers, identifying a suspect and a motive, the shooter remained at large—and had the advantage of knowing her, while she remained clueless to his face and name and whether he was coming after her to finish the job he'd started.

"I know what fear is." Gina stood when Frannie resumed folding the towels, probably thinking the long pause meant the conversation was over. "You just have to decide you're not going to let it rule your life."

"That's easier said than done."

"I know. You have to keep trying—every day—to be stronger than the fear. If it gets you one day, then you wake up the next and you try harder." Frannie hugged a towel to her chest again and nodded, trying to internalize the hard-won advice that Gina had learned in No-Man's Land. Gina smiled and added a little practical advice to that philosophical wisdom. "If Leo does come to see you, call 9-1-1. If he physically threatens you, fight back. As hard as you can." She gestured as she gave each instruction. "Stomp on his instep. Gouge his eyes. Ram your hand against the bottom of his nose. And, of course, there's always the old goodie—kicking him where it counts." Frannie silently repeated each hand movement. Gina repeated them for her, encouraging her to use more force. "Scream your head off, too. Help will come running. At least around here. Either Troy or Mike has his eyes on you whenever I'm here. Probably when I'm not, too. Those two have a good-guy streak in them a mile wide."

Frannie nodded. "I know. They've been through so much, and they're still so nice. Any girl would be lucky to…" Her cheeks turned pink as she swallowed whatever emotion she'd been about to share. "Mike's like a big brother to me."

Gina wasn't forgetting where this conversation had started. "And Troy?"

Frannie's blush intensified. Interesting. Maybe she wasn't so keen on Troy seeing her shortcomings, either. "They're the best. I'll talk to Mike and call Leo's parole officer." She divvied up the clean towels and put half away before carrying the basket to the locker room door. She paused there, looking to Gina before repeating her advice. "Feet. Eyes. Nose. Family jewels."

Gina grinned. "And scream like crazy."

"Thanks."

For what? All she'd done was give the woman a few tools to use if she ever needed to defend herself against her ex. It was what any cop would do. Acknowledging that it felt good to do something that made her feel useful again, Gina quickly finished dressing. No doubt Mike would have some comment about missing her ten-minute challenge to be ready. He'd expect her to laugh. And if she wasn't careful, she probably would.

They've been through so much...

What had Frannie meant by that comment? What could Troy and Mike, especially Mike, have endured that would make the other woman sound surprised— almost awestruck—that the two men would end up being such nice guys? Such hero figures to her?

And why was Gina so curious to find out the answer to that question?

"I'd like to check in with my partner first." Gina stepped into the elevator and pushed the 3 button on the panel, taking her and Mike upstairs instead of down to the shooting range in the basement. "Our desks..." Hopefully hers hadn't been filled yet, but she knew her partner had been temporarily reassigned to ride with someone else until she could get back to patrol duty. "Derek's desk," she corrected, "is on the third floor." She checked the time on her phone before tucking it into her back pocket. "They're probably getting out of morning roll call about now."

"Not a problem. My schedule's flexible." Mike joined her at the back railing. "Today is all about taking your recovery to the next level. Making that hand usable again."

Gina inhaled a deep breath. "I hope there's a level after that. *Usable* doesn't sound like it'll get me the job I want."

"The healing part I can't control. But I'll teach your body to do everything it's capable of. I promise. It's just a matter of time and training." Even leaning against the car's back wall, Mike was a head taller than she was.

Gina was used to being shorter than most men, often shorter than anyone in the room except for her great-aunt. But her bulky uniform vest, gun and determined attitude usually beefed up her presence. Yet there was something about Mike Cutler that seemed to fill up the limited space of the elevator and make her feel tiny, fragile, more feminine than usual. Perhaps it was the lack of the uniform and gear she usually wore. Or perhaps it was the protective way he opened doors for her and stood on her right side, shielding her injured arm now that she didn't have to wear the sling around the clock anymore. Although she might be vertically challenged, Gina had never considered herself delicate in any way. Not since she was a child had she needed anyone to protect her. Back then, an absent father and an ailing mother had forced her to grow some tough emotional armor and learn to fight and stay smarter than any adversary. Gina took care of herself and her family all on her own. She didn't need a man taking care of her.

Even if he did smell good and generate the kind of heat she fantasized about on chilly spring mornings like this.

"Am I your only patient today?" she asked, needing to start a conversation before she did something damsel-like and leaned into that body heat.

He tucked his fingers into the pockets of his jeans and answered. "Yeah. Business has been slow."

She wasn't blind to the lack of company at the CAPT Center in the mornings. "You didn't exactly pick the most lucrative area of the city to set up shop. Have you ever thought of affiliating with a hospital? Even moving the center a couple of blocks over to Westport would make it appealing to a broader audience. Not everyone feels safe spending a lot of time that close to No-Man's Land. You know, that part of the city where urban renewal hasn't quite reached—"

"I know what No-Man's Land is. Son of a cop, remember?" He tilted his face down to hers. "I've done the hospital thing. We're exactly where we want to be, offering physical therapy services to an underserved part of the city. We're our own bosses now. Troy grew up in the neighborhood, and I've had my share of experience there."

"Your share of experience?" Gina scoffed. "You're telling me you've been on the mean streets of the city? You've broken the law? I pegged you for a middle-class suburbia guy all the way."

Was that a scowl? Did Mr. Good Guy have a secret sore spot she'd just poked? He straightened away from the railing. "I'm not the *choir boy* you think I am. I've done things."

"Like what? Cheat on a test? Run a red light?"

The scowl deepened. Gina felt a stab of guilt, thinking back to Frannie's comment about Mike going through something terrible in his past. Had her smart mouth just crossed a line?

"You don't live in the suburbs? Have enough land that you can't touch your house and the neighbor's at the same time?" Good grief. Was she actually making light of the topic to try and restore that goofball smile to his face? "I was really hoping you had three bathrooms because I was totally going to come for a visit and spend the afternoon soaking in one of those tubs."

She heard an exhale of breath that sounded like a wry laugh.

"You want to get in my bathtub?" There was the glimpse of white teeth amid the sexy dusting of his beard. His voice dropped to a throaty whisper as he leaned in. "I wouldn't object to that."

Gina couldn't remember the last time she'd blushed hard enough to feel heat in her cheeks. "I meant…our house is small. I share one bathroom with four… I can't take my time…" She growled at her flummoxed reaction to his teasing innuendo.

Not a boyfriend. *Not* a lover. *Not* a man who should be getting under her skin.

Thankfully the elevator doors slid open, and she could escape the sound of Mike's laughter.

But she never got the chance to get her armor fully in place again. A trio of SWAT cops waited just outside the elevator, greeting Mike with a chorus of "Mikey,"

handshakes and a ribbing about an upcoming barbe-
cue contest.

Gina knew the three officers, dressed in solid black,
except for the white SWAT logo she coveted embroidered on their chest pockets. These were her trainers.
Members of KCPD's elite SWAT Team One, led by
Captain Cutler. The one with the black hair, Sergeant
Rafe Delgado, was even slated to lead the new tactical team she wanted to be a part of.

Clearly, they were all longtime friends, with Mike
giving the jokes right back, teasing Holden Kincaid,
the team's sharpshooter, about the dogs living at his
house who were all smarter than him. He asked about
Sergeant Delgado's son, Aaron, and pointed to the
baby bump just beginning to show on the woman with
the long ponytail, Miranda Gallagher. "They're not letting you out into the field, are they, Randy?"

Gina admired the tall blonde who had been KCPD's
first female SWAT officer. She'd shared a couple of
private conversations with Gina about the challenges
and rewards of being a woman with her specialized
training. Officer Gallagher cradled her hand against
her belly. "For now, these bozos are letting me drive
the van. Pretty soon, though, I'll be relegated to equipment maintenance, and then it's maternity leave."

Gina felt like an afterthought, and considered duck-
ing back into the elevator with the two detectives who
snuck in behind her to go downstairs. She hadn't even
realized she'd been backing away from the animated
reunion until she felt Mike's hand at the small of her
back, pulling her forward to stand beside him. "You
all know Gina Galvan, right?"

Sergeant Delgado nodded. "Of course, we know our star recruit. We miss you at training."

Holden agreed. "She keeps us on our toes."

"Hi, Gina." Miranda Gallagher smiled down at her.

Apparently, she was going to be a part of this conversation after all. "Officer Gallagher."

Miranda tilted her head. "We talked about that."

Gina nodded. "Randy."

Sergeant Delgado pointed to her arm. "I heard you were at Mike's clinic. How's the recovery going?"

"Fine." She glanced up at Mike. *Was* she getting any better?

Mike's hand rubbed a subtle circle beneath her denim jacket, and she nearly startled at the unexpected tendrils of warmth webbing out across her skin and into the muscles beneath. "She's progressing nicely. Slowly but surely, I'm seeing improvement every day."

"That's good to hear." Holden tapped his thigh. "You willing to give out some free advice to the guy who once saved your life?"

Saved his life?

"What's up?" Mike asked. "And I thought I saved myself."

Saved himself? *I'm not the* choir boy *you think I am, Gina. I've done things.* She still couldn't get her head around what kind of secrets a guy like Mike might have.

"You wish," Holden teased before getting serious. "My knee hasn't been right since I took a tumble off a roof doing sniper duty last week. Anything I can do besides load up on ibuprofen?"

"You should go to Mike's clinic." Gina wasn't sure where the suggestion had come from, other than a deep-seated need to keep things even between them.

If Mike was supporting her in a moment of social discomfort, then she'd support him. "The location's not that far from headquarters. You could stop in over lunch or right after work."

"I'll do that." Holden smiled at Gina. "He's obviously doing something right with you, so that's a good recommendation."

Mike's fingers pressed into her back. The tension flowing from him into her didn't exactly feel like a thank you. "Call for an appointment. My assistant will make sure we squeeze you in."

"I'll do that. Thanks."

Sergeant Delgado checked his watch and hurried the conversation along. "I hate to break up the party, but we've got an inspection this morning. We'd better get down to the garage and secure the van."

"Good to see you guys."

"You, too, Mikey."

There was another round of handshakes, and a hug with Miranda before the three uniformed officers got on the elevator and Mike pulled Gina aside to whisper, "I don't need you to drum up business for me."

"And I don't need you to stand up for me."

He shrugged. "It's what people do. Make everyone feel included. What is your hang-up with me being nice to you?"

She propped her hands at her hips and tilted her face to his. "You know those are my superior officers, right? I shouldn't be socializing with them."

"I practically grew up with those guys. That was running into family, not socializing."

"You weren't including me in the conversation to curry favor with them, were you? I want to earn my spot on the new team on merit, not because I'm friends with the captain's son."

Suddenly, the hushed argument was over. He straightened. "So, we're friends now? And here I thought you were going to fight me every step of the way."

She stared at his hand when he reached for hers, overriding the instinctive urge to close the short distance and lace her fingers together with his. No, she couldn't start leaning on Mike just because he made it so easy to do so.

Gina heard a wry chuckle, although she didn't see a smile, as he curled his fingers into his palm and turned toward the desk sergeant's station to check in and get visitor badges. "Right. Just friends. Come on. Let's find your partner."

Chapter 6

"Did you talk to the man who had his plates stolen?" Gina asked, scrolling through the sketchy details of the report on Derek's computer screen. Had he always been this lax about following up with paperwork on the calls they handled? Had she been too obsessive about her own A+ work ethic to notice his borderline incompetence? Or was he skating by on minimal effort without her at his side every day to push him into being the best cop he could be? "Could you tie him to the Bismarck brothers or Bobby Estes?"

Derek perched on the corner of his desk, looking over her shoulder at the screen. "It was just me running a plate for you. I didn't follow up because there wasn't any crime."

Gina shook her head, closing down the page. At least a mouse was easy to control with just her thumb and index finger. It wasn't frontline action, but she could make herself useful doing a little research. "Um, theft? Maybe tell one of the detectives working that stolen-car ring? You know I think Bobby is involved with something like that. How else could he afford the different cars he drives? And, clearly, Denny Bismarck is a motor head. You saw that bike he was riding. Does he work in auto repair? A guy like that could easily lift plates off another vehicle."

Speaking of detectives, her gaze slid across the maze of desks and cubicles to spot Mike chatting with a plainclothes officer she recognized as one of the department's veterans, Atticus Kincaid. Was he related to Holden Kincaid, the SWAT sharpshooter? From senior officers down to the administrative assistant in the chief's office, they'd all said hi or waved or nodded or smiled. He was a law-enforcement legacy more at home at Precinct headquarters because of his father's seniority than she was after six years of scratching her way up through the ranks. If she needed any more evidence that they came from different parts of the city, from virtually two different worlds, that comfortable-in-his-own-skin, one-of-the-boys conversation was it.

"You're right." Derek interrupted thoughts that felt melancholy rather than envious, as she would have had seven weeks ago. Either Mike had social skills she could never hope to possess or she truly was an outsider fighting to find her place among an elite group of cops. "I did mention it to a detective."

Gina spun the chair to face her partner. "What did they say?"

Derek shrugged his broad shoulders. "I just gave him the message."

Gina combed her fingers through her hair and clasped the nape of her neck, biting down on her frustration. "Well, has there been any progress on the shooting investigation?"

Surely, he'd be right on top of the case that was so personal for both of them. He nodded, moving off the desk to open the bottom drawer and pull out a file folder. "Detective Grove and his partner brought Denny Bismarck and his biker buddies in for questioning. Other than the verbal threats they made at the house, we can't get them on anything. They all alibi each other. Said they left the Bismarck house and went straight to the Sin City Bar."

"Can anyone at the bar confirm that?" Gina picked up a notepad and copied names and contact information. Holding a pen was a skill she'd worked on with Mike. The handwriting wasn't pretty, but it was legible, and learning these details was making her feel like a cop again.

"You'd have to ask Grove. Whatever he found out is in that file."

"You didn't follow up?"

"I was in the hospital."

"I know. But after that?"

"No."

"Four suspects accounting for each other's whereabouts is hardly a solid alibi. And that wasn't the first time we stopped Gordon Bismarck from hurting his ex-wife. What if that call was a setup to get us shot all along?"

"What's with all the questions?" he snapped, lowering his voice when the officers at the nearby desks looked his direction. "Look, G, I'm not trying to be a detective. My goal is SWAT."

"Your goal should be being the best cop you can be." Gina stood, tucking the notes into the pocket of her jeans. There had to be something else going on here. "Don't you want to find out who shot you? I want to see that guy behind bars."

"I just want to put it behind me." Derek skimmed his hand over the top of his light brown hair, a look of anguish lining his face. "I can't solve the case for you. Hell, G, I don't remember anything of that afternoon after being shot. The doctors said I hit my head. I remember getting shot, going down, and then..." He shook his head, his frustration evident. "You're not the only one who lost something that day."

"Why didn't you tell me?" She squeezed her hand around his forearm, offering the support she hadn't realized he needed. "I'm so sorry. I didn't know. I'm not criticizing. You must be as frustrated as I am. But I want answers. Justice. For both of us."

"I know." Derek patted her hand. "I didn't want to do anything that would get Vicki hurt either, so I kind of let things slide."

"Vicki Bismarck?" Gina frowned as she remembered a detail from the moments before they'd been shot. "You two were calling each other by your first names that day. Is there something personal going on between you two?"

He shrugged and pulled away to shuffle some papers on his desk. "We may have gone out a couple of times. Nothing came of it."

"You dated a victim you met on a call? A domestic-violence victim? Was that before or after someone tried to end us?"

"Vic is really sweet. Once you get past the shyness."

Gina's mouth opened. Shut. Opened again. "Derek—you know what a jealous idiot Gordon Bismarck is. Going out with his ex-wife could have been the motive to make him go ballistic and target us."

Derek spun around, his tone hushed but angry. "We don't know if that's what happened."

Gina pushed the papers back to the desktop, wanting some concrete answers. "Did you follow up on Gordon? Find out if he saw the two of you together?"

"No. And if I make a stink of it, he might take it out on her."

"Does Vicki mean something to you?"

"I haven't seen her since that day. Let it go, G."

"I'm not blaming you, especially if you're trying to protect her. I just want answers. I want to put someone away for trying to end our lives. Don't you?"

"Sure." Derek dropped his head to stare at the spot where her hand rested on his desk beside his. "Don't you think I feel guilty? I don't remember enough about what happened that day to ID the guy—and now you're suggesting I may have triggered the incident in the first place? I just thought some crazy was targeting cops."

And maybe that *was* the answer. But how could he not be using every spare moment to find the truth? Would guilt, amnesia and worry about a victim's well-being be enough to stop her from pursuing every possible lead?

The telephone on his desk rang. He inhaled a steadying breath before picking up after the second ring. "Officer Johnson. What? Right now? Just what I need," he muttered sarcastically. "No, that's fine."

"Is something wrong?" she asked once he'd hung up.

Derek smoothed the long black sleeves of his uniform and straightened his belt. "Let's drop this conversation for now, okay? I've got a visitor. They're sending him back." He made an apologetic face. "Fair warning."

"Huh?"

And then she understood the cryptic comment. A man wearing a visitor's badge, looking like a hippie version of Derek, with faded jeans, a stained fringed jacket and a graying, stringy ponytail hanging down the middle of his back, came around the cubicle wall. "Dad? What are you doing here?"

"There's my boy." The two shook hands before Harold Johnson pulled Derek in for a black-slapping hug. When he pushed away, he was grinning down at Gina. "Senorita Galvan. What are you doing here?"

Gina remembered the ruddy cheeks, leathered skin and inappropriate comments from her earlier encounters with Derek's father. All the years he'd spent outdoors working at a junkyard between stays in jail or rehab seemed to be aging him quickly but hadn't put a dent in his oily charm. "It's *Officer* Galvan, Harold. Or Gina. Remember?"

"My apologies. But you remind me so much of that *chica bonita* who used to serve me tequila shots at Alvarez's outside Fort Bliss." He chuckled at the memory of the pretty girl who used to wait on his table. "And she was just as insistent I call her Senorita."

Derek shook his head at the tired old joke. "You

said that was because she didn't want you calling her after hours."

Harold swatted Derek on the shoulder and told him to get a sense of humor. "Forgive an old man. I know it's not politically correct, but some habits are hard to change. Come here, honey."

Honey? Like that was any better. Gina went stiff as the older man leaned in for an unexpected hug.

"I'm just glad you and my boy are okay. Scariest moment of my life was when I got that phone call that he'd been shot. I'm glad his mama didn't live to see…"

A hand came over Gina's shoulder, palming Harold's chest and pushing him out of the hug and out of her space. "Easy. She's injured."

Gina didn't need to hear Mike's low voice to know who'd rescued her from the unwanted squeeze. She recognized his scent and the heat of his body against her back. Her breath came out in a huff of relief. She hadn't even been thinking about her rebuilt shoulder. She'd been bothered by the same overly familiar discomfort she got when Derek talked about her sister, Sylvie, as if he wanted to date her. But, not wanting to insult her partner's father and drive a rift between her and Derek, she was glad for the physical excuse. "Sorry, Harold. I've got to watch the arm while it's still healing."

He settled for a loose handshake that extended the awkward moment when he pointed out her limp fingers. "That's too bad about your hand. I guess you didn't see the man who shot you, either. Derek had his back to him but said you were facing him."

Pulling away, Gina tucked her hand inside her jacket against her stomach, surprised by the indirect accusation. Of course, a father would want his child to be safe. Even if that child was a grown man, a good father would want to know why his son had gotten hurt. "I heard the shots. I didn't see—"

"Of course you didn't. Otherwise, you would have warned my boy. He wouldn't have gotten hurt."

"Dad," Derek warned.

Mike moved to Gina's side, positioning his body in a way that forced Harold back another step. He was shielding her again, even as he thrust out his hand. "I'm Mike Cutler."

Harold's bushy brows knotted with confusion as they shook hands. "Harold Johnson. I'm Derek's daddy. You a cop?"

"I'm a friend. And you're out of line."

Derek finished the introductions with an embarrassed sigh. "This is Captain Cutler's son, Dad."

"You're Captain Cutler's boy?" *Boy* wasn't a term Gina would ever use to refer to Mike, especially when he was a solid wall of defense between her and any perceived threat or insult as he was now. Harold's frown at Mike's intrusion flipped into a beaming smile. "I see the resemblance now. Your daddy's got my boy on a short list for his new SWAT team. That means a promotion and more money."

"Gina mentioned it." Mike nodded to Derek. "Congratulations. My dad doesn't make decisions lightly. I understand he's narrowed it down to ten good candidates."

Harold tilted his head to offer Gina a sympathetic frown. "Looks like it's down to nine, unfortunately."

"Harold," Gina chided, "Captain Cutler isn't making his final decision for another week. I have every intention of giving your son and everyone else a run for their money. And I'm as much a victim of that shooting as Derek was."

"Ooh, touched a nerve there, didn't I?" Harold laughed, elbowing Derek's arm before apologizing. "I'm sorry, honey. I just assumed—"

"'I'm sorry, *Officer* Galvan,'" she corrected with the most precise articulation her subtle accent allowed. How had Derek grown up to have any charm at all with a father who didn't possess an ounce of empathy or respect for personal boundaries?

Harold retreated a step as Mike leaned toward him. "Watch your mouth, Johnson."

But Derek had it handled. After sliding Gina an apologetic look, he pulled his father around the corner of the desk. "Why are you here, anyway? What do you need?"

"A place we can talk in private? Family business." Derek seemed relieved to usher his father toward an interview room. "I've been talkin' to a lawyer…"

That's when she discovered she'd latched on to the back of Mike's shirt. Tightly enough to feel the flex of muscle through the cotton knit. Had she really thought Mr. Nice Guy was going after Harold and she'd have to stop him? Or had she subconsciously realized she needed the anchor of his solid presence to get through this difficult visit to Precinct headquarters after all?

She quickly released him and tilted her face to meet Mike's sharp blue gaze when he turned. "You ready to go?"

Gina patted her pocket with the folded notes. "I got enough information that I can follow up a few leads myself."

He arched an eyebrow that was as sleekly handsome as Harold's had been a bushy mess. "Need I remind you that you're on medical leave?"

"It doesn't hurt to make a few phone calls."

"What if you stir up the wrong kind of interest— like that driver who threatened you last week? What if he's the shooter, trying to figure out whether you recognize him? If you start poking the bear, he might stop the next time and finish what he started. You don't have a gun or a badge right now."

"You don't have to remind me of *that*," she snapped, turning toward the elevators. He followed in that long, loose stride that forced her to take two steps for every one of his to beat him to the elevator's call button. "I can't stand by and do nothing. I can at least make a pest of myself with the detectives investigating the shooting."

They had to wait long enough that logic had the chance to sneak past Gina's flare of temper. Mike was right about starting something she couldn't finish. What if she did manage to identify the man who'd shot her? She wouldn't be able to do anything more than call someone else at KCPD to make the arrest. If she confronted him herself, she'd be at a disadvantage. She hadn't been able to protect her partner back when she'd been at 100 percent. What did she think she could do now? Not only could he hurt her again, he could hurt the people around her—her family, innocent bystanders, this tall drink of annoyingly right catnip standing beside her—and she couldn't do anything to stop him.

She was worse than useless as a cop right now. She might well be a danger to everyone around her.

The elevators were busy enough that Gina and Mike were standing there when Derek came around the corner of the last cubicle wall, pulling his father by the arm, hurrying him toward the exit. Whatever *family business* Harold had wanted to discuss, it wasn't going over well with Derek. Words like *lawsuit* and *easy money* popped out of the hushed argument. Was he suggesting that Derek sue the department? The city? Her? To make a profit off getting shot?

Although she was getting used to Mike positioning himself between her and anyone who might accidentally bump into her arm, his protective stance couldn't stop Harold from tugging free of his son's grip and addressing her. "Talk some sense into my boy, *chica*. Do the right thing."

"What are you talking about?"

"Leave her out of this, Dad. You've embarrassed me enough with your get-rich quick schemes. I'm sorry, G. Are we good?"

Gina nodded. Derek was her partner and a friend. He needed her support—not someone grilling him for answers or blaming him for whatever nutso scheme his dad had come up with.

"Come on." Derek snatched Harold by the shoulder of his jacket and pushed him toward the stairwell door. He shoved the door open and pulled his father inside, for privacy to continue the argument as much as the apparent need for speed in making an exit.

She was still staring after them when the elevator arrived and Mike's hand at the small of her back nudged her inside. She crossed to the back of the car and leaned against it, feeling her energy ebbing from the unexpected emotional onslaught of this morning's visit to the Precinct building. "That man is stuck in the Dark Ages. I suspect feminism and ethnic equality aren't part of his vocabulary."

"Derek's dad?"

"The only other Hispanic woman he knows is a bartender from a cantina during his army days? That's how he thinks of me? He blames me for Derek getting shot. No way could a *little woman*, much less one from my part of town, be a good cop and a good partner who could protect his son."

Mike pushed the button for the basement level before resting his hip against the back railing beside her. "He got to you. You don't blame yourself for getting shot, do you?"

Did she? Gina shook off the misguided guilt. "No. I know there's only one person to blame—a wannabe cop killer I can't identify."

"But Johnson made you *feel* guilty." The elevator lurched as it began its descent. "From the way that conversation started, I assumed he must always be a jerk and you were accustomed to blowing him off."

"Usually, I do. But…" Her mood descended right along with the elevator. "I feel out of step here today. Like I don't belong anymore. I don't know the facts of the most important cases. I can't maintain a conversation with people I've worked with for six years. Harold is always going to say something that gets under my skin, but I try to be civil about correcting him for Derek's sake. Yet today, I let him get to me. For a few seconds there, I thought you were going to do what I wanted to."

"Punch him in the mouth?" Gina groaned at his deadpan response. Besides lifting her spirits, the heat of his body standing close to hers was comforting, even though she hated to admit it. She watched as he slid his finger across the brass railing until his pinkie was brushing against hers. She couldn't feel that lightest of touches with her fingertip, but she felt the connection deeper inside. She felt his strength, his easy confidence, his caring. "Have you been back to HQ since the shooting?" he asked.

"Only to sign my incident report and fill out some insurance forms in the administrative offices. A few of the guys stopped by the hospital to see how I was doing. But I haven't done much to keep in touch since then. I've just been so focused…" She looked down at their hands, studying the differences in size and strength, the contrasts of male and female, the olive sheen of her skin next to his paler color. Mike Cutler was different from any man she'd ever taken the time to get to know. Not just on the outside. Somehow, her physical therapist had become her friend. A good friend. Her savior had become a trusted confidant who'd seen her at her worst and motivated her to be her best. He was honest and funny and strong in ways that went beyond his obvious athleticism. "I used to go toe-to-toe with those guys. Today, I feel like a rookie. Like I have to prove myself all over again just to keep my badge."

His pinkie brushed over the top of hers and hooked between her fingers, holding on in the subtlest of ways and deepening the connection she felt. "I bet there's not a one of those guys who could handle what you've been through and come back the way you are."

"They're KCPD's best."

"They're men. Men are terrible patients."

"I'm a terrible patient," she admitted.

"Yeah, but you're cute." Mike's voice had dropped to a husky timbre that skittered along her spine.

"*Cute?* No one has ever called me *cute*. Except maybe Harold Johnson." Although she'd never developed her flirting skills the way her sister had, Gina could hear the huskier notes in her own voice. "Strong. Stubborn. Temperamental. But not *cute*."

"I figured you'd punch me if I called you *sexy* or *built like a fine piece of art*. And I don't want you to injure that arm."

Gina felt herself blushing for the second time that day. But with an infusion of Mike's humor and compassion and that delicious heat she craved, she could also feel her strength coming back. "Stick with *cute*, Choir Boy. That may be the best I can do for a while."

"I'll take that bet." Mike slipped his broad hand beneath her smaller one, turning his palm up to meet hers. "Squeeze my hand. Hard as you can."

Gina straightened at the challenge. "Another exercise?"

"I'm warming you up for the shooting range. Just hold on to me." Her thumb and forefinger easily latched on, but she had to concentrate to move the other fingers. She wasn't sure if it was simple gravity or her own effort, but the last three fingers trembled into place, curling against the side of his hand. When she would have pulled away, he tightened his hand around hers. "Do you feel that?"

"I feel the heat coming off your skin." His grip pulsed around hers. Gina straightened as a renewed sense of hope surged through her. "I felt that." His deep blue eyes were watching her excitement, smiling. So was she. "Does that mean I'm getting the sensation back in my fingers? Am I improving?"

He squeezed her hand again. "Baby steps, Gina. I saw you writing with that pen. Picked it up without hesitation. That's definite improvement."

A dose of reality tempered her enthusiasm. "A gun is going to be a lot heavier than a pen. Losing control of a weapon is far more serious than making a scribble on a page."

One by one, Mike laced his fingers between hers. "My money's on you, Tiger."

He raised her hand to his lips and kissed her knuckles. She gasped at the surprising tickle of his beard stubble brushing across her skin. Were her nerves finding new pathways to bring sensation back to her hand? Or was that flush of warmth heating her blood a sign that Mike was starting to mean more to her than just a friend?

Gina knew the strangest urge to stretch up on her tiptoes and feel the ticklish sensation of his lips on her own. The elevator jostled them as it slowed its descent, and the tiny shake reminded Gina that this man was all kinds of wrong for her. Any relationship was, at this point in her life. But she could appreciate his friendship and support. "You didn't have to defend me against Derek's dad."

"Maybe I was protecting him from you."

A long-absent smile relaxed her lips as she leaned back, letting her shoulder rest against his arm. "You're a good man, Mike Cutler."

He shrugged. "It's what nice guys do."

Chapter 7

The following Monday afternoon, Gina was back in training. After her regular session at the CAPT clinic, Mike took her back to the Precinct offices for another round at the shooting range. He was a taskmaster, and she loved the challenges he set up for her. Running. Light weights. Flexibility. Although she still didn't believe they had much in common beyond these sessions, she enjoyed the time they were spending together—Mike the physical therapist putting her through her paces, Mike the friend making her laugh, Mike the protector watching her every move to make sure she didn't injure herself, even as he pushed her to do more.

Today, her hard work and his patience were going to pay off. She was going to shoot her gun, instead of merely manipulating the weapon as she had during last week's session. This time Mike was giving her a baseline test to see how much progress she was making toward returning to active duty.

Other than the officer manning the door to the shooting range, she and Mike were alone and could take their time going through the dexterity exercises they'd practiced last week. She cleared and unloaded, then reloaded her gun twice—once using both hands, and a second time that took several frustrating minutes, while Mike held her left hand down on the counter, forcing her to do more of the work with her right. Now, with their noise-cancelling headphones hanging around their necks, Mike picked up her service weapon.

"You're sure you know what you're doing?" she asked. "It's loaded today."

With an efficiency she envied and respected, he demonstrated that he knew exactly what to do with a Glock 9 mil. "I'm the son of a cop and grew up with guns in the house. Dad always made sure my brother and I knew gun safety and how to handle a weapon."

She put on her ear protection when he did and stepped to the side of the booth as he fired off five rounds. And, if she wasn't mistaken at this distance, he placed all but one of the bullets center mass of the target.

"Show-off," she teased, when he caught her staring in openmouthed admiration.

He grinned, unloading the Glock and setting the gun and magazine on the counter. "Your turn."

He pulled her in front of him, in that protective stance that surrounded her with his warmth. But this wasn't an embrace. It was a physical therapist supporting his patient. She needed to focus on her physical training.

Still, it was hard to miss the intimacy of their positions when her hip brushed against his thigh and his arm reached around her to tap the weapon. "I don't want you to fire any rounds yet. Let's practice raising and aiming the weapon."

Before last week, Gina hadn't handled her weapon since an embarrassing fiasco shortly after she returned home from the hospital. She'd thought she could suit up like any ordinary day and resume the chaos of her life without missing another step. But the heavy Glock had slipped from her grip and bounced across her bedroom floor. Thank goodness the safety had been on. That humbling morning when she realized that all of her cop armor, both figurative and literal, had been stripped away from her by a gunshot was the day she started her determined journey to return to the job and to the protector and provider her family needed her to be.

Realizing the extent of her impediment had been a shock to her sense of self that morning. Today, she knew better than to expect a miracle. But she didn't intend to humiliate herself, either.

She'd ask for a little backup before she put her hand on that weapon again. Crossing her fingers, she raised them to her lips before brushing them across her heart.

"You superstitious?" Mike asked.

"It doesn't hurt to ask for a little luck before doing something new or difficult." She closed her thumb and finger around the grip of the gun before wrapping her left hand around that to seal her grip.

Feeling a gentle pressure at the crown of her hair, Gina paused before lifting the weapon.

"For luck." Mike's gentle kiss and the husky tremor of his deep voice vibrated across her skin and eardrums, seeping inside her like the warmth of his body. Any trepidation she felt was under control, thanks to the support of this unexpected ally. "Let's do this."

She raised the weapon, tilting her head slightly to line up the sight and aim it at the paper target at the end of the firing lane. The gun dipped slightly when she moved her finger to the trigger guard, but she stabilized it with her left hand. The gun clicked when she pulled the trigger.

"Again," Mike instructed, sliding his hand beneath her elbow to steady her arm.

Gina aimed the empty weapon. *Click.*

"Again. Control it."

Click.

"Now use your left hand just to steady it, not to keep your fingers on the grip." Her right hand shook as she made the adjustment. Mike's fingers stroked along her arm as he pulled away. "This one's all you."

Gina pressed her lips together, willing her grip to remain fixed as she took the whole weight of the weapon on her own. "Bang."

Steady. Her strength hadn't flagged.

"There you go." Mike praised her, setting the new clip of bullets on the counter. "Clear it and load it while I bring up a new target."

With Mike's hand at her shoulder to support the extra kickback of firing real ammo, Gina took aim at the target and fired off six shots. By the fourth bullet, she could feel the strain in her shoulder. By the sixth one, her hands were shaking.

"Easy," Mike warned, catching her right arm beneath the elbow to control the weapon as her hands slumped down to the counter.

But she kept hold of the gun, kept it pointed safely away from them. She batted his helpful fingers away to expel the magazine and clear the firing chamber herself before setting the gun aside. Gina exhaled an elated sigh as she pulled off her earphones. "I did it."

"That you did." Mike's hand settled at her hip, his long fingers slipping beneath her jacket, spanning her waist with a familiar ease while he nudged her to one side to secure the Glock. Whether casually or with a purpose, he touched her often, as if he had the right to do so, and she wasn't complaining. "Have you considered using a lighter weapon?"

She shook her head as she removed her goggles and set them on the shelf beneath the counter. "I need one with stopping power." When she straightened, she asked, "So how did I do? I was six for six, center mass before I was injured."

Mike laughed as he pushed the button to bring the target up to the counter. "Give me a minute to check, Annie Oakley."

"I could learn to shoot left-handed if I have to."

But Mike pointed out the challenge in that solution. "How would you steady your grip and secure your aim? It's smarter for the strong to support the weak."

Was that supposed to be a metaphor? That he was strong and she was weak? Or that he believed she had the strength to overcome this setback? Mike was too nice a guy to give her a veiled put-down, so she chose to believe the latter.

Mike stowed his earphones, his body brushing against hers in the tight quarters of the booth. This was crazy, this distracted feeling she got whenever Mike was around. From the first moment she'd seen his long, powerful stride eating up the sidewalk on his afternoon run, there'd been something about him that pulled her attention away from the laser-sharp focus that had ruled most of her life. He was still a little too Dudley Do-Right compared to her streetwise bad girl persona for her to think they'd have any chance at making a relationship work—or even surviving a regular date. But she couldn't deny that he'd been a solid and dependable teammate since he'd taken over her recovery program. And for a woman who'd had very little *solid and dependable* in her life, Mike Cutler seemed an awful lot like that dream of peace and space and security she'd been chasing for so long.

She could count the individual holes in the target before it stopped in front of them, and some of her excitement waned. "I'm not six for six, anymore, am I?"

There was one hole right through the heart, the ultimate target for stopping a perp when cops fired their weapons. There were two more holes in the stomach area, two more in the left thigh and one completely off the map beneath the target's elbow. But the goal was to stop the assailant when threatened, not just to slow him down or give him a bellyache.

"At least they're all on the paper, and you didn't put a bullet in me or you." His humor eased some of her disappointment.

"You're right. Seven weeks ago, I couldn't even hold

that gun." She tilted her gaze to Mike's clear blue eyes, his optimism feeding her own. "I am getting better. I just have to be patient."

"*Patient?* I didn't know that word was in your vocabulary."

"Ha. Ha. After all my hard work—*our* hard work—" she admitted, "I feel like celebrating."

"Celebrating?"

Gina reached up to stroke her fingertips along the chiseled line of his jaw, her hormones enjoying the perfect blend of ticklish stubble and warm skin. His eyes darkened to a deep cobalt at her touch. "Catnip." He shook his head slightly, his lips thinning into a smile. But before that smile fully formed, Gina's fingers were there, tracing the supple, masculine arc of his mouth. She heard a low-pitched rumble in his throat. Or maybe that visceral sound was coming from her. "Thank you."

She was stretching up on tiptoe as his mouth was coming down to meet hers. His lips closed over hers, and Gina slipped her left hand behind his neck, holding on as they dueled for control of the kiss. She delighted in the rasp of his beard against her softer skin as his mouth traveled leisurely across hers, pausing to nip at her bottom lip. When she mewed at the tingling stab of heat warming her blood, he grazed his tongue across the sensitive spot, soothing the sting of the gentle assault. But *leisurely* was frustrating, and *gentle* only made her hungry for something more.

When his tongue teased the curve of her mouth again, Gina parted her lips and thrust her tongue out to meet and dance with his. She slipped her right hand up around his neck as well, her sensitive thumb and finger learning the crisp edge of his short hair. When his fingers tunneled into her hair to press against her scalp and angle her mouth more fully against his, she didn't protest. When her hips hit the countertop and Mike's thighs trapped her there, she reveled in the feel of him surrounding her, consuming her. He tasted of rich coffee and man and desire, and Gina demanded the liberty to explore his mouth and learn his textures and delight in the chemistry firing between them.

"I like the way you celebrate," Mike growled against her lips before slipping his hands beneath her denim jacket to skim the length of her back and the curve of each hip through the cotton of her blouse. When his thumbs spanned her rib cage to catch beneath her breasts and tease the subtle swell there, she moaned in a mix of pleasure and frustration. What would it be like to feel his hands on her bare skin? To eliminate the barriers of clothing that kept her from touching him?

But even as she clutched at his shoulders, relishing the rare satisfaction of feeling warmth in every part of her body, from her taut, aching breasts to the tips of her toes, she knew this was a mistake. This kiss was moving too fast. Moving them in the wrong direction. Changing their relationship and jeopardizing every goal on her life list. "Mike…"

She made a token effort to push him away and ended up curling her fingers into the front of his polo shirt, latching on to the skin and muscle underneath.

"Tell me what *catnip* means." He reclaimed her mouth.

She helplessly answered his kiss.

"Hey, G. You in here?" A familiar voice shouted from the doorway, followed by the noise of heavy boots and other voices.

Gina shoved Mike back, abruptly ending the kiss. Even as his hands closed around her hips to steady her, she was twisting from his grasp.

"Gina?" Although he must hear the footsteps approaching, too, Mike's hoarse, throaty whisper demanded an explanation. Did he want an apology for cutting short that ill-advised make-out session? A reassurance that she had no regrets the kiss had happened? She wasn't sure what her honest answer would be. He tugged her jacket back into place and smoothed the wrinkles she'd made in the front of his shirt. "I get that the timing sucks, but we need to talk about this."

"What *this*? There is no *this*." With the walls of the booth granting them a few precious seconds of privacy, Gina wiped her copper lip gloss from his mouth, regretting the defined line her hasty withdrawal had put there. She swiped her knuckles across her own mouth, willing the nerve endings that were still firing with the magnetic need to reconnect with his lips to be still. "You're not my…" Boyfriend? Temptation? Best decision? He had to understand that she'd never meant her thank-you kiss to go that far. "I have to focus on me right now. On taking care of my family. I—"

He cut her off with a tilt of his head, warning her that they were no longer alone.

"There you are." Derek appeared around the corner of the booth. His gaze glanced off Mike and landed on her, his eyes narrowed as if he suspected something more than firing a gun had happened here. "Everything okay?"

"Of course," she answered a little too quickly. Although she could feel Mike's blue eyes drilling a hole through her, Derek seemed to buy it. She needed to change the subject before she admitted something she might never want to. "What are you doing here? Did you get things straightened out with your dad last week?"

"Yeah. He had another harebrained scheme to make easy money. I told him to stick with restoring the junk he finds in the scrapyard. I talked some sense into him. Sorry that he was being such a jerk." Grinning, he rattled on. "I heard you were down here, training with the captain's son. Brought you a surprise."

"A surprise?" she echoed.

Derek stepped aside to usher two other men, dressed in their distinct black SWAT uniforms, over to join them. "She's here, guys."

Mike moved out of the booth as a compactly built man with black hair joined them. Alex Taylor, one of her SWAT team trainers, grinned. "Hey, Galvan, we heard you were on the premises. Thought we'd stop in and say hi, see how you're doing."

As he stepped aside, another SWAT officer appeared. Despite the blond man's intimidating facade, she knew Trip Jones was a gentle giant until he went into SWAT mode. And then he was all serious business. His big hand swallowed up hers in a light grip as he smiled. "Look what the cat dragged in. Good to see you without the sling and hospital gown."

"Good to be seen. Thanks."

By the time she'd stepped out of the booth to join the minireunion, Alex was shaking hands with Mike.

"Michael Cutler Jr. How'd you get involved with this fireball?"

"I'm her physical therapist." Apparently, Mike *did* know everybody at KCPD. Although the tension from that kiss and the guilt she felt at ending it so quickly still vibrated through her, making it difficult to think of what to say to these men she hoped to serve with one day, Mike didn't seem to have any problem joking with them as equals. "We're getting her back into fighting form."

"Don't do too good a job," Alex teased, including Gina in his smile. He swatted the big man beside him. "Trip's been practicing that takedown maneuver you used on him in training so you can't knock him over again."

Trip gave the teasing right back. "I stumbled over her. Didn't see her down there. Same problem I have when I'm sparring with you, Shrimp."

"You know I can take you out at the knees," Alex challenged.

Trip didn't bat an eye. "You know I can take you out, period."

Mike and Derek laughed, although both responses seemed forced to her. Mike wasn't in a laughing mood, and Derek was trying too hard to fit in as one of the team.

Gina inhaled a deep breath, determined to be a part of this camaraderie the men all seemed to share. "How do you all know Mike? Captain Cutler's summer barbecues?"

Trip splayed his hands at his waist, considering the answer. "Well, let's see. We first met when that creep had a bomb at Jillian's clinic. SWAT Team One was deployed, and Mikey here got up out of his wheelchair to get us inside to defuse the situation."

"Bomb?" Derek asked.

Gina looked up at Mike. "Wheelchair?"

She felt the sharp dismissal of Mike's blue eyes. He'd claimed she didn't know him, that he'd chosen to embrace his nice-guy persona *despite* his background, not because of it. What had confined him to a wheelchair and put him in the middle of a Bravo-Tango, or bomb threat?

Alex snapped his fingers. "No, wait. It was before that. We had to clear a building in No-Man's Land. Remember? There were a couple of druggies, and we were off the clock, but the captain called us in." Alex swatted Mike's arm. "You and Troy were outside in Captain Cutler's truck. Hey, how is Troy, anyway? The new business taking off for you two?"

"We could use a few more patients," Mike confessed, ignoring her silent questions. "As Gina pointed out to me—we didn't exactly set up shop in the most profitable part of the city. But we're making do. We'll turn the corner soon."

While they chatted, Derek stepped into the booth to pick up the discarded target paper on the floor. He let out a low whistle of appreciation. "Whoa, G. Is this your score? Looks like you're ready to come back to work."

"No. That's Mike's." Swallowing her pride in front of her peers, she pointed to the mutilated paper still hanging in the firing lane. "That guy's mine."

"Oh." Derek was at a loss for words. Alex covered the awkward moment with a cough.

Trip Jones, ever the practical one, stated the obvious. "You're going to have to do better than that to make SWAT."

Mike interrupted before she could acknowledge that she knew that score probably wouldn't qualify her to wear a sidearm for even regular duty. "Gina's improving every day. This is only her second time on the shooting range. Give it a couple more weeks and she'll be beating your scores."

"No doubt." Alex smiled, and Gina's spirits lifted a little. "This woman can do anything she puts her mind to."

Trip extended his hand to shake Mike's, bringing the brief reunion to an end. "You do good work, Mikey." He glanced down at Gina. "Heal fast," Trip said with an encouraging smile. "We need more good cops like you."

The door to the shooting range swung open at the same time as the radios clipped to Alex's and Trip's shoulders crackled to life.

"Taylor. Trip." SWAT Team Captain Michael Cutler strode across the room, the clip of authority in his tone and demeanor making Gina snap to attention. "Time to roll. We need to clear a neighborhood. Armed suspect at large."

"Yes, sir." Alex and Trip muted the same information coming over their radios, nodded their goodbyes and jogged from the room, heading toward the Precinct garage, where their SWAT van was located.

"You're the one I've been looking for, Johnson. Why aren't you at your desk?"

Derek pulled his shoulders back, too, at the direct address. "I was just heading up when I ran into Alex and Trip in the locker room."

"You're up to do a trainee ride on this call. You want to join us?"

"Definitely."

Gina's hand fisted with the same anticipation charging through Derek's posture.

"Gear up on the van. We're leaving as soon as I get there. This is an observation opportunity only," the captain reminded him. "You stay behind the front lines unless I tell you otherwise. Understood?"

"Yes, sir." Derek jogged off after the others, and the impulse to follow the action jolted through Gina's legs.

The older man backed toward the door. "Gina. Son."

Gina took half a step after him. "Any chance I'll get the opportunity to ride on a call with you again, sir? Keep my tactics skills fresh?"

Captain Cutler halted, his face lined with an apology. "I'm sorry, but you're a liability right now. Until you're declared fit for duty…"

"I understand." She nodded toward the door. "I'll let you go."

Mike's fingers curled around hers, down at her side between them. Holding her back from embarrassing herself? Or comforting her obvious disappointment over yet another reminder that right now she wasn't good enough? "What's up?" Mike asked.

The captain's pointed gaze landed on her, sending a silent message. "Somebody shot another cop. Frank McBride."

Gina's blood ran cold. First Colin Cho was shot. Then she and Derek were hit. And now this? With each incident, the injuries had grown more severe. "Is Frank…?"

"Ambulance is on the scene. No report yet."

"Go." The urgency of Mike's command matched her own sentiment. "Keep us posted. And be safe."

Captain Cutler's expression was grim as he hurried out behind his men.

Three assaults on police officers since the beginning of the year. Gina drew her hand away from Mike's, pacing several steps toward the door, needing to do something more than accept his comfort. She should be out there, protecting her brethren on the police force.

"Who's shooting cops?" she wondered out loud.

"I don't know," Mike answered. "But it sounds to me like KCPD is under attack."

Chapter 8

"Could these incidents be related?" Mike speculated on the phone with his father. "They're all Kansas City cops."

His visit with Gina to the KCPD shooting range had stretched into the evening as they waited at headquarters for word on the injured officer. Once the news that Frank McBride had come out of surgery in fair condition, triggering a collective sigh around the Precinct offices, she'd agreed to let him drive her home. Troy would escort Frannie to her car and lock up the clinic, freeing Mike to stay with Gina. Now the city lights were coming on and streets were clogging with rush-hour traffic as the sun warmed into a glowing orange ball in the western sky. And though he hadn't followed his father's footsteps into the police force, Mike was just as eager as the woman sitting across from him in the cab of his truck to find out who the shooter might be and put a stop to these crimes against cops.

Gina leaned against the center console, following his half of the conversation. "Not just KCPD," she whispered. "The victims—Cho, Derek, McBride and me—we're all candidates for the new SWAT team."

Michael Sr. continued. "It sure feels personal to me. Every person hit since the beginning of the year has been one of the candidates we've been training for the new SWAT team. Maybe he's challenging himself to take down the best of the best."

"Gina was just mentioning that connection."

His dad's voice hushed. "She's with you now?"

Mike slowed for a stoplight. "I'm giving her a ride home."

"Good. I've put my team on alert and am in the process of notifying all the candidates to keep their guards up. Keep an eye on her for me, will you, son? This guy might just be toying with us, taking potshots at random cops. But I'm guessing there's something else at work here we don't understand yet. I'd like to think he can't bring himself to actually kill a cop. But more likely, he's working up his nerve and fine-tuning his MO. Once he's made one kill, he might decide he has a taste for it and come back to finish what he started."

The sunset warmed Gina's cheeks as Mike glanced across the seat at her. He didn't have to wonder at the twisting in his gut at the thought of the shooter making another attempt on her life. He had feelings for her. And her giving him the cold shoulder after that kiss wasn't making them go away. "Thanks for the update, Dad. Give Frank and Mrs. McBride my best."

Mike disconnected the call and placed the phone

in the cup holder in the center console. "Dad noticed the same thing you did. The victims aren't just cops, they're all SWAT contenders."

She sat back in her seat with a deep sigh, giving him a rare glimpse of fatigue. "That has to be a co-incidence. We're all uniformed officers. We haven't earned our SWAT caps and vests yet, so there's no way to distinguish us from anyone else at KCPD. How would this guy know?"

Mike shrugged as the light changed. He could think of several possibilities. "What about the car you've seen following you? Could be he's staked out the training center or Precinct headquarters. Maybe he's in the crowd when you go on observation calls with SWAT Team One and has seen you in action. Or he's hacked the KCPD computer system? There are a lot of ways he could get that information."

She grunted a sound that could have been a reluctant laugh. "You're not making me feel better."

"I'm not trying to. You're not the only one who wants to nail this guy and put a stop to the assaults on cops. It's personal to me, too."

Reaching across the center console, she patted his arm, as if she thought *he* needed comforting. "Your dad is too high-profile of a police officer. A highly trained veteran, to boot. I'm sure the perp wouldn't go after him."

Unless a high-profile officer like his father *was* the ultimate target, and Gina, Derek and the others were a diversion to make KCPD think the attacker was hunting cops, in general, and not a specific target. Mike captured her hand against the warmth of his thigh. "I hate to think of someone hurting you as simple target practice until he works up the nerve or the skill to make an actual kill shot."

Gina pulled her small, supple hand from his, as if even that small intimacy made her as uncomfortable as that kiss they'd shared. At least she wasn't discounting the attraction simmering between them, but she sure as hell didn't want to be feeling that way about him. Or maybe the aversion to the growing closeness was about something else. Bad luck with relationships. No interest in relationships. Or maybe the vulnerability that naturally arose when two people cared for each other was the thing she wanted to avoid.

The petite beauty studiously ignoring Mike was turning out to be as complex a mystery as the recent spate of attacks they both wanted to solve.

She pointed out the next intersection where he needed to turn and watched out the window as they entered the older neighborhood. The street narrowed and the houses got closer together and more run-down. The arching maple trees littered the small yards and sidewalks with their messy buds as leaves started to sprout. Gina shivered, and Mike discreetly turned on the truck's heater, although he suspected it was something mental, not physical, that had given her that chill.

Just as he thought they might reach her house in silence, Gina spoke again. "If the other incidents have all been a misdirection to throw the investigators off track, then who's his real target? Or if he just hates cops, why hasn't he killed any of us?"

"Thank God for that small favor."

"Seriously. Is it ineptitude? Is he toying with us?" Her shoulders lifted with a deep breath as she continued to speculate about the possibilities. "What if this has nothing to do with us being cops at all? What if it's something personal—that there's something besides a badge that connects all four victims? Or they're not connected at all? What if he's going after cops to make us think it's the uniform he's targeting and not a specific individual? How do we figure out who to warn? Who to protect?"

"Right now, we protect you."

"I can take care of myself."

"Right. While you're busy trying to find answers to these attacks, taking care of your family, vying to make the new SWAT team, and, oh, yeah—healing—you really think you have the capacity to watch your back, as well?"

She shook her head, stirring her dark hair around her face. "*Not* my bodyguard, Choir Boy."

Mike exhaled an irritated sigh. "That tough-chick shtick is getting pretty old."

"Look around you." She nodded toward the trio of young men hanging around a jacked-up car. "I have to be tough."

The young men, smoking cigarettes, all wore ball caps with the same telltale color underneath the brim, labeling them as gang members rather than a baseball team. Their souped-up car and air of conceit reminded Mike of his dangerous forays into No-Man's Land half a lifetime ago, when he'd sought out teens like that, instead of hanging with his true friends. He hoped it wouldn't take a tragedy like the ones he'd faced to convince them to make better choices and see the hope in their future. If Gina was the real target, and the other assaults were planned diversions, could the real threat be from someone close to home, like these guys?

"Gangbangers," Gina pointed out unnecessarily. She waved as they passed. Two of the boys waved back. One flipped them off.

Mike's hands fisted around the steering wheel as he remembered the faceless driver who'd pantomimed shooting Gina that morning outside the physical therapy clinic. "I assume they know you're a cop?"

"Uh-huh." He noticed her good hand fisting in her lap, too. "The one with the rude salute is in my sister's high-school class. My brother used to run with the other two. They're low-level members of the Westside Warriors, more bark than any real bite. I doubt they'll try anything unless their captain gives them the order to do so."

"Are they a threat to your brother or sister?"

"Not them." But someone else was? Gina's mouth twisted with a wry smile. "Can you see why I need that promotion at KCPD? It's so I can get my family out of this place."

Mike didn't have any platitude to offer. This *was* a dangerous part of the city. But it hurt to see that brave tilt of her chin and how all her responsibilities and the danger surrounding her day and night changed her posture. If he could make that smile a genuine one, for a moment, at least, he'd feel as though he was easing her burden. "And here I thought you just wanted a private bathtub."

Her dark eyes snapped to his before he heard the laughter bubbling up from her throat. "I'm a very serious woman with a very serious set of troubles. I don't have time for laughing with you."

Mike grinned. Fortunately, she'd said *with* him and not *at* him. "That's officially part of my recovery prescription for you. Laughing at least once a day."

She settled back into her seat and pointed out the window. "Turn here. It's the brick house with white trim and black shutters in the next block."

Mike spotted a row of three small houses whose owners seemed determined to maintain a clean, respectable appearance. The lawns were greening up, and there was a lack of junk or old cars sitting on the grass or at the curb. Gina's home was the one in the middle.

But the respite from worry and wariness was short-lived. "Did Captain Cutler say anything else about today's shooting?" she asked.

Mike nodded. "SWAT One did a building-to-building search in that block. Stopped traffic and checked vehicles. No sign of him."

"Any leads?"

Obliquely, Mike wondered if Gina had ever considered aiming for her detective's badge rather than SWAT. Although he suspected, with her position as the major breadwinner for her family, she didn't have a college degree yet, a prerequisite for becoming a detective. However, she was a natural at asking questions and observing the world around her. "It was an ambush from an unidentified vehicle, just like with you and Derek. McBride was answering a call on a fight at a bar and grill downtown. Not far from Precinct HQ. Still, the shooter was gone before backup got there."

"No description of the shooter or vehicle either, I bet."

"The only witnesses were a drunk still sobering up from last night and the bouncer. He was busy breaking up the fight. The two perps, of course."

When there was no empty spot to pull up in front of the house, Gina pointed him into the driveway. "Any bystanders hurt?"

Mike pulled his truck up to the garage door. "The only casualty was Officer McBride. Looks like the man in uniform was specifically targeted."

Unhooking her seat belt, Gina sat forward, facing him. "Wait a minute. Was the incident at the Sin City Bar and Grill?"

"Yeah. How'd you know?"

She pounded her fist on the console. "That's the bar where the bikers we chased away from the Bismarck house allegedly went before Derek and I were shot. I'd love to talk to the patrons there. See if the Bismarck brothers and their buddies were there today—maybe even part of that fight. They don't like cops. Maybe the whole fight was staged."

"How would they know Frank McBride would respond?"

"Maybe the guy was willing to shoot at any cop who responded to the call. Or maybe he scouted the place out and knew that was Frank's beat." Her voice trailed away as she thought out loud. "Did he know the streets Derek and I patrolled? Or Colin Cho?" She was in full voice again as she turned to the door. "I need to see if anyone's followed up on this."

She tugged on the door handle and muttered a curse in Spanish when her recovering hand didn't cooperate quickly enough.

Mike caught her left wrist before she could reach across to open the door with both hands. "I know what you're thinking."

She tugged on his grip. "No, you don't."

Mike tightened his hold on her. "You aren't talking about making a phone call. You're planning on going to the bar yourself to investigate. Not tonight. You're home. You're staying put."

The tension left her arm and she smiled for a split second before forcing her right hand to fumble with the handle. "You're not the only means of transportation available to me. I can call a cab."

"The bar will either be closed or the cops investigating the shooting will have already talked to everyone."

"I'd be in the way. No help to anyone. Is that what you're saying?"

"What I'm saying is that it'd be a fool's mission right now. Plus, you need your rest and some dinner because I know you missed lunch."

"Not my nursemaid, Cutler."

"Not your chauffeur—yet here I am driving you. Not your friend—yet I'm the one thinking of your best interests. Not your lover." Her head snapped toward him, her startled eyes wide and dark as midnight. "And yet you kissed me like—"

She jerked her arm from his grasp. "Forget that kiss. I got carried away. I just wanted to thank you."

"A tough chick like you couldn't be interested in a nice guy like me, huh?" Why was he pushing this sore spot? Probably because his heart and ego had been battered one time too many. And a little of that rebel he used to be was getting tired of taking hit after hit. He reached across her, ignoring the clean, citrusy scent coming off her hair and skin, and pushed open the door. "Run if you want. You'll face down anything except what's happening between us."

Gina climbed out and circled around the hood of the pickup. But Mike was there to block her path.

She propped her hands at her hips and tilted her chin to face him. "Fine. Let's hash this out, Choir Boy. Is this where you tell me why you hung out in No-Man's Land as a teenager? Why you were in a wheelchair? Where you prove to me you're not so nice and that the two of us have enough in common to make something work after all?"

An image of his teenage friend Josh's mangled body flashed through Mike's thoughts, followed by the familiar upwelling of guilt he'd known since he was sixteen years old. The grief of his mother's death to cancer had sent him spiraling out of control, and the boozy haze of those wild months had cost him a football scholarship, the use of his legs and his best friend's life.

But the pricks of fear and grief and guilt were manageable now. He could acknowledge those feelings and lock them away before he did damage to anyone else's life. Or he allowed anyone else to be hurt when he could damn well do something about it. Including the stubborn Latina facing off against him. Gina needed to see him as her equal, as a partner who could help her if she'd only let him beneath that proud, protective armor of hers. "Let's just say I made some bad choices after my mother died. I found the solace I needed in No-Man's Land."

That took her aback. The sparks of defensive anger in her eyes sputtered out. "You did drugs? You had a dealer here?"

Alcohol had been his drug of choice. "I had *friends* willing to sell liquor to an underage drinker. I was happy to take them up on the offer. Defied my dad's rules, trashed my chance at a football scholarship, got a friend killed."

Gina's gaze dropped to the middle of his chest as she reassessed her opinion of him. Was she trying to realign her image of Mr. Nice Guy Choir Boy with an out-of-control teen who lived with baggage from No-Man's Land the same way she did? Was the real Mike Cutler someone she could relate to and admire for getting his act together and making amends to the world for his mistakes every day of his life? Or did she now see him as the very kind of thing she was trying to get away from?

But Gina Galvan was nothing if not boldly direct. She tilted her gaze back to his. "How did your mother die? My mother had cancer."

All the no-one-can-hurt-me attitude had left her posture. Her voice warmed with compassion and understanding.

At the balm of that hushed, seductively accented tone, Mike wanted to reach out to her. He rested his hand on the hood of his truck, mere inches from where her fingers now rested. He stretched out his fingers, brushing the calloused tips against hers. When she feathered her fingers between his to hold on, something eased inside him. There were some understandings that crossed the barriers of backgrounds and economics and skin color. "Cancer. It was long and painful, and I didn't handle it well."

"Is that where you met Troy? Was he in a gang?"

"Nope. But that's where he got shot. In the wrong place at the wrong time during a drive-by shooting in the old neighborhood."

Her fingers danced against his palm, spinning tendrils of warmth, desire and healing into his blood with even that gentlest of connections. "How did you end up in a wheelchair? And why aren't you in one now?"

Gina's persistence would make her a fine detective. But Mike hadn't forgotten where this conversation had started. "If I answer all your questions, will you answer one of mine?"

She held his gaze expectantly, considering his request. Then she pulled her hand away and squared off her shoulders. Even without her flak vest, that woman's armor was locked down tight. "All right. What's your question?"

"Will you go to the Sin City bar on your own tonight after I leave?" She didn't need to say the word *yes*. He could read the guilty truth all over her face. Mike angled his gaze toward the orange glow of sunset on the horizon, shaking his head at the symbolism of his chances of making a relationship work with Gina going down right along with it. He'd better reel in his emotions like the champ here, and settle for finding answers and keeping her safe. "How about I pick you up in the morning and we go to Sin City together after your training session. Somebody should be there setting up by ten. And you won't be stepping on anybody's toes at KCPD then."

"Are you going to park outside my house tonight to make sure I stay put?" She'd barely uttered the flippant accusation before her expression changed. "Oh, my God, you are. You do know a truck this nice could get stripped in this neighborhood."

"I'm not leaving."

"Fine." Her cheeks flushed with irritation that he could be just as stubborn as she. "I promise to wait until you drive me in the morning if you promise to go home and not put yourself in danger because of me."

He couldn't make that deal. Mike planted his feet, tucking his hands into the pockets of his jeans and standing fast. If she was going into a dangerous situation, then he wasn't letting her do it alone.

"I'm going inside." She nudged his shoulder brushing past him, and Mike turned to follow her to the porch. "What are you doing?"

"Making sure you get inside safely."

"Nothing's going to happen to me between the curb and the front door."

He waited for the import of what she'd just said to sink in. A quick glance out to the street and he knew she was reliving the day she'd been shot. That short distance between the safety of her police cruiser and Vicki Bismarck's front door was exactly where she'd gotten hurt.

One look at the color leaving her cheeks and Mike turned her to the front door of her own home, sliding his fingers beneath the hem of her jacket and resting a supportive hand at the small of her back. He scanned up and down the block and through the neighboring yards, ensuring they were safe before nudging her forward. "Indulge a nice guy the manners his mama taught him, okay?"

Gina shivered at the polite touch but fell into step beside him as they climbed the single step onto the porch. "And here you are insisting over and over that you aren't so nice. Which Mike Cutler am I supposed to believe?"

"Both." Mike was grinning as they reached the door.

Gina pulled her keys from her pocket, but the door swung open before she could insert them into the lock.

A portly man with a strip of gray hair circling from his temples to the back of his head leaned heavily on his walker as he backed out of the doorway. "Gina, *la niña*. You are so late. We were getting worried." The elderly man raised his dark gaze to Mike. "You bring us a friend?"

"Tio Papi." Gina stepped inside to kiss the man's pudgy cheek while Mike waited in the doorway. A tiny woman with snow white hair that curled like Gina's dark mane tottered up behind the man, drying her hands on a dish towel. She gently chastised Gina's tardiness in Spanish before the two women exchanged a hug. Keeping her arm around the older woman's waist, Gina made the introductions. "This is Mike Cutler. My great-uncle, Rollo Molina. My great-aunt, Lupe."

Mike nodded a smile to each. "Ma'am. Sir."

"*The* Mike Cutler?" In addition to being overweight, Rollo Molina was a tad sallow-skinned. The man must be struggling with circulation or heart issues. But that didn't stop him from grinning from ear to ear and extending his beefy hand. "I like to meet the man who saved my girl's life. Now you see her every day. More than we do. We worry, but not when she's with you."

Mike accepted the vigorous handshake. "She's mentioned me, huh?" Why did that surprise him? More importantly, why did knowing that she'd talked about him with her family fill him with a warmth and sense of connection that eased the lingering sharpness of that argument they'd had outside? Gina's dark eyes bored into his, as if daring him to make something out of knowing she thought enough of him to tell her family about him. Oh, he was making something of it, all right. He'd been recognized as "*The* Mike Cutler," so she must have done more than simply mention his name. Mike winked at Gina. "I imagine she's a hard one to keep track of."

Rollo laughed, pulling Mike into the entryway and shutting the door behind him. "She has a mind of her own, *sí*?"

"Yes, she does."

Those dark eyes rolled heavenward. "Tio Papi…"

Gina started to explain something, but diminutive Lupe, a good three to four inches shorter than her great-niece, pushed past Gina to stand in front of Mike. She grabbed hold of his forearm, her body swaying slightly as she tilted her head back to study him through narrowed dark eyes. "You are Gina's friend? The young man who makes her well?" She tugged on the sleeve of Mike's jacket and he instinctively grasped her shoulders to steady her balance. "*¡Dios mio!* You are so tall. Your eyes are so *azul*, er, blue. Very handsome."

Mike glanced past her to Gina. *She* was the one blushing at her great-aunt's compliments. "Tia Mami… Mike was giving me a ride home. He can't stay."

"He doesn't eat dinner?" The fragile woman's grip on his arm tightened as if he'd imagined Lupe's balance issues. "I made chicken pozole soup. I put on a fresh pot of decaf coffee. And I have cheesecake empanadas for dessert. You like empanadas?"

"Yes, ma'am. But I don't want to intrude—"

"Come in, come in. You join us." A twenty-something man with a curling black ponytail strolled out of the kitchen, munching on an empanada. With her fingers latched on to the sleeve of Mike's jacket, Lupe pulled him past Gina and Rollo to swat the young man's arm. "Javi, those are for dessert."

"I'm hungry," he whined around the doughy sweetness in his mouth. "Who's the big dude?"

"This is Gina's friend, Mike."

He glanced up, then down at the white-haired woman. "*The* Mike Cutler?"

"My brother, Javier," Gina explained. "Where's Sylvie?"

"Yo, Mike."

Mike chuckled. "Yo."

Javier stuffed the last bite into his mouth and looked to his sister. "She's out."

Gina came up beside Mike, tension radiating from her posture. "Out as in running an errand? Or...out?"

Between Javier's darting glance at his great-aunt and Rollo's weary sigh as he shut the door, Mike could guess that, wherever Sylvie Galvan had gone, it didn't meet with the family's approval. Gina pulled out her cell phone. "Maybe I should go," Mike offered.

"Put that away." Lupe touched Gina's phone. "We have a guest. Sylvie makes her choices. She can eat without us." Then she shooed her great-nephew out of her path. "Go wash up. You need good food before you go to work. Not sweets." When she looped her arm through Mike's and pulled him into the kitchen, he rethought his first impression that she was a fragile grandmother. Lupe Molina ran this home in a way that made it easy to see why Gina was such a determined woman.

"Tia Mami—"

"Senora Molina, really, you don't have to—"

"You saved my Gina's life." Lupe patted a chair at one side of a rectangular white table. "You sit. I feed."

Short of wrestling all one hundred pounds of the elderly woman out of his way, Mike had no choice but to do as she asked.

Once he took a seat as the honored guest, Lupe bustled around the kitchen. By the time she'd set an extra place setting and the fragrant, steaming food was on the table, Rollo, Javier and Gina had joined them.

Mike enjoyed Gina's family as much as he enjoyed the spicy, hearty soup. Although his understanding of Spanish was limited to the classes he'd taken back in high school, he had little trouble following the mix of English and Spanish and the teasing, loving conversation. Lupe and Rollo were animated and charming. Javier was interested in Mike's truck and Chiefs football. Gina was quiet in the chair beside him and, though Mike suspected that wasn't typical, at least she'd stopped glaring a silent warning that he needed to leave as soon as possible.

If anything, she seemed to be assessing his response to her family and circumstances. He could understand her concern for her family's well-being. He could also understand her devotion to this tightly knit group.

Maybe she was chalking up the apparent success of this dinner to him being a nice, polite guy, or maybe she was finally beginning to believe that he was more complex and able to relate to her and her background than she'd given him credit for.

Javier popped a third empanada into his mouth and took off for the bus stop a couple of blocks from the house to get to his job as an overnight custodian at a downtown office building. In between, Mike answered a barrage of questions: no, he wasn't married; yes, his father was the man Gina wanted to work for at KCPD; no, he didn't live with his dad and stepmom and brother; and, yes, he owned his own home off Blue Ridge Boulevard. Yes, he thought Gina was making a good recovery that would get her back on the police force, although he wouldn't promise how long it might take or if he could guarantee her a place on a new SWAT team.

They answered a few of his questions, too. He heard a bit about how Gina, Javier and Sylvie had come to live with their great-aunt and -uncle, and a lot about how proud they were of each of them. Gina had gladly taken on the job of supporting them, in addition to Rollo's pension check. Javi had enrolled in tech classes at one of the city's junior colleges. And Sylvie, who was as pretty as their late mother and prone to being late, was set to graduate from high school in just a couple of months.

Mike was sipping a cup of coffee that was richer and smoother than anything Frannie brewed at work and bemoaning the fact that he'd eaten that second empanada, when he heard the screech of tires braking on the street in front of the house.

He couldn't miss the instant bracing of alarm around the table, or the exchange of worried looks between Rollo and Lupe. Gina shoved her chair away from the table and hurried out of the kitchen.

"Gina," Rollo warned, reaching for his walker.

Mike stood, putting up a cautionary hand to keep the elderly couple in their seats. "I'll keep an eye on her."

The older couple reached for each other's hands across the corner of the table and muttered a prayer as he went after Gina. Not good.

He heard the slam of a car door and raised voices outside and saw Gina's curvy backside storming out the front door. Even worse.

"Gina?" Concern lengthened Mike's stride, and he caught the storm door before it closed in his face.

Ignoring him, Gina stepped off the porch and marched down the walk toward a cream-colored luxury sedan parked catty-cornered across the end of the driveway. Outside the front passenger door of the slick, pricey car, a black-haired man was kissing a young woman with long, curling dark hair.

"Sylvie!" Gina called.

Sylvie? *That* was Gina's younger sister? The ankle boots and mini skirt showed so much leg that he'd question a grown woman wearing that outfit out of the house—much less a teenage girl.

Although the man who'd mimicked shooting Gina outside the clinic had driven a darker tan car, Mike found himself checking the license plate for a familiar 3-6. No match. Different car, different plate number—didn't mean Loverboy there wasn't a threat. And judging by the money invested in that car, he could afford more than one vehicle. "Gina, stop."

She didn't. Mike doubled his pace to catch up to her.

"I'll call you tomorrow," the would-be lothario murmured, looking over the girl's head to note their approach before adding an endearment in Spanish.

The teen pushed away from her adult boyfriend and hurried up the driveway. Although the sun had set and the street's tall maple trees blocked the moonlight, the glare of a nearby streetlamp cast a harsh glow across Sylvie Galvan's pretty face. The streaks of mascara running down her cheeks indicated she'd been crying.

The smudge of violet on her cheek bone hinted that she'd been hurt, too.

Gina noticed the mark, too, and caught her sister by the arms. She looked up into Sylvie's face, brushing the long hair away from the tears and the bruise. "Did he hit you?"

Sylvie sniffled. "I'm fine."

"Tell me what happened."

"Let it go, okay?" Then she tilted her gaze up to Mike. The young woman wiped her nose on a tissue and smiled, dismissing Gina's maternal concern and cop-like probing. "Who's this? You've been holding out on me. I thought you didn't have time for a man." She shrugged off Gina's grasp and circled around her older sister. "Wait. You've only talked about one guy lately—are you Mike Cutler? *The* Mike Cutler?"

"Guilty as charged." He took the hand Sylvie offered, noting the bruises on her wrist that were only slightly smaller than the span of his own fingers before turning her toward the yellowish streetlight to inspect the injury to her face. Although he kept his smile friendly, he was fuming inside. He'd seen marks like that on Frannie, courtesy of her ex, when she'd started working for him. "You hurt anywhere else?"

Sylvie tucked her hands inside the cuffs of her jacket, avoiding his questions, too. "You're cuter than Gina told us."

And Gina was angrier than Mike had ever seen her.

"Bobby Estes!" Gina whirled around and charged at the compact, muscular man in the black leather jacket. She spewed out a stream of Spanish Mike couldn't follow, but he could guess it had something to do with accusation and condemnation.

"Get inside the house," Mike ordered Sylvie before running after Gina. "Go."

When Sylvie started to protest, he glared her toward the front door, throwing out any essence of Mr. Nice Guy and replacing him with the stern taskmaster who wouldn't take no for an answer. With Gina's protective instincts raging like a mama bear protecting her cub, Mike had a sick feeling this confrontation was going to escalate into something a lot more serious than a lovers' quarrel.

The black-haired man leaned against his spotless car, laughing at Gina's approach. "You want a piece of me, Big Sister?"

That's when Mike spotted the telltale bulge beneath Bobby Estes's black leather jacket. Aw, hell. "Gun!"

Gina wisely backed off a step, her hand at her waist where her own weapon had once been. "I see it. Keep your hands where I can see them, Bobby."

While Bobby raised his hands into the air with a smug grin, the situation skipped from bad to worse and went straight to hell when a second man climbed out of the back of the car. He was armed, too. Mike shifted in front of Gina.

Gina shifted right back. "Hands on top of the car," she ordered. "Who's he?"

"A friend," Bobby answered. "I have a lot of friends. They protect me when I need it."

"Protect you from what?"

"People who threaten me?" With a gesture from Bobby, the second man held his position on the far side of the car, but did as she'd commanded, resting his hands on top of the car. "They're jealous of my success, or they want what I have."

Mike's stomach knotted right along with his fists at the obvious taunt.

But Gina kept her cool. "Like my sister? She's not a possession. If you really cared about her you'd leave her alone."

Bobby's arrogant amusement turned smarmy with a purse of his lips. "Maybe she's not the Galvan I want."

"You're using her to get to me?"

"Is it working?" he mocked, brushing his fingers against her hair.

This was a neighborhood power struggle, not a romantic foray. Still, it stuck in Mike's craw that the other man was putting his hands on her. He was already moving forward when Gina grabbed Bobby's wrist and flipped him against the car. "Stay away from Sylvie. Stay away from my family."

"See? Can't keep your hands off me." Bobby laughed. Mike turned his attention to the young man on the far side of the car, who looked more alarmed than amused by the wrestling match.

Gina bent Bobby's arm into the middle of his back,

shoving him against the vehicle. That spike of jealousy instantly switched to concern that she would get hurt if this physical altercation escalated any further. "Get in your car and drive away," she warned, twisting his arm. "Lose Sylvie's number. Get out of our lives."

She pinched his wrist tightly enough for Bobby to curse in pain and, suddenly, the joke was over. "*My* neighborhood. *My* girl. Get your damn cop hands off me."

Bobby jerked his hips, knocking Gina back a step. Then he swung back with his free arm, the point of his elbow connecting squarely with her bad shoulder. Gina grunted with pain, grabbing her arm as she stumbled to the sidewalk.

Mike was right there to shove Bobby back against the car, his forearm pressed against the bully's neck as he reached inside the leather jacket to pull the gun from Bobby's belt. "Leave. Now." With the smooth ease his father had taught him, Mike pointed the weapon over the roof of car at his buddy, who was reaching for his own gun. "Put it on the ground."

From the corner of his eye, he saw Gina scrambling to her feet and hurrying around the car to pick up the gun. Was she hurt? How badly? And just how much trouble would he get in if he pressed his arm more tightly against this sleazeball's windpipe?

Once Gina had the weapon trained on the other man and he'd wisely linked his hands over his head in surrender, Mike pulled back the Smith & Wesson pistol he was holding and leaned into Bobby's ruddy, angry face. "You got a license for this?"

"You a cop, white boy?" When Bobby shoved against him, Mike shoved right back.

The tendons in his back and legs strained as he kept the shorter man wedged in place. A zap of electricity shot down his leg as one of the old nerves pinched. Pain gave way to numbness in his right hip and thigh and would eventually settle into a dull, bruising ache if the injuries he'd lived with for more than a decade followed their usual pattern.

Mike gritted his teeth against any discomfort and kept Bobby a prisoner while he watched Gina cover the second man. "You okay?" he asked.

"I'm fine," she ground out, grimacing with the strain of keeping the gun pointed at Bobby's friend. She needed both hands to keep the weapon from shaking, but there was no mistaking the authority in her tone. "Get back in the car. Get in!" The man didn't need a nod from Bobby to obey the order this time. Once he was in the backseat, with his hands out the window as she'd instructed, Gina lowered the weapon and circled around into the driveway again. "Let him go, Mike."

"You're sure?"

"Keep the gun, and let him go."

Bobby was laughing again as Mike released him and stepped beyond his reach. "You sure you can handle Officer Gina?" The neighborhood thug straightened his shirt and jacket as if this had been a civilized encounter. "I know how feisty Sylvie can be. All the Galvan women have fire in them."

"If you're so good at *handling* women, why did you need to hit a teenage girl?"

"Prove that I did." Bobby winked at Gina before circling around the hood and climbing behind the wheel of the car. He leaned toward the open passenger door.

"May I have my weapon back, Officer?" When Gina hesitated, he added, "If you arrest me, I'll file assault charges against your boyfriend here."

As far as Mike was concerned, anything he'd done to Estes was justified. Hitting a girl? Assaulting a police officer? But he wasn't the cop here, and he'd defer to however Gina wanted to play this. He was right beside her as she dumped the bullets from each gun into her palm and tossed the empty weapons back into the front seat before Mike closed the door.

"You'll be seeing me again, Gina," he promised before backing out into the street and speeding away.

The car veered around the corner and out of sight before Gina moved again. She stuffed the bullets into her jeans and turned back to the house. "I want to get these to the crime lab. See if they match the bullets from any of the police shootings. Bobby might have been targeting me and using the other incidents as decoys to throw the investigation off track."

Checking one last time to make sure Estes and his buddy stayed gone, Mike followed, wincing at the nerves still sparking through his hip and thigh. A hot shower or a long run would ease the kinks out of those muscles and tone down the minijolts. It had been a lot of years since he'd gotten mixed up in a physical confrontation that twisted his body like that, and he'd be paying for it later.

But he wasn't the only one in pain here. Although Gina was booking it up the driveway, he could hear the soft grunts with every other step and see her rubbing her shoulder.

"Are you all right?" he asked, catching up to her.

"Bruised my shoulder. My fingers are a little tingly. At least I'm feeling them, right? I'll be fine. I want to talk to Sylvie and find out what happened. If she presses charges, I'll serve the warrant on Bobby myself." She jumped onto the porch and reached for the storm door. "Could you drive me to the lab tonight? I don't want to have any issues with chain of custody—"

"Gina. Stop." Mike put a hand on her arm. "Take a breath. Everyone is safe."

"Are they?" Gina whirled around on him, and he spied something he'd never expected to see in her beautiful eyes. Fear. "I couldn't protect my family, Mike. I couldn't defend myself tonight. How the hell am I ever going to be a cop again?"

Chapter 9

Mike closed the door to Lupe and Rollo's dimly lit room and moved down the hallway toward the bedroom Gina and Sylvie shared. It had been a long night at the Molina house. The family had gone through a second pot of decaf coffee, a phone call to Rollo's doctor, plus lots of tears, terse words and hugs. He peeked through the open doorway to see Sylvie perched on the corner of her daybed, dressed in black-and-gold sweats from her school, while Gina stood behind her, arranging her damp hair into a long braid.

As soon as her dark eyes made contact with his, Sylvie set down the ice pack she'd been holding against her swollen cheek and sprang to her feet. "How is Tio Papi?"

Leaning his shoulder against the doorjamb, Mike crossed his arms, hoping the relaxed stance would ease some of the worry and regret from her young face. "I checked his BP on the monitor again. He's resting comfortably now."

"But his pressure *was* elevated," she confirmed with a woeful sigh. "That's why he got dizzy."

Gina followed behind, winding a rubber band around the end of the braid. "His heart can't take much more of this kind of stress."

"I'm sorry, Gina. I never meant to upset him. Or Tia Mami," Sylvie apologized. "Is she okay?"

Mike nodded. Nothing that a little less worry and a good night's sleep couldn't fix for any eighty-year-old. "I encouraged her to lie down, too. She's getting ready for bed now."

"But she's upset?" Sylvie looked more little girl than woman without the heavy liner and mascara she'd worn earlier.

"Those bruises and guns would scare anyone."

Gina hugged an arm around her sister's shoulders and guided her back to the bed. "Come on. You should rest, too."

"Do we need to call anyone?" Mike asked, knowing Gina had asked Sylvie some pointed personal questions about the nature of her assault while he'd helped their great-aunt and -uncle settle in for the night.

"We're good," Gina assured him, meaning there'd been no sexual assault. She cleared the ice pack and some first-aid supplies off the top of the purple comforter, while Sylvie stacked a rainbow of pillows against the wall. "I think the shower helped, but she hasn't shared many details yet."

Sylvie sat on the bed and reached for Gina's hand, pulling her to a seat beside her. Mike would have excused himself from the private conversation, but Sylvie's eyes filled with tears as she raised her gaze to his. "I love Bobby, but he… His friend Emanuel…"

Since she was including him in this conversation, Mike took a step into the room. "The other guy in the car?"

She nodded. "Emanuel said I was pretty and that he wanted to kiss me. Bobby said I had to let him." Gina's curse echoed the thought going through Mike's mind. "I didn't want to. But Emanuel grabbed me, and Bobby didn't try to stop him. Not at first. He laughed. I slapped Emanuel, and then Bobby…" She touched her cheek, and Mike's hands curled into fists. "He said I'd embarrassed him. That's when they got into an argument. Emanuel said the Lexus was his car, and if Bobby wanted to drive it then I had to… I was a bargaining chip," she sobbed. "I'm worth the price of a stupid car to him."

Gina wrapped her arms around Sylvie, rocking back and forth with her. "You can't see him again. You just can't."

How often had Bobby Estes promised Sylvie's affections in exchange for a fancy car? The image of a tan Mercedes circling around the PT clinic so that the driver could threaten Gina filled his thoughts. "Does Bobby borrow his friends' cars a lot?"

Although Gina shook her head, warning him away from asking questions related to *her* troubles, Sylvie answered, anyway. "Bobby has a different car about every week, I guess."

"Do you remember what he was driving two weeks ago?"

"Mike…" Gina chided. But the phone rang in her pocket, and she pulled away to check the number. "It's Derek calling me back. I need to take this." She wiped the tears from her sister's cheeks before standing and turning toward the door. Mike spotted the hint of moisture sparkling in her own eyes and started to reach for her. "No more questions," she mouthed before putting the phone to her ear and hurrying past him into the living room. "Hey, buddy, where were you? I called a couple of hours ago… Yeah, she's fine—or she will be. I need to ask a big favor…"

With a nod, Mike excused himself, too. "I'll let you get some sleep."

But the teenager popped to her feet. "Will you stay for a while?"

Mike supposed Sylvie didn't want to be alone until her sister returned. "Sure, kiddo."

She plucked a tissue from a box on the dresser and wiped away her tears. "I know Gina tries to be all badass. But I think Bobby scares her. I know he scares Rollo and Lupe. But things are a little calmer with you here."

"He scares her because you got hurt and she couldn't stop it. Doesn't mean she's going to back down from any of his threats. Your sister's a brave woman."

"I know." She rolled her dark eyes. "And I know I'm…a headache for her. But we're all trying to find our own way out of this part of town."

"Bobby isn't your way out."

Sylvie shredded the tissue in her fingers before tossing it into the trash. "Maybe not. But I thought he cared about me. Until tonight. And there aren't many guys like you around here."

"White guys?"

She smiled at his teasing chuckle. "Nice guys." Maybe that was a compliment, after all, because she padded across the rug and wrapped her arms around Mike's waist, squeezing him in a hug. "Don't let Gina scare you off. She really likes you, you know."

He knew. But did Gina? And given the career and family priorities she pursued to the exclusion of anything personal, would it make any difference if she did?

He pressed a chaste kiss to the crown of Sylvie's head. "You're going to be okay."

"I know."

"I'll be out on the couch tonight. Don't worry about Bobby or your aunt and uncle or Gina. Sleep tight."

He patted her shoulder before she moved away and crawled onto the daybed, leaning back against the pillows. After pulling a fuzzy blanket over her lap, she grabbed her phone, plugged in her ear buds, turned on her music and tuned him out the way a normal teenager would.

Mike grinned as he pulled the door shut, liking this version of Sylvie Galvan a lot better than the frightened young woman who fancied herself in love with Bobby Estes.

He found Gina in the darkened living room, sticking her cell phone into the pocket of her jeans. She flipped on a lamp beside the sofa where Lupe had set out a pillow and a blanket. He recognized the tight set of her full, bow-shaped lips as she waged an internal battle between the urge to tell him to leave and the desire to give her family the reassurance his presence here seemed to provide. Although hushed, so as not to disturb anyone else in the house, her tone was strictly business. "Derek said he'll do the paperwork for the lab and file a report on the assault."

Mike whispered back. "The one on you? Or the one on your sister?"

"Both."

"Good."

Gina nodded as she circled around the couch and gestured for him to follow her toward the front door. "Thank you for staying so long, but it's late. You have work in the morning and need to get some sleep. I've checked the doors and windows twice already. Sylvie's not sneaking out, and I'm not letting anybody get in. We'll be all right."

"I know you've got your bases covered. I'm staying, anyway."

She tilted her proud chin to his. "Because I'm weak?"

"You're the strongest woman I know." He reached out to brush his knuckles across her soft cheek, not liking the chill he felt there. "I don't want anything to happen to this family. Another set of eyes and ears can't hurt. If I can help—"

"You have helped. You always help." She tipped her cheek into his hand, and the silky curls of her hair tickled his skin, waking the nerve endings that flared to life whenever she got close. "Sometimes I wonder if you're for real. You're just too damn—"

"Don't you dare say *nice* again, like it's some kind of plague." Gina's pupils dilated in the shadows, turning her eyes into rich pools of midnight. She fisted her hand in the front of his shirt, and Mike knew he was in for another argument as she tugged him toward the privacy of the kitchen. "What now? I swear, woman…"

Once his shoes reached the tile floor, she yanked harder, untucking the front of his shirt and pulling him off balance as she bumped into the lower cabinets. Mike braced his hands against the countertop on either side of her so he wouldn't crash into her. But before he could ask what this sudden escape from the living room was all about, she slipped her damaged hand behind his neck and pulled his mouth down to hers.

The unexpected contact shot a bolt of lightning through him, igniting an urgent heat. There was something purposeful, maybe a little angry, in the way she clung to him and fused her mouth to his. Where that anger was directed, Mike couldn't tell. And, at the moment, Mike didn't care. Instinctively, his mouth moved over Gina's, claiming what she offered. Her lips softened, parted. With a husky gasp that went straight to his groin, Gina swept her tongue between his lips. Her fingers clutched at the edge of his jaw, stroking across his beard stubble, holding their mouths together. This wasn't anger; this was need. This was attraction simmering out of control. This was the inevitable release of every emotion roiling through this house tonight.

Mike understood that fire. That desperation. That crazy need to connect to the one person who could ease the fear, the anger, the need and the passion that had grown too powerful to control anymore.

Slipping his hands to her waist and pulling her body into his, Mike took control of the kiss, suckling on her sweet bottom lip, soothing the trembling response with his tongue. She pulled at the hem of his polo until she could slip her hands inside to palm the skin of his chest and stomach, branding him with her desire. He returned the favor, tugging her blouse from her jeans and splaying his fingers over the smooth curve of her back.

He felt the chill of her skin as he explored the length of her spine and flare of her hips. He dropped gentle kisses against her eyebrows and cheeks and the rapid beat of her pulse beneath her ear. The woman was responsive in a way that made him feel powerful, male, whole. Gina warmed at every spot he touched and cooed soft, excited moans that hummed in her throat. Her fingers raked through his hair, roamed over his shoulders, traveled inside his shirt, kindling an incendiary response that made him want to reclaim her lips and loosen the snap of her jeans and tug down the zipper so he could dip his fingers beneath the elastic band of her panties and fill his hands with that irresistible backside.

"Is Sylvie okay?" she murmured against his mouth, running her fingers along the column of his throat, nipping at the point of his chin, turning his response into a hoarse growl.

"You want to talk *now*?"

"Yes." She tipped her head back as he trailed his lips down the arch of her throat, seeking out the source of those sexy hums. She whimpered when he found a particularly sensitive bundle of nerves. "No. Is she?"

Mike chuckled his response against her skin. "She'll be fine. The bruises on her cheek and wrist are superficial. It might not hurt to talk to a counselor, though."

"I'll arrange it." Gina stretched up on tiptoe, her small breasts pillowing against his chest as she guided his mouth back to hers for another hungry kiss.

Mike indulged himself in the pleasure firing throughout his body. He grabbed her sweet, round bottom and lifted her, thinking he was never going to get enough of this woman until he was buried deep inside her. His hard length pushed against the zipper of his jeans, seeking out the heat of her body.

This make-out session was going from zero to sixty in a matter of seconds. And while their bodies were definitely willing, Mike had to wonder if their brains were on board with where this was headed. He moved his hands up to feather his fingers into her hair and rested his forehead against Gina's, sucking in a deep breath of much-needed air. "I need to understand the rules here. There is no *this*, no *us,* yet it's all right for you to kiss me like I'm the only snack on a deserted island?"

"Forget the rules. Just…" She tipped her head to seal their lips together in brief kiss. "I don't like being scared or vulnerable."

"Tell me about it." He welcomed the cinch of her arms around his waist, as he took her mouth in a leisurely kiss. "Sounds like you've talked to your family about me. Maybe said a couple of nice things."

"Don't let it go to your head, Choir Boy."

Oh, but there were a lot of other things going straight to his head.

Her hands slipped beneath his shirt, singeing the skin on his back. "I don't like feeling as if I can't handle myself in a fight."

"You'll get there. I promise."

The kiss jockeyed back and forth with forays and acceptance, with tantalizing discovery and revisiting a favorite angle or caress. "I'm glad you were here, that you had my back."

"Anytime."

"No. Not any—" she gasped as his palm settled over her breast, squeezing the proud nipple between his thumb and palm through the lace of her bra. She buried her face against his chest, pushing the pert handful into his greedy hand, her soft gasps belying her breathless words. "I want this, but… I can't do a relationship. I don't have time. It wouldn't be fair to you… all my responsibilities—"

"Do you hear me complaining?" He squeezed her bottom and lifted her again. She wrapped her legs around his waist, and Mike's pulse thundered in his ears. He wanted her. She wanted him. "There's just now." He spun around, leaning against the sink. But her knees butted against the countertop. "We're both adults. We're safe." He spotted the chair sticking out from the table and carried her toward it. "Don't overthink this."

He sank onto the seat, pulling Gina into his lap. He couldn't help but push against her as her thighs squeezed around his hips. They kissed as their hands fumbled between them. Mike spread his thighs to ease the tightness in his jeans. But he'd miscalculated his position on the chair, and his right leg slipped off the seat. Gina shifted. Mike caught her, planting his foot to keep her in place. He moaned against her mouth, a blend of anticipation and frustration as the inevitable jolt of electricity sparked down his leg.

Hugging her tight to his body, Mike winced as he stood to alleviate the pressure on the pinched nerve. His broken body was betraying him. Just when Gina was letting him get close. Ah, hell. Now the leg had gone numb.

"Mike? Put me down." Gina scrambled out of his grasp, pushing away but clinging to his arms until she found her balance. No, she was steadying him. "Are you hurt? Do you need to sit down?"

"Standing is better." He pulled Gina back into his chest, dropping his chin to the crown of her hair. "I'm sorry. Nothing like a twinge of the old bursitis and my leg going numb to put a damper on things. Just let me hold you for a second, okay?"

But the woman couldn't keep still. Now he'd just added himself to the long list of things she had to worry about. "What happened? Did Bobby hurt you?"

"Be still for a sec. I'll be fine. It's an old war wound acting up."

"Huh?"

When she stilled and leaned into him, Mike pulled her arms back around his waist and breathed deeply against her dark, fragrant hair, willing the numbness and the lingering desire still firing through his system to abate. "I was in a car wreck when I was sixteen. A friend was driving me home because I was too drunk to be responsible for myself. He died. Helping me. Pretty much every bone below my waist was shattered. Tore up muscles and nerves. The doctors weren't sure I was going to walk again."

Her arms tightened around him. He felt both hands hooking into the back of his belt as she nestled her cheek against his heart. "Your friend died?"

"Leave it to you to pick up on the important detail." Mike distracted himself from the guilt and regret by sifting her hair through his fingers. Although this stance gave him a bird's-eye view of that sexy bottom he wanted to grab again, he ignored the impulse and savored her willingness to simply be close to him without any kind of protest. "There's some residual nerve damage I deal with. Regular exercise keeps the weight off the joints and the muscles strong, but sometimes I'll twist wrong or even sleep wrong and tweak a nerve. Or the weather changes and all the metal pins and wires inside let me know it. But I'm walking now, with no braces and no cane. I can make love to a beautiful woman again—on most nights." His wry comment only made her snuggle tighter. "I can run again. So I'm not complaining. Sorry to start something I couldn't finish."

She shook her head. "*I* started it. And I'm not complaining. I'm just glad you're here."

"Me, too."

"We're a pair, aren't we? Gimpy and Hopalong. Maybe between us there's a whole person who can take down the bad guys." She released his belt to rub her hands over the backside of his jeans. Whether consciously or unconsciously done, the tender strokes across the muscles at the small of his back and hips felt good. The physical tension in him eased and the air around them cooled, even as something warmer and more profound than the desire they shared took hold inside him. "I'm sorry for all of the trouble I've brought to your life."

"Trust me, Tiger. I know trouble. You ain't it." He leaned back against her arms, framing her face between his hands and tilting those rich brown eyes up to his. He dipped his head to press a firm kiss to her beautiful lips before reluctantly pulling away. "You need to go to bed. Alone." He pulled her hands from his hips and backed away before he couldn't leave her. "Do not sneak out of this house and go to that bar by yourself. Do not take on Bobby Estes by yourself. Take care of your family tonight. Rest. I'll be here in the morning when you wake up."

"You can't stay." Despite her words, she pawed at him, buttoning his shirt, smoothing down the spikes of his hair. If she kept touching him, they were going to end up right back where they'd been a few minutes ago. "You shouldn't."

Mike listened to what she needed, not what she wanted. He stopped her hands from their busywork and squeezed them in his grip. "This is moving too fast, and you're not comfortable with that. I get it. I don't want you to regret anything that happens between us."

She nodded. "I don't want you to regret anything, either. I'm kind of a mess tonight."

"Join the crowd. The timing sucks. That's all." He released her hands and brushed a thick curl off her cheek, tucking it behind her ear. "Mind if I call a couple of friends at KCPD and ask them to make a few extra passes through your neighborhood tonight?"

This time, she pulled his hand away. But she was smiling. "I'd appreciate it."

"Consider it done." He leaned in for one more peck on the lips, thought better of it considering his willpower around Gina and turned her toward her bedroom. "I'd better go to that couch now, or I never will."

He followed her into the living room, pausing at the couch as she quietly opened the bedroom door and peeked in. Even through the shadows cast by the lone lamp, he could see her smiling.

"Sylvie asleep?" he whispered.

Gina nodded before opening the door wider. Mike glanced down at his wrinkled shirt, grinning at the mismatched buttons and buttonhole Gina had missed in her haste to redress him.

"Mike?"

He glanced up to see her padding back across the hall to meet him. "Something wrong?"

She drew her shoulders back, steeling her posture before speaking. "It's the five o'clock shadow. The way it's just enough beard to be interesting, but not so shaggy that it obscures your face." He frowned in confusion. She touched his face, running her fingertips along the line of his jaw. "Catnip," she explained. "That's my catnip. What I find attractive on a man. Something about the angles and the rawness is *muy masculino*. There's something a little bad boy about it that I want to touch."

He didn't need to be fluent in Spanish to understand that compliment. His face eased into a smile beneath her touch. He turned to kiss her palm before she pulled away. "Happy to oblige. Now get some sleep. I'll stay up and keep an eye on things until the first black-and-white drives by. See you in the morning."

Mike waited for the bedroom door to close behind her before he went back into the kitchen to splash some cold water on his face, tempering those last vestiges of desire lingering from that kiss. He called a couple of friends from his father's SWAT team and explained the situation, needlessly promising a free lunch or workout at the clinic in exchange for their help watching the house.

Once his friends Trip and Alex had arrived and parked their truck across the street from Gina's, Mike peeled off his shirt, belt and shoes and stretched out on the couch that was too short for him. It was after midnight when he heard the hushed sound of a door opening and closing. More curious than alarmed, he peeked around the end of the couch to see Gina in a long-sleeved T-shirt and pajama pants. Instead of heading for the bathroom, as both Lupe and Rollo had done earlier, she kissed her knuckles and rubbed them against her heart.

Mike remembered the superstitious action from the shooting range. "What do you need luck for at this time of night?"

She didn't startle at his teasing voice from the shadows. "Not luck. Courage."

He sat up, concerned by her answer. "Gina?"

"I saw the men out front. Thank you." She circled the sofa and sat beside him. "I don't want to have sex. I'm not ready to complicate us like that yet. But… could we snuggle for a little bit? I can't seem to get warm again, and I can't sleep when I'm cold, and…"

Relieved to know that Sylvie and everyone else in the house were safe, he wrapped the blanket around her and pulled her into his arms. "You don't have to be the strong one all the time. Take a breather tonight. I've got you."

Turning onto his side, he stretched out on the couch behind her, spooning his chest against her back. "This doesn't mean anything," she insisted. "I'm just cold."

"Understood." Grinning at the tough act he wasn't buying, Mike draped his arm around her waist and tucked her as close as the blanket and dimensions of the couch allowed. "Warm enough?"

She nodded, resting her head on his arm. "This doesn't make your legs cramp or hurt, does it?"

"Nope. Your shoulder okay?"

"It doesn't hurt at all when I lie on this side." Several seconds passed before he felt her body relax against his. "Sylvie gets up at seven for school."

He ignored the bottom nestling against his groin and reached for his phone. "I'll set my alarm for six."

"You're driving me to the crime lab and Sin City Bar in the morning."

"Yes, ma'am."

"Could we do that before my therapy session?"

Mike's laugh was as hushed as the shadows surrounding them. "Only if you stop talking and get some rest."

"*Not* my mother, Choir Boy." Her answering laugh faded into a yawn.

He nudged aside the dark curls at the nape of her neck and pressed a kiss there. "How about your partner?"

She brushed her lips across the swell of his bicep. "Deal. For now."

The strong fingers of her right hand latched onto his. In a matter of minutes, the tension eased from her body, and her soft, even breath against his skin let him know that she'd finally fallen asleep. "I'll be your armor tonight, Tiger," he whispered.

Mike settled into the most comfortable position he could manage and drifted toward sleep himself, knowing three things. One, Gina liked to keep things even between them—he'd revealed a secret, so she had, too. Two, there was far more danger surrounding this woman than even he'd realized. And three, the attraction simmering in his veins, the unexpected caring that took them beyond therapist and patient, or even friends, was mutual, no matter how stubbornly independent she tried to be.

Logically, he could see the pattern of his life repeating itself: play Knight in Shining Armor to a woman who needed him. Stir up his hormones and get his heart involved. The next inevitable step would be her realizing she no longer had a use for the strength and support he provided, and him getting hurt again.

But he couldn't stay away from Gina. Out of all his relationships—Caroline, Frannie, others who'd grown tired of Mr. Nice Guy before anything real had started—none of them had gotten him twisted up inside as fast and feverishly as Officer Gina Galvan. Her bravery and vulnerability, her fierce determination to improve her standing and protect her family, her passionate impulses and the stubborn emotional shield she couldn't quite keep in place—all got under his skin and inside his head and into his heart, refusing to answer to caution or logic.

He was falling for Gina Galvan. Falling hard and fast. And the closer he got, the more he realized there were too many ways he could lose her.

Chapter 10

Gina fingered the badge clipped to the belt of her jeans, trying not to feel as if she was impersonating an officer this morning, as she stared out the window of Mike's pickup at the heavy steel door below the Sin City Bar sign. Technically, although she was on medical leave, she was still a member of KCPD, and she'd earned the right to wear this badge. And, until that losing skirmish with Bobby Estes last night, she'd believed she was always going to be a working cop again. An elite cop. A SWAT cop.

Now she was feeling a bit like Sin City's fraudulent facade. At night, their sign lit up with red and yellow bulbs, bathing the entryway in a warm color, welcoming patrons. But the bright sunlight of a chilly spring morning revealed chipped white paint on the outside walls. Rust at each corner of their sign stained the painted brick and faded awning over the door. With the blinds drawn at every window, there was no promise of a party at a friendly bar to draw in customers.

Just like wearing the badge didn't mean she could do this job the way she wanted to again.

Looking at the row of motorcycles and the beat-up van in the parking lot beside the bar, she was certain she was about to get another opportunity to chat with Gordy and Denny Bismarck and their biker buddies. And she suspected them being here at this time of day meant they were either very good friends with the manager and bartenders she'd hoped would break their alibi—which meant that probably wasn't going to happen—or they had gotten wind of KCPD looking into them as the potential cop shooters and they were here to make sure that no one gave them up. Either way, she was on their turf. Asking questions and getting straight answers wouldn't be easy, even on her best day.

"You ready to go play good cop/bad cop?" Mike's angular features crooked into a teasing smile as he pulled in beside the van and turned off the engine.

Drawn from the doom and gloom of her thoughts, Gina smiled back. One more day and that sexy beard stubble of his would cross the line into scruffy.

But in the dark hours of last night, she'd admitted there were plenty of other reasons why Mike Cutler was her catnip. Her family had felt reassured by his presence at the house, and anyone who was that kind and patient with her family was a hero in her book. That long, hard, rebuilt body had been a furnace at her back, keeping her warm and secure enough to enjoy the best night's sleep she'd had since the shooting. His hands had awakened an answering need inside her with each purposeful touch. And she shouldn't even think about the gentle seduction and commanding firmness of his mouth moving over hers. Even his do-the-right-thing stubbornness that matched her own was becoming less of a frustration and more of a type of strength she respected. She'd lowered her guard with Mike last night, both physically and emotionally. She'd felt normal, free of all her burdens, for a few hours. Mike Cutler managed to be strong for her without making her feel weak or foolish or at any kind of disadvantage.

She'd never expected that a man could make her feel like that—like she could fall in love with him if she wasn't careful.

She reached over the console to brush her fingers across his jaw. *Sí.* She had definitely developed a craving for that handsome face. "Not a cop, Choir Boy."

The color of his eyes darkened like cobalt at her touch. Just like that, with a piercing look and the ticklish caress of his beard beneath her sensitive fingertips, her stomach tightened with desire.

But she was here to work. She hadn't been lying when she'd said she couldn't fit a relationship into her life right now. If she could, there would be only one candidate. But reality made falling in love low on her priority list. It made falling in love with Mike nearly impossible. She pulled her fingers away and unbuckled her seat belt. She eyed the officer stowing the last of the yellow crime scene tape from Frank McBride's shooting into the trunk of the black-and-white police cruiser already in the parking lot.

"Looks like Derek's ready for us." Having her partner here made this interview sanctioned, despite her own self-doubts. He'd met them at the crime lab earlier so she could deliver the bullets she'd taken from Bobby's and Emanuel's guns to the ballistics tech. He would run a comparison between them and the spent rounds recovered from the police shootings, including her own. "You wait in the truck."

Mike shook his head, pocketing his keys in his jacket. "I can't very well watch your back from here."

Gina paused with her hand on the door handle. "Derek will have my back. I'm guessing the Bismarck boys aren't going to cooperate, and I need you to stay safe."

"How about we double our efforts?" He pointed through the windshield to the garage on the opposite side of the bar's parking lot. "An auto-repair and customization shop right next door to their hangout? Want to bet that one or more of them works there? I can wander in and ask if anyone there remembers them from the day of your shooting, or if they saw them here yesterday when Frank was shot. Maybe I'll get an estimate on rotating my tires."

"And, while you're in there, see if you spot any familiar vehicles like the rusty old SUV the shooter used or the tan Mercedes that's been following me?"

"Is that a bad idea?"

"No. It's a smart one." Derek was out of the cruiser, heading toward the truck. As uneasy as the thought of Mike investigating on his own made her, she couldn't deny that he had inherited all the right instincts about being a cop from his father. Other than the fact he was unarmed. But then, so was she. "All right. You check out next door while Derek and I see if we can break anybody's alibi. But if the Bismarcks or their friends *are* there, I don't want you to engage any of them. Turn around and get out of there. I'll meet you back here."

"Ten minutes give you enough time?"

Gina nodded. "No heroics, okay? Just get information."

"Yes, ma'am."

Derek was waiting beside the truck when she shut the door. He rested an arm on the butt of the gun holstered at his waist, his eyebrows arched in confusion as Mike jogged across the parking lot and entered the automotive shop. "I thought Cutler was just driving you around until you're cleared to do it yourself. What's he up to?"

"Detective work." Kissing the back of her fingers and rubbing them against her heart, she sent up a silent prayer that Mike wasn't on a mission that could get him hurt. Then she butted her elbow against Derek's and headed for Sin City's front door. "Come on. We'd better do the same."

On a different day, if she was in uniform and back on patrol, Gina would have run in the bar's owner, Vince Goring. The myopic manager was already serving a drink to a dazed old man who, judging by his ratty appearance and eye-watering stench, had probably been sitting on the same barstool since closing time the night before. She wondered if he was the drunk who'd allegedly witnessed Frank McBride's shooting yesterday afternoon.

Nothing about this quest for answers was going smoothly. The deep voices and laughing conversation from the back of the bar fell silent by the time her eyes had adjusted to the dim lighting. She'd been hoping she could talk to the owner alone, find out who'd been tending bar that wintry afternoon when she'd gotten shot. But Vince was carrying a tray of coffee mugs to the back booth, where Gordon and Denny Bismarck, Al, Prison Tat Guy and one of their potbellied buddies were sitting. Denny pulled his flask from his pocket and doctored his coffee before passing the container around the table. Oddly enough, none of them seemed to be sporting a black eye or broken nose, or other signs that'd they'd been involved in the fight that had lured Frank McBride here. But in this dim lighting, it was hard to tell.

Still, she wasn't here about serving drinks to someone who'd already had too much, or citing a barkeep who allowed patrons to bring in their own alcohol. Letting the glare from Denny Bismarck's dark eyes fuel her resolve to conduct this interview, she ignored him and the whispered conversations at the table, while Vince shuffled back to the bar where she and Derek stood.

"Mr. Goring." Gina made no effort to whisper. If Bismarck and company knew she was here, then they had to suspect she was asking questions about them. "That group of men at the back table—are they regulars?"

Vince pushed his thick glasses up onto the bridge of his nose before answering. "Sure. Al and Jim work next door at the body shop."

Gina had done her homework. She pointed to her neck. "Jim Carlson is the guy with the tats?" She remembered Al Renken, the van driver. He was bald.

"Yep. You friends with them?"

The last man, Aldo Pitsaeli, was the guy who'd been worried that day about getting in trouble with his wife. Denny and the others had been with Gordy at the Bismarck house before the shooting. Did the five men always travel in a pack? Would they alibi any member of their group who wasn't there? Even if he left to go shoot a couple of cops? "We're acquainted."

That seemed good enough for the barkeep to start talking. "Gordy got his bike customized at the shop. Denny, too. Although they sometimes drive a '75 Bronco SUV they inherited from their daddy. If you ask me, they ought to take that wreck to the scrap-metal yard, or else get *it* customized. All painted up with a couple new fenders, folks might go for it."

She wasn't here for a lesson in auto mechanics, either. "They come in here a lot?"

He picked up a rag to wipe down the bar around the drunk who never moved. In fact, she could hear him snoring. "They hang out with Al and Jim when they're workin'. Sometimes do odd jobs over there. They're all motor heads. They come over here a lot when Al or Jim go on break or have a day off."

Derek tapped her on the arm and straightened behind her. But Gina was already aware of Denny Bismarck standing up and his younger brother sliding out of the booth behind him. She doubted they'd do anything stupid like attack a uniformed officer so soon after yesterday's shooting, but she still felt the urgency to ask her questions faster. "Do they ever come into the bar in the afternoon?"

"I guess." He snapped his fingers. "Oh, you mean like those cops were asking yesterday?"

"I'm more interested in seven weeks ago, January twenty-sixth," she clarified. "Were you working the bar that day? Were they all here?"

Vince nodded. Then frowned and shook his head.

Gina's hand curled into a fist. "Yes or no? Were they here that afternoon?"

"Seven weeks is a long time to remember something."

As far as Gina was concerned, seven decades wouldn't be long enough for her to forget that day. "Well, can you remember yesterday? There was a fight in your bar. A black police officer responded. He was shot out front."

"Oh, yeah. That was real bad. I didn't know what was going on until I heard the shots. Thought it was an engine backfiring next door."

"Who was in the fight?" She pointed to the back of the bar. "Was it any of those guys?"

"G?" Derek's hand brushed the small of her back, alerting her to the group of men ambling their way.

Gina caught and held Denny's glare as she asked Vince a follow-up question. "Are they always here together? The brothers, their friends—in a group like this morning?"

"I guess."

"Was one of them missing?"

"Yesterday?" He looked at the group of approaching men, as if seeing their faces for the first time. "As I recall, they were out front by the time I got there. Fight was over. The officer was writin' folks up. Maybe they were in the bar. Guess they could have come out of the shop."

Gina bit down on her frustration and kept a friendly smile on her face. "All of them? What about seven weeks ago?"

Vince adjusted his glasses again. "Come to think of it, Gordy wasn't here that day."

No. He'd been sitting in the back of her police

cruiser. "But the others were all here at the bar? Could you swear to that in court?"

Vince's eyes widened behind his glasses. "Am I going to court? Lady, I don't want to testify against anybody. That's bad for business."

Derek put up a warning hand. "You boys keep your distance. We don't want any trouble."

Denny snickered. "You're the only one making trouble, Johnson. Moving in on my brother's wife?"

"Ex-wife," Derek reminded him. "I only went out with Vicki twice."

Jim Carlson moved within chest-bumping distance. "That's two times too many as far as we're concerned. You're taking advantage of my friend's unfortunate situation."

"Back off, Carlson," Derek warned. "Assaulting a police officer and impeding an investigation will land you back in jail."

"Were the others all here that afternoon, Mr. Goring?" Gina needed an answer. "Even Denny?"

Jim Carlson's skin reddened beneath the tats on his neck. But even as he wisely retreated a step, Denny slipped onto the barstool beside Gina, brushing his shoulder against hers. "You checking up on me, *querida*? I heard you weren't a cop no more."

Gina plucked her badge off her belt and slammed it on top of the bar in front of him. "Touch me one more time and I'll arrest you."

Derek held his ground behind her, but she heard the urgency in his tone. "G, we need to get moving."

Denny wiped his mouth, leaving a dot of spittle on his scraggly beard. "You think I shot you?"

"Doesn't seem like Vince here is much of an alibi.

And I think your buddies are scared to say anything you don't want them to. Maybe you wanted revenge on us for arresting your brother? For me bossing you around? Or you were after Derek for dating Vicki, and I was collateral damage."

"And I shot all those other cops, too? Why would I do that?" Denny snorted and reached for his flask. "I watch the news. I know you ain't the only cop who got hurt. As far as I know, ain't none of them boinking my brother's wife."

"That's enough, Bismarck," Derek warned him.

Bobby Estes was more likely to have premeditated the shooting, setting up the diversion of attacking other cops before going after her. The Bismarcks were heat-of-the-moment types of criminals. But she and Derek had been to the Bismarck house before on previous calls. Were these bozos smart enough to stage another assault on Vicki to set her and Derek up as targets? They sure seemed to have plenty of time on their hands to follow her to the physical therapy clinic or drive by her home or hang out here.

Denny had taken a swallow and tucked the flask back inside his jacket before Gina realized the place had gone quiet, except for the snoring coming from the end of the bar.

Gina backed away from the bar and surveyed the rest of the interior. There was nothing but a circle of abandoned coffee mugs at that back table now. "Where are your friends?"

Denny shrugged. "Al had to go back to work."

And she hadn't seen him leave. She clipped her badge onto her belt and pointed to Vince. "Is there a back door to this place?"

"Yeah."

She didn't know if she was madder at Derek for not telling her the men had slipped out or at herself for not noticing. She was damn certain she was mad at Denny for setting up the diversion while his comrades snuck out, knowing her suspicions were centered on him. "You could have left here that afternoon and come back to shoot up the Bismarck house without anyone seeing you leave."

Denny wasn't fazed by her brewing temper. "You saw me leave on my bike that day. Did you see me come back?"

She remembered the rusty old SUV with frozen, dirty slush thrown up around the wheel wells and masking the license plate. "You could have dropped your bike off here and come back in your '75 Bronco."

Gina held her ground when Denny stood and towered over her. "I could have, *querida*."

It didn't feel like a confession so much as a taunting reminder that she still had no answers. Only too many suspects with motives and opportunities.

The front door banged opened, flooding the bar with light. Gina squinted Mike's tall frame into focus. "Your ten minutes are up. We need to go."

"Mike—"

"Now." He sounded as if he'd just run a wind sprint. He backed out the open door, letting her know this wasn't that overprotective streak kicking in but something else.

She was smart enough to follow him. "Did you find something out?"

Denny's laughter confirmed her suspicion that he'd been diverting her attention for a reason. While Derek shoved him back onto his barstool and warned him to shut up, Gina hurried outside and ran to Mike's truck as he climbed in behind the wheel. "Mike?"

"That guy who was in the backseat of your cruiser the day I rescued you is leaving in a mighty big hurry." He turned the key in the ignition and shifted the pickup into Drive.

She was climbing onto the running board between the open door and frame of the truck, when she heard the growl of an engine revving up to full speed. When a big motorcycle roared out of the garage next door and jumped the curb before skidding into a sharp turn, Gina dropped into the passenger seat and slammed the door. "Go! Don't lose him."

Derek ran out of the bar behind her, shouting through the open window. "I'll call it in. If you get the plate number, let me know." Mike's tires spit up gravel before they found traction and they raced down the street after the motorcycle. "I suspect that place next door was a chop shop. They had an awful lot of car and motorcycle parts in the back room that belonged to high-end vehicles. Not the kind of stuff you see in this neighborhood."

Gina reached across the console to buckle him safely behind the wheel before sitting back to buckle herself in. "What were you doing in the back room?"

"Chasing the guy who ran in while you were next door asking questions."

"You were supposed to stick to getting your tires rotated." He was intent on dodging in and out of traffic and honking to warn pedestrians before they stepped into the street. Apparently, it was useless to argue the idea of staying away from danger with this man.

"You're certain it was Gordon Bismarck? Big guy? Needs a haircut?"

He nodded, skidding his truck in a sharp right turn to follow the motorcycle around the corner. "The boss yelled 'Gordy' when he flew out of the garage. Thought that was a pretty good clue."

Gina frowned. Out of all the members of that aging biker gang, she'd figured Denny would be the one to come back and take potshots at the cops arresting his brother. She eyed the spinning lights of Derek's police car taking the corner behind them. Gina gripped the center console as Mike's truck sped through the next intersection. Denny was the one who should be running now. Was this chase the real diversion? Was Denny Bismarck slipping away into hiding right now?

"We should get back to the bar."

"You want me to turn this truck around?"

"Gordy Bismarck couldn't have shot me. He's the only one with an airtight alibi."

Mike skirted through another intersection as the light was turning red. "I'm staying on this guy's tail. Why run if he's got nothing to hide?"

Why wouldn't the answers she needed fall into place? "If that place was a chop shop for stolen car parts, then Gordy's violating his parole by being there. Maybe that's why he's running. It might not have anything to do with me."

"And it may have everything to do with you." Mike leaned on his horn and ran a second red light. "Maybe he knows who shot you and doesn't want you asking questions. Put a call through to my dad."

"I'm not calling in SWAT for a car chase." Gina's bottom left the seat as they bounced over a pothole.

The motorcycle swerved around a delivery truck. Mike followed, nearly rear-ending the slow-moving car in front of it. "Look out!"

"I see it." He cut into the opposing lane of traffic, coming nose to nose with an oncoming bus.

"Mike!" He swerved at the last second, knocking Gina between the door and the console.

"You okay?"

"I'm fine. Just don't lose him." Her heart pounded against her ribs. "And don't do that again."

He steered his truck around another corner and sped up the hill, trying to catch the racing motorcycle before it disappeared over the crest. "Call Dad and tell him to send somebody back to Sin City. We'll stay on this guy. And I want someone to know that we're chasing down a suspect. We're flying through town in an unmarked truck. Why hasn't anyone stopped *us* yet?"

They shot over the top of the hill and veered down the other side. Downtown traffic gave way to underpasses, railroad tracks and the warehouse district near the confluence of the Kansas and Missouri rivers. She should be seeing some neighborhood black-and-whites by now. Roads should be blocked off. A wary sense of unease that had nothing to do with the dangers of this daring thrill ride shivered down her spine. "Where's our backup?"

"Call Dad."

"Derek already called—"

"Your buddy Derek lost us after we nearly hit that bus. If we catch this guy, we'll need help. Call."

"What?!" But her partner's black-and-white wasn't in the rearview mirror. "Where…?"

"Call!"

She pulled out her phone and dialed Dispatch. "This is Officer Gina Galvan. I'm an off-duty cop." She gave her badge number and recited the partial license plate she'd gotten off the motorcycle, along with Gordon Bismarck's name and a description of the rider. "He's moving west on Twelfth. Suspect is in violation of his parole. I am in pursuit in a black pickup. Unit 4-13 has been notified of our intent and is also in pursuit. Although, I've lost sight of him. Please verify that he hasn't been in an accident."

"Acknowledged." The dispatcher's efficient monotone put out an APB over her headset before coming back on the line. "Notifying units in area of high-speed pursuit."

"No one's called this in yet?"

"I'm sending out a notification to all units now."

An all-call warning officers of the dangerous traffic situation in the area should have gone in five minutes ago. "What about sending a unit to the Sin City Bar?"

The dispatcher hesitated. "That's where Frank McBride was shot."

"Yes. I was questioning suspects there."

"My records show there's already a unit assigned to watch the bar."

"What?" She hadn't seen any police car in the area. "Then call them."

"Unit 4-13 was assigned that duty this morning. 10:00 a.m. to 2:00 p.m."

"4-13 is with me." Only he wasn't. Gina inhaled a deep breath, quashing her emotions. "I need you to send a new unit to Sin City Bar to round up Denny Bismarck, Al Renken, Jim Carlson and Aldo Pitsaeli for questioning. And send an alert to Michael Cutler of SWAT Team One that his son is with me."

"Copy that. Unit dispatched. Message sent."

"Galvan out." Gina's phone tumbled out of her hand as they bounced over a railroad crossing and followed the motorcycle into the West Bottoms area of the city. Once a teeming center of commerce, the monoliths of rusting metal and sagging brick walls stood like looming sentinels beside the river. Although much of the district had been bought by investors and was slowly being transformed into trendy art houses, antique shops and reception halls, the buildings were only open on weekends. In the middle of the week, there were only a few lone cars on the streets, and one small moving van backed up against a concrete loading dock.

It should have made it easy to spot Gordy. But he'd steered the more maneuverable motorcycle up and down side streets and alleys, and they'd lost him. Mike slowed his speed as they drove down Wyoming Street, each checking every alleyway and open warehouse door on their side of the street.

"Where did he go?" Gina heard the distant sound of police sirens a split second before she heard the familiar sound of an engine revving. When Gordy shot out of the cross street in front of them, Mike floored the accelerator. "There he is!"

"Hold on!" Mike's big pickup left the stink of burned rubber behind them as he took a hard turn to the left.

Gina spotted the wall of chain link fence and piles of plastic trash bags stacked between it and the food truck at the loading dock behind a café where two men were hauling out crates of produce. "Blind alley!"

Mike stomped on the brakes. Gina's shoulder protested bracing her hands against the dashboard. The truck skidded to an abrupt halt while Gordy gunned his bike up the concrete ramp to leap the security fence. But he hit a dolly loaded with lettuce and tomatoes and spun out. The bike crashed into the fence and Gordy rolled across the concrete, sliding off the edge into the bundles of trash.

Before Gina could get unbuckled, pull out her badge and warn the two workers to stay inside the café, Mike was out of the truck, racing down the alley toward Gordy Bismarck as he scrambled to his feet. But his limping gait didn't stand a chance against Mike's long legs. Gordy abandoned his bike and was halfway up the fence when Mike leaped up, grabbed the other man and pulled him down. They tumbled into a sea of restaurant waste, but Mike had Gordy's face pressed against the pavement by the time Gina caught up to them.

"KCPD!" she announced. "Stay on the ground!"

Mike was breathing hard from the exertion. But given Gordy's deep gasps, and pale, oxygen-deprived skin, she knew Mike clearly had the upper hand. Still, Gina wasn't about to trust any perp's cooperation at this point. After a quick assessment of their surroundings, she shut off the motorcycle's engine and pulled the strapping tape from one of the broken crates to wind it around Gordy's wrists, securing him and checking his pockets for any weapons before she gave Mike the okay to release him.

"I'm getting tired of arresting you, Gordy. Why did

you run from us?" Gina demanded, stowing the pocketknife she'd found on him before rolling him over and showing him her badge.

When he didn't immediately answer, Mike grabbed him by the shoulders of his jacket and sat him up against the fence to face her. "Answer Officer Galvan's question."

"I'm not going back to prison," he answered on a toneless breath.

"You will if you shot a cop," Mike reminded him, his usually friendly voice low and menacing. "We were just there to ask questions. You look guilty making us chase you all over town."

Gordy tilted his gaze up to Mike, evaluating his younger, fitter, more ready-to-do-battle posture before deciding to talk to Gina. "I didn't shoot you, lady. You know I didn't. Hell, I was in the backseat of your car. I got shot at, too."

"But you didn't get hit. You were protected while my partner and I were out in the open. What about Officer McBride?"

"Who?"

"The cop who was wounded yesterday at Sin City."

Silence.

Mike tugged Gordy forward by the collar of his jacket. "Do you know who shot Gina?"

Gordy glared at Mike but didn't answer.

Refusing to speak wasn't an option as far as Gina was concerned. "Did Denny come back to the house to shoot us? Is that why you ran? To protect your brother the way he protected you that day? Or are you just worried about you and your boys getting caught working in a chop shop?"

She must have struck a nerve with one of those questions because Gordy's gaze dropped to the pavement. "I want my attorney."

Gina turned at the blare of sirens at the end of the alley as two black-and-whites pulled up. Two officers climbed out of the first car, one radioing in the situation report, while the other hurried over with a proper pair of handcuffs to secure Bismarck and drag him to his feet.

Gordy looked down at Gina. "A man's got a right to protect what's his."

Was he confessing a motive for the shooting? Or was he defending his actions to protect his brother?

While the officer led Bismarck to the backseat of the cruiser, Derek jogged around the corner. "G? You all right?"

Her voice was sharp when he reached her. "Just how many times did you sleep with Vicki Bismarck?"

"Whoa." Derek put up his hands, stopping just short of touching her. "That came out of left field."

"Not really. Gordy and Denny seem to think you're a motive for their behavior. Beating up on Vicki. Threatening us. Maybe even firing a gun at us. Because you moved in on Gordy's woman."

Derek propped his hands at his waist, alternately smiling and looking as if he was about to cuss up a blue streak. "That is out of line, G. Bismarck's got no claim on her. They're divorced. And I told you, I went out with her twice."

"The Bismarcks seem to think it was more than that."

"The Bismarcks are wrong. Whose side are you on, anyway?"

Gina shook her head. "You should have recused yourself from that interview this morning."

The smile didn't win. "Hey, you were the one who called me for the favor."

"That was my mistake. My second mistake was counting on you to help me round up Bismarck." She took two steps toward Mike's truck and spun around to face Derek. "Where were you? What if he'd gotten away?"

"I circled around to Thirteenth to cut him off when I lost you. I thought he was heading for the interstate. How was I to know he'd do a U-ee and head toward the river?"

"What about sealing off traffic corridors and keeping everyone else safe while we were in pursuit of a suspect? I called Dispatch myself."

"I called it in," he insisted.

"When? Dispatch hadn't gotten your call yet."

"So it wasn't the first thing I did. I was focused on driving. Everybody has an off day."

An off day? She was done with him settling for being an average cop who lived by an ambiguous moral code.

"You should have stuck to stakeout duty at the bar." He'd have to be blind not to read the disappointment screaming from her body language. She marched back to Mike's truck, aware that Derek was hurrying after her.

"I'll go back to the bar and round the Bismarcks up for questioning."

Gina waved off the offer and kept walking. "Already taken care of. If they're not long gone."

"Did you want me to take care of *them*? Or take care of *you*?"

Gina whirled around on him. "I don't need to be taken care of. I need you to do your job."

He thumped his chest. "I'm the one still wearing a uniform."

Gina shoved her fingers through her hair, muttering a curse, before inhaling a deep breath so she could speak calmly. "Well then, Mr. Uniform, notify the auto-theft team that that place next door to Sin City may be housing stolen vehicle parts. If Denny and his gang haven't cleared them out already."

"Stop giving me orders, G. Look, it's not like we were chasing some piece-of-junk Chevy."

"Why would we—?"

"You were after a guy on a motorcycle. A wild-goose chase that steps on the toes of some other department's investigation. You've got me running errands and filing reports on KCPD time, when I'm supposed to be doing my job at the Precinct." He gestured to the empty belt at her waist. "You're not even cleared to wear your gun, much less run your own investigation. I'm the one trying to cover your backside so you don't get in trouble with the brass."

"Me?"

"Yeah. Haven't you heard? My dad talked to a lawyer about suing you and the department for allowing me to get shot."

"Allowing…?" She'd suspected as much. Didn't stop her temper from flaring. "He has no case. There is only one person responsible for you and me and Frank and Colin getting shot. I'm doing everything I can to find this guy before he shoots someone else—

before he kills one of us. I thought that was what you wanted, too." She turned toward the truck, then faced Derek one last time. "And why would you say 'piece-of-junk Chevy'? Are you remembering something from the shooting? Did you see the shooter's vehicle?"

That seemed to genuinely take him aback, knocking the anger out of his voice and posture. "What? I don't think so. It's just a figure of speech."

"No, it's not."

She was aware that Mike had followed them and spoken briefly to the officers in the first police cruiser to arrive on the scene. It wasn't the hole ripped into the knee of his jeans or the unidentifiable glop of food staining the sleeve of his shirt or even the subtle limp she detected in his stride that proved he'd gone above and beyond to protect her and help track down the man who might hold the key to the truth. Now he circled to his side of the truck, giving her some space to deal with her partner. But his watchful blue eyes never left her. He was ready to intervene if she needed him—and willing to step back if she didn't. *That* was the kind of backup she expected from anyone she called *partner*.

But Derek just didn't get it. He didn't understand fire and dedication and getting the job done the way she did. "G, you're a little obsessed. Maybe we're never going to catch the guy who shot us. Maybe we just need to move on. I can handle my dad. You need to go home and heal. We need to focus on keeping our noses clean and making SWAT."

She shrugged off his placating touch and climbed in beside Mike. "You quit if you want, Derek. I never will."

Chapter 11

"Here's a clean shirt from my locker, son." Mike caught the black KCPD polo his father tossed to him and straightened away from the wall outside the Fourth Precinct's third-floor conference room as several more officers, both uniformed and plainclothes, filed out of the room behind him and moved on down the hallway to their various work stations. Michael Sr. wrinkled his nose at the stain on Mike's shoulder, which could be the remnants of spoiled pasta sauce or a really old tomato. "You're a little fragrant."

"Thanks, Dad." Ignoring the protest from joints that weren't used to duking it out with armed bullies or tackling a man off a concrete loading dock, Mike unbuttoned his soiled shirt and shrugged into the clean one. "What's the verdict?"

Although the captain was just *Dad* to Mike, Gina

hurried over from pacing up and down the hallway and practically snapped to attention. "What can you tell us, sir? Did Gordy Bismarck say anything else after lawyering up? No one else was hurt during that chase, were they? What about Denny Bismarck? Did we find him?"

The Precinct's top brass and investigators from various departments had been called in for a briefing on everything that had happened between the confrontation at Gina's home last night to the Sin City Bar and stopping Gordon Bismarck in a pile of trash near the river this morning. Michael Sr. splayed his fingers at the waist of his dark uniform, looking down at her with a boss-like seriousness. "Denny Bismarck has gone to ground, but there's a citywide APB out on him. We've got unis checking their regular haunts. We've arrested Al Renken on trafficking stolen goods and Gordy on his parole violation and resisting arrest."

"Even though I was the officer in pursuit?" A worried frown marred Gina's beautiful eyes. "Technically, I'm still on leave. The arrest is good? Am I going on report?"

Mike felt the same paternal, perhaps reprimanding, glare fixed on him for a moment before his father answered Gina's concern. "You're still KCPD. You identified yourself with your badge—Bismarck said as much. Your instincts were good about the Bismarcks and their buddies hiding something. The auto-theft team wants to buy you a drink down at the Shamrock for breaking one of their investigations wide open. I think I've got some competition for recruiting you."

The compliment didn't seem to register. "But I'm no closer to finding out who's shooting cops."

"None of us are." The grim pronouncement hung in the stuffy hallway air. "But there are a lot of officers in there who'd like to get Denny in an interrogation room. I'm confident we'll figure this out."

Gina rubbed her shoulder through her denim jacket. Mike wondered if she was in pain, or if that was becoming a habit of the self-doubts and second-guessing that were new to her. "Hopefully, before anyone else gets hurt."

He agreed with a nod. "We're all working this case, Gina. When you attack one cop, you attack all of us. You and Mike have given the detectives several leads to follow up on, including your buddy Bobby Estes. But you need to step back and let Detectives Grove and Kincaid take the lead on this. Go home. You've earned a good night's rest. We'll get this guy. I promise."

"Yes, sir."

Michael's face relaxed into a smile for Gina. "Mind if I borrow my son for a moment?"

Gina's dark gaze darted up to Mike's. "I didn't mean to get him into trouble, Captain. No one's issuing Mike a reckless driving ticket, are they? If I'd been able to drive myself—"

The captain raised a reassuring hand. "Mike's a grown man. It's kind of hard to reprimand him. But we decided not to issue any tickets since he was assisting a police officer." It probably didn't hurt that he was Michael Cutler's son, either. "We do, however, have some things to discuss. Personal things."

But Mike could see his father's explanation had only made Gina straighten to a more defensive posture. Defending him? Or worried that causing friction between father and son would further jeopardize her chances of making the new SWAT team?

"This is nothing for you to stress over," Mike assured her. "We're just two guys having a conversation."

"I'll give you some privacy then." Gina reached over to brush her limp fingers against his knuckles before turning her hand into his and squeezing it. The gesture was shyly hesitant—if he could believe anything about this brave, direct woman could be shy—but it meant the world to Mike. Was that an apology for getting him into any kind of trouble? A thank-you? Maybe her only hesitation was that she was confirming the connection between them in front of his father. "I want to read over my statement again before I sign it. I'll be downstairs in the lobby when you're finished."

"I'll find you there."

He watched her cross to her desk in the main room, pick up the printout of the statement she'd typed earlier and sit down to read it before his father nodded toward the break room. "Buy you a cup of coffee?"

Mike followed his dad inside and closed the door, although he questioned the privacy of this conversation since the walls on either side of the door were glass windows with open blinds hanging in front of them. "*Personal* things?"

When had his dad gone all touchy-feely?

His father pulled out a couple of insulated paper cups and poured them both some hot coffee. "The auto-theft team impounded Denny Bismarck's '75 Bronco. They'd like you to look at it to see if you recognize it from that day at the shooting."

"Not a problem." He took the cup from his dad. "Let's hear the real reason you wanted to talk without

Gina around. You think I'm getting in too deep with this. Too deep with her."

"She's getting her grip back?"

He wasn't surprised that his dad had noticed the way Gina had reached for his hand. "I don't know if it'll ever be one hundred percent, probably not steady enough to hold a sniper rifle. But I still wouldn't count her out in a fight. She's already good enough to pass her competency exam on the shooting range."

"Have you told her that?" His dad arched a questioning brow. "I need better than competent for SWAT."

Mike took a sip of the steaming brew, thinking the bitter sludge beat Frannie's coffee but wasn't anywhere near the smooth delight Lupe Molina's coffee had been. But he knew this conversation wasn't about father-son bonding or evaluating caffeinated drinks. This was Captain Michael Cutler, KCPD, asking for a report on the recovery of a wounded police officer he wanted to recruit. "She's still a good cop. You haven't seen her out in the field, Dad. She's fearless. Gina knows how to handle herself in an interview. She's got good instincts about protecting people. And she's kind and strong and inspiring with the victims I've seen her talk to."

"She wants to be SWAT. Not a victim's advocate."

"She wants to be a cop."

His father nodded, considering the update on Gina's progress. He took a drink before changing the subject. "How do you figure into all this? Are you looking to be a cop now, too?"

Mike chuckled, hearing the fatherly concern about risking his life, yet knowing exactly from what gene pool he'd inherited this strong urge to help others and protect the people he cared about. "That's your calling, Dad. Not mine. Business has been slow at the clinic, so I've had time on my hands. Gina's going to chase this guy down whether or not she has anyone watching her back. I prefer she not take on the whole world alone and aggravate her injury before she's completely healed." He shrugged, instantly regretting the twinge through the stretching muscles of his back. "I help out where I can."

"Driving eighty miles an hour through downtown Kansas City is your idea of helping out? I didn't know your big dream was to drive for NASCAR one day."

Nah. His big dream was to find the man who'd shot Gina so that she'd give up this crazy investigation and give them a chance at being a couple. "I couldn't lose that guy, Dad. He knows something that could help her. For all we know, he's the key to stopping whoever is targeting cops. Or who might be targeting Gina specifically. That's a theory we're working on."

"A theory?" Those observant blue eyes, so like his own, narrowed, no doubt suspecting the pain he was in. "You look a little beat-up yourself. Fractured nerves and steel pins doing okay?"

Mike admitted to the electric shocks sparking intermittently through his lower back and the ache in his right leg that had been numb when they'd left the crime scene earlier. "I've had better days. Some ibuprofen and a hot shower ought to take care of it."

"I wanted you to help Gina get fit enough to come back to KCPD—not for you to get caught in the cross fire. I nearly lost you once." He wandered over to peer through the blinds beside Mike. "Trip and Alex told me about the run-in at Gina's place last night. Your truck never left the driveway. Just how serious has it gotten between you two?"

"We've become friends." Standing beside his father and fingering the visitor's badge hanging around his neck, Mike studied the main room. More accurately, he studied the dark-haired woman at the far end of the sea of desks between them. Gina methodically read through the printout, making notations. "I was giving her a break from having to be responsible for her family, her neighborhood, this whole city for one night. She's such a tiny thing, and yet she carries the weight of the world on her shoulders." Mike grinned, trying to make light of the truth his father was no doubt reading between the lines. "And her great-aunt Lupe sure can cook. Her coffee's a damn sight better than this stuff."

The joke didn't work. He felt his father's hand on his shoulder. "You are never going to be so old that I won't worry about you. If she's using you to get into SWAT—"

"Gina wouldn't know how." Mike pulled away from his father's hand and poured out the last of his coffee into the sink before dropping the cup into the trash. "She's honest to a fault, Dad. Good, bad or ugly. She says what she means, and anything she gets she wants to earn on her own merit."

"I thought as much. But I had to ask."

Mike headed to the door, thinking this tête-à-tête was over. But before he turned the knob, he saw Derek Johnson perch on the corner of Gina's desk. She tipped her head up to her partner as they chatted, then pushed to her feet as the conversation grew heated. Derek pointed toward the break room, and Mike had to wonder if the disagreement had to do with him or his father. But whatever they were arguing about ended quickly. Gina tucked her report into a file folder and carried it over to Kevin Grove and Atticus Kincaid, the detectives leading the investigation, and dropped it on Grove's desk. Mike glanced back to her desk to see Derek watching her, too. When she excused herself and headed to the elevators, Derek sank into his chair, slumping like a pouting boy. He wasn't thrilled with whatever she'd said or written. Gina had disappeared around the last cubicle wall by the time he sat forward and picked up the phone on his desk, punching in a number as if an idea had suddenly entered his head.

Mike was about to overstep a line with his father, taking advantage of his KCPD connections. "Dad, I know you're not an investigator, but could you check out Derek Johnson for me?"

"Gina's partner?"

Mike wondered how much of that argument he'd just witnessed had to do with the accusations she'd made that morning after the car chase through downtown. "I've seen rookies who make fewer dumb moves than that guy does. It's almost like he's sabotaging anything Gina tries to do. I wonder if he blames her for getting shot."

"That's a serious accusation. Not every partnership works out," his father conceded. "Maybe there is some tension between them—especially if someone was targeting her and he feels like collateral damage. Or vice versa. I heard about his fling with Bismarck's wife. But his work history is clean. He came recommended to me for SWAT training, so I know he hasn't been written up for anything."

"What kind of cop do you think he is?"

Michael Sr. considered his answer before speaking. "He's in the top half of every test I've given him. He takes orders. Does what I ask of him in training. He gets along with everybody on the team."

"What about his personal life?"

"I don't know him that well, but I can poke around. No one will question me looking more closely at any of the SWAT candidates. What am I looking for?"

They both watched the animated phone call as Derek smacked the desktop and argued with whoever was on the other end of the line. "I'm not sure. I can't put my finger on it. But something's hinky with that guy. I don't think Gina trusts him any more than I do. Maybe that's one reason she's so damn independent. She doesn't believe Johnson's got her back."

"But you do?" His father crumpled the empty coffee cup and tossed it into the trash. "Need I remind you, you don't wear a uniform? You've got no responsibility here. Gina has a whole police department she can call on for help. Last I checked, putting your life on the line for a woman in trouble isn't part of a physical therapist's job description. You took on Leo Mesner when he was hitting Frannie. Caroline's parents were controlling every aspect of her life until you…" He saw realization dawn in his father's sharp blue eyes. "You're in love with her. Mike, I wasn't matchmaking when I asked you to help—"

"This isn't like Caroline or Frannie, Dad." He didn't need to be reminded of his past mistakes. "They needed a support system—someone who would put their needs first."

"Isn't that what you're doing for Gina?"

"She won't let me half the time." He laughed, but there was no humor in the sound. "She was a fighter before I ever met her. Strong and confident. This injury is just a temporary setback until she figures out a new way to move forward. That spirit is still inside her. She doesn't need me to hold her hand or build up her ego, she just…needs me. For how long, I don't know yet, but—"

"I like Gina well enough." His father looked him straight in the eye, wanting him to really hear what he was saying. "Whatever you decide, you know I'll back you all the way. But I don't want to see you get hurt again."

Yeah, the pattern of Mike's woeful love life did seem to be repeating itself. Maybe he was the one who needed to be rescued from the mistakes he kept making. But not yet. He wasn't giving up on Gina or his feelings for her. "She says she doesn't have the time or space in her life for a relationship right now. But everything in me says that she's the one. That we could be really good together if she'd give us a chance."

"From what I've seen, she cares about you. But caring isn't the same as—"

"Just check Johnson out for me, okay? If his partner can't rely on him or his priorities are somewhere else besides his job… She doesn't need that right now."

"That kind of behavior is troubling when it comes to building a SWAT team, too." With a nod, his father became a cop again. "I hope you're wrong. But I'll see what I can find out. I'll give you a call the moment we take Denny Bismarck into custody, too. In the meantime, keep your head down. I'm not explaining it to Jillian and Will if you get hurt again."

"Thanks, Dad." He pushed open the break-room door to go after Gina and run interference between her and Derek if she needed it.

"Mike?" He stopped and turned as his dad caught the door behind him. He turned for one last piece of paternal advice. "Falling for your stepmother was a complete surprise for me. I thought I was done with love until Jillian came along. And then I nearly lost her."

"I know Jillian's been good for you, Dad. She's been good for all of us. Hell, she's the one who finally got me up out of that wheelchair. She made our family complete."

"If Gina's the one, you need to be a fighter, too." That was the voice of experience that Mike took to heart. "Fight for her with everything you've got."

"I intend to."

Why the heck were they running the air conditioning this early in the spring? Maybe it was the cold marble walls of the Precinct's first-floor lobby that made Gina shiver. But looking through the reinforced glass and steel-framed doors, she still saw more brown than green in the grass outside. And even without a cloud in the sky, the afternoon sun couldn't quite seem to reach her skin through the glass.

She was practical enough to know the chill came from a place inside her. But as to its cause? Where to begin?

She worried that she'd gotten Mike into trouble with his dad by involving him in this private investigation into the cop shootings, along with the rest of her screwed-up life. Not that she'd invited him to be a part of any of it. But now she couldn't imagine *not* having Mike around as her chauffeur, friend, sounding board, protector and catnip. On paper, he was every kind of wrong for her. Wrong background. Wrong neighbor-hood. Wrong skin color.

But in reality, everything between them felt right. Gina shook her head. How could she ever make a re-ality with Mike work? Chemistry alone couldn't sus-tain a relationship. Their personalities clashed. Her family was a responsibility she would never give up. His father might be her boss one day. But the thought of Mike Cutler not holding her for another night, or never kissing her again or never even butting heads with her made her feel empty. And cold.

Maybe the lack of warmth stemmed from the fact that she'd probably irreparably damaged her relation-ship with Derek by promising to report his less-than-stellar performance on the job to their superior officer and Captain Cutler if he didn't get off his lazy butt and start doing his job the way they'd been trained at the academy. Today she'd been reminded that, technically, it wasn't her job to solve this case. But she knew they could find the shooter if they stayed sharp and ran down every lead. Maybe she'd called in one favor too many, and Derek was right to be angry about helping her. But why couldn't he have just told her *no* instead of stringing her along with his half-hearted assistance? When had they stopped being able to trust each other and communicate like partners should? Maybe Derek had moved on from the shooting. But she needed clo-sure. She needed to know why someone had wanted to change her life so irreparably.

Maybe those answers would finally erase the sense that an enemy was watching, circling, drawing ever closer. And she wouldn't be able to recognize him until it was too late.

Gina moved closer to the rays of sunlight streaming in through the windows and rubbed her hand up and down the sleeve of her jacket while she waited for her great-aunt or -uncle to pick up the phone.

Knowing how slowly Lupe and Rollo moved, she waited patiently through several rings. Still, she breathed an audible sigh of relief when her great-aunt picked up. "*Hola*, Gina."

"*Hola*, Tia Mami." Some of the pervading chill left at the cheerful sound of Lupe's voice. She was glad to hear that someone in her family was having a good day. "I'm calling to see if you're all okay after last night. Mike and I had to leave before everyone was up. Did Sylvie get to school okay?"

"*Sí.* I let her drive the car so she wouldn't have to call Bobby. She wore blue jeans and looked like a teenage girl. So pretty."

"Good." Hopefully, her sister would be smart enough to come straight home after school, too, even if Bobby tried to contact her. "And Tio Papi? How's his blood pressure?"

"He is taking it easy today. He found the Royals playing a preseason game on television. Javier is watching with him." She could hear the laughter in Lupe's voice. "In truth, they are both napping. They wake up when there's a big play."

The gentle normalcy of such a report made Gina smile, too. "And you're checking Papi's pressure every hour?"

"He fusses at me. But I remind him that Mike said to do so, and he stops arguing with me."

Gina's attention shifted and her smile faded when Harold Johnson, Derek's father, loped up the front steps. The fringe of his brown leather jacket bounced with every stride. Since they were both on their cell phones, intent on their own conversations, Gina turned away from the door, letting the people milling through the lobby and Harold's hurry to get to the elevators prevent him from seeing her. She'd already had enough unpleasant conversations today. Did he really think he had a legal case against her? Was the idea of suing her and the department on Derek's behalf just his way of showing his son he cared? Or were the accusations an idle man's latest idea on how to get some easy money, as Derek claimed? Should she be worried that he was running upstairs to see Derek now?

Gina gradually tuned back in to Lupe's list of errands she needed to run when Sylvie or she got home. "Will Mike be coming to the house again tonight? Should I set him a place for dinner? He has a good appetite, that one."

"Tia Mami…" Suddenly, Harold Johnson's reflection loomed up behind her in the front window. So much for avoiding unpleasant conversations.

"I know, I know. He is not your boyfriend. But he could be. You are being nice to him, yes?"

A shiver ran down her spine like a wintry omen. But having Derek's father intrude on her personal phone call only made Gina stand up straighter. She turned to face him, keeping her voice calm even as she felt the glass behind her back and knew she was trapped. "I have to go. I'll call you later. *Te amo.*"

Harold flipped his oily, gray ponytail behind his back and leaned in toward her. *"Hola, traidor."*

Traitor. Gina tilted her chin, refusing to be insulted or intimidated. "Mr. Johnson."

"I just got off the phone with Derek. Just because you got crippled up doesn't make it fair to file a complaint about my boy."

Crippled up? Is that how Harold saw her? Gina glanced around either side of his worn jacket, wondering if anyone else—maybe the two men coming off the elevators, maybe the elderly couple chatting with a public information officer at the front desk, maybe Derek or even Captain Cutler—saw her as crippled, too. Her damaged hand curled into a fist down at her side, the only outward sign that anything Harold Johnson said could get to her. "Mr. Johnson, you need to take a step back. You're in my personal space."

"Is that so?" If anything, he moved closer.

"Maybe you shouldn't be talking to me. Especially if you're filing a lawsuit. Derek told me. You know what part of town I live in. Even if you had a case, you wouldn't get any money out of me." More than anything, she wanted to shove him back a step. But she suspected turning this battle of wills into a physical confrontation would only add fuel to his irrational fire. "Maybe you should be supporting your son, encouraging him to be a better police officer, instead of making excuses for him or blaming other people when things go wrong."

"Ooh, now the pretty little *chica*'s got her dander up." Harold placed his hand on the window beside her head, smudging the glass. His clothes smelled of grease and dust and had the burnt odor of acetylene from the blow torch he must use at the junkyard to disassemble cars, appliances and old construction materials into scrap metal. Not that she had anything against a hardworking man, but she doubted this life-long schemer and champion of political incorrectness qualified. "I talked to a lawyer. I'm going to prove my boy is a better cop than you are."

"You're doing it to make a buck and retire at the department's expense. Think about Derek's reputation. No one is going to want to partner with him if they're afraid you're going to sue them over any grievance or mistake they make."

"You admit you made a mistake that got my boy shot?"

She was admitting nothing. Harold could twist the truth any way he wanted, but Gina knew there was only one person to blame for her and Derek's injuries—the gunman who'd fired those bullets. "Your son will get the job on SWAT if he earns it. If someone else is more deserving, then they will be put on the new team."

"Like you?" He snorted and backed away. "You immigrants are all alike." *Immigrant?* She and her siblings had been born right here in Kansas City. Not that it was worth arguing that point with a man who wouldn't listen. "Thinking you're entitled to something just because you're a girl or a minority. If you've done anything to hurt Derek's chances of that promotion—"

"Dad." The stairwell door off to Gina's right closed behind Derek as he strolled over to join them. "You need to back off before you get me into more trouble."

Harold ignored his son's stern warning. "No. If she can't do the job, she can't do it. She needs to step aside and let a man take her place on the team."

The stairwell door opened a second time, and Mike entered the lobby. He strode straight to Gina, made no apology for nudging Derek aside, reached for her hand

and pulled her away from the window and uncomfortable closeness of Derek's father. "Everything okay?"

He'd followed Derek. He'd probably been suspicious of her partner taking the stairs instead of coming down on the elevator. Why was Derek here, anyway? He should still be on duty. Was he following her? Did he know his dad had her cornered down here? Had he summoned his dad to do just that? Or was he truly worried about his father making his situation worse by showing up here?

Gina squeezed Mike's hand, glad for the subtle show of support. "I'm fine. Mr. Johnson was just expressing an opinion. I disagreed."

Derek propped his hand on his father's shoulder, uniting them as a team, too. "Gina never gives up, Dad. She made that perfectly clear." He turned that smug, mocking smile on her. "Well, you should know, G, that I don't, either. I deserve to be on that SWAT team. I'm the one who's still training with them every week. I'm the one going on calls with them." He cupped his arm where he'd been shot. "I'm the decorated cop who's returned to duty. When Captain Cutler posts the list, I'll be on it." He snorted through his nose, sounding just like his father. "You'll still be on medical leave. Unless you think sleeping with your boyfriend here will get you that SWAT badge. I can't compete with that."

Gina felt the instant tension of Mike moving forward. She latched on to him with both hands and held him back. "*Not* my bodyguard," she whispered against his shoulder. "If anybody's going to punch this guy, I want it to be me. You'd better get me out of here."

Chapter 12

Gina scooped up the last handful of bubbles in her wrinkled fingers and blew them across the top of the water. She should feel guilty for stepping away from her responsibilities for any length of time. But technically, she was following orders.

Captain Cutler had told her to take the night off. Give other officers a chance to do their job. Mike had told her she needed to rest, that she'd been pushing herself physically more than he thought wise at this stage of her recovery. And since that was the only thing he'd said during the first ten minutes of their drive after pulling out of the KCPD parking garage across from headquarters, she was quick to agree.

Mike's silence wasn't something she was accustomed to. No comment on her stowing her gun and badge in the glove compartment of his truck. No admonishment over pushing so hard on this investigation that they could have both been injured or killed more than once. No explanation for how she'd been ordered to stand down by a superior officer—Mike's own father—and then Mike was the one who'd been taken aside for a private conversation.

A few weeks ago, she would have relished not having him tell her what she could and couldn't do. She would have been more than happy for him to drop an argument when she suggested he do so. But now, after spending so much time together, after drawing on the strength and support of a true friend, after developing these feelings that went beyond friendship—feelings which she was certain would get her into trouble somewhere along the way—his silence worried her. Was Mike angry? Deep in thought? Worried about something he didn't want to share? Did this have to do with the insults Derek had slung at her? Frustration with the investigation? Was he in pain?

Why would the man who prodded her about everything suddenly go silent?

When she'd admitted that she'd like to wash up before dinner, Mike had responded with a simple, "Me, too." Although she hadn't taken the brunt of the garbage outside the West Bottoms café this morning, she felt soiled and slimy just from her conversations with Denny and Gordy Bismarck, and then with Derek and his father. A quick cleanup and fresh change of clothes sounded wonderful.

She thought he'd take her to her house. Or maybe once he'd charmed the socks off her great-aunt during a quick phone call, saying not to hold dinner for them but that they'd be there for dessert, she thought

Mike was taking her out to eat someplace, making the break his father had ordered them to take sound very much like a date. She wouldn't have complained if that had been his plan.

But Mike Cutler knew her far better than she'd realized. They drove through a burger joint for takeout and ate in the truck before ending up at his ranch-style home in the suburbs. The neighborhood was quiet except for the kids playing a game of hide and seek across the street. Traffic was light. There weren't cars parked bumper-to-bumper at the curb. The yards were well tended and, though they had mature trees, the street itself was wide, allowing plenty of late afternoon sun through to warm her skin as she tipped her face up to the sky and breathed deeply.

The house itself needed a little work—probably why a single man struggling to make his fledgling business a success could afford to buy a home here—but the space was more than double the size of the home she shared with her family. The fenced-in backyard was made for barbecues and swing sets and gardens. And even though much of the house was stuck in the 1970s or was in the process of being remodeled, he showed her three different bathrooms where she could freshen up.

Three bathrooms. Heaven.

Other than the green and gold of the '70s decor, this place was everything she wanted for her family. It was as suburban and perfect and interestingly unexpected as Mike himself was.

When the tour was finished, Mike left her with a fresh towel and new bar of soap in the tiny powder room off the modern white kitchen. "Make yourself at home. I'll take a fast shower. If you get hungry or want something to drink, help yourself to whatever you can find in the fridge."

While she liked the retro look of the new black and white tiles and nickel-finish faucet, the pedestal sink just wasn't calling to her. "Do I have to use this bathroom?"

Mike shrugged. "I haven't had time or money to remodel the guest bathroom in the hallway yet."

"But it has a bathtub. Could I…?" She tilted her face up to his. "Instead of just washing my face here, would it be a horrible imposition if I took a bath?"

"And I thought *I* was your catnip." Mike smiled at her request. Really smiled. Then he dipped his head to capture her mouth in a kiss that heated her blood but left her little time to respond. Instead, he turned her around, gently swatting her bottom to nudge her down the hallway into the guest bathroom. "Towels are in the cabinet. Some of my little brother's bubble bath, too, if you want. Enjoy yourself."

"I'm sure I will. Thanks."

He closed the door. She heard the shower running in his own bathroom off the master bedroom before she turned on the faucets in the tub to let it fill while she quickly shed her clothes.

She was still lounging in the tub when the shower next door stopped. Gina checked the time on her phone on the towel shelf beside the tub where she'd stowed her folded clothes. Fifteen minutes. She sighed in contentment, closing her eyes and leaning her head back against the tub wall. She hadn't relaxed like this in weeks, months maybe.

This was no five-minute shower and dash to her bedroom to dry her hair so that someone else could get into the bathroom. This was fifteen minutes of pure heaven, soaking in a bubble bath. Even the fruity smell of the child's soap bubbles couldn't diminish the dreamy satisfaction of hot water turning every muscle into goo and the delicious quiet of long-term solitude, interrupted only by an occasional dribble of water as she shifted position.

Had anyone ever pampered her like this? She was a warrior. A protector in every sense of the word. No one ever saw the girly-girl inside her. Had anyone outside of her family ever cared enough to indulge her feminine side? Growing up in a life so full of need, had she ever opened herself up enough to allow an outsider to know her foolish secrets? It was a little unsettling to admit that Mike knew her like that. When had she allowed herself to become so vulnerable to a man? Why wasn't she more frightened by the inherent risk of allowing a man to see her as a woman? Not a cop. Not a big sister or neighborhood protector or family breadwinner. Not a patient or even a friend.

With Mike Cutler, aka Choir Boy and Mr. Nice Guy, of all people—she felt like a woman.

Gina heard a whisper of sound from the doorway behind her.

Make that a desirable woman.

She'd been so deep in thought that she hadn't heard Mike open the door. "I knocked. You've been in here so long and it was so quiet that, when you didn't answer, I'd thought I'd better check to see you hadn't fallen asleep in the tub and drowned."

"Sorry to worry you. But I'm fine." She crossed her arms over her chest, inhaling a satisfied breath. "More than fine, actually."

"Very fine, from this angle." Mike shifted, leaning his shoulder against the door jamb. From the corner of her eye, she could see he'd only been out of the shower long enough to towel off and pull on his jeans. Droplets of water still glistened in the dark spikes of his hair. He'd trimmed his beard back to sexy perfection.

The only bubbles that remained were clinging to the edge of the tub. Gina smiled, not feeling the water's cooling temperature at all. If anything, her temperature was rising. "A nice guy wouldn't stand there staring."

"Told you I wasn't a nice guy."

She found his gaze, dark blue and unabashedly focused on her, in the mirror. The message she read there was crystal clear, and it thrilled her down to her very core. Last night, the timing had been off. She'd been emotionally exhausted and worried about her family. But this evening was a different story. There weren't family members here they had to tiptoe around. Other cops were handling the bad guys tonight. And Mike had been so sullen earlier, to see him engaged and talking again like the man she'd gotten to know made her want to savor this charged moment. "How are your hips and legs? Did the hot shower help?"

"I'm okay."

"Okay enough to climb in this tub with me?" she invited.

Mike walked over to the tub, holding out his hand to her. "Okay enough to help you into my bed in the next room."

"Deal." She curled her fingers around his and stood, proudly showing her body as she stepped out of the tub. "Want to hand me a towel?"

"Nope."

Gina Galvan did not blush. She didn't embarrass easily or feel self-conscious beyond her injury. Yet this man, with a hungry look and a single word, could set her on fire from the inside out.

Gina Galvan *did* know how to go after what she wanted, though. Her skin flushed with heat from head to toe. For once in her life, she felt uncomfortably warm.

While Mike's hungry perusal dappled her skin with a riot of goose bumps, that long, leanly muscled chest beckoned to her like real catnip. His attentive blue eyes told her he wanted her as much as the bulge at the front of his jeans did. She slid her arms around his waist, pressing her naked, wet body against his. She nearly lost her breath as an intense awareness sparked through every cell of her body, lighting her up from the inside out.

The tips of her breasts pebbled with the teasing caresses of his wiry chest hair and solid muscle underneath moving against her as he swept his hands down her back. He paused a moment at her waist before he curved his shoulders around her and reached lower to squeeze her bottom. The soft denim of his worn jeans stroked against her thighs as he spread his legs slightly, lifting her onto her toes and pulling her into his body. The masculine swell of his desire filled the indention between her legs and Gina pressed her face into his chest, letting her body adjust to the ribbons of heat coursing through her from every spot he touched. Matching goose bumps pricked his chest and abdomen as the cooling water dripped from her skin onto his and rivulets of moisture soaked into his jeans. Gina pressed a kiss to one chill bump, and then another, inhaling the clean scents of spicy soap and man, following a path to the firm swell of pectoral muscle. She closed her lips around the taut peak of the nipple she found there. "Now show me how bad a guy like you can be."

His muscles jerked beneath the stroke of her tongue, and Gina felt powerful, sexy, loving that he wasn't afraid to respond to her overtures. But if she thought she was in charge of this seduction, Gina was mistaken.

"Only if you promise to show me how good you can be."

Mike reached beneath her chin and tilted her face up so he could claim her mouth. He tongued the seam of her lips before thrusting between them, telling her with every stroke of the deep, drugging kiss exactly what he wanted to do with her body. Gina released his waist to wind her arms around his neck and hang on as he lapped up the droplets of water clinging to her face and neck. She willingly tipped her head back, giving his lips and tongue access to her throat and the mound of her breast before he dug his fingers into her bottom, lifted her off the floor and took the aching nipple into his mouth. Gina cried out at the fiery arrow of need that shot from the sensitive nipple deep into her core.

"Mike…" she hissed, clawing at his shoulders. She'd thought the hot, sudsy water had turned her bones to mush, but she knew if Mike let go of her now, she wouldn't be able to stand. She wrapped her legs around his waist, clinging to him as he turned his attention to the other breast. Between gasps of pleasure, she dropped kisses anyplace she could reach. The point of his chin. The strong column of his neck. She nibbled her way along the perfect line of his stubbled jaw until his hands and mouth made it impossible for her to think. "Mike... I want... Can we...?"

His lips came back to smile against her mouth and plant a kiss there. "Yes."

Despite her protests that she could walk and that she didn't want to risk aggravating his injuries by carrying her, Mike tightened his hold on her and hauled her down the hallway to his bedroom. Although he laid her gently on top of the bedspread, Gina scrambled onto her knees to maintain contact as he tossed his billfold onto the bed and shucked out of his jeans.

"I hate that you got hurt." Her fingers tangled with his, pushing the waistband of his shorts down over his leanly muscled backside. She found the ridges of scar tissue at his lower back, tracing them over his hips and partway down each thigh. Her heart constricted with compassion, then beat with admiration, over the pain he must have endured and overcome. Leaning forward, she pressed a kiss against one particularly wicked looking web of scars at the juncture of his back and hip. "I didn't fully understand how badly you'd been injured."

His skin jumped at the brush of her lips against the next scar and he turned. He grasped her by the arms and hunkered down to eye level. "This isn't pity, is it?"

"No." The intensity in those cobalt eyes was impossible to ignore. But she held that gaze, willing him to understand the depth of need and admiration she felt. "Is it for you?"

"Never." He dipped his head to kiss the newer, pinker scars on her shoulder before pushing her down on the bed and lying on the covers beside her. She trembled as he nudged his long thigh between hers to rub against that most sensitive place. He threaded his fingers into her hair and kissed her eyelids, her cheeks and the tip of her nose. "I hate that you got hurt, too. But we're not damaged goods, Gina. We're a man and a woman. Every part of me that counts is perfectly healthy. And if you can't tell how badly I want you…"

Gina pushed at his shoulders, turning him onto his back, bracing her hands against his chest, straddling his hips. "Like this?"

His answering laugh was more of a groan as she leaned over him to retrieve a condom from his billfold. His hands played with her breasts and tugged at her hair, making it difficult to concentrate on sheathing him. When his thumbs found the juncture of her thighs and pushed against her, a feverish riot of sensations bloomed like heat lightning. For a moment, she couldn't see, and her hands shook. She could barely stay upright.

Mike sat up, catching her in his arms as she tumbled into his lap. He nipped at the lobe of her ear, whispering against her skin as he lifted her slightly and slipped inside her. "Your secret is safe with me, Tiger."

"What secret?" she gasped, her body opening as he filled her, then tightening again to keep him intimately close.

He framed her face between his hands and claimed her mouth as he moved inside her. "That you're not always a tough chick. Let this happen." He kissed her again. "I've got you."

Gina nodded, believing him as she rocked over his lap in a matching rhythm that stoked the fire between them.

There were no more words. Only touches and kisses. Gasps and moans. Strokes and shivers. The friction between them turned to passion. The teasing words became an answer to every temptation. The understanding they shared transformed into a connection that bound them closer than she'd ever been to any man. Gina had never felt so deliciously warm. She'd never felt so thoroughly loved, so completely vulnerable without feeling afraid. She buried her face in Mike's shoulder as a consuming heat blossomed in her core and seeped with delicious abandon through every part of her. She was still riding the fiery waves of pleasure when he clutched her in an almost unbearably tight embrace and found his release inside her.

Then he fell back against the pillows, pulling Gina on top of him. As she rode the deep rise and fall of his chest, he pulled the edge of the bedspread over her back, securing her against the heat of his body.

"You okay?" he whispered, feathering his fingers into her hair and tucking it gently behind her ear.

"Very okay." Gina snuggled beneath his chin. "You?"

"Very." He kissed the crown of her hair before tugging loose the other edge of the bedspread and wrapping them up in a cocoon of heat and contentment. "I'm always good when you let me get close."

Sometime later, Gina was snuggled up against Mike's chest. His arm anchored her in place as he spooned behind her. He dozed, his soft snoring stirring the wisps of hair at her neck. Gina was wide awake as darkness fell over the city. She traced the dimensions of Mike's long, agile fingers that had brought her such pleasure and ran her tongue around the abraded skin of her mouth, remembering each and every kiss they'd shared.

What was she going to do if she fell in love with Mike? How was she ever going to fit this strong, funny, brave, stubborn, generous man into her life? How could she and her needy family and demanding job be good for Mike? She wanted to be a helpmate, not a hindrance, to any man who cared about her. How would they handle children? Where could they all live without him thinking that all she wanted from him was a house with three bathrooms? What if her hand never got any better than it was right now and she couldn't return to the job she loved? What if she couldn't contribute her fair share to a relationship? Knowing Mike, he would shoulder any burden. But she didn't want to be a burden. She wanted to be his equal, the way they were right now.

She should have a plan in place for falling in love with Mike.

Because Gina knew she already had.

Mike knew Gina was awake the moment he opened his eyes. Even though she was facing away from him in the bed, he could tell by the repetitive circles she traced on the back of his hand that she was deep in thought. That couldn't be a good sign.

He brushed his lips against the nape of her neck so his words wouldn't startle her. "Having regrets?"

The circles stopped. She rolled over to face him, letting him see the troubles that formed shallow lines beside her beautiful eyes. "No, but…"

"A *but* can't be good."

She patted the middle of his chest, warning him

he might not like what she had to say. "Where is this leading? What kind of future can you and I have?"

Mike inhaled deeply as the familiar hints at not being good enough or no longer being necessary to a woman chafed against his ears. He wondered at the irony of his guarded sigh pushing his heart against her hand. "What kind of future do you want?"

"I have so many responsibilities. I have plans."

"And they don't include me?" He wasn't particularly proud of the bitterness that crept into his voice. But some scars were slower to heal than others. He pulled his hand from the nip of her waist and rolled onto his back. "For what it's worth, I'm not sorry we made love. I'm only sorry you can't see the possibilities between us."

She pushed herself up onto her elbows beside him. "But you can? Derek said I would sleep with you to get closer to your father and improve my chances of making SWAT."

Mike's thoughts burned with the sick idea that her partner had put into her head. "He knows he screwed up. He was lashing out at you."

"Is that why you were so quiet on the ride here? Did you think his words had hurt me?"

"I didn't like the way the Johnsons talked to you." His hand fisted over his stomach, remembering the blinding urge to ram his fist down her partner's throat for saying such hateful, untrue things. "It's one thing to hear crap like that from a stranger. But from someone you're supposed to trust?"

Gina rested her hand over his fist, willing the tension in him to relax. "I know. I thought Derek was a better man than that—a better friend. Everyone reacts differently when they feel threatened. Fight. Flight. Meanness. Fear. But in one way, he was right." She shrugged, steeling herself for some unpleasant truth she was determined to share. "There are all kinds of advantages to me being with you. But what benefit could there possibly be for you to get involved in my life?"

Mike looked up into her beautiful dark eyes. "You're kidding, right?"

She didn't think a sense of being valued, shared understandings, her great-aunt's coffee, this undeniable attraction and filling the hole in his heart were good enough reasons for a relationship? He turned his palm into hers, lacing their fingers together, trying to convey how her straightforward words and these rare glimpses of tenderness were gifts he would always treasure.

"You're Michael Cutler's son. A fine man in your own right. You have a college degree, own your own business, possess an unshakable sense of right and wrong and could have any woman you wanted." That part clearly wasn't true. But he suspected he would be even less thrilled at what she'd say next. "I grew up in No-Man's Land. I can't afford the time or money to go to college. I've got crazy stress in my life, and I'm…" her gaze shifted away to study some nameless point on the headboard as her voice trailed away "… an immigrant."

He cupped the side of her face, forcing her gaze back to his. "That's Derek and his dad talking."

Infused with a sudden energy, she rolled over and sat up, pulling the bedspread up to cover herself. "Harold Johnson called me an immigrant."

Mike sat up beside her, not understanding why the insult was something to get excited about. "He's a classless SOB. Don't let him get to you."

"He doesn't." Her animated expression told Mike this conversation was no longer about them and their apparently lousy chance at a future. "That's another way all the cop shootings are connected. Colin Cho. Frank McBride. Gina Galvan. Other than Derek, the victims have all been minority cops." She tilted her gaze to his. "Is that a coincidence?"

He shifted gears back to work with her. "Or a sad statement about some of our world today." Apparently, the discussion about a future together had ended.

"So many possible motives. So many reasons one person would want to hurt so many others." When she linked her arm through his and rested her cheek against his shoulder, the edgy frustration he'd felt a moment earlier abated. "Mike?"

"Hmm?"

"I'm sorry I called you *Choir Boy*. That probably didn't feel any different than Harold or Bobby Etes or the Bismarcks calling me *chica* or *querida*. They're labels. Assumptions. Even in jest, those nicknames show a lack of respect. Men like that—they don't care enough to get to know me. I don't want you to think I feel that same way about you. I'm sorry."

He turned his head to kiss her temple. "Apology accepted."

Her soft, lyrical laugh vibrated against his skin. "You *are* too nice."

Mike was beginning to think that there could be a way for the two of them to make this work, when Gina's phone rang.

"Sorry," she apologized, pulling away. "Hazard of the job."

But she got tangled in the covers. Mike pulled the quilt up to her neck and motioned for her to stay put, while he slipped out of bed. "I grew up with Michael Cutler. I understand interruptions. Dinners. Football games. Driving lessons." He grabbed his jeans and jogged down the hall to retrieve her phone from the guest bathroom. She followed right behind him, two silly grown-ups running naked through his house.

When he handed her the phone, Gina saw the number and frowned. "Hazard of my family," she corrected. She offered him a silent apology as she swiped the answer icon. "*Hola?* This is Gina."

Since he couldn't understand the frantic, high-pitched tones, he assumed the caller was speaking in Spanish. But there was no second-guessing the color draining from Gina's olive skin. Before Mike could ask what was wrong, she was moving, grabbing her clothes, sliding into her shoes, putting on that tough-chick armor that couldn't quite mask the stark fear in her eyes. "Call 9-1-1. Is anyone hurt?" She was visibly shaking by the time she responded to the answer. "Tell them to send an ambulance. Lock the doors, and stay inside. Stay away from the windows. I'm on my way."

Mike had already pulled on his shorts and jeans by the time the conversation had ended. "What's happened?"

Gina reached for his hand, holding on tightly, pulling him toward the front door. "Someone shot up my aunt and uncle's house."

Chapter 13

For the second time in as many days, Gina raced across Kansas City with Mike at the wheel.

An ambulance was already pulling away from the scene by the time Mike screeched to a stop at the end of the block. Gina was already on the ground and running before the truck stopped rocking. *"Mami! Papi!"* She spotted her brother and sister just outside a strip of yellow crime scene tape, wrapping up a conversation with Detective Grove. The overbuilt detective thanked them and moved away to take a phone call. "Javi? Sylvie? What happened? Who's hurt? Is this Bobby's doing?"

"Whoa!" Javier caught her briefly against his stocky chest before she turned away to hug Sylvie. But Mike had followed right at her heels, and now Sylvie was attached to his waist, wrapped up in a brotherly hug. "Nobody got shot, sis. We were all back in the kitchen eating dinner. We heard the gunshots and dove for the floor."

She glanced over at the bullet-ridden front porch and shattered windows at the front of the house. "But the ambulance?"

Javier tightened his arm around her shoulders. "It's Tio Papi. He had a heart attack."

Gina's stomach fell. "Is he…?"

Suddenly, she felt Mike's warm hand slide beneath the curls at the nape of her neck. His tone was as grounding as his touch. "Let's get the facts before we react to anything."

Sylvie pulled away from the anchor of Mike's chest and sniffed back the tears she'd been crying. "The paramedics said he was alert and responsive."

"That's a good sign," Mike agreed.

Sylvie nodded. "He was so pale. He couldn't catch his breath. I gave him a baby aspirin, just like the 9-1-1 lady said."

Mike kept Sylvie turned away from the officers securing the chaotic scene. The CSI van had arrived, too, and the techs were gearing up to remove bullets and analyze any usable foot prints or tire tracks. Kevin Grove was still on his phone, while his partner directed two other officers to close off either end of the block with their cruisers. Neighbors were at their windows or peeking out front doors, too afraid to step out into the night.

"Good girl," Mike praised Sylvie. Gina appreciated that he was keeping her siblings calm and focused, while she was a roiling mass of suspicion and fear and protective anger. "A stressor like having his home attacked could certainly cause it. Are they taking him to St. Luke's?"

The nearest hospital made sense. Javier nodded. "I was just about to drive over there with Sylvie. They look Tia Lupe in the ambulance, too, to monitor her blood pressure, they said. She was sitting up."

"That's standard precautionary procedure once you reach a certain age," Mike said. "It's good for both of them to be together at a time like this." He clapped Javier on the shoulder. "It'll be even better once they're surrounded by their family. You two go on. We'll meet you there later."

Javier frowned at Gina. "You're not coming with us?"

Gina had only been half listening to the conversation. Her attention had shifted to the flashing lights of a criminologist snapping photo after photo of the bullet holes in the posts and siding and chipped bricks on the front porch. And to Detective Grove's clipped conversation that included words like *Bismarck* and *BOLO* or Be On the Lookout For. On the lookout for who?

"I think your sister is in cop mode right now." She was. Mike told Javier and Sylvie to call them as soon as they learned more about their great-aunt and -uncle, then shooed them toward the car. "Don't worry. I'll stay with her. We'll be there as soon as we can."

By the time Javier and Sylvie had taken off, Gina had done a complete 360. Every cell in her body was screaming on high alert. The street and yards were already crowded with cars and junk. There were too many people here. Too many distractions. Too many places to hide. "This is a setup. This whole thing is a trap." The moment Kevin Grove hung up the phone, she ducked beneath the crime scene tape and marched over to him. "Detective Grove? You need to get your men out of here."

He didn't seem fazed that she'd entered the crime scene without permission. "This is the home of a cop, Galvan. Another attempted murder. Of you."

Gina shook her head. "No one was shot here. Not yet." She could feel the truth in her bones as clearly as if she was reading the information off a computer screen. "Have you recovered any of the bullets yet?"

The detective pulled a plastic evidence bag from his pocket for her to examine.

"These aren't like the bullets we took from Bobby Estes. These are rifle caliber."

"Estes carries a hand gun?"

Gina nodded as he pocketed the slugs. "The shooter is here. I know it. This is exactly the kind of chaos he thrives on. The perfect cover. While you and your people are focused on doing their jobs, he's picking out his target." She scanned the chaos and shadows around them. "Whoever he's after this time, he already has them in his sights."

Kevin Grove might be as stubborn as they came, but he was one of the best detectives in all of KCPD. He listened to Gina's take on the situation and started shouting orders. "I want a car-to-car search of anything parked within targeting distance. Clear all nonessential personnel out of here. Everyone on the scene wears a flak vest." He pointed to the porch lights across the street. "Let's get these civilians away from the windows and kill some of these lights. I don't want this guy having any advantage we don't." After the uniformed officers and CSIs scrambled away to do his bidding, Detective Grove looked down at Gina. "You got your badge on you? We can use every available cop right now."

"She's ready." Gina turned to see Mike holding out her badge and holstered Glock that she'd stowed in his truck. His half grin belied the serious warning in his eyes. "I figured you were going to jump into the middle of this, even if you are still on medical leave. I'd rather have you armed and able to defend yourself than be a sitting duck."

"Works for me." Grove nodded toward one of the officers jogging to the house next door. "Since you know these people, why don't you make the rounds and warn your neighbors to keep their heads down until we're finished."

"Yes, sir." Gina took the badge and gun and slipped them onto her belt. Mike's understanding of who she was touched her. Strapping the Glock onto her hip for the first time in almost two months was both empowering—like putting on a favorite pair of jeans—and a little unnerving. This wasn't just a good luck charm she was wearing. It was a loaded lethal weapon. And she was responsible for her use of it.

"You can do this, Tiger." She tilted her gaze up to those piercing blue eyes. Mike Cutler believed in her. So she believed, too. When Gina nodded, Mike reached for her damaged hand and squeezed, reminding her that she could feel with those fingers, she could control her body. She could do this.

She quickly squeezed back. "Thank you."

"Let's go."

"Go? Where are you going?" she chided, hurrying her steps to catch up with his long stride. "Not a cop,

Cutler. You need to go back to your truck and get out of here."

But once she slipped under the crime scene tape he held up for her, he fell into step right beside her. "We're partners, remember?"

"Not when it comes to something this dangerous."

"You're not getting rid of me," he insisted.

"Fine. Just keep up."

Gina coordinated the contact with and notification to the residents of the nearby houses with the other officer, taking the east end of the block. She knocked on the doors of two houses, asking the residents if they'd seen anything, then warning them back into interior rooms of the house until KCPD had fully cleared the scene.

She'd just headed up the next front walk when Mike stopped at the edge of the driveway. "Gina."

She followed the general direction of his gaze to the north–south side street. A familiar tan Mercedes cruised slowly through the intersection. The driver watched the police cars blocking the street and the officers still moving around her great-uncle's house.

"That's your stolen license plate."

She spotted the last two digits, 3-6, as the car passed beneath the glow of the streetlamp at the corner. A shiver ran down her spine. Along with a sense of finality and purpose.

Mike was already moving toward the slow-moving vehicle when she joined him. "That's Bobby Estes." What was he doing here? Could he have something to do with the attack on her family, after all? It wouldn't be that hard for him or one of his friends to get a different weapon. Gina tossed Mike her phone as she quickened her pace to keep the car in sight. "Detective Grove's number is in there. Call him and let him know. I'll track the car as long as I can."

By the time Gina reached the corner, Bobby picked up speed. She ran across the street, chasing him past Mike's truck and down the sidewalk to the next intersection. But Bobby gunned the powerful engine and careened out of sight, leaving her no chance of catching him on foot. She stopped at the curb, breathing hard at the full-out sprint, her mouth open, her nostrils flaring. Her only hope was that Mike had gotten through to Detective Grove and an APB on the car and license would stop him before he got too far away. "You son of a…"

As her breathing eased and the urge to curse faded, Gina realized that she'd just run past a piece-of-junk Chevy. She let go of her enmity toward Bobby Estes as a chilling suspicion took its place.

Piece-of-junk Chevy. Derek's particular choice of words rang in her ears. He *had* remembered something from the day of the shooting. Gina slowly turned as the ghost of a forgotten image filled her head. There. A dented 1500 pickup with a faded red side panel and rusted wheel wells was parked up the street, lost among the bumper-to-bumper heaps that littered the neighborhood. It was far enough away from her house not to be caught in the grid of police officers blocking out a crime scene, but it sat at an angle that gave its driver a clear view of everything happening along the street. Its unremarkable appearance had camouflaged it from notice. But she saw it now. Saw it clearly. She took one step toward it. Two. She saw the tip of the rifle balanced through the open window. Aimed right at her.

"Gun!" Gina yelled a split second before she saw the flash of gunpowder lighting up the night.

The boom of the big gun's report hit her a nanosecond later. Before she could react, a long, broad chest slammed into her, tackling her to the ground. Mike. Of course. Rescuing her. Again.

She heard a rare curse against her ear. A second gunshot split the air. With his long arms snaked around her, they rolled, scraping across the unforgiving concrete before they hit crinkly brown grass and slammed to a stop against a fire hydrant. Mike's back took the brunt of the impact, and he swore again.

"Mike! Are you hurt?"

But he was pushing her out of his arms. An engine roared to life in the distance. He pushed her to her feet as he sat up. "Go!" Tires squealing against the pavement, fighting for traction, drowned out the engine noise. Mike shoved her away from him. "Go get him!"

Gina shook off the dizziness from their tumble and started moving. By the time she saw the other officers running toward the intersection, the Chevy had already bashed in the bumper of the car in front of it and was flying down the street. He was getting away. He couldn't get away.

Gina unhooked her holster and stepped into the middle of the street.

"Gina!"

"KCPD!" she shouted. "Stop the car!" She pulled out her Glock. "Stop the car!"

It picked up speed and raced toward her in a deadly game of chicken. No more wounded cops. This guy wasn't winning. Not on her turf.

Gina raised the gun with both hands, willed her

shaky fingers to be strong, slid her finger against the trigger. "Stop the damn car!"

When the driver answered by gunning the engine, Gina squeezed the trigger. She felt the kick in her shoulder and steadied her aim, firing again and again. She took out one headlight, shattered the windshield, popped a tire and kept firing until the truck spun out of control and crashed into a row of parked cars.

The other officers were on the scene in an instant. Kevin Grove pulled the driver out of the car and put him down on the ground, cuffing him. Several other officers had rushed in to turn off the Chevy's motor and assist Grove with dragging him up onto the sidewalk before Gina reached the wreck.

Gina's hand, still holding the gun, was shaking down at her side. She recognized the oily gray ponytail and interrupted the detective charging the perp with numerous crimes. "Harold? Harold Johnson?"

"I didn't kill anybody," Derek's father protested, spitting his anger at everyone around him. "I didn't kill anybody. You can't get me for murder."

Gina shook her head. The adrenaline that had charged through her system a moment ago was draining away, leaving her stunned by the discovery of the man who'd hurt her. "You shot four cops. You shot your own son."

"That was a decoy. A flesh wound. I knew he'd recover. You were the one I was aiming for. Maimed you good, didn't I? Turned you into a cripple."

"You son of a…"

She startled at Mike's touch on her arm, urging her to holster her weapon. "Why?" he asked. "What do you get out of this?"

"It's what Derek gets. What my boy deserves." Gina still didn't understand. "They were going to promote you and that—"

"Shut up, Johnson," Mike warned.

"—ahead of my boy. You immigrants don't deserve a better job. You get special treatment you haven't earned. Just because your skin's a different color or you got boobs instead of—"

"He said to shut up." Grove dragged him to his feet. "Did Derek know about this? Know how you were stacking the odds in his favor?"

"Not at first. But he figured it out." He pointed his nose at Gina since his hands were bound. "Because of all that poking around that you were doing, he figured it out. He knows where his loyalties are. Unlike his lousy partner, who files complaints on him." Harold's face had been cut by some broken glass. His cheek was already swelling from where he must have smacked into the window or steering wheel when he crashed. But his injuries didn't stop him from spewing his vile prejudice. "I screwed up a lot in Derek's life, but I could do this for him. Made it so you couldn't be a cop no more. I got rid of the competition." He snorted a curse. "I thought you couldn't handle a gun no more."

Gina looked right into those bloodshot green eyes without blinking. "I got better."

"Someone take this jackass off my hands. I want to see Officer Johnson at my desk before the night's over," Detective Grove ordered. "Call Impound. And let's contain this scene." While others hurried to carry out his orders, the burly detective smiled down at Gina. "Good work, Galvan. Welcome back. I'd put you on my team any day. I'll get a report from you later." Then he nodded up to Mike. "In the meantime, you'd better get him to the hospital."

"What? Mike!" Gina spun around. Mike was holding on to his left bicep and blood was oozing between his fingers. More than the shock of learning the identity of the man who'd shot her, more than the disappointment of knowing Derek had hidden the truth from her, seeing Mike bleeding because of her might be the one thing she couldn't handle. "You need to sit down." She slipped her arm around his waist and started walking toward his truck. "What were you thinking?"

"That you are the most magnificent woman I've ever known. Facing Johnson down like that."

"I don't mean that. Harold was shooting at *me*. At cops."

"I didn't want you to get hurt."

"It's not okay for you to get hurt, either."

"It's just a graze. A few stitches and a shot of antibiotics and I'll be good."

Even though he seemed to be walking fine under his own power, Gina kept a steadying arm around him. Maybe she was steadying herself because her vision was blurring and her heart was breaking and she couldn't stand that she was falling apart. He sat on the running board of the truck, while she rummaged beneath the front seat to find his first aid kit.

When she knelt in front of him, he captured the side of her face in his hand and wiped away the tears with the pad of his thumb. "Hey. What are these? I didn't think tough chicks cried."

She unbuttoned his shirt and gently peeled the cotton sleeve off his shoulder and away from the wound. "I hate you, Michael Cutler Jr. I hate you for making me cry."

"Um, okay?"

She dabbed at the blood with a wad of gauze, relieved to see it was just a flesh wound. "I'm crying because you're hurt and I'm in love with you."

"You're not selling me on this, Tiger." He pulled her hand away from stanching his wound and dipped his head to meet her gaze. "Does it help if I tell you I'm in love with you, too?"

"You are?" The man had such incredibly blue eyes.

"Has there been one moment when you doubted that I cared about you?"

Gina stretched up to press a hard kiss against his mouth. When she pulled away, his lips followed hers to claim another kiss. Then she caught his stubbled jaw in her hand and kissed him again, feeling the fear fading and the emotional strength this man inspired in her returning. "I don't know yet how we're going to make this work. But we are going to make it work. Understand? You know how good I am at fighting for what I want."

"Do you mind if I fight for us, too?"

"But no more jumping in front of bullets, okay? No more running down bad guys." She poked a finger in the middle of his chest. "Not a cop. Even if I don't make SWAT, I'm going back to a beat or working with domestic-violence victims or earning my detective's badge. That's my job."

"If we're going to be a partnership, what is my job?"

Those blue eyes mesmerized her. Treasured her. Believed in her. "To love me every day of your long and healthy life."

Mike wound his uninjured arm around her and pulled her in for a kiss. "Deal."

Epilogue

Two months later

Mike would never tire of seeing Gina in her starched KCPD uniform. She walked into the CAPT clinic with takeout and drinks to share lunch in his office and his heart did a familiar tumble of love and pride. She carried herself with confidence when she wore the blue-and-black with her badge, gear belt and holstered gun. And her sweet figure filled it out in a way that was anything but mannish.

He waited while she greeted Troy and leaned in to give him a hug. Mike dutifully raised his gaze to her dark eyes when she turned to include him in her announcement. "Did I tell you I've already got three people signed up to take my self-defense training class here? Vicki Bismarck, Frannie and Sylvie. Lupe said she's going to bake cookies and bring them down to watch. Says maybe she's not so old that she can't learn a thing or two."

"Lupe's baking cookies?" Troy raised his hand. "Anything I can do to help with your class?" When Mike and Gina laughed, Troy pressed his hand against his heart. "Hey, I'm serious. She's brought food to each of the sessions where I've been helping her work on her balance issues."

Mike took the bag from Gina before teasing his friend. "You know that's not how we get our bills paid around here, right?"

"Yeah, but don't tell her that. That woman can cook."

Although Gina smiled much more often these days, she was serious for a moment. "So, it's okay if I set up my class here? I know it's not physical therapy, but you are in the neighborhood."

Mike read the agreement on Troy's face and nodded. "I think feeling safe and building self-confidence all fits into that wellness goal we strive for. Just let me know when and I'll schedule the gym for you."

Frannie came out of her office carrying a computer pad. "As long as you leave Monday and Wednesday nights open. That's when Colin Cho and Frank McBride are coming in for their PT."

Mike couldn't deny the recent upturn in business. Or the credit Gina deserved for helping him. "I wouldn't have thought you'd be the best PR person. But you've brought in a half dozen new clients from KCPD."

Gina shrugged. "Cops have a lot of back and joint issues. I just suggested they come here."

Troy rolled his chair up beside Frannie. "Hey, you signed up for Gina's class? You gonna wear those tight shorts you had on the last time you worked out?"

"Troy!" Her freckles disappeared beneath a healthy blush.

"Like I'm not gonna notice." Troy grabbed Frannie around the waist and pulled her into his lap before wheeling them both into the gym. "C'mon, Sunshine. Let's get you warmed up."

Once they were alone in the hallway, Gina smiled. "They seem happy."

"They do." Mike led her into his office and set lunch out on his desk while Gina closed the door. "What about you, Tiger? Are you happy?"

"What do you think?" Gina was right there when he faced her. She nudged him onto the edge of the desk, moved between his legs and kissed him very, very thoroughly.

Mike returned the favor, pulling her onto her toes and taking over the kiss. When she mewled that tell-tale hum in her throat that told him they were about to take this embrace past the point of no return, Mike set her back on her feet. He settled his hands at her waist, resting his forehead against hers as they both struggled to return their breathing to normal. "Do you like working the special victims unit? I know how badly you wanted SWAT."

"There'll be other SWAT teams. The guys who made it deserve the honor." She tilted her gaze up to his, sharing an honest, beautiful smile. "Maybe one day my shoulder will be good enough so I can make the cut. If not, I'm okay. I think I'm really good at what I'm doing now."

"You'd be good at anything you set your mind to."

"Your dad doesn't still feel guilty about not putting me on the new SWAT team, does he?"

"No. I think he's happier to know he's got you for a future daughter-in-law."

Resting her hand against his chest, Gina eyed the simple solitaire he'd given her. "Me, too."

They shared another kiss before sitting down to lunch. As it often did between them, the conversation turned to her work and family. By the time they'd finished, she'd updated him on the Bismarck brothers, who were both in jail now. Rollo Molina's health was still a concern, but his stress was more manageable now that Mike had moved the family into his home. Lupe cooked, Javier helped with the yard and Gina had planted a garden. Bobby Estes was still trading favors for fast cars in No-Man's Land, but at least he'd stopped pestering Sylvie. "We'll have to catch him at something where we can make the arrest stick," Gina groused. "But I like a project."

"Just say the word and I will help you do whatever is necessary to get Estes off the streets." Mike stood as Gina circled the desk to meet him.

"Not a cop, Cutler."

"No, but *you* are, Gina Galvan." He leaned in to kiss the teasing reminder off her mouth. "You're my cop."

* * * * *

Janie Crouch has loved to read romance her whole life. This *USA TODAY* bestselling author cut her teeth on Harlequin Romance novels as a preteen, then moved on to a passion for romantic suspense as an adult. Janie lives with her husband and four children overseas. She enjoys traveling, long-distance running, movie watching, knitting and adventure/obstacle racing. You can find out more about her at janiecrouch.com.

Books by Janie Crouch

Harlequin Intrigue

The Risk Series: A Bree and Tanner Thriller

Calculated Risk
Security Risk
Constant Risk
Risk Everything

Omega Sector: Under Siege

Daddy Defender
Protector's Instinct
Cease Fire

Omega Sector: Critical Response

Special Forces Savior
Fully Committed
Armored Attraction
Man of Action
Overwhelming Force
Battle Tested

Visit the Author Profile page
at Harlequin.com for more titles.

ARMED RESPONSE

Janie Crouch

This book is dedicated to my sister-in-law, Kimberly. Thank you for always being such a source of joy and encouragement, not just to me, but to everyone around you. And for making Mark read my books. I love you.

Chapter 1

The way some women felt about that perfect little black-dress-and-heels ensemble—ready for anything, able to handle themselves, *bring it on*—Lillian Muir felt about her SWAT cargo pants, combat boots and tactical vest.

The heavy clothing and gear she wore might have felt burdensome at one time on her five-two, one-hundred-pound frame, but she had long since adjusted. Now she almost felt more comfortable with the extra thirty pounds weighing on her than she did with it off. The weight was a comfort. A friend.

Her HK MP5 9mm submachine gun rested against her shoulder, just grazing her chin. Her fingers curled gently around it as she moved through the silent winter air of this Colorado night. A shotgun strapped around her back and a Glock pistol low on one hip provided further assurance she could handle what was ahead.

More than a pair of high heels ever would.

And what was ahead was pissing her the hell off. A man—a *father*—holding his ex-wife and their two children hostage at gunpoint.

"Bulldog One, status."

Lillian tapped the button that allowed her to speak into the communication system attached to her ear under her helmet. "Approaching back door, TC."

"Roger that. Hold for entry." One of the team's newest—and temporary—members, Philip Carnell, was acting as Tactical Command. Carnell wasn't the team's usual TC and his presence added to Lillian's unease about the mission. Not that Carnell wasn't brilliant when it came to planning and calling the shots. He was. Had an IQ of about a million and was able to process tactical information and advantages faster than anyone Lillian had ever seen. His mind was like a damn computer.

But he wasn't part of the usual team. And moreover, he was pretty bitter about that.

They were shorthanded from recent attacks by criminal mastermind Damien Freihof over the past few months. Team members had been hurt and even killed as they battled one assault after another. Explosions. Bullets through windows. Sliced throats. Even assailants at weddings. Freihof had made it his mission in life to wage war on Omega Sector.

Lillian herself had been injured in a mission just two weeks ago, shrapnel from an explosion catching her in the shoulder. She ignored the slight discomfort now. She had bigger things to worry about.

"Bulldog Two, report status," Carnell said.

"I have a visual on the suspect. Single tango. He's pacing. Three hostages. Mom and two kids. All in the kitchen." Bulldog Two's voice was a little too high, too excited. Another person that damn sure wasn't part of the normal elite Omega Sector SWAT team. Damn Damien Freihof and his mole inside Omega.

Lillian ignored that discomfort for now, too.

"I have a shot. Repeat, I have a shot," Bulldog Two said.

Lillian held her tongue. New Kid wasn't her problem.

"Negative, Bulldog Two. Hold your position," Carnell told him.

"I want to take this bastard out," the trainee guy said again. What was his name? Paul?

"Hold, Bulldog Two." This time it was team leader Derek Waterman on the comm unit. He was also out in the darkness surrounding the house.

Lillian's lips pursed. "Derek, request channel change."

"Roger that. Go to channel three, Bulldog One."

Lillian clicked the dial that turned the comm device to a channel so she and the team leader could talk without anyone else listening.

"Go, Lillian," Derek said.

"We going to have a problem with Newbie?"

"His name is Saul. Saul Poniard."

Generally Saul was a good guy. Friendly, surfer-boy looks with a ready smile. He was also pretty excitable, which might have been the reason he was turned down for final SWAT training multiple times. The only reason he was here now was the injuries on the team.

Lillian sighed. "I just don't want him shooting those kids' dad in front of them."

"Roger that," Derek said. "No deadly force unless we have no other options. TC knows that. Carnell won't make that call unless there are no other options and things are escalating."

"I know that. You know that. Just want to make sure New Kid knows that."

Derek grimaced. "Don't worry. I've got him under thumb. I'll pull him out if I need to. Switch channels."

Lillian did so. She'd said her piece, and really didn't have a problem with Saul Poniard except for his excitability, and lack of experience. Derek would handle it. Which was good because she didn't want to have to go take out baby-SWAT wannabe before taking down that scumbag dad on the inside.

Who she could now hear screaming at his wife.

"Tactical Command, this is Bulldog One. I am at the back door. I have visual on the mom and kids but not the tango."

She could see them in the kitchen, the woman and children sitting at a small round wooden table. The mom had both hands reached out toward her children, a boy around nine and a girl around seven, and they sat on either side of her, but not near enough to be touching her.

The tango paced into view, gun in hand, but at least pointing down, and he smacked the mom in the head with his bare hand as he stormed past and out of sight from where Lillian crouched at the window. Guy was still shouting.

"I still have a shot. Repeat, Bulldog Two has a shot," Saul said. He was in a tree on the east side of the house, so Lillian had no doubt the angle gave him a tactical advantage. And yes, if Psycho Dad's actions escalated, then Saul would need to take him out.

But otherwise Lillian would do everything she could to make sure these kids didn't see a parent—no matter how terrible he was—die right in front of them.

Not here. Not today.

"Negative, Bulldog Two," Philip said. "Bulldog One, can you infiltrate without exposure?"

"Affirmative," Lillian responded. "Especially with all the noise this guy is making."

"Everyone is in position. Go at your discretion," Philip told her. The rest of the team—as well as the new kid—was ready to back her up and take out the tango if needed.

Lillian waited until the guy went on another tirade, screaming right in the mother's ear, both kids sobbing, as an opportunity to slip inside a small crack when she opened the door. The Omega SWAT team regularly used Lillian's small stature to their advantage. This was no different.

She kept to the shadows as she made her way closer to the kitchen.

"Tango is starting to wave the gun again." Saul's voice had reached an excited pitch again. "He's got it to the wife's head."

"Roger that, Bulldog Two. Your shot?"

"Still clear, TC. Just give me the word." Saul was damn near panting with excitement.

Damn it. She'd rather the team take out the father than have the mother die.

"Bulldog One?"

"I have no visual," she muttered.

"Okay, Bulldog Two, you are cleared to—"

Lillian saw movement again in the kitchen. "Hold," she said. "Tango is on the move again. Back to pacing."

"I've still got the shot, TC."

The frustration was evident in Poniard's tone, and Lillian couldn't blame him. Preparing to fire, and being cleared to fire, but then having the order rescinded at the last second, was irritating. But exercising control was also an important part of being a SWAT team member.

"Bulldog One, can you beanbag him?" Carnell asked.

"Roger that, TC. Moving into position." Lillian grinned, replacing her HK MP5 with the shotgun strapped behind her back. The beanbag round was only accurate up to about six meters, but she was within range. Its blow was designed to cause minimal permanent damage while rendering the subject immobile.

The fact that it would hurt Screaming Dad like hell didn't bother Lillian a bit. She crawled forward. She was going to have to pull some sort of Tom Cruise roll-and-shoot nonsense in order to get into position in the quickest way possible. She usually went for much less drama. But not today.

Guy started screaming again. Lillian had had enough. *You want to dance, buddy? We'll dance. Together.*

"On my mark," she whispered to the team. "Three, two, one."

Lillian pushed herself from her crouched position in the shadows, twisting her body into a roll as she cleared the wall and came into the opening of the kitchen, landing in a kneel.

She saw surprise light the tango's face. He was

swinging his gun around toward her when her finger gently squeezed the trigger on the shotgun, her aim perfect.

The beanbag round hit him square in the chest, propelling him back through the air and away from the table and hostages. The gun fell out of his hand.

Less than two seconds later Lillian was on the tango and the rest of the team was filing through the door, grabbing the children and wife and leading them to safety.

Screaming Dad groaned as Lillian grabbed his hands to cuff them. "Tango is secure."

"You're a woman!" The man's outrage couldn't be more clear.

Lillian arched a single eyebrow. "Yeah? Well, you're an idiot. Turn over."

"I think you done broke my ribs."

Lillian didn't give a rat's ass whether this jerk had a couple of cracked ribs. He was lucky Philip hadn't turned the trigger-happy new kid loose on him. "Shut up. I'll break more than your ribs."

Within a few more minutes the perp was loaded into the back of a squad car and the wife and kids were handed over to the paramedics.

"Nice work, everyone," Derek said over their comm unit. "Let's get packed up and back to HQ to debrief."

Lillian bumped fists with everyone as they made it back to the car. Even Saul, who was smiling like an idiot. Everybody was walking away today. No one seriously injured, even the tango.

That made today a good day.

"Beers on me," Derek said.

That made it an even better day.

* * *

Later that night after the debriefing and the beers, Damien Freihof sat in an abandoned warehouse across town, staring at "Mr. Fawkes." Damien had made it his mission over the last six months to destroy Omega Sector, piece by piece, in payment for taking the life of his beloved wife.

Fawkes, as he so cleverly liked to be called, had proven very useful over the last few months in that endeavor. Fawkes's inside information on Omega had been quite helpful indeed.

Fawkes still wouldn't give Damien his real name. Damien wondered how upsetting it would be to the younger man to know that Damien had figured it out weeks ago. The man might be brilliant, but Damien didn't work with people he didn't know.

Damien's and Fawkes's ideologies were different. Fawkes looked to destroy and rebuild all of law enforcement. Damien just wanted Omega to suffer the way he did when he'd lost his Natalie. Wanted them to know what it meant to experience unbearable loss.

But if Damien could bring chaos across the country by destroying the foundation of all law enforcement, as was Fawkes's plan, then hell, he was up for that, too.

"It's time," Fawkes said as he paced back and forth hardly visible beside a window, even in the full moon. "You'll be ready, right? We only have eight days."

Damien sat perched against a desk. "Yes, I'll be ready to do my part in your master plan."

"We've gotten rid of two of their team members completely. Another is injured and not fully up to speed." Fawkes continued his pacing.

"It's a mistake to underestimate the Critical Response Division, even when they're weakened." Damien had learned that the hard way.

"They brought in a new guy on the SWAT team. That was unexpected." Fawkes stopped and studied Damien as he said it, as if gauging his response.

Damien knew all about the new guy. "Is that a problem?"

"No." Fawkes resumed his pacing. "The team thinks they're so smart, but they're not. I've left a trail. It's going to lead right to the very heart of the SWAT team. The sweetheart."

"Lillian Muir?" Damien raised an eyebrow.

"I've got special plans for her. Have already left clues in the system that lead back to her as the mole I know they're searching for."

Damien had to admit Fawkes's computer skills were impressive. He'd provided information that had helped Damien a great deal. Most particularly two weeks ago, when Omega had almost captured him at his own house. Without a warning from Fawkes, Damien would never have made it out.

Nor taken one of the SWAT team out of action in the process.

Fawkes might not be the easiest person to work with, but he definitely knew how to manipulate a computer system. And how to manipulate people, for that matter. People didn't take him seriously enough, including those at Omega Sector.

Which was probably why he was trying to blow up—*literally*—all of law enforcement.

Or maybe he just had mommy issues. Whatever. Damien didn't care why Fawkes was doing it, he just wanted to see Omega Sector destroyed. If Lillian Muir was going to take the fall for that, even better. Damien would do a little checking up on her himself.

Fawkes wasn't the only one with computer skills and digging-up-info skills.

"Is there even going to be anyone left to search for the villain after you get through next week?" Damien asked.

Fawkes stilled. "I'll be left. I will be one of the few tactically trained agents left in the whole agency. Hell, in the whole country. And all the destruction will lead right to Lillian Muir's door. She'll be dead and unable to open the door, but the destruction and blame will still lead right to her."

Damien grinned. One thing Fawkes had was exuberance. "Sounds like a perfect plan to me."

Chapter 2

Jace Eakin stretched his long legs out in front of him in an office chair that probably hadn't been comfortable even when it was new. Now that it was ratty and at least a dozen years past that, it was even less so. His knee was stiff from too many hours cramped in a plane, his shoulder vaguely ached from a bullet he'd taken years ago in Afghanistan. Thirty-two was too young to feel this old.

He was in an office that looked like it was out of some old gumshoe movie, complete with dirty windows and low ceilings. The man sitting behind a desk looked almost as rumpled as the office itself.

Jace knew Ren McClement was anything but.

Jace had first met him ten years ago when they served together in the US Army Rangers in the Middle East. Working side by side with someone in daily life-or-death situations showed that person's true colors. Ren McClement was one of the few people in the world Jace trusted without restriction. He knew the feeling was mutual. Which was why he was here now in this godforsaken seat in some out-of-the-way office in Washington, DC, rather than putting the finishing touches on his ranch in Colorado.

"Ren, seriously, dude, you've got to get some chairs not built for midgets."

Both Ren and the other man in the room, Steve Drackett, chuckled. Ren had gotten out of the army not long after the time he spent in Afghanistan with Jace. Because of his skills and security clearance, Ren had immediately been brought into Omega Sector, a joint task force made up of the best agents the United States had to offer.

Jace knew Ren was one of the highest-ranking members of Omega, and that he worked mostly in covert missions.

Nothing surprising about that. Ren had had the ability to blend in with almost any situation even back in his Ranger days. That the government was smart enough to use him for clandestine work wasn't surprising to Jace.

What was a mystery to him was why Ren had asked *him* here to begin with. Although always happy to see his old friend, Jace was not an Omega Sector agent. He wasn't an agent at all.

"Yeah, budget for this place wasn't very big," Ren said. "Not that I'm in here enough to worry about that anyway."

Ren could probably have a very high-end government office with a million-dollar view of DC, but chose not to. Jace knew for a fact that Ren never entered a government building unless he had to, and even then it wasn't through the front door. The undercover nature of his job prohibited it.

"I can see why you wouldn't want to be here often. And speaking of, why am *I* here? I'm assuming there's a reason other than reliving old times."

Ren nodded. "We have a situation in the Omega Critical Response Division out in Colorado Springs. A mole who is leaking information to a terrorist named Damien Freihof. We know the mole is someone inside the SWAT team. Steve—" he gestured to the other man, who was leaning with one shoulder against the wall "—has requested that I send in someone I trust to help find the mole."

Steve pushed himself away from the wall and handed Jace a thin file with some papers inside. "We found this Manifesto of Change document hidden in one of our Omega computer servers."

On my honor, I will never betray my badge, my integrity, my character or the public trust.

I will always have the courage to hold myself and others accountable for our actions.

I will always uphold the constitution, my community and the agency I serve.

Jace looked over at Ren, then Steve. "This looks like some sort of law-enforcement creed."

Steve nodded. "It's the oath of honor that law enforcement officers take at their swearing-in ceremony. But keep reading."

We all took an oath to uphold the law, but instead we have allowed the public to make a mockery of it. Where is the honor, the integrity, the character in not using the privilege and power given to us by our training and station to wipe clean those who would infect our society? We were meant to rise up, to be an example to the people, to control them when needed in order to make a more perfect civilization.

But we are weak. Afraid of popular opinion whenever force must be used. So now we have changed the configuration of law enforcement forever.

And now, only now, will you truly understand what it means to hold yourselves accountable for your actions. Only with death is life truly appreciated. Only with violence can true change be propagated. As we build anew, let us not make the same mistakes. Let the badge mean something again.

Let the badge rule as it was meant to do.

Jace shifted slightly in his chair. "Okay, I'll admit, this is scary. And I sympathize, I really do, that this has come from within your own organization, but I'm not an agent. There's got to be other people you trust who could do a better job than I could."

Ren glanced over at Steve and then back at Jace. "We're not looking for someone long-term. This is a time-sensitive op."

Steve nodded. "I would've bet my life that the traitor was not one of my SWAT team members. I've known most of those people for years. But intel has suggested that not only is the mole a member of SWAT, but also has a plan that will involve a massive loss of life."

"Do you have details about how? When?" Jace asked.

Steve nodded. "Within the next two weeks. Our strong suspicions are that it has to do with a law-enforcement summit scheduled in Denver next week. It will have police chiefs and politicians in attendance from all over the country."

"That would definitely make a good target." Jace looked back at Ren. "And if you need an extra hand with a rifle, I'm more than willing to help out, especially since I'm headed out to Colorado anyway."

"Still planning on breeding and raising dogs?" Ren asked. "Horses? Opening your ranch?"

"Hey, don't mock my dream." Jace had always wanted to own a small parcel of land where he could raise animals, particularly dogs, that could be trained for service members and veterans who suffered from PTSD. Maybe even make it into a place where vets could come and enjoy space and quiet for a temporary stay when they needed it.

Jace had made some savvy financial investments in his twenties that had given him the means to make this dream a reality now. He'd be able to cover himself financially until he was able to make a living from his business. He was looking forward to working outside, with the land and animals. He also looked forward to not having to be constantly worried about being in danger.

Although risk cognizance had been a part of his life for so long it was second nature to him now.

"I wouldn't dream of mocking it." Ren smiled.

"Hell, I may be joining you before this is all over. But I was hoping you would help me out before you got out of the game for good."

"We don't need an agent," Steve said. "We just need someone who can come in and pass for a SWAT team member. Somebody who has the qualifications and physical prowess to join the team. Because of attacks by Damien Freihof, we're down a couple of members, so bringing in someone from the outside wouldn't be unheard of."

"And then once I'm in there?"

"Then there's one person particularly under suspicion who we need you to get close to." Ren leaned forward on his desk, watching Jace closely. "Lillian Muir."

The name had Jace actually rising from his seat before he even knew it.

"Lillian Muir?" He looked from Ren to Steve. "Lillian Muir is a member of the Omega Sector SWAT team?"

"Not only a member, one of the *best* members. One of the most gifted SWAT personnel I've ever known," Steve said.

Jace began pacing back and forth behind the chair he'd just vacated.

Lillian Muir.

He'd be lying if he said he hadn't wondered what had happened to her over the years. He hadn't seen her in twelve years, since he was twenty and she was eighteen. The day they were supposed to leave to join the army together, to get out of a pretty rotten living situation in Tulsa. To figure out their future together, which for Jace had always meant marriage as soon as he could talk her into it.

He hadn't seen her since the day he'd found her in his brother's arms.

Jace looked at Ren. "You know, of course, that Lillian and I have a history."

Ren nodded. "You and I talked about a woman you cared about a great deal back when we served together. And you'd mentioned her name was Lillian. When I found out the Omega Lillian was the same as your Lillian, I thought we could kill two birds with one trusted stone."

Jace shook his head. "You also know things didn't end well between the two of us. I'm probably not the most neutral person. She decided she'd rather have my brother than me."

Daryl had died in a fire not long after Jace joined the army, but that didn't change the fact that Lillian had chosen Daryl, not him.

"I just want to say officially and on the record that I do not think Lillian is the mole," Steve said, conviction clear in his voice. "As a matter of fact, I'm hoping you'll be able to come in and clear her."

"Clear her? Why me? There's got to be someone better."

"It's a perfect storm of problems," Ren said. "We need someone we can trust. We need someone who has the skills to infiltrate a SWAT team. And we need someone Lillian may be willing to get close to."

Jace shrugged. "The first two I might fit. But Lillian won't get close to me. There's got to be someone else. Friend. Boyfriend. Somebody."

"I recruited Lillian basically off the streets nine

years ago." Steve shook his head. "She's got a tactical awareness and physical control of her body that has only improved over the years with training and education. But, despite being an excellent team member, Lillian has never gotten close to anyone since I've known her."

Jace scrubbed a hand over his face. "Even more reason why she's not going to get close to me. Some people are just lone wolves."

Jace knew enough about Lillian's upbringing to not be surprised that she kept to herself. She wasn't ever going to be the life of the party. But never having gotten close to *anyone*? The two of them had been plenty close at one time. Or so he'd thought.

"Our division psychiatrist was killed by Freihof two weeks ago," Steve continued. "Her case files are confidential, even with her death. But I do know for a fact that Lillian was seeing Dr. Parker regularly. And Dr. Parker believed there was a sexual trauma of some kind in Lillian's history."

Ren leaned back in his chair. "Honestly, we were hoping maybe you knew something about that and could use it to foster a closeness between the two of you."

"I don't. If that happened, it happened after she and I…separated." Jace grimaced, tension creeping through his body. Despite her leaving him for his brother, Jace would never have wished something like that on her. Couldn't stand the thought of someone hurting her that way.

"Like I said, I don't have any details. And it may not even be accurate. But I know Dr. Parker had suggested that finding someone from her past, someone she knew before the trauma, might be the key to helping her overcome it." Steve gestured toward Jace. "Maybe you could be that person. Help us find the real mole. Help her work through whatever is in her history."

"What if she is the real mole?" Jace asked. He didn't want to believe it. He *didn't* believe it. But it could still be the truth. He'd known her twelve years ago and she cheated on him. Had that developed into even darker tendencies as she'd gotten older?

Steve took a step forward. "She's not."

Ren held his hands out in front of him in a soothing gesture. "Steve, you're too close to this. You know you are."

Jace jerked his chin at Steve. "You involved with Lillian?"

"No, happily married and a new father." Steve's eyes narrowed. "Plus, did you not just hear what I said about her not getting close to people? That particularly goes for men."

Jace shrugged, studying Steve with hooded eyes. "Thought maybe you might be the exception to that."

"Steve cares about the entire team," Ren insisted. "He wants to catch Freihof and the mole more than anyone else, especially given the people they've lost. And the mole doesn't know that we're on to him. Or her, as it may be. So we want to use that to our advantage. Steve poking around will draw attention. Not to mention he's not neutral."

Jace sat back down in the uncomfortable chair. "And you think I am?"

Ren stared him down. "I think I would trust you with my life—and have—multiple times over. I think you have an innate situational awareness that was only honed in your years as a Ranger. I think you will be fresh eyes and able to pinpoint specifics others may have missed."

Ren leaned back in his chair but didn't lose eye contact as he continued. "And I think this is a chance for you to finally put your history with Lillian to rest and move on. She's not the only one who hasn't gotten close to anyone else in the last twelve years."

Jace was also a loner. Lillian hadn't had anything to do with his choice not to settle down with anyone. But that was irrelevant to the situation at hand.

Ren was right—it was time to leave Lillian Muir behind for good.

"Fine. I'll do it. Another couple of weeks isn't going to change my plans for the ranch. I just hope I'm able to do what you guys think I can."

Ren nodded. "Your best has never once not been good enough."

Jace just shrugged. That wasn't true. They'd lost men in the line of duty whom Jace wished he could bring back. "I appreciate the sentiment."

Steve stepped up and shook his hand. "Welcome to the team."

Chapter 3

Lillian had been quick and wiry her whole life. Not just fast with running, although she could average a six-minute mile for ten miles in a row, but swift with everything. Her hand movements, her body movements, how she processed info.

A lot of it probably came from early in her life, when if she wanted to eat, she'd had to steal food from the grocery store or local market. And if she wanted to sleep safely, away from her mother's drunken wrath or boyfriends' wandering hands, she'd learned how to move quickly and silently out the window.

Those lessons might have been hard to come by, but each of them had made her into the woman—the *warrior*—she was today.

Whatever didn't kill her had better start running.

The SWAT team was sparring and doing some gen-

eral workouts in the training area until the new guy
got there. *Another* new guy. Evidently this one had a
little more experience than Saul, the friendly yet trigger-happy newbie who had been filling in for the last
couple of weeks. Or anybody was better than Philip
Carnell, the computer whiz who had been working
with them as an analyst in hostile situations for the
last two months.

Carnell had a mind like a steel trap, but the person-
ality of a horse's ass. Which was probably an insult to
the hind end of a horse. Nobody liked Philip and he had
a bone to pick with everybody about seemingly every
damn thing. Lillian avoided him whenever possible.
Hell, everybody avoided him whenever possible, unless he was acting as Tactical Command, as he had been
a couple of days ago. Carnell was great at finding fast
solutions in dangerous tactical situations, but he wasn't
physically adept enough to be a part of the tactical team.

He'd only sulked about that fact and gave his opinion about "the unfairness of elitist practices" of the
SWAT team about once every hour. Lillian was glad
to not have to deal with him in training or in the field.

Saul wasn't so bad. He tried to get a little too
friendly, and grinned a little too much for her taste.
But at least Surfer Boy didn't make her want to lock
him in a trunk, like she did with Carnell.

Right now she brought her leg around in a vicious
roundhouse kick and hit the punching bag. Roman
Weber, her teammate holding the bag for her, took a
quick step back.

"Trying to take out all your aggression on one
poor defenseless piece of canvas?" He chuckled as he
grabbed the bag more firmly.

"Too many new people, Roman. I don't like change."

"Oh, yeah? Try finding out you're about to be a dad. Now, *that's* change."

Lillian grinned at him. "Yeah, every time that happens to me I swear it's not gonna happen again."

Despite his wounds from an explosion two months ago, she knew Roman couldn't be happier about Keira being back in his life and the baby they had on the way. Hell, it seemed like just about everybody on the SWAT team had found romance-novel-type true love within the last year.

Lillian was thrilled for them, she really was. She liked each and every one of the women her teammates had fallen for. But love and marriage weren't in the cards for her. She'd long since accepted that. Emotional attachment just wasn't her thing.

But she had a career she savored and kicked ass at. That was enough.

"I hear this new guy is actually qualified to be on the team. An Army Ranger. Steve Drackett vouches for him personally," Roman said.

Lillian punched the bag again. "I just wish Liam was back in action." Their teammate had almost been killed by a biological weapon three weeks ago.

"He's alive and going to recover. That's what matters."

Omega Sector's casualty list at Damien Freihof's hand was getting too damn long.

Liam Goetz, SWAT team member: seriously injured via chemical inhalation. Hospitalized two weeks.

Roman Weber, SWAT team member: seriously injured via explosion. In a coma for more than a week.

Tyrone Marcus, SWAT team member-in-training: killed in action via explosion.

Grace Parker, Omega psychiatrist: murdered in cold blood.

And those were just the worst of the worst.

Especially Grace. *Damn it.* Lillian forced herself to push away the grief that threatened to suck her under at the thought of losing the other woman and the close friend she had become.

She switched with Roman and held the bag as he went through a series of kicks and punches, at a slower speed and with less force because of his recent injuries. As soon as the new guy came in, they'd be doing some training with him. Running the SWAT obstacle course, some sparring, throwing him immediately into the mix.

"Hopefully this new guy won't crush on you like Saul," Roman said between punches.

She rolled her eyes. "Yeah. I don't think Saul understands that I don't date work people."

"You don't date anyone."

This was an old argument. "I do date. I just don't announce it around here like all you lovesick fools. There's enough swooning going on around here without adding me to the mix."

"I'd like to meet a boyfriend of yours just once."

Lillian took her turn at the bag. "Fine. I'll bring the next one around for approval, okay?"

She wouldn't. Roman was right, she didn't have boyfriends. She had sex with random guys, probably too often, but she tended to check out mentally in the middle of the act itself. Then immediately left afterward. Not being able to remember any part of the sexual act did not lend itself toward building a relationship.

She and Grace Parker had been working on some of Lillian's issues before Grace had died. Lillian's triggers. The fact that she'd *never* been able to have sex and remember it clearly afterward.

Disassociation due to acute sexual trauma. That was what Grace had told Lillian was the clinical term for it. And that it was treatable. That they would continue to work together so that Lillian's mind didn't try to escape every time she became intimate with someone. They'd made progress over the last year.

And now Grace was dead.

Lillian attacked the punching bag with renewed vigor. "I just want SWAT to be ready for when we get the call to go take out Freihof. I'll even date the new guy if he can help us be ready for that."

Roman chuckled. "Hell, *I'll* date the new guy if he can help with that."

"I'm sure Keira won't mind, considering Freihof nearly got her killed."

"If Steve vouches for this guy, then that's all I need to know," Roman said.

Lillian trusted Steve completely also. "Yeah, me, too. What's the guy's name? I promise I'll make an effort at learning it."

"Jace Eakin."

Lillian's head snapped up and she glared at Roman, about to make him repeat the name.

Roman gestured to the door. "Here he is."

It could not possibly be. There was no way. She turned, slowly. No. Way.

Yes way.

"Jace. Jace Eakin," she whispered.

"You know him?"

"I did. A long, long time ago."

She felt like her heart had completely stopped beating. *Jace* was the new guy? Part of her wasn't surprised that he was qualified. He'd been strong, fast and smart when she knew him twelve years ago. Evidently the army had turned him into someone even more dangerous.

And he was particularly dangerous for her. He knew every secret she'd gone to such lengths to keep hidden from the team. He knew how she used to steal and run illegal items all over town for the gang they'd both been in. She'd been fast, trustworthy and had looked innocent. She'd never once gotten caught.

Jace Eakin knew every secret she'd made sure no one else at Omega Sector knew.

Except one. And he would never know that one.

She kept him in her peripheral vision as she returned to her assault on the punching bag.

"If you know him, don't you want to go talk to him?" Roman asked, grabbing the bag.

She shook her head. It was all she could do to not run from the room. And Lillian was known for not running from anything.

She saw Jace put his bag on the floor and talk to Derek. A few minutes later he was headed toward the locker room.

Fifteen minutes after that Derek was calling the entire team together, including Jace.

"Everybody, this is Jace Eakin. Eakin, the team." Derek looked around at everyone. "They'll all introduce themselves individually."

So far Jace had avoided looking at her directly, but

Lillian had no doubt he was aware of her presence. She could almost feel his awareness of her.

The same way she was aware of him.

"Jace is coming in to help us with the Law Enforcement Systems and Services Summit next week in Denver," Derek continued. "The LESS Summit, as everyone knows, is going to bring in the bigwigs from all over the country. Our job is to provide internal protection for that event."

Ashton Fitzgerald, team sharpshooter and general smart-ass, spoke up. "LESS is more."

Everybody echoed Ashton's statement, the slogan for LESS, as they always did. LESS was a system that would link together law-enforcement-agency computers all over the country, providing valuable instant connectivity and the ability to share data.

"Denver is also expecting a number of demonstrators and protesters, so if needed, we'll help out with that. Everybody knows we're a little undermanned right now. Roman and Lillian are both coming off injuries. Jace is joining us as temporary replacement for Liam. Saul is also going to be joining us as a full member for the LESS Summit."

Everyone was quiet at those words. Building the cohesion needed for the team to run smoothly in just a week wasn't going to be easy. Lillian shifted restlessly. She wasn't the only one.

Derek looked at each one of them. "You're angry at Damien Freihof. All of us are angry after what happened to Grace Parker, not to mention our team. We all want to get our hands on Freihof and make him pay. And that time is coming. But our focus right now is on the LESS Summit. It's about keeping those attending safe. So I want everyone to stay frosty and focused. We have a job to do."

Lillian raised her hand halfway. "What about the rumor that there's a mole inside Omega providing Freihof intel?"

She wanted to nail that traitor bastard just as much as she wanted to nail Freihof.

"I know a mole is suspected," Derek responded. "But to date, no official evidence has been found to support that rumor. We all know Freihof loves to play head games. Getting us to turn on each other, go on witch hunts, is exactly what he wants. So we're not going to do that. If you see anything suspicious, you report it to me, but we don't go around accusing each other of anything."

Lillian nodded. She glanced over and found Jace openly studying her. Their eyes met and she was determined not to look away first. Jace, damn his still gorgeous blue eyes, seemed to have the same determination.

Derek saved them both from their battle of wills.

"We're going to get into training immediately to get us working as a team. And this week we're going to put in long, team-building hours." Derek turned to Jace, who had changed into workout clothes from the khakis and collared shirt he'd arrived in. "Eakin, although you come recommended from a man we all highly respect, if you don't mind, we'd like to see what you're capable of."

Jace nodded. "You'd be a fool not to."

Lillian froze at the sound of Jace's voice. The deep timbre still did something to her. Nudged at parts of her that had been sleeping so long she'd thought they were dead. The most feminine parts of her. For a moment she couldn't breathe as her mind attempted to figure out what she was feeling.

Desire.

It had been so long—twelve years, in fact—since she'd felt clear, untainted desire for a man.

And she was feeling it for the man who, with just a sentence or two about her past, could destroy the rapport she'd taken years to build with her team and probably cost her her job.

Omega Sector generally frowned upon employing people who were once part of an unofficial gang in the streets of Tulsa. While their gang hadn't had turf wars and drive-bys, she'd definitely broken the law multiple times throughout her teenage years.

"We'll hit the team obstacle course this afternoon," Derek continued. "But I thought we'd begin with some sparring."

"Sounds good to me." That deep voice again.

"Who would you like to start with?"

Jace's full lips were turned up at one corner as if he knew some private joke. "Why don't you just pair me with your best close-quarters fighter and I'll go from there."

Everybody chuckled at the new guy's guts.

Even Derek smiled. "Even better, why don't you tell me who *you* think our best close-quarters fighter is?"

Surely Jace would pick Roman or Derek. Both of them were big—over six feet tall with biceps the size of tree trunks.

Lillian could take down both of them. Had done so, in fact. She was pretty damn fast, stronger than she looked, and had spent the last twelve years making sure no man—no matter what his size—would be able to force her to do something she didn't want to do.

Never again.

"Sure." Jace looked at everyone around the circle, as people started stretching and warming up while listening. "There's a number of people who I think could give me a run for my money. But if I had to guess who's most capable of kicking someone's ass, I think it would be this one."

He pointed straight at Lillian.

She could hear the soft chuckles of her teammates, and felt Roman pat her on the shoulder. They didn't know why Jace had chosen her. Because he really thought she was the best close-quarters fighter? Because he thought she'd be easy to take down? She wasn't.

Damn it, she didn't want this. Didn't want to touch Jace Eakin in any way. But she'd never been one to back down from a fight.

She wasn't going to start now.

Stretching her shoulders, she put on the sparring mask and gloves and met Jace in the sparring ring. They gave each other a brief nod and then began.

They spent the first couple of minutes dancing around each other, throwing a jab here and a few kicks there. Lillian felt herself loosening up. She excelled at close-quarters combat. Her body knew what to do from muscle memory.

Jace got a little more serious, sending a spinning back kick in the direction of her head. She dropped low and hooked the back of her leg behind his, bringing him to the mat with a thud.

For just a moment they were face-to-face near the floor.

"I taught you that move," he whispered.

She leaped up to her feet and he followed, pushing off from his shoulder and straight onto his feet.

Lillian didn't let him get resituated. She used her greatest advantage—her speed—and flew at him with a series of punches and kicks. Jace was forced to go on the defensive, and did a damn good job of it.

She stepped back as he nearly backed out of bounds, ending her attack. "You didn't teach me that."

He grinned. "I sure as hell didn't. Impressive." Without warning he came at her, forcing her to go on the defensive this time.

All in all, they were pretty evenly matched. Derek eventually called the match to a halt when it became apparent neither of them was going to win easily. "Let's save some energy for the rest of today's training. There's a lot of hours still left."

Jace took off his gloves and held his hand out to shake hers. "Nice job, Tiger Lily. Although I'm not surprised."

You could've heard a grasshopper karate-chop a fly. *Tiger Lily.* Nobody ever called her Lily, not if they expected to live to see the next sunrise. And no one had ever called her Tiger Lily—the beautiful and exotic flower—but Jace. Hearing the words did something to her she couldn't explain and didn't want to delve into too closely.

So she kept her cool.

"Welcome to the team, Jace. And it's Lillian. Just Lillian, nothing else."

Chapter 4

"Lily, hold up."

He smiled as he saw her shoulders stiffen at the name. Her curt instructions on the sparring mat not to call her anything but Lillian had just spurred his desire to call her by her old nickname.

But it was her whispered words as they had left the sparring area that had really caught his attention.

Don't say anything about who we were.

Jace wasn't sure if that meant their personal history or the gang-related activities they'd participated in during their youth. She might not have ever told anyone about that, especially the latter. Since she had never been arrested, nor had he, it wasn't in either of their permanent records. She didn't have to worry about him spilling her secret. Not that one anyway.

Working with her today, fighting with her, seeing

how everyone else interacted with her... Jace couldn't help being impressed. She had taken all the natural physical skills she'd had as a teenager—speed, flexibility, sheer grit—and had formed herself into nothing short of a warrior.

He'd known it from the first punch she'd thrown in the sparring ring. She'd always been feisty, but now she was deadly. Small but fierce.

She'd been the only woman in the room or on the field, and that hadn't seemed to bother her at all. The men hadn't treated her any differently than they treated each other. Even with their limitations because of injuries, the team members had relied on and functioned around each other's strengths.

No point in Lillian being the one on the bottom hoisting her teammates up the fifteen-foot wall that was part of the obstacle course. Could she have done it if she needed to? Jace had no doubt. But it wasn't her specialty, so instead the team had sent her up and over first. Nobody in this close-knit group played politics: you weren't given an assignment just because you were a man or a woman, you were given an assignment because of your strengths and talents.

Part of the course had also involved an underground tube, which there was no way in hell Jace was ever going to fit through. Neither were most of the men on the team. But Lillian had no problem. So she was sent.

Again, nothing to do with gender, everything to do with what was best for the team.

The men respected her, she respected them. Even the outsiders, the couple of guys besides Jace who obviously weren't regular members of the team, respected her.

And Jace would bet his next paycheck that everything Steve Drackett had said was true. Lillian had not been intimate with any of these men. There was no flash of recognition, no secret smiles…

No nicknames that had been only for them twelve years before. Like Jace had just said to her again.

"I told you, it's Lillian now. Not Lily. Nobody ever called me that but you anyway. And definitely not Tiger Lily."

He jogged the rest of the way to catch up with her. "Old habits. You know how it is."

"It's not like you've been saying my name very often in the past twelve years, so it shouldn't be too difficult for you to make the change."

"I'll do my best." He held his hand up with his fingers open in Mr. Spock's Vulcan *V* symbol. "Scout's honor."

She thawed minutely. "Jackass." She shook her head. "You were never a Boy Scout *or* a Vulcan."

And he wasn't going to stop calling her Lily, either.

They reached her car, a gray Honda Civic. About as unflashy a vehicle that was made. She opened the trunk and set her duffel bag inside. Then turned to him.

"Why are you here, Jace?"

Giving her as much truth as he could was probably his best option. "Ren McClement asked me. He and I served in the army together for a few years. You know him?"

She shrugged. "Not personally. But everyone knows *of* him. He's pretty much an Omega Sector legend."

"Steve Drackett and Ren said the team needed someone with experience who could jump right in.

To help with this LESS Summit thing." Jace looked over to where some of the others were coming out of the building. "No offense, but your team is a little shaky right now. And the two new guys are not exactly anything to write home about."

Lillian rubbed her fingers against her forehead. "That's for damn sure."

"Carnell doesn't play well with anyone. And that guy Saul Poniard is a little too flippant for my taste. That could be disastrous in a lot of situations."

"I agree. Steve recognizes it, too, but right now we don't have a lot of options."

He took a slight step closer to her, unable to stop himself. "Exactly. Ren knows me and knows he can trust me. And you guys needed someone with my skill set."

Talking coming from the parking lot caught their attention and Jace took a step back. They both waved to the other members of the team as they got in their vehicles one by one.

"And did you know I would be here when you said yes to Ren?" Lillian finally asked as her teammates drove away.

This was a much trickier question to answer. He knew he shouldn't have any qualms about lying to her. After all, she had been the completely dishonest one all those years ago. But he found the thought of telling her lies to be more difficult than he expected.

"Ren mentioned there was someone else here from Tulsa. A Lillian. But I couldn't be one-hundred-percent sure that it was you. You were impressive out there today, Tiger Lily."

She glared at him but didn't press the nickname issue. "Thanks."

"Seriously. You can handle yourself. I mean, you've always been able to handle yourself, but this was so much more than that."

Lillian leaned back against her car but didn't meet his eyes. "Thanks. You, too. Of course, I'm not surprised or anything. You were always built like a military man. Physically and mentally. I guess you just honed that over the years. So you got out?"

He nodded. "Yeah. For almost a year now. I loved the army, but it was time."

"Moving back to Tulsa?"

"No. Nothing for me there anymore. I actually bought some land here in Colorado. I'm opening a ranch of sorts."

Her brown eyes got big. "A ranch? I didn't know you had any interest in animals."

"I didn't, really, not when you knew me before. Not that there was much space for animals in downtown Tulsa anyway. But we had bomb dogs when I served over in the Middle East. Really found I had a love for them. So I'll be raising them and some other animals. Working with vets, too."

Hopefully providing people with PTSD a place to come and heal for a little while when things got to be too much.

"That sounds amazing. I'm glad your experience in the military was a good one."

"You would've done well in the military, too." The words were out of his mouth before he could stop them. Lillian should've gone into the military with him. That had been their plan. The military had catered to both of their strengths.

Now she *really* wouldn't look at him. "Yeah. I always thought so."

He had to decide right now whether to battle this out—what had happened between her and his brother—or leave it alone. He didn't want to fight with her the entire time he was here—that would be counterproductive to his ultimate mission of getting closer to her—but he didn't want to leave Daryl as the elephant constantly in the room between them.

He leaned in just slightly closer to her. "Twelve years was a long time ago. I think it's safe to let bygones be bygones, right?"

Now her brown eyes peered up at him. "Yeah, I'm sure that's true."

"And if it means anything, I'm sorry Daryl passed away so soon after the two of you got together. I don't know if it would've lasted or whatever, but I'm sorry you didn't get the chance to find out."

Jace had never seen the blood drain from someone's face so quickly. Lillian's slight weight fell back more heavily against her car. Jace couldn't help himself. He reached toward her. "Are you okay?"

Did the thought of Daryl's death still hit her so hard?

"Daryl and I would never have made it as a couple." Her laugh was bitter. "If there's one thing I'm sure about, that's it."

She pushed herself away from the car and he could almost see her withdraw into herself. Part of him wanted to press, but on the other hand, he *really* did not want to know intimate details about her relationship with his brother.

She turned and reached for the car door, opening it. Jace took a step closer, boxing her in.

They both felt it. The attraction between them. Daryl or not, it was still there. It had been buzzing around them all day, and now it was pooling in the air between them.

It didn't matter about twelve years, it didn't matter about Daryl, it didn't matter that they didn't know enough about each other now to be sure if they even liked each other.

The heat was still there, just like it had always been.

"You need to talk to Ren," she finally said, her back to him.

With his hand on the frame of her door and the other on the roof of her car, she was, in essence, trapped in his arms. If she turned around, it would almost be like in an embrace.

But she didn't turn as she continued. "Tell Ren this won't work. Help him find someone else."

"Why do I make you so uncomfortable, Tiger Lily? You're the one who gave me up, remember? And like we said, it was over a decade ago. It shouldn't matter now."

She shook her head with a little jerk. "It'll be easier for both of us if you're not here."

"Since when have you or I ever done anything the easy way? We are a good team. You had to have seen that out there today."

She nodded stiffly. Jace took a step forward, which caused Lillian to turn around. Suddenly all he could see was her mouth.

Cursing himself, he brought his lips down to hers.

He couldn't help himself, it was like being caught in some tractor beam from a science fiction movie.

Her lips were as soft as he remembered. As sweet. Sweeter, if possible.

She held herself stiffly for the first few seconds, as he teased her lips slowly, nibbling at them, but then he felt her give in. She sighed as if she couldn't fight it, either.

Her fingers slid into his hair, pulling him closer, and a sound of hunger left him, his mouth moving more hungrily on hers, their tongues twining. The attraction and heat pushed at them in waves.

When Jace finally stepped back, they both just stared at each other. Then, without another word, Lily got in her car and started it, pulling away so quickly that if he hadn't stepped back she might've run over his toes. All he could do was watch her drive away.

He muttered a curse under his breath. He'd been sent here to do a job, get more info, find out if Lillian had anything to do with this mole. Not kiss her senseless within the first few hours of his being back in the same general vicinity as her.

He'd counted on his sense of betrayal to help him keep his distance from her. To be able to remain objective and even cold.

Jace should've known better. He'd been many things around Lillian Muir, but cold was never one of them.

Seven hours into this mission and already things had become a hell of a lot more complicated.

Chapter 5

Showing up at Omega HQ the next day knowing Jace would be part of the team, part of her inner circle after twelve years of not having seen him at all, was pretty much inconceivable to Lillian.

And the fact that they'd made out yesterday? She couldn't even wrap her head around that. She didn't make out with people. Making out was for teenagers.

And she especially didn't make out in the Damn. Parking. Lot. Sure, the entire team had left by then, but still. What would people say if someone had seen her lip-locked with the new guy just a few hours after meeting him?

After the Tiger Lily comment, plus the fact that she'd mentioned it to Roman, everyone had heard or figured out she and Jace had a history. But that still didn't account for her sucking face with him.

And hell if heat didn't course through her at that thought. Again. Like it had done all night long.

Lillian had a lot of sleepless nights. But never had they involved being so caught up thinking about a kiss that she couldn't get to sleep. It was like something out of a Sweet Valley High novel.

She wished she could call Grace about it. Get her opinion as both psychiatrist and woman. Although she knew what Grace would tell her.

To take a chance. To be willing to leave herself unguarded for once.

But Lillian couldn't call Grace. Because Freihof had killed her.

That was enough to wipe all thoughts of teen-romance-books-style kisses out of her mind. Jace was here for a purpose. That purpose had nothing to do with Lillian and everything to do with keeping the LESS Summit safe, especially if Freihof decided to make some sort of play.

She would do well to remember that.

Jace Eakin was now, at least temporarily, taking up residence in her home—Omega HQ was much more home than the one-bedroom apartment that basically just housed her stuff. She would work with him. Get him up to speed. Keep it strictly professional. Definitely no more kissing.

In the locker room she changed out of her civilian clothes and into her training fatigues. She arrived in the SWAT station house living room thirty minutes before she was scheduled to be there. Derek was already there sitting at the conference table that took up a good section of the room, looking over paperwork for the team.

Jace was there, too, on the opposite side of the room.

Ignoring Jace, she walked over to Derek and sat down next to him. Derek slid a file over to her.

"Today's schedule."

Nothing out of the ordinary. Some PT, time to go over the building plans of the LESS Summit and one of Lillian's favorite drills.

"The Gauntlet. Haven't done that one in a while. Pretty brutal."

Derek grinned. "I thought it would be a good team-builder. Trial by fire." He glanced over his shoulder. "I'm going to have you pair up with Eakin."

"For the Gauntlet?"

"That and for the summit."

"Seriously?"

Lilian glanced over at Jace, who was leaning against the wall messing with his phone. The slight smirk lifting the corner of his mouth let her know he could hear everything being said.

She made a show of looking over the schedule again. "Maybe you should assign Jace to someone else. Team me with Saul. Or even Carnell." She swallowed her grimace at both offers. She didn't want to be assigned to either of them. It would limit her effectiveness at the summit.

"No. Carnell will be tactical command and computers only. He's not ready for active missions. Saul is better, but he's still not top-tier. Unless I see something over the next few days that makes me think Eakin doesn't have the skills I think he has, you two will be the Alpha team."

Everybody was important on a mission like protecting the LESS Summit, but the Alpha team was second in command to Derek, able to make judgment calls and decisions without approval when needed.

"Is that going to be a problem?" Derek asked when Lillian didn't respond. "There's obviously history between you two."

Yes, there was history, but she wasn't going to let that stop her from being as effective as possible. From making the entire team be as effective as possible. They'd need to be as strong as they could for whatever Damien Freihof had planned. Putting ancient history aside would be no problem.

Lillian glanced at Jace again, his blue eyes now piercing hers. She didn't look away. "No—no problem," she told Derek. "Our past was a long time ago. It's over. It was over before it even started."

It was over before it even started.

Lillian's quiet words stung even hours later. They shouldn't; after all, they were only the truth. Their relationship—at least the sexual side of it—had ended almost as soon as it began.

Trying to stick to the letting-bygones-be-bygones promise he made yesterday was proving a little more difficult than he had expected.

Jace pushed the entire conversation from his mind. There was no room for worrying about the distant past out here on the Gauntlet, which was a glorified obstacle course full of real-life dangers—fire, barbed wire and paintball-type ammunition that wouldn't seriously wound someone, but would hurt like hell if you got hit.

Harsh words were the least of his problems right now. Evidently there was some sort of multimillion-dollar training simulator nearby, but the way everyone had started crossing themselves and balking when it was mentioned made him think it wasn't very popular.

So here they were, out in a wooded area, having just crawled 500 yards under barbed wire. He and Lillian were a team, moving together. There were four other two-person teams made up of the various SWAT members he'd met yesterday. This exercise was part race, part team-building.

It wasn't unlike some of the obstacles and exercises he'd been a part of as an Army Ranger. He understood the importance of pushing the body and the mind, and doing it with the person who was going to have your back when you went into battle. It looked like he and Lillian would be that person for each other.

And she wasn't too happy about it.

Unhappy because she was being forced to work with an ex? Or unhappy because that ex was a new person on the team who might recognize some suspicious behavior on her part that her other colleagues could miss?

Either way, she was pushing those feelings aside now. She seemed vaguely surprised that he was able to keep up with her rapid crab-crawl pace under the barbed wire, roughly eighteen inches over the ground. Her small stature gave her a decided advantage for an obstacle of this type, and Lily knew how to use it.

But Jace knew how to make his body move quickly also. Even though the wire was sometimes only an inch or two over his shoulders and back, he used his abdominal muscles to keep himself straight and low, speed from his long reach making up for the caution he had to use because of his size.

As they reached the last of the wire and rolled out, they took cover behind some trees.

"You're fast," she said.

"Not my first rodeo."

The rest of the teams were making their way along the ground, Philip Carnell having the most difficult time.

"Do we need to go back in and help Carnell?" he said.

Lillian gave a brief shake of her head. "No. Normally Derek doesn't even allow him to do this sort of training even though Carnell insists he should be given the chance. But he may be needed to do something besides provide tactical assistance next week in Denver, so today he's in."

"Is he going to make it?" Carnell's partner was Saul Poniard, who might also be new, but was light-years ahead of Carnell when it came to physical abilities.

"Saul will get him through hopefully. And we'll get Philip out as a team if he needs it. Not that he'll thank us for it." Lillian shook her head. "As Alpha team, we're going to have our own problems. We'll need to take out the sniper before he picks everyone off."

"Sniper?"

Lillian grinned. "You didn't think Derek was going to miss the fun, did you? That man loves his paintball gun. You and I will have to take him out before everyone else gets there. That's Alpha team's primary challenge."

"Then let's get moving."

They navigated a series of obstacles, including a fifty-foot rope climb, before coming to a pile of five large, heavy logs.

"Each of these has to be maneuvered through this next section." Lillian referred to the logs. "Every two-person team is responsible for one log. We choose to make it either hard on us or hard on the other teams coming behind us."

Jace raised an eyebrow. "So…heaviest?"

Lillian's smile was huge and he had to fight to keep it from taking his breath away. "I was hoping you'd agree. But it's not going to be easy."

"Then I guess you better stop grinning like an idiot and get to it."

Jace couldn't stop the grin on his own face, either. Lily wanted to push herself. That was something he understood. He had known it about her even back in the day, and it was one of the reasons he had thought the army would be such a good fit for her also.

He tamped down the spring of bitterness over the way things had turned out. Bygones. Much more important to focus on the problems at hand.

The log was damn heavy. The exercise required them to lift the log over some obstacles, under others, and even carry it over their heads as they crossed a small creek.

Lillian never complained, never slipped in supporting her part of the awkward piece of wood. By the time they threw it down half a mile later, they were both pushing the edges of exhaustion. They slumped together against the back of a tree, shoulder to shoulder, so they could each catch their breath.

"Now we have to take out Derek and his evil paintball gun." Her eyes were closed as she allowed her body to attempt to recapture some of its strength just as he did.

"How do we do that with no gun of our own?"

"Technically for this exercise, all we have to do to defeat him is for one of us to make it over the finish line without getting hit." She didn't sound very enthused about the idea.

"Easier said than done?"

Those brown eyes opened. "Derek is a mastermind at this. Plus, he knows all our strengths. We have about a five-percent success rate when it comes to getting past him."

"What about splitting up and running from two different directions?"

She shook her head. "We've tried. It's such a narrow strip of land, he can cover it and almost always get both people before they get across. We don't have very much cover."

"What are the rules about just one person getting across? If that's all we need, we should wait for everyone else, protect one person and everyone else can take the hits."

"First, the hits aren't gentle. They hurt like hell." She obviously had firsthand knowledge. "Second, to keep us from always grouping, the rule is, whoever makes it across the finish line unhit has two minutes to get the wounded the fifteen yards across no-man's-land. Almost impossible if it's one person trying to get multiple people across. And particularly impossible with the group coming up behind us."

Jace leaned his head back against the tree. He could hear the frustration in her voice. The Omega SWAT team was not up to the level it usually was. Too many new people. Too many wounded.

"I have a plan," he said.

Now he had her full attention.

"We'll use Derek's assumptions against him, with a little bit of trickery thrown in. But I'll warn you, this won't be easy. Particularly on you. We won't be playing to your strengths. But we will be using your strength."

She sat up. "Okay. I'm game. What's your plan?"

"Derek expects you and me to make a break before the rest of the team gets here. To try to overcompensate for their limitations. To use your speed and my strength to get everyone else through."

"And we're not going to do that?"

Jace just smiled.

Ten minutes later the other members of the team began catching up with them. Jace explained his plan. Everyone stared at Lillian once Jace told them what she would need to do.

Even Lillian looked a little skeptical.

"You can do it," he said.

"You're going to take a lot of hits," she responded. "Derek won't like it and won't show any mercy."

Jace grinned. "I can handle a few bruises."

"Are you sure you don't want me to make a dash for it?" Saul asked, enthusiasm fairly radiating from him. "I'm fast."

Jace shook his head. "No, that's exactly what he's expecting. For you or Lily to run, to try to use your speed. And you're too big for me to use in this plan."

Saul grimaced. "Are you sure she can handle her end of this?"

Jace shook his head at the same time Lillian's eyes narrowed. Saul might be new, but he would learn fast not to underestimate Lillian if he wanted to stay part of this team. "Don't worry. I'll do my part."

It was a pretty damn big part.

Jace turned to Philip. "You've got to sell it, to get us more time. Derek will come after you just to teach you a lesson."

Philip didn't look thrilled, but then again, Jace wasn't sure he ever did.

"I can handle a few bruises," Philip echoed.

Jace nodded at the other team members. They weren't excited about being left out of most of the action, but they understood the advantage of his plan. Of keeping Derek off balance as long as possible.

"Remember." Lillian turned to him. "Rules are that you can only take five more steps after you're hit. Make them count."

They all stood and made their way closer to the twenty-yard square area Derek was guarding. There was some cover of trees and boulders, but not a lot. Derek definitely had the tactical advantage.

Jace and Lillian separated from the rest of the team. Philip and Saul would be drawing Derek's attention—hopefully—from the other end of the field.

"If Saul gets all gung-ho and takes off, then gets hit, this isn't going to work," Lillian whispered. "I'm not sure it's going to work even if he doesn't."

Jace couldn't help himself—he bent down and kissed her, fast and hard. "If there's anyone I would trust to get me out of a situation when I'm wounded, it's you."

"You're nuts, Eakin." She shook her head. "Let's try this crazy plan."

They waited for the signal. It came just moments later.

"Because we have to stick together, Poniard, don't you dare leave me here to get shot." Philip's words were soft, like they weren't meant to be heard. Jace and Lillian could barely make them out.

But that meant Derek could, too.

Jace didn't wait. He scooped up Lillian—she rolled herself into as tight a ball as possible—and he ran. He only had to make it halfway before he got shot. Far enough that his back would be to Derek, and the team leader wouldn't see the hidden person Jace had curled in his arms. Derek would be expecting Lily to try to run her own route and make it through. Wouldn't expect her to agree to be carried.

"Damn it, Saul, wait!" Philip again, hopefully going from the script, and not saying it because Saul really had taken off.

It bought Jace the few extra seconds he needed. He kept Lillian tucked high against his chest as he felt the first paintball hit his back. Three more followed rapidly.

Damn, those *did* hurt.

This whole plan was relying on the fact that Derek wouldn't stay and watch Jace "fall" onto the boulder in front of him. He had too much else he had to keep track of. Jace got his five more steps in, then set Lillian on the ground. She immediately began sprinting toward the finish line.

Whooshes of air blew as more shots were fired from the paintball gun. But not at Lillian.

Philip squeaked, "Ow, damn it." He took his five steps closer to the finish line, then fell.

Jace turned to watch and saw the exact moment Derek realized he'd been played. He turned and aimed his gun at Lillian, but she was already crossing the line.

Derek smiled and looked down at his watch. "Okay, Muir. You've got two minutes to get them both across if you want to claim your victory."

Lillian sprinted back to Philip first. She sat him up and then swung his arm over her shoulder, dragging him across to the safe area.

She stopped to take a breath, looking Jace in the eye. He weighed significantly more than Philip did.

But Jace had no doubt she could do it—that she would get him over to that safe zone. Especially now, with the entire team looking on.

She jogged back to him and got down to business. The boulder helped, putting Jace more upright. But she would still have to fireman-carry him. There was no way she could drag him like she had done with Philip.

He could hear the cheers of their teammates as she pulled his torso around her shoulders and slipped her hand through his legs and wrapped her arm around his knees. A huge groan came out of her small body as her legs straightened and she took his whole weight, lifting him off the ground.

She couldn't walk straight, and she might not have been able to walk for long—especially after the grueling workout they'd already gone through on the course—but Lillian got them both over the finish line just as the time was running out.

Jace immediately dropped his leg to the ground and took his weight as the rest of the team ran over, hooting and hollering. Even Philip was grinning. Lillian dropped back against a tree to get her breath. Everyone was slapping both of them on the back until Derek came over and told them to complete the rest of the course.

"Good job, you two," he told them as they walked to the next section. "Completely had me fooled. Some partnerships are just meant to be."

Jace didn't say anything. He'd once thought that exact same thing also.

He'd been wrong.

Chapter 6

Everything seemed to take a turn for the better after the Gauntlet in terms of team building. The paintball win had given them all the boost they'd needed and the confidence that they could work together success-fully. Lillian was glad to see it.

What she wasn't quite so glad about was that Jace seemed to be within arm's reach every time she turned around for the next five days.

All the damn time.

Admittedly, a lot of it was the training they were doing as a team. More obstacle courses. The shoot-ing range. The different scenarios within the multi-million-dollar simulator on the outskirts of the Omega Sector campus.

It came as no surprise to her that Jace fit right into the team as if he'd been there all along. He'd always been charming and affable even back when they were teenagers. The polar opposite of his bastard brother. Tension coursed through her body at the thought of Daryl, so Lillian pushed him from her mind. She'd had twelve years of practice doing that.

But charm meant nothing to a SWAT team without the skills to back it up. Jace had those in spades, too, and they'd been especially evident when he'd proven himself with the Gauntlet plan. His sharpshooting abilities impressed even Ashton Fitzgerald, the team's sharpshooter. Jace's close-quarters fighting skills she already personally knew about. He also had a specialty in explosive devices.

When Ashton, team clown, asked Jace if he would go steady with him, Lillian knew Jace had won over the team.

Saul and Philip weren't too happy about Jace's instant inclusion into the inner circle, when they'd both been fighting so hard for that same acceptance. But there was just an innate authority with Jace that neither Saul nor Philip had. Nobody said anything about it, but they all knew it.

The parts of Jace that had drawn her when they were both teenagers were even more prevalent now. His strength. His focus. His dedication.

Add that to the fact that he was opening a ranch where he would raise animals that would help soldiers with PTSD? How was she supposed to process that?

She wanted distance from him but couldn't get it. There literally was no time. The LESS Summit was coming up in just days and they would all need to function seamlessly as a team by then.

They trained day and night, since the summit would

require them in both daylight and nighttime hours. Sometimes that meant little sleep or crashing on whatever couch or floor was available in the team break room.

Jace definitely wasn't a diva. Just like everyone else, when they had a break in the middle of a twenty-four-hour training session, he found a spot, curled his head back and promptly fell asleep.

But damn it, that had ended up being right next to her every single time.

Just like how every time they were at the practice range he ended up next to her.

And every time they were in the SWAT van traveling somewhere, it was his leg pressed up against hers.

When they ate. When they did their ten-mile runs.

Always there. Always next to her.

He never did anything to make any sort of big deal out of it, hadn't kissed her again or made any moves on her since that brief kiss at the Gauntlet. But he didn't have to. Lillian was aware of him in a way she hadn't been aware of someone…for twelve years.

And it felt good. In the scariest way possible.

Her body and mind trusted Jace in a way she hadn't been able to trust another man in twelve years…actually her whole life. She wasn't well versed in psychology—damn, she missed Grace Parker—but Lillian knew enough about her own mind to know that the passion between the two of them a dozen years ago was the only untainted memory of sex that she had.

Sometimes she still thought about those nights they'd had together. How uninhibited and all-encompassing her feelings had been. They'd had the entire world and forever in their future. No grasp at all of how quickly life could change.

She and Jace had been friends for a long time before they were lovers, since Jace was older than her and refused to sleep with her until she turned eighteen. Then they'd only had about a month after her eighteenth birthday before…

Before he left for the army. Before everything in her world crumbled. Lillian felt her body turn cold even now.

Jace seemed to have forgiven her for *leaving* him—God, the thought still made her want to vomit—for Daryl.

It was good that he'd forgiven her, without even having one iota of understanding about the true circumstances.

Jace was a good man. He'd been a good man then, and he was still a good man now. So she was glad he had gotten over his sense of betrayal at her perceived actions.

And if she had any choice in the matter, Jace would go to his grave being the man who was good enough to forgive an ex-girlfriend for running off with his brother. He would never know the truth.

Because that would just hurt him so much worse.

"What are you thinking about over there?" Jace's voice broke in to her thoughts. "Whatever it is, it can't be good."

This time he was across the table from her in the Omega canteen. It was lunchtime, and while they had been here all night for a dark-based training op, they'd all be leaving to go home for a break soon. The team would be going to Denver tomorrow.

She shrugged, ignoring his question, since there was no way in hell she was going to answer it truthfully anyway.

"You worried about something concerning the summit?" he asked between bites of his sandwich.

This she could answer. "To be honest, I'm concerned about everything to do with this summit. Hitting something this high-profile may not align perfectly with Damien Freihof's MO, but I think it aligns with his mind-set."

"I thought Freihof had been using other people to do his dirty work. Stirring up the pot with people in the past who had an ax to grind with Omega agents and helping him try to get their revenge."

"He has." Lillian's hands balled into fists. "But then he killed Grace Parker, our team psychiatrist, himself. Brutally, and in front of everyone. I think he's escalating. And I think trying to humiliate Omega by attacking the summit would definitely suit his purposes."

"Sounds like he has it in for you guys. What's that about?"

"Evidently we had a hand in his wife's death. She was killed when Omega went in on a bank raid."

"Freihof brought his wife along when he robbed a bank?"

"No. Freihof has been involved with a lot of different criminal activities for the last fifteen years. But in this case, evidently they both just happened to be in the wrong place at the wrong time. Someone was robbing the bank, the wife freaked out and tried to make a run for it when SWAT arrived, and she got shot and killed. By us. And Freihof has decided to make everyone who has ever been a part of Omega Sector pay for that mistake."

Jace seemed to process all that as he ate. "And he maybe has someone helping him? Someone inside Omega?"

Lillian shrugged. "There's been no official word, but a lot of rumors. And some of the stuff Freihof has known, he couldn't possibly have known without help from the inside. I have no doubt there's a traitor within Omega, as much as I hate to say it. But like Derek said, we can't all go around accusing one another of being the mole and expect to work effectively as a team."

Jace nodded, studying her.

It had been a long few days and they were all supposed to go home and rest. They would all need to be on high alert at the summit.

If Lillian was Freihof, the summit was where she would strike. If he could take down the LESS device, he would be serving a great blow to law enforcement all over the country. Doing that while humiliating Omega Sector seemed to be cut directly out of his playbook.

Not to mention the summit would be crowded with politicians, law-enforcement leaders and ordinary people there to observe or protest. Plenty of people to try to hurt or kill.

"You headed out?" Jace asked as they finished up their food.

She wasn't particularly interested in going back to her empty apartment. She tended to spend as little time there as possible. But no need to advertise that fact. "Absolutely. We all need to get a little R and R before heading to Denver."

The rest of the team had already left. Most of the guys had families now. A lot of times Lillian was invited over to their houses for meals or just to hang out. But not right now. The wound of losing Grace Parker was still too fresh, too open. All the guys just wanted to be with their wives and children and hold them close and thank God for them.

Lillian wasn't going to boo-hoo just because there was nobody thanking God she was alive. If Jace wasn't here, she would probably head out to a bar and find a guy to hook up with for a few hours. It was never fulfilling, and sometimes it was downright scary the way she checked out emotionally during sex, the way she didn't remember any of it even though it had happened just a few minutes before.

But anything was better than sitting at home alone.

Yet something about Jace being nearby made the thought of some random, emotionless hookup seem even more unappealing.

"How about you?" she asked him. "I don't even know where you're staying."

"Hotel a few blocks from here. There didn't seem to be much point in renting a place, since I was only going to be here a couple weeks. And I didn't want to have to drive back and forth every day from my ranch."

That made sense. And they were probably paying him enough to make it worth his while anyway.

"Okay." She nodded. "I guess I'll see you tomorrow."

"Yeah, see you tomorrow."

They dumped their trays and headed off in separate directions for the men's and women's locker rooms.

Lillian was used to being in here by herself. It usually didn't bother her. As a matter of fact, there had been plenty of times when she had to change clothes in front of the guys. She honestly didn't even think they saw her as a woman anymore.

She hardly saw *herself* as a woman anymore. She had all the woman parts but didn't tend to have many of the emotions that were tied to the female gender. She couldn't remember the last time she had cried.

She didn't mind being the only female on the team. She respected her colleagues, they respected her and they trusted her to do her job. She would die before she let down the team. She was part of something bigger and more important than herself, and she loved that.

But right now she just felt pretty damn alone. Not to mention all ramped up to get to the action tomorrow.

So she might as well stay here for a while longer and look over again the plans of the Denver city hall, officially known as the Denver City and County Building, where the summit would take place.

The LESS device was something that would change the face of law enforcement forever. Would allow a true merging of technology in all branches. The ramifications would be significant. Interstate cooperation would be much easier with the LESS system.

It was her job—the team's job—to make sure that happened. Studying the building plans one more time could only help.

She brought her duffel bag out of the changing room with her and moved to the main computer work space area in their building. SWAT members didn't have their own desks, but they had computers available for the team's use. They were mostly used for training, updating education, or situations like this, where someone wanted more details about the particulars of an op.

The big desk gave her plenty of room to set up a notebook and take some notes, as she brought up the building plans.

The 3-D replication of the building allowed her to take a virtual tour. Extremely helpful. But she knew that whatever she could find on a computer, Damien Freihof could, too.

She studied the plans for nearly an hour, going over each window, doorway, elevator shaft and staircase. She wanted to be able to find her way around the building even if she was blindfolded.

She closed down her browser and drew the plans of the first floor from memory, then compared it back to the actual drawing. Pretty close.

Lillian sat back in her chair, stretching her arms over her head and her legs out in front of her. That was enough for today. She'd already been up all night with the training. It was time to go home.

She just wished she had someone to go home to.

She shut down the computer and stood up, giving a small gasp when she saw Jace leaning against the wall a few feet behind her.

"You're lucky I didn't have a weapon, Eakin. What the hell are you doing standing there all stalker-like?"

"I didn't want to interrupt your memorization exercise."

"I wanted to make sure I was as familiar with the building as I could be. I thought you had already left."

"Smart. And no, not yet. I had a little bit of work to do here."

She couldn't help noticing how good he looked in jeans and a black long-sleeved shirt rolled up at the wrists. He even had his boots on. He'd owned similar ones back in the day.

His brown hair was cut shorter than it had been then, closer to military regulation, although it had obviously grown out a little bit. The tips of her fingers itched with the need to run her hands through it. Those icy blue eyes stared at her with a touch of friendliness and something she couldn't quite discern.

But one thing she could discern for certain: he was the sexiest-looking thing she had seen in a long time. Whatever she was feeling right now definitely wasn't emotionless. The opposite, in fact.

There would never be anything emotionless when it came to her and Jace Eakin.

The thought of feeling something—something *real*—while a man touched her had Lillian crossing to Jace. Just once she wished she was more of a high-heels-and-short-skirt sort of girl. A girl who knew how to do something with her hair besides pull it back in a ponytail. A girl who knew how to put on makeup to cause her eyes to look mysterious and sultry.

A girl who knew how to seduce a man like Jace.

But she wasn't that girl. All she could do was make her offer straight up with no pretense.

She stopped when she was directly in front of him. From this close, all she could do was remember that kiss from a few days ago in the parking lot.

"If you're done with your work, why don't you come over to my apartment? We've got eighteen hours before we have to report back here. Seems like we ought to be able to find something to do with that time."

Passion—the same heat she felt—flared in his eyes for just a moment as he eased closer to her. She felt his fingers grip her hips and knew she would feel those lips on hers again any second. There was nothing she wanted more in the world. Those kisses, as much as she'd tried to tamp them down, had never been far from her conscious mind.

But then his fingers clenched on her body for just a second before letting her go. He stepped back. Her eyes flew up to his, but his handsome face was carefully masked.

"I don't think that's such a good idea. For a number of reasons."

Everything that had been burning inside Lillian turned to ice. She took a step back, feeling like he'd slapped her.

"Tiger Lily, it's not that I don't feel the attraction," he continued.

Maybe she'd been wrong, maybe he hadn't truly been able to forgive her for leaving him. "It's about before. About Daryl. Right?"

He shook his head. "No. It's not even that. It's about now, and us being a team and…"

She waited for him to finish, but he didn't. Whatever he *wasn't* saying was just as important as what he was. But ultimately it came down to one thing, didn't it?

She took another short step back from him. "And we really don't know each other, do we? Not anymore." Something flickered in his eyes and he reached for her again, but Lillian moved smoothly out of his reach. "You're right, Jace, this is probably a bad idea. The team has to come first. And casual hookups probably just aren't your thing."

His dark head tilted to the side. "Are they yours? They weren't at one time."

She knew he was talking about how she had felt about her mother when Lillian was growing up. How she'd disdained her mother's constant revolving door of men. How she swore she would never be that way. That sex would never be a meaningless act.

She laughed softly even as she felt the wounded heart she hid deep inside crack a little further. For a long time, Lillian hadn't thought about that promise she'd made to herself. How she'd utterly broken it. She couldn't even blame it on Daryl. That had been all on her. "I guess we all change. Grow up. Face the real world."

"Lily…"

Lillian knew she had to get out of here. She couldn't continue to face his blue eyes without crumbling. Knew that if he asked her about her secrets now she would tell him.

She closed her eyes and regrouped. When she opened them a couple seconds later, she was able to put a smirk on her face. She punched Jace good-naturedly on the arm. "Get some rest, Eakin. I'll catch you tomorrow. Big day."

Without another word she turned, grabbed her bag and walked out the door.

Alone. As always.

Chapter 7

The next morning when the team met at Omega Sector headquarters in preparation to depart to the LESS Summit, Jace wanted to punch a wall.

Still wanted to punch a wall. He'd wanted to do so ever since yesterday afternoon, when Lillian offered... whatever it was she had offered.

He hadn't known how to handle it. On one hand, there was nothing he wanted more than to get Lillian in his bed. His body didn't seem to care what had happened between them twelve years ago, or care that she might be the traitor.

But he found that he couldn't betray her in that way. Couldn't take her to bed just to get close to her to find out more about her activities. Ridiculous that he would take her feelings into consideration when it came to the issue of betrayal.

He'd watched her yesterday on the computer for a long time. She'd been so focused she hadn't even realized he was there. She'd studied the building plans, examining them over and over until she was able to draw them without looking.

Unfortunately, the action didn't necessarily prove her innocence. Maybe she was studying the plans because she wanted to be as prepared as she could possibly be as a member of the SWAT team.

Or maybe she was studying the building plans because she had nefarious reasons of her own.

All Jace could say for sure was that she had not tried to communicate with anyone or leave any sort of cryptic messages while he'd been watching, as the mole had been known to do.

Jace's gut said the same thing about her now that it had said about her back in Ren's office: she was not the traitor. But God knew his gut had been wrong about Lillian before.

He'd basically glued himself to her side for the past week and all he'd found was that she was a damn fine SWAT team member. He hadn't found anything else that would suggest she was the mole. Lillian had secrets, Jace had no doubt whatsoever that she had secrets. But he didn't think those secrets had anything to do with national security.

That look on her face when she'd mentioned casual sex was still haunting him. Hell, Jace hadn't been a saint for the last decade. He'd had plenty of casual relationships with women in that time. He didn't hold a double standard. If Lillian had chosen to have a slew of casual sexual encounters, that was her prerogative.

What gutted him had been the look in her eyes,

the completely humorless laugh, when she said that those sexual encounters had been her choice. Obviously somewhere deep inside she wasn't okay with it. She was hurting herself.

Steve Drackett's words of concern about possible sexual assault in her past had been echoing in Jace's mind for the last eighteen hours. Ever since Lillian had offered a casual hookup with eyes that told him she hated herself.

He was back to wanting to punch a wall again.

Not to mention he'd turned her down, which had probably stung also, even though he was doing it—or *not* doing it—for the right reasons.

Regardless, Lillian was now in a different vehicle on the way to Denver this morning. She'd been coldly polite to him as they'd all worked together to pack up equipment. Not unfriendly or rude, just obviously not interested in prolonging any conversations with him. The closeness they'd been building through sheer proximity over the last week was now completely gone.

Jace had no doubt Lillian would be coolly professional to him throughout the mission. That wasn't going to help him get close enough to her to find out if she was the one sabotaging Omega Sector. But he wasn't going to sleep with her to get that info, either.

Especially not after how she had looked at him yesterday, with such shadows in those brown eyes.

Jace was going to have to concentrate on the mission in front of him. At this point, if the mole was going to strike, and Lillian was that mole, all he could do was be close enough to stop it. After that, hell if he knew what he would do if she was the mole.

The LESS Summit started in two days. Already people were gathering in Denver. It was going to be crowded, full of angry and excited people. The situation was already hectic; throw in a potential terrorist attack and the situation became even worse.

They didn't even make it all the way into downtown Denver before they hit trouble.

"Change in plans, everybody," Derek said from the front seat as the SUV picked up speed. "Just got a call from Denver PD. Evidently, as expected, all the crazies have rolled into town with word of the LESS Summit. There's a jumper on a highway bridge and we're closest. They need our help."

Jace could see the shift come over the team, especially the more experienced ones.

"A jumper? As in someone trying to commit suicide?" Philip asked. "Why the hell is SWAT being called in? Just let the person jump."

Nobody responded. Being part of a SWAT team was not just about hunting bad guys, shooting and securing buildings. Sometimes it was about defusing situations. Helping people who didn't know how to help themselves. It had been the same for the US Army Rangers.

If someone couldn't understand that, they probably shouldn't be on the team at all. This was probably a big part of the reason Carnell was only temporary.

"Shut up, Philip," Saul muttered, rolling his eyes. Everyone else was obviously thinking the same thing.

They pulled up at the bridge crossing the highway. Local police were stopping traffic on either side of the road, where a man was standing on the highest part of the overpass, on the outside of the railing, one arm around a light post.

If he let go, there would be nothing to stop him from flying onto the busy highway below.

As they got out of the vehicle, a uniformed officer came running over to them. Derek showed him credentials and the officer fully admitted to being in over his head.

"He's been out there for about ten minutes. Hasn't said a word."

Lillian and the rest of the team from the second vehicle jogged over to where they were.

"Okay." Derek glanced at the man's chest to get his name. "Officer Milburn, we're going to take over if that's all right with you."

Milburn nodded enthusiastically.

"Everybody on open comms, channel A," Derek continued. "Ashton, Saul, Jace—you need to clear everyone else off this bridge. Everybody wants to be a YouTube sensation, but let's not make it easy. Carnell, get on the laptop. As soon as we can get this guy's name, you find whatever info you can on him. Lillian, you're with me."

Lillian shook her head. "Derek, you know I'm no good with the touchy-feely stuff."

Derek nodded. "Just in case he responds to a woman better than a man. Lillian and I will be on open comms. None of us deal with this sort of situation a lot, so if you've got insight, let us have it."

The open comm channel meant that everyone could hear anytime someone else spoke without them having to press a button. It could be chaotic, but in a situation like this, also useful. Jace jogged over to the other side of the bridge and moved the barrier back farther. They couldn't stop people from recording what was happening, but like Derek had said, they could make it as difficult as possible.

Jace heard Derek ask the man his name. Ask if it was okay if they stood there and talked. Explained that they wouldn't come near him.

Derek did everything right. But the man wasn't interested in talking.

"Hey, guys." It was Saul. "I've got an empty vehicle over here that doesn't belong to anyone. Registration of the vehicle says it belongs to an Oliver Lewis."

"Start running the name, Philip," Derek said softly. "You try talking to him, Lillian."

Jace watched as Lillian took her turn, easing a little closer to the man. "Hi, sir, my name is Agent… Lillian. My name is Lillian. Can you just tell us your name?"

The man shook his head.

"Is your name Oliver Lewis?" Lillian continued gently. "There's a car registered to someone named Oliver Lewis. Is that you?"

"Don't come any closer," the man said even though they hadn't moved. "You can't stop me."

"No, sir," Derek said immediately, hands out. "We won't come any closer. We just want to know if that's your name."

The man gave the tiniest of nods.

"That was a confirmation on the ID," Jace said so Derek wouldn't have to take a chance on talking and spooking the guy. "Run everything you have on him, Carnell. Hurry."

Derek and Lillian continued to try to get Oliver to talk, but without much success. Finally Philip came back on the comm.

"Oliver Lewis. Twenty-seven years old. Married. Got out of the army six months ago after nine years in."

Lillian turned away from Oliver to look over at him. "Jace, you try."

He met her eyes from across the bridge, but spoke softly into the comm unit. "I don't have any background in this sort of thing."

"But you're military. Maybe he'll respond to you."

"Yes, Jace," Derek whispered. "We're not getting through to him at all. If anything we're doing more harm."

He could at least try. He jogged up, slowing to a walk as he neared.

"Oliver," Derek said, "this is Jace Eakin. Jace isn't a normal part of our team, he just stepped in to help out."

"Yeah," Jace agreed. "I just got out of the service. They needed some help here with all the protests and stuff happening in Denver this week, so I'm assisting."

"You were in the service?"

"Army. Tenth Special Forces group."

"Ranger," Oliver whispered, turning to look at Jace for the first time.

Lillian and Derek were backing away to give Jace and Oliver some semblance of privacy. Jace nodded. "That's right. You army also?"

"How did you know that?"

"Not many people would know that the Tenth Special Forces group are Rangers unless they'd been in the army themselves. How long have you been out?"

"Six months."

Jace took the slightest step closer. "How long were you in?"

"Since I was eighteen. Was the only thing I've ever known. And now…" He trailed off.

Jace nodded. "Adjusting back to civilian life can be really difficult. Especially if you did some hard tours."

"Two back-to-back in Afghanistan."

Jace asked Oliver questions about his tours. Where he'd been located. Tried to get him to talk about friends, other men and women who'd served in his unit. He continually shifted closer under the guise of discussion, or leaned against the railing, or just listened.

Although it really wasn't a guise at all.

Jace would've sat and listened for however long Oliver wanted. People like him were the reason he was opening his ranch in Colorado. For guys like Oliver, who just needed somewhere to go for a while as they sorted out the mess in their head, tried to adjust back into a world that didn't always fit how they'd been trained.

"Oliver," Jace finally said after they'd talked for nearly twenty minutes. "Why don't you step back over the railing? Whatever it is you're feeling? Let's just wait it out, try to find another way. A less permanent solution to whatever's going on with you."

"I hit my wife," Oliver responded, his tone dripping with remorse. "I freaked out during a nap and punched her in the face. She's pregnant, Jace. How can I be trusted to be around her? To be around a baby, for God's sake. I'm toxic."

Jace tensed, prepared to make a dive for Oliver if he let go of the railing right now. He was almost close enough to pull back.

"We've already got the wife on the way, Jace." Derek's voice came through the comm. "She's been frantic looking for him. Definitely doesn't want him to do this."

"That's really hard, man." Jace might not be schooled in talking down a potential suicide victim, but he knew enough not to discount Oliver's feelings. "Have you talked to her since it happened?"

"Why would she ever want to talk to me again?"

. "How long have you two been married?"

Oliver glanced at him. "Four years."

"Well, maybe your wife doesn't want to throw out four years' worth of good, just because of one moment of bad."

"She woke me up in the middle of a nightmare and I hit her. Hard. Before I even knew what was happening. Could've broken her jaw. She was scared of me. I could see it."

Jace nodded. "Yeah, but knowing she might have to give you space and wanting you to end your life are two different things. You can see that, right?"

Oliver shrugged. But at least he was holding on to the railing again.

"Listen," Jace continued, "I know this isn't an answer to all your problems, and you and your wife are going to need to work through a lot, it sounds like. But I have a ranch I'm setting up, just outside Colorado Springs. Horses, dogs, hell, even a few cats. It's a place for vets to come, spend some time."

"You're just making that up. Just trying to get me to come down."

"No, man, I'm not. Like Derek said, I'm just helping out with law enforcement temporarily. The ranch is going to be my full-time work. Soldiers can come, sort stuff out in their head while riding or walking or just hanging out with the animals. People like you, Oliver. Because if you feel this bad about what happened with your wife, that means you want to do what's right. I can't guarantee the ranch will help, but it's at least worth a try before you leave your unborn child with no father at all."

"You're not lying?" For the first time, there was the slightest bit of hope in Oliver's voice. "This place really exists?"

"I give you my word, as one man who served to another, I am not lying. You can be the first person to come visit. Hell, you can come help me get everything set up."

Oliver just stared at him.

"This bridge is always going to be here, Oliver." Jace knew this might not be the right thing to say, but it was the truth. "There will always be a way to kill yourself if you want to go that route. But today why don't you choose to do something different? To give life a chance and see if there's any way to fix things that maybe a few months from now might not be as broken as you think."

Oliver stared at him for a long time before finally nodding and stepping one leg back on the safe side of the railing. As soon as his other leg was also over, Jace crossed the few feet to the man and pulled him in for a hug.

"I was telling the truth," Jace said. "I don't know what happens now, but I'll make sure you get the information about the ranch."

Jace stepped back when he heard a woman screaming Oliver's name and running toward him. She didn't give him any choice but to catch her as she leaped at him, sobbing.

The size of the bruise covering half her face left no doubt that this was Oliver's wife. But instead of being mad, she pulled back from him and cupped his cheeks in her hands. "Together. Whatever it is, we get through it *together.*"

As he walked back to the rest of the team, Jace realized Oliver probably wasn't going to need his ranch. He was one of the lucky ones. Oliver had the support he needed right at home.

Chapter 8

Lillian punched the lumpy pillow under her head as she lay in the too-soft hotel bed. Damn things were keeping her from getting any sleep.

Who was she kidding? The bed and pillow had nothing to do with her not getting rest. She never slept well outside her own bed. Hell, she didn't sleep all that great in her own.

Too much time, alone, in the dark, to think…to remember? Not her friend.

Daytime and her job at Omega Sector allowed her to stay busy, to stay focused, to push herself to her limits.

To keep the demons at bay.

But nighttime, especially after a day like today, when she hadn't expended a great deal of physical energy? Not as easy. The darkness seemed to press in on her.

How many times had she come back to her senses in a bed sort of like this one with a guy she didn't quite remember, her skin crawling with the knowledge of what she'd done? Again.

Jace had been right to turn her down. She was damaged in ways that would taint every relationship she had. And it might have started with Daryl, but Lillian couldn't deny that her own choices, the patterns she allowed to take over in her sexual escapades, were what had perpetuated the problem.

And watching Jace today, talking to that vet, connecting to the man on such an honest, authentic level… Lillian rubbed her chest in the general vicinity of her heart. He was going to raise dogs, horses. Animals that would help people who'd been traumatized by war.

She couldn't help wondering if a dog might help her through the trauma of a different kind of war. Maybe it could provide the companionship she'd refused to acknowledge she so desperately needed.

Who was she kidding? She couldn't take care of a puppy. A dog needed attention. Love. A regular schedule. She wasn't capable of any of those.

She glanced at her watch to find it was 3:30 a.m. and swung her legs around to the floor. She might as well get up. She knew well enough she wouldn't be able to get back to sleep.

Knew that it was just a matter of time before the darkness around her—even though she had a light on in the bathroom—started to eat at her sanity. Lillian *never* slept in the dark

She would go for a walk. It was what she usually did. Although sometimes those walks led her to a local bar and then to the home of some nameless guy for meaningless sex. She always hoped that it might be different. That she might connect. *Feel* something.

She had no desire to go find some random guy now. The kisses with Jace had just reminded her how utterly empty those other encounters were. Attempts to punish herself, Grace had said. Lillian had scoffed. What did she have to punish herself for? she'd argued.

But Lillian knew the list was long and never far from her mind. And growing.

For not being able to fight back against Daryl.

For not being strong enough to escape and go to Jace.

For not having the guts to admit to him—then or now—what had happened and why she was so broken.

For not being able to stop Freihof from killing Grace and hurting others.

Lillian was dressed in her cargo pants and T-shirt in under a minute. She grabbed her jacket from the closet and left the voices behind.

The chill of the February air helped chase away the voices. There weren't many people around this area of downtown at this hour. The bars had already let out, and most of the buildings were government or offices anyway—no one was burning the midnight oil.

Lillian found herself wandering down toward the Denver City and County Building, the picturesque government building where the LESS Summit would be taking place.

The massive white marble building was iconic in the state of Colorado, beautiful and dignified. Although she knew the plans almost by heart, she wandered around it slowly, getting a feel for it from the outside. It would not be an easy building to secure. Multiple entrances and exit points in the form of doors and windows. The doors would need to be secure, although the windows had alarms and none of them would be open.

Lillian did a double take at one of the windows she was just thinking about on the far side of the building from where she stood.

Someone was easing themselves inside one of the windows lowest to the ground. The same windows that Omega, with the help of Denver PD, had secured earlier today after they'd finished with the attempted suicide.

Someone had missed a window. On purpose?

Was this Freihof entering the building now? The mole?

Silently, Lillian crouched down to grab her backup sidearm from its ankle holster in her boot and took off in a sprint toward the window. If this was Freihof, she was going to catch him and nail the son of a bitch.

Right. Damn. Now.

The window was still missing part of the grate that should've been covering it to stop this sort of entry into the building. Staying low, she gazed inside. The small basement storage room was dark and she couldn't see anyone. Whoever had entered had proceeded into the hallway.

Lillian holstered her weapon and edged herself through the window, thankful her size made it easier. Once inside, she crouched low again, weapon back in hand, looking and listening. She was fairly certain no one was in the room, but she didn't want to take a chance.

Once she knew the room was secure, she moved quickly to the door, opened it and glanced up and down the darkened hallway. This wasn't an area of the building used for daily government purposes. The hall was littered with unused desks and furniture, cleaning supplies and bookshelves.

Plenty of places for someone to hide. And damn well too many areas where someone could leave an explosive device.

Lillian looked up and down the hall, trying to ascertain which way the suspect had run. This was a virtual maze of connected halls and doors. Was the perp trying to get up to the main section of the building?

She heard a muffled noise farther down one of the hallways and began to move toward it, stepping quickly but silently.

Now would be a good time for backup, but by the time they got here it would be too late. And the three-man private security force who patrolled this building at night wouldn't be much good against Freihof.

Lillian could still remember watching Freihof pull the knife across Grace Parker's throat, helpless to do anything to save her friend. If Freihof was in this building, Lillian wasn't going to lose him calling for backup. She'd take him down herself.

She eased farther down the hallway, coming to an intersecting one. She didn't know which way the perp had gone. She moved quickly down one hallway, only to find it came to a dead end at a locked door. Cursing, she spun around and ran back down to where the halls crossed, hoping the perp hadn't made it out. She wished she'd studied this floor's plans as much as she had the other levels.

She took the corner too quickly and wasn't expecting the assailant to be right there. Mistake. She'd been too desperate to catch him to be as careful as she should have been.

She swallowed a cry as the perp hit her arms with a hardcover law book, knocking her gun to the floor and sending it skidding across the hall. Pain radiated through her right forearm at the force of the blow.

Mistake on his part, too. He should've clocked her with that book and knocked her out while he had the chance. He wouldn't get a second opportunity. Lillian spun back toward him, already perfectly balanced on her feet.

Her opponent was around six feet tall, probably close to two hundred pounds, and he was wearing a mask. Lillian was determined that would be coming off.

The guy dropped the book—smart, it would slow him down—and Lillian went on the offensive. She kicked him in the midsection, then used her momentum to swing her other leg around in a roundhouse kick to catch him in the head.

He blocked her kick at the last second, bringing his own fist around in a hook that would've knocked her to the floor, if not unconscious, if it had hit her jaw, where he was aiming.

Guy wasn't playing around.

Neither was she.

As always when fighting someone bigger and stronger, Lillian used her speed and agility to her advantage, keeping out of reach of his blows and using her legs and kicks as much as possible. The guy adapted quickly, bringing himself closer to her, so her legs couldn't inflict any damage. Also meant she had to stay focused in order to not get caught by one of his fists.

He had some skills.

She had more.

Lillian spun, her elbow connecting with the perp's jaw as she flung around. Momentum propelled him backward, allowing her to hit him with a right upper-cut and then a left hook. He was going down and they both knew it.

Too late Lillian heard the click of a Taser and felt the voltage run through her body. Was there a second person here or had she just missed it?

She fought the blackness but it overcame her.

As soon as she came to, Lillian realized the direness of the situation.

A noose wrapped tightly around a neck had a very distinct feel.

She was sitting on a crate that rested precariously on a step in a stairwell. Her arms were tied behind her back. A few moments later the rope attached to her neck began to move upward as it was hoisted from the other side. Lillian could stand or she could suffocate.

The rope continued to move upward, pulling her up, until she was standing on the crate, then it kept going until she was on her very tiptoes.

The bands restraining her arms behind her back weren't that tight, but weren't so loose that she could get out.

"Someone has to take the fall," a voice whispered from the other side of the stairwell, near the door. Lillian couldn't tell whose it was. Someone she knew?

And that was why the restraints weren't tight on her arms. This needed to look like a suicide.

"This isn't going to work, you know. Whatever you have planned."

Lillian winced as the rope jerked the slightest bit higher as the masked man tied it to the door. The door pulled to the outside, which meant if someone opened it she was a goner.

So much for yelling for help.

She was on the very tops of her toes, the square crate balancing precariously on the rectangle step that was much more narrow.

"No one is going to believe I killed myself with my arms tied behind my back." The words came out in breathy gasps as she focused on holding herself steady.

Masked Man just tilted his head, studying her. But she knew if he didn't cut her arms loose she had no chance of survival.

The box tipped forward and she felt sweat drip down her forehead as she attempted to get it back straight with what little leverage she had. She wasn't sure she had much chance for survival anyway.

The man moved away from the door and came up the stairs, giving her a wide berth—as if she could kick him and still maintain balance on the crate—and without another word cut the cord from her arms.

Lillian immediately brought her hands up above her head and took her weight from her legs, then swung her legs back down, twisting and using momentum to propel them toward Masked Man, hoping to catch him around the shoulders.

But he was expecting it and had moved up the stairs out of her reach. Her legs fell downward to the crate again, to give her arms supporting her weight a rest.

"Goodbye, Omega Sector."

She heard the whisper from behind her and saw an envelope drop to the floor before the crate was kicked out from under her. Immediately her arms took the weight of her body. She swung her legs up to try to wrap them around the rope, but couldn't, with the length and angle of the noose. She reached her foot out to the side, trying to reach the banister, and cursed when her legs weren't long enough to reach it.

She couldn't see the bastard behind her but knew he was waiting. Waiting to watch her die as her strength gave out and she couldn't support herself anymore.

She tried to yell—even if someone came rushing into the room, it wasn't going to do much more damage than her swaying here until her strength gave out—but the sound was cut off by the rope over her vocal chords. If she wanted to yell, she was going to have to use one hand to pull the rope away from the front of her throat. That meant supporting all her weight with one arm.

Her muscles were already straining from the constant state of pulling up. Supporting her weight with one arm wasn't going to work.

But she'd be damned if she was just going to die in front of this bastard.

She swung her legs up, trying to catch the upper part of the rope, but failed again. Even if she could get her legs hooked up there, she wasn't going to be able to get herself released.

She heard a low chuckle to her side. Bastard. He was enjoying this.

And then the alarm started blaring.

Masked Man muttered a curse and took off up the stairs. Lillian felt her arms begin to shake as the exhaustion from holding her own weight began to take its toll. If it wasn't for the rigorous SWAT training, she'd already be dead.

But even training wouldn't be enough. Physics would win. Her arms began to tremble more and she was forced to let go of the rope to give them a break.

Immediately the rope cut off all oxygen.

When everything began to go black, she reached up and grabbed the rope again. It wasn't long before the tremors took over.

She didn't want to go out like this. Wished she hadn't squandered this second chance she'd had with Jace in her life.

But even thinking of Jace, with his gorgeous blue eyes and cocky grin that still did things to her heart after all these years, couldn't give her any more strength.

She reached back up with her arms and found them collapsing before she even took her weight. Then the noose tightened and jerked around her neck, pulling her body forward, all air gone.

Blackness.

Chapter 9

The door to the stairway was heavy as Jace opened it. Abnormally heavy, like someone was slumped against it. Fear coated his throat. Was it Lillian against the other side of the door, unconscious?

What he found when he pushed it open was much worse.

Jace immediately took in the situation, cursing violently as he flew up the steps toward Lillian's swinging form. "Lily!"

He dove to get himself under her legs and lift her, taking the weight off her throat and airway.

"Lillian? Lily? Come on, baby, talk to me."

His heart was a hammer in his chest as he wrapped his arms around her thighs and hoisted her up.

God, he couldn't be too late.

"Lily!" he yelled, shaking her and tapping her leg,

trying to get her to wake up. The only thing he could hear was silence and the desperate beating of his own heart.

"Come on, Tiger Lily, damn it. Fight." Lillian Muir was nothing if not a fighter.

Jace reached into his pocket for his army knife, trying to position himself where he could hold her weight and saw through the rope above her head. He still couldn't tell if she was breathing or not.

Holding all her weight while on the awkward stairs made cutting the rope nearly impossible. But there was no way in hell he was going to let her go.

"Hand me the knife."

Lillian's hoarse whisper sent relief flooding through Jace. He gave her the knife, lifting her body farther to provide her the slack in the rope she needed. A minute later she fell completely into his arms as she finished cutting the binding around her throat.

He set them both on the stairs and pushed her clawing fingers away from the noose, loosening it and lifting it over her head. She slumped back against the wall.

There was already angry red marks and bruising on her neck and throat where the rope had been suffocating her.

"Jesus, Lily." Jace hauled her to him in a fierce hug, swallowing the terror that still scratched at his insides. "What the hell happened?"

He was thankful when she didn't try to pull away. "Masked man." Her voice was painfully hoarse. "Saw someone crawl through a window and I followed him. He must've had a partner. Bastard Tasered me. When

I woke up, he had me strung up, standing on a box. Then he tipped it."

"Damn it." Jace's eyes closed again. "You were holding your own weight up?"

She nodded and silence fell between them as Jace realized how close to death she'd really been. The fact that she was sitting here alive right now was a testament to both her physical and mental strength. Strength very few people had.

"Sick bastard. Why didn't he just shoot you?"

She pulled back from him and grabbed a note from behind him on the stairs. He unfolded it.

I CAN'T LIVE WITH WHAT I'VE DONE. WITH BETRAYING MY COLLEAGUES. SO MY FIGHT ENDS HERE.

It was written in block letters, which had been smart. It would've been difficult to prove whether Lillian had written it or not, which was exactly what the killer wanted.

"He wanted to make it look like a suicide," she whispered.

"We need to get you to a hospital and report to Derek. Let him know what's going on."

She pulled away from him, shaking her head. "I don't need a hospital. We go to Derek first. I'll get the team medic to check me out."

Jace grimaced but knew Lillian was probably right. There wasn't much a hospital could do for her except help her manage her pain. "Fine. But if your throat starts feeling any worse, you have to let someone know immediately. Swelling could still be an issue. And swelling could mean airway blockage."

She tilted her head, studying him. "How do you know that?"

"I had a little bit of medical training in the army."

She nodded and he could tell even that small movement caused her discomfort. "Okay, I'll tell you if it gets any worse."

"We need to let the building guards know about that window. It shouldn't have been missed in the security sweep."

He kept a hand at the small of her back as they moved through the door and toward the elevators.

"Maybe they weren't missed." Her voice was low, husky. "Maybe someone deliberately left it unsecured."

"You think the mole is here in Denver?"

"I think it's awfully suspicious that the guy who broke in was wearing a mask. He would've blended in better without it."

"A mask definitely screams *bad guy*."

"Exactly. Why bother with it at all if nobody's going to recognize you anyway?"

Jace nodded as he led Lillian into the main lobby of the building. The guards were surprised to see them, and they had to show their identification quickly to keep the security team from calling backup.

Backup Lillian could've desperately used twenty minutes ago.

Without going into too much detail—particularly until they could talk to Derek and figure out a plan—Jace informed the guards about the unsecured window and that Lillian had followed someone in.

Lillian and Jace waited as the security team followed their protocol and brought in other members of the staff, as well as police. They showed them the window so it could be secured, and the area was swept for possible DNA. Whomever Lily had fought would be long gone by now, but maybe they would get lucky and get some sort of forensic clue to point them in the right direction.

Ultimately, there needed to be a great deal more security in this building, but not just the type that was barely paid more than minimum wage. City hall would need to be reswept. If Derek didn't make the decision to move the LESS Summit to the secondary location.

Jace kept an eye on Lillian as they left the building and walked back toward the hotel, carefully watching for signs that her throat was swelling and closing off. Although she moved stiffly—he couldn't even imagine what sort of trauma her upper body muscles had been through trying to hold her own unsupported weight for that long—she didn't seem to be suffering from shortness of breath.

He hated what she'd been through, what had almost happened, and it had damn well taken twenty years off his life seeing her swinging there unconscious. But tonight had also proven one thing beyond a shadow of a doubt.

Lillian was not the mole.

There was no way she could've faked what had happened tonight. No way she could've known that Jace would come through that door when he did. If he had been another minute later, just *one* minute, she would've been dead.

And if someone was leaving a suicide note on her and trying to kill her, then Lillian Muir was not the mole.

The relief coursing through Jace now was almost as prominent as the relief of knowing she was alive after he'd seen her hanging there in the stairwell.

The proof of her innocence changed damn near everything for him. Every single reason he had for not giving in to the attraction that sparked between the two of them vanished as soon as he'd cut her down from the rope that had almost taken her life.

Jace couldn't stop himself from staring at her. She was alive and she was *innocent*.

"I'm not going to collapse, Eakin, so you can stop ogling me."

She had no idea why he couldn't drag his eyes away from her. She would soon.

If she would still have him.

They went straight to Derek's room. The sun was already coming up and he was awake. One look at Lillian's neck had his eyebrow raised, and he eased his door open farther for them to enter his room.

"You two get a little too excited with the sparring?" Derek asked.

Jace explained what happened, with Lillian filling in details, speaking as little as possible to protect her strained voice.

Jace sat down at the edge of the bed and pulled Lillian down beside him. She was starting to look a little paler. Was probably in a lot of pain.

"We told the building's security team about the break-in and unsecured window, but didn't give them much info about what happened to Lillian. I wasn't sure how you wanted to handle that. They brought in locals to process the scene and woke up every guard who's ever worked there to get them on-site."

Derek rubbed a hand across his face. "It's still not enough. I'll make a call. We're going to need further backup for the summit. We'll also need to move the summit to the secondary location. The bigwigs won't like it because it's not nearly as picturesque as city hall. Plus, we'll need to lock down an entirely new building." He turned to Lillian. "You need a hospital? You've been Tasered and strangled. Maybe you need to sit this event out."

Lillian stood. "I'm going to pretend I didn't even hear that. Bastard got a lucky shot, but it won't happen again. And I'm damn well not going to miss the LESS Summit. We're shorthanded enough as it is."

The tough-person speech would've been much more convincing if her voice hadn't broken three times during it.

Jace couldn't help himself—his hand moved to her back to rub gentle circles. The fact that she didn't pull away both thrilled and worried him. "She's agreed to let the medic examine her. Then she'll be in my room."

He ignored Lillian's raised eyebrow.

Derek nodded. "I don't want to see either of you before thirteen hundred hours at the secondary location. We'll start the security lockdown and then prep for a run-through of the summit."

Jace and Lillian both stood and headed toward the door. Lillian turned back to Derek.

"You know what the mask means, right?" she croaked.

Derek rubbed the back of his neck. "It means Omega definitely has a mole, and that you would've known his face. We'll be sure to keep an eye on any reactions today when you show up. Because as far as that person knows, you died in that stairwell."

Jace's fists clenched. They'd come so damn close to that being the truth.

"Freihof is making his move, Derek. The summit is too good a target for him to pass up," Lillian whispered, her voice almost gone.

"And we'll be ready for him," Derek responded. "This is going to end. But first, go to the ER or at least go see the medic, get checked out. Then try to get some rest. Because you're right, we do need you. I have a feeling we're going to need all the help we can get."

Chapter 10

Everybody needed to stop telling her to go to the ER. Jace. Derek. The medic. She was fine.

Lillian was angry as hell, but physically she would be fine. So the medic informing Jace—as if Jace was the boss of her—that she needed to be under constant supervision for the next twenty-four hours didn't do much for Lillian's temper.

"I'm fine," she muttered as they left the medic. "I don't need to stay in your room."

Jace looked at her calmly as he used the card key to open his hotel door. "Less than two hours ago you were unconscious from lack of oxygen. Your body is depleted. Exhausted. I understand you not wanting to go to the hospital, but please humor me on this. Stay with me."

His voice rolled over her like gentle waves, soothing her. Calming her.

But she also knew even soothing, calming water could drown her if she wasn't careful.

Lillian wanted to stay. And wanted to run. Maybe she was more injured than she thought, because she truly couldn't decide.

But finally she admitted to herself that the reason she wanted to run didn't have anything to do with proving her health and everything to do with how sexy Jace looked standing there against the wall in his jeans and shirt, holding the door open for her.

Holding the door open to the room that had one king-size bed as the main piece of furniture.

Lillian wasn't a coward, so she walked through the doorway, feeling Jace's hand at the small of her back as she did. Just like she'd felt it as they'd walked down the hall.

She knew she shouldn't read into it. He'd already made it quite clear he wasn't interested in anything more than a professional relationship. Working together. That was it. Being a friendly colleague was enough for her with everyone else. It would be enough with Jace, too.

Plus, she owed him. If he hadn't gotten there when he had, she'd definitely be dead now.

"Thank you for saving my life." She stood staring at the big bed for a moment before a thought occurred to her and she turned to him. "What were you doing at city hall anyway?"

She expected an immediate quip about insomnia or the problem with having a job that wasn't nine-to-five—with SWAT, probably the same as his time in the army, daytime and nighttime hours could run together.

Instead, Jace stepped closer. Directly into her definitely-more-than-just-professional space. There weren't a whole lot of things that threw Lillian off balance. This was one of them.

"I was looking for you."

Lillian took a slight step back, Jace's proximity a little too much for her system. "Okay. I'm glad you found me or else I'd—" She stopped, realization dawning. "You were following me?"

He nodded, features unreadable.

She tried to process the possible reasons why Jace would be following *her*. "Why?"

Now he stepped out of her space slightly, eyes shuttered. He paused so long she thought maybe he wasn't going to answer.

"I'm not just here to fill in for the SWAT team. I was also sent in by Ren McClement to look for the mole working with Freihof."

The mole. Lillian stepped away from Jace and walked over to the window that didn't provide much of a view. She leaned her forehead against the cool glass, taking in all the ramifications of Jace's statement.

"They sent you in because they think I'm the mole," she finally muttered. Somehow she'd always known there was a deeper purpose for Jace's sudden infiltration into the team.

She could hear him move closer behind her, but she didn't turn around. "They sent me in because Ren trusts me, they needed someone with a particular skill set and because…yes, they know there's a mole."

"And your past with me had nothing to do with them sending you in?"

Jace sighed. "No. They knew we'd known each other before when they asked me to join the team.

You were one of the suspects. Although if it helps, your boss, that Steve Drackett guy, was adamant you weren't guilty."

"And you?" She hated the weakness in her voice as she whispered the question. Hated that the answer mattered so much to her. "Did *you* think I was guilty?"

She knew it was unfair. After what had happened between them twelve years ago—or what Jace *thought* had happened—expecting him to trust her carte blanche just wasn't fair. But God, how she wanted to believe he would find it impossible to conceive she was a traitor of that magnitude.

"Never mind," she said before he could answer. Before he could say the words she knew would tear her apart even though they shouldn't. "We don't really know each other, and what you did know about me wasn't complimentary. Of course you thought I was guilty."

She tried to give a lighthearted laugh, but it came out a brittle croak even to her own ears as she continued to stare out the window with no view. When he didn't respond, she continued, moving into a deeper register of her voice so it wouldn't crack. "We should get some rest like Derek said. Obviously we've got a ton of fortification work to do in a few hours now that we're moving to the secondary location."

"Tiger Lily…"

Damn it, he could *not* call her that. Not right now. Not when every part of her felt vulnerable.

She turned from the window but didn't meet his crystal eyes. She couldn't. Not right now. "You know what? I really am fine. I'm just going to head on up to my own room. I promise if I feel even the slightest bit—"

"No," he interrupted before she got any further. "I never thought you were guilty of treason. I didn't think it when Ren recruited me a couple of weeks ago. Hell, Lily, I didn't even think that when I felt the worst about you."

God, she wanted to believe that more than anything. "But yet, you came here, because of me. Followed me because you thought I might be up to something."

He took a step closer and ran a hand through his brown hair, causing short pieces to stick up at crazy angles. "I came here because of you, yes. Because, despite everything, I've never been able to stop thinking about you. Because I wanted to put you—put the *past*—behind me once and for all."

That hurt almost as much as him thinking she was the mole. "Yeah, I can't blame you for that, either. Although I guess I'm glad you don't think I'm trying to kill my friends and betray my country, even if you don't like me personally."

His fingers gripped her upper arms. Not hard enough to hurt, and they both knew she had moves that could get her away from him if she wanted, but a firm enough touch to let her know that he was serious.

"It took me about three and a half minutes after seeing you to figure out that this heat between us was very definitely not in the past."

She couldn't look away from those eyes. "But what about the other day at HQ? You turning down my offer to come over? I thought you weren't interested."

He stepped closer. All Lillian could feel, smell, breathe…was Jace.

His volume dropped to a husky whisper. "I didn't want to be with you that way under false pretenses. I didn't want to have sex with you and then you think I had used it to get close to you to see if you were the mole."

"You *did* want me?" It had to be the near strangulation that made her voice so weak. So thready.

His hands moved up from her arms to cup her face. Her eyes closed and she breathed him in. He smelled of heat and desire and a scent that was pure male. Not just any male. *Jace.*

It had always been Jace. *Only* been Jace.

"Oh, hell yeah." His deep whisper sent chills across her skin. "But not with lies between us. And so while I hate what happened to you tonight, I'm also thankful for it. Because now there's no doubt in my mind you aren't the mole."

He was so close Lillian couldn't think clearly—all she could do was feel. And it felt so different than most interactions Lillian had with men. By this point of closeness she was normally checking out mentally. Fading away to some place in her mind that no one could touch. Even though her encounters with men weren't violent, her brain just wasn't able to process the intimacy.

But not now. She wanted to be here. With Jace. In every way.

She almost felt giddy. The desire coursing through her veins like a fire was heady. She felt almost tipsy on it.

"I'm a little nervous about that smile," he said, lips so close to hers she could feel the hot sweetness of his breath. "You look like the cat that ate the canary."

"I just want to be with you." She couldn't help it, her smile grew wider as she pulled him closer. She wanted to revel in this feeling. "And it sounds like you want the same."

"Oh, you better believe it."

She let out a soft gasp as her body was pushed up against the window while his mouth came crashing down on hers. This kiss wasn't gentle or searching. Wasn't the kiss of the two teenagers they'd been.

It was hot. Forceful. Encompassing.

Everything about Jace demanded that Lillian's mind and focus stay here with him in the room. On him. On *them*.

Not that she wanted to be anywhere else. And hell if it wasn't the most authentic emotion she'd had in years. In twelve years.

Desire.

He kissed her with utter absorption, as if he couldn't get enough of her. Her fingers threaded in his hair as his hands slid down her back to her hips and he jerked her against him.

Lillian couldn't hold back the moan that broke free.

"I want you, Lily," he said against her lips.

Good, because she wanted him, too. In ways she thought had died long ago. She kept herself plastered against him as he picked her up by bending his knees and wrapping his arms around her hips. Then he lifted her and carried her to the bed.

He laid her down gently, without breaking the kiss, bringing his weight down on top of her. Lillian tensed.

She knew a man's form resting on her was one of her triggers—she and Grace had talked about it in depth in therapy—and Lillian waited for numbness to inch through her mind as it always did so she could fight it off.

But it didn't come.

All she could do was feel as Jace's lips moved over her jaw, taking special time to gently kiss down her injured throat. Finally he reached that most sensitive point, where her shoulder and neck met. He bit down gently and a soft cry escaped her.

She was feeling a million things. Numbness definitely was not one of them.

Jace's weight wasn't frightening, wasn't overwhelming her senses in a way that caused her mind to switch off in order to survive. That frightening place she'd barely survived as an eighteen-year-old wasn't looming in the distance.

Instead his weight was comfortable, as if her mind knew him, her body remembered him. Knew she was safe. And she was. Lillian knew that on every level.

Jace equaled safety.

As his hand ran down her body from her shoulder to her waist, unbuttoning her shirt as he went, she gripped his hair so she could see him face-to-face.

"I want you," she said, staring into those blue eyes that had once meant everything to her.

He gave her a half grin that stopped her heart and seemed to have a direct link to the most feminine parts of her. "You seem a little surprised by that statement."

"I just want to be here with you, all the way with you. Here and now." She knew she was being cryptic, that he couldn't possibly understand what she meant. And she definitely wasn't about to explain, especially not now.

But Jace just nodded. "Then stay with me, Tiger Lily. Here and now, in this bed. Just you and me." He bent down and brought his lips to hers again tenderly.

And she did. For the first time in twelve years she stayed—mentally—in a bed with a man. Not just any man. *Jace*. Experienced every kiss, every touch. Every moan and lick and sigh. Things she'd thought she was long past able to feel.

And found there was nowhere else she would rather be.

Chapter 11

"What the hell were you thinking, Freihof? If I hadn't come in and saved your ass, you'd be arrested right now."

Damien stared at "Guy Fawkes," his eyes narrowed to slits. The hell of it was, the younger man wasn't wrong. Damien had made a mistake. Had miscalculated. It didn't happen very often, but it had this morning.

It was the anniversary of his beloved Natalie's death. The day Omega Sector had swept in six years ago and taken her from him. Killed her in their heavy-handedness.

Damien hadn't planned to do anything about it. Moving on a day connected to Natalie would be too obvious. But he hadn't been able to stop himself.

They needed to pay.

He'd been toying with them for months, chasing and killing their loved ones so they could know the pain that he'd known from losing his Natalie.

But it was no longer enough. It was time for them to stop feeling the heartache of death and start feeling death itself. One by one… Groups… Damien didn't care which.

He just wanted them all to die.

Setting a trap in city hall—a bomb that would take out the entire SWAT team—had seemed like the perfect plan. Yes, it would've messed up some of Fawkes's destroy-all-of-law-enforcement plan, but Damien didn't care. He was tired of the game. Tired of Fawkes and his grand scheming. Tired of Omega Sector cheating death every time.

Tired of the same old story, so Damien was planning to turn some pages.

For Natalie. He could still picture her in his mind. Her blond hair and blue eyes. The perfect all-American girl. And she'd been all his. His most prized possession. Until they'd taken her away forever.

"Freihof!" Fawkes slammed his fist down on the table in the small apartment Damien had rented. "Are you listening to anything I'm saying? I took a big risk helping you and then again getting here to talk to you in person. You've probably ruined what I've taken months to set up."

The temptation to end Fawkes's life right now was almost more than Damien could bear. But it would be a mistake and Damien had already made one of those several hours ago. Fawkes was still useful and Damien needed to get his emotions under control.

A time and a place for everything. That was what he'd always told his beloved Natalie, and it was still true now.

"It won't happen again," Damien muttered through tight lips.

"It doesn't matter if it happens again!" Fawkes began pacing back and forth. "Thanks to your stunt, they're moving the summit to the secondary location. This changes everything for my plans. Networks I've painstakingly linked together for months ruined because you had to sneak in through a damn window in the middle of the night."

Damien watched the younger man pull at his own hair. Damien wouldn't have to kill him. He was going to give himself a stroke. "Fawkes, I will fix this."

"How?" Fawkes glared at him. "How exactly will you do that?"

"You let me worry about it. You concentrate on keeping your team from figuring out your grand scheme. From figuring out who you are."

Fawkes pulled at his hair again. "We have a limited window, Damien. If all my systems are not aligned when LESS goes live in thirty-six hours, my plan fails. And city hall is the center of everything. Ground zero."

Damien nodded. "Like I said, I will make sure the summit is returned to the original location."

It would take work, but Damien already had a plan in mind.

"And Lillian Muir? She didn't die despite me stringing her up. I'm lucky I borrowed your mask because she would definitely be able to identify me, since she didn't die. And now she's even more suspicious."

"Yes, she's suspicious, but she's not suspicious of *you*. That's all that matters right now. She doesn't know who she saw entering that window. She doesn't know who strung her up in that hallway and she doesn't know any of the plans. Besides, I have something very special in store for her. And her boyfriend."

"Damn Eakin. Everybody accepted him into the SWAT team like he was some sort of god. I even saw Lillian making out with him in the parking lot last week."

The words fairly dripped with jealously. In just over a week, Eakin had done what Fawkes had been trying to do for months: make the team, get the girl. And, more importantly, gain respect. But pointing that out to the young Mr. Fawkes wasn't going to do any good.

Damien could see he'd been wrong to get so impatient. To want to jump straight to killing the SWAT team rather than torture them. They would still die, but first they would suffer.

Lillian Muir would especially. He had something special planned for her.

"I was wrong." Damien's voice was full of sincerity that for once he wasn't faking. "I shouldn't have tried to circumvent the plan. I will make sure we get back on track."

Fawkes nodded, somewhat appeased. "Good. What I'm doing is important, Damien. It's going to reshape law enforcement all over the world. The badge will mean something again. The badge will rule as it was meant to do from the beginning."

Ah, quoting the infamous "Manifesto of Change" once more. Fawkes constantly hid behind it, allowing it to mask his jealousy, fear and ineptitude. After all, killing thousands of people because you just couldn't make the SWAT team didn't have the same ring to it. But this manifesto, which he planned to release publicly after his massacre at the LESS Summit, made Fawkes feel more legitimate.

But Damien wasn't about to try to convince Fawkes of his own folly. He just nodded. "Change is necessary. There's a time and a place for everything. Omega Sector's time and place has come and gone. Together, we'll destroy them."

"There are things you don't know, Freihof. Plans I've made beyond what I've told you that even the precious SWAT team won't figure out."

"Are you sure they're not on to you?"

Fawkes just shrugged. "They suspect damn near everyone. But they'll never have proof. And soon they'll all be dead."

"Maybe it's time you let me know all the details of your plan. I'm sure I can help."

Fawkes grinned, but anger laced the expression rather than joy. Anyone who couldn't see that had to be blind. Then Fawkes began to tell Damien his entire plan. Damien just listened.

He realized that *everyone* had underestimated this young man.

And they all would burn.

When Jace woke up after a couple hours of sleep, Lillian was gone. He wasn't surprised. The medic had told him to keep an eye on her to make sure she was okay.

Jace had kept a very close eye on her. On *all* of her. For hours.

It was like they were trying to cram twelve years of not making love into a few short hours. *Intense* was an applicable term for the last few hours they'd spent in bed, but would be an understatement.

Mind-blowing, earth-shattering, game-changing—those would be closer to the truth.

Jace wasn't so naive as to think that everything was perfect between him and Lillian just because they'd had some awesome sex. There were still a lot of years and a huge betrayal between them. He'd told himself—and her—that he was going to let the situation with Daryl be left in the past, but he had to admit he wasn't one-hundred-percent sure he was there yet.

Lily had seemed as enraptured in their lovemaking as he had been. She'd actually seemed a little surprised at their connection. At the heat. Had mentioned more than once how she wanted him, as if the notion caught her a little off guard.

A heat that all-encompassing after twelve years *was* a little surprising. Of course they'd had heat at the beginning, too.

That hadn't stopped Jace from finding Lily in his brother's arms a few days later. So there was no reason to think something similar wouldn't happen again. He needed to remember that. Keep his head on straight when it came to her.

Mind-blowing sex? No problem. Jace would partake as often as possible during this mission.

Giving Lily a piece of his heart? Absolutely not. He couldn't allow this to become more than a burn-the-sheets-off-the-bed sexual encounter between two friendly colleagues who would go their separate ways.

He brutally squashed the niggling voice that tried to tell him that Lillian Muir had always held a piece of his heart.

Jace showered and grabbed a bite to eat before dressing in full SWAT gear. He knew Lillian would meet at the secondary location at 1300 hours, like Derek had requested. Knew she would act as if nothing had happened, in both her near-death experience and the passion between the two of them. Lillian was never going to be one to wear her heart—or her weaknesses—on her sleeve.

Jace would be professional, too. Because although he definitely planned to have Lillian back in his bed, they couldn't deny that there was a very real threat here at the LESS Summit. Freihof and his crony might not have succeeded in making it look like Lillian was the mole, and taken her out of the picture, but that didn't mean they would turn their backs on an opportunity to do damage.

By surviving, Lillian had just upped the ante for whatever they had planned.

Omega would need to be ready.

Chapter 12

Jace was making his way to the federal building serving as the secondary location when the call came through. The entire team was to stop what they were doing and head to the lobby of the adjoining building. Some sort of elevator emergency.

He met Lillian as she was running from the federal building. Roman Weber and Saul Poniard were just two steps behind.

"Why the hell are we being brought in for a stuck elevator? Why didn't they call the fire department?" Jace asked as they ran, having to dodge picketers holding signs and chanting. The summit didn't start until tomorrow, but the public and news crews were already out in full force.

"Maybe the fire department has more on their plate than they can handle. But you can believe that Derek wouldn't call the entire team from our current assignment if we weren't needed."

Jace already knew that they were needed. It was confirmed a few minutes later as they all met up in the lobby. People were rushing by them, not screaming in panic, but not calm, either.

The presence of a SWAT team wasn't helping. People could tell something was wrong.

Derek spoke fast. "As we knew, the summit is bringing out the crazies. We've got four different bomb threats across the city, all tied to elevators. People are stranded in them all, and the guy is threatening to detonate all the bombs in thirty minutes if he doesn't get his demands met."

Saul cursed next to Jace. The ugly word very neatly summarized how he was feeling also.

"A police negotiator is talking with the bomber, criminal psychiatrist assisting, but they both have already signaled that they think the bomber has every intention of killing people today. Wants the attention, not the three million dollars he's demanding. Local police is spread thin, so we're working this building."

Now muttered curses could be heard all the way around.

"What's the plan, Derek? If he's going to blow it, let's get the people out before he can," Lillian said, her small body already strumming with energy.

"Elevator is caught between the sixteenth and seventeen floors. Eight people inside. We're going to have to jimmy the door open and pull the people out. But our clock is limited, especially if this guy is wanting to kill people solely for the attention. We have twenty-two minutes exactly."

The entire team set their watches. Anybody who was crazy enough to plant a bomb that would kill innocent people wasn't someone who could be trusted to keep his word, but until they had other intel they would move as if they had twenty-two minutes.

"Roman, Ashton, you need to help clear the stairwells and keep people moving without panic. Especially if this thing blows." Both men nodded and moved toward the main stairwell.

"Jace, Lillian, Saul," Derek continued, "you're with me."

The entire team sprinted to the stairwell and up the sixteen flights, the benefits of their daily physical training kicking in. Jace worried for a moment that Lillian might not be able to keep up because of her injuries, but she never faltered.

Less than three minutes later they were in the hall of the sixteenth floor. Derek used the elevator-emergency drop key to release the outer doors and pried them open.

Immediately they found the elevator car was over three quarters of the way up from the building doorway. There was no way anyone would be able to fit through the small space. They would have to go to the next floor.

Jace let out a curse, doing the rough math in his head based on the height of the stairwell.

"What?" Lillian asked.

"That car is too high on this floor to get them out here, but based on the height of the ceilings and stairwell, it's going to be damn tight trying to get them out on the next floor as well."

"We've got to try," Derek said. "We're down to seventeen minutes."

Immediately everyone sprinted to the next floor. The emergency drop key was reapplied on both the outer and inner doors and Jace's theory was unfortunately proven true. There was less than fifteen inches of space for the trapped passengers to fit through.

The passengers inside were talking, but weren't hysterical. They probably thought it was just a malfunction rather than a deliberate act of terror.

"This is the SWAT team," Derek called out. "We're going to pry open the door. Please stand back."

A small cheer went up from inside the car as force was applied to the inner door…until the door was pried open and the passengers could see the small space they'd have to get through.

"Can't you get the elevator up or down farther to give us more room? Some of us aren't going to fit."

Fourteen minutes.

The team looked to Derek. Nobody wanted to cause a panic, but they were going to have to work pretty damn fast to get all eight people out of there in time. And the guy who spoke up was right, it was going to be tough for some of them to fit. Jace himself would have a hard time.

But not everybody. Before they knew it, a petite woman was being hefted by someone in the elevator and was easily sliding through the fifteen-inch opening. One down, seven to go.

"Good!" Derek called out. "Send up as many people as you can."

Two more women and a skinny teenager were sent through next. Jace helped the team pull them out. Lillian, knowing her lack of upper body strength was a hindrance rather than a help, particularly after what she'd been through less than twelve hours ago, scooted out of the way. She eased her head inside the elevator car to get a good look at the remaining four passengers.

When she pulled back out, she was shaking her head, lips pursed. Her eyes met Jace's, but she spoke to Derek. "That last guy isn't going to fit," she said softly so only the team could hear.

"He's going to have to," Derek muttered, pulling passenger number six through.

"He's three hundred pounds, Derek," Lillian replied. "There's no way he's going to make it through that opening, even if we could pull him up."

Before Jace knew what was happening, Lillian gracefully poured herself through the opening and into the elevator car.

"Muir, what are you doing?" Saul yelled.

Jace met Derek's eyes as they hoisted the seventh passenger—a large man who barely fit through the opening—out of the elevator. Jace already knew what Lillian was doing. She knew they weren't going to be able to get the last guy out, so she was looking for other solutions to the problem.

"She's searching for the device," he muttered to Derek.

"What device?" the man they'd just pulled through asked. "A *device*? Like a bomb?"

The other people gasped and the elderly lady grasped her chest. "There's a bomb?"

Derek and Jace ignored them. "Disarming is the only option if we can't get everyone out," Jace said. "I'm going in with her."

Jace glanced at his watch. Eight minutes.

The civilians were now crying. Derek turned to Saul. "Lead them down the stairs."

The older woman gripped her chest again, her breathing ragged. Jace studied her briefly before turning back to Derek. "Saul isn't going to be able to get them all down."

Derek nodded. "I'll help him. You're the explosives expert. I sure as hell hope you can work a miracle."

Jace did, too.

Derek stepped closer. "But if you can't, then you make sure the body count is as low as possible, you understand? One is bad enough. We don't need to make it three."

"Agreed."

"Lillian won't see it that way."

"Lillian already almost died once in the past twelve hours. I'm not going to let it happen again now."

Derek nodded curtly and moved to help the other civilians. Jace lowered himself into the elevator.

"What the hell is going on here?" the man too big to fit through the opening said loudly, sweat pouring down his face. "Why is SWAT here rather than the fire department?"

Lillian was ignoring him. She was using an electric screwdriver to open panels on the elevator, searching for the bomb.

"Fire department is busy in other parts of the city, sir," Jace responded to the man.

"Well, then get a damn elevator repairman out here. Whatever this girlie is doing can't be helping. A woman with power tools always makes me nervous. One in a broken elevator is downright terrifying."

Now Jace understood why Lily was ignoring the sexist jackass.

She turned to him. "These panels are all clear. Nothing. I didn't think it would be here, but it was worth a shot, since that would've been the easiest access." She pointed to the roof panels. "Hoist me up."

They both ignored the man, who was still spouting off from the corner. Jace linked his fingers by his knees and Lillian immediately stepped into his hands. He lifted her until she could reach the ceiling panels and unscrew them. A few moments later she grasped the sides of the opening and lifted herself through.

Her muttered curse told him the news was not good.

"Tell Derek to let the other locations know there's a primary device on the main cable and a second one on the emergency break," she said down to him.

"Device?" the guy yelled. "What kind of device?"

They ignored him again.

Jace relayed the message to the team leader, then continued, "This is beyond my pay grade, Derek. No way I'm going to be able to defuse this in time."

The big guy went crazy, became livid. "There's a bomb up there? Don't you think you should've told me about that, you bitch?"

What was it with this sexist freak? Jace pointed a finger right in the middle of his chest. "You know what? There's only one person stuck in this elevator without a way out. It's not me and it's definitely not her." He pointed up to where Lillian was on the roof. "So shut the hell up and help us save your life."

The man shut up and nodded, thankfully.

"Lillian, I'm coming up." Jace crouched and jumped, catching the opening in the ceiling and pulling himself the rest of the way through. Lily was shining her flashlight on the small explosive device.

"Four minutes." He shone his own light at the secondary device on the emergency brake.

"Hell, I don't even know what I'm looking at, Jace. The entire team knows that explosives aren't my specialty. I don't have the patience for it. Tell me what I need to do."

Jace studied the bomb in front of him. There wasn't time to inspect both separately. He would have to work on his and walk Lillian through hers at the same time. "Tell me what you see."

What was in front of him was a hot mess. Definitely not something crafted with care. It almost seemed to have been thrown together.

Derek's voice came in through his earpiece. "Report, Jace. You're running out of time."

"This device isn't what I was expecting, especially for someone we would've thought had been planning this since the summit was announced. This device is almost haphazard."

"The other three buildings couldn't find any explosive devices in the elevators. Looks like the bomber was just using those as decoys to spread rescue personnel more thinly."

"It worked," Jace muttered, still studying the messy IED in front of him. "Something about this whole thing is off, Derek."

"That's not going to stop us from being less dead in three minutes if we don't get this figured out," Lillian quipped.

"You focus on the task at hand," Derek's voice said in his ear. "We'll figure out what doesn't fit later."

"Roger that," Jace muttered, clicking off his transmission. "Lil, I need you to figure out the four main parts of your bomb. Main charge, a trigger switch, the ignitor and the power source for the switch."

"Okay."

"We've got to separate the trigger switch from its power source."

Lillian blew out a frustrated breath. "So this is going to be more than just cut the red wire or the blue wire?"

"Actually, believe it or not, it is a case of just cutting a wire. But if your IED is anything like mine, it's a mess. Bomber didn't take much care with this explosive. But like you said, it will still get us just as dead."

"We're under two minutes, Jace. Which wire am I supposed to cut?"

They both heard the guy in the elevator start crying, promising God he would go to church every day for the rest of his life if he survived this.

"Tell Him you'll stop making sexist remarks, too. Maybe that will help," Lillian called down to him.

Jace grinned. This woman.

He couldn't wait to get her back in his bed. All the thoughts about keeping his distance from her seemed ridiculous now.

The bomb was messy, but still cleverly put together. Not easily disarmed. Jace gently pried the battery—the trigger switch's power source—away from the main charge. He barely saw the tiny aluminum wire attached to the bottom of the red wire—the one that would need to be cut to separate the trigger from its power source.

A fail-safe. If that tiny wire got cut by accident—by someone who didn't see it—the explosive would detonate. The person who built this might have been in a hurry, but he was very smart.

They were in serious trouble.

"Lil, you need to go."

She didn't even look up. "Like hell I will. Especially not without you."

"Negotiator was right. Whoever rigged this didn't plan on anyone surviving here today, no matter what demands he gave."

Guy below them began crying louder.

"Is it possible to defuse it?" she asked. Their eyes met across the roof of the elevator. Hers were calm, like his. Lillian could handle it.

"Yes, but it's tricky."

She grinned. "Tricky is my middle name, Eakin. What do I do?"

He quickly explained about the aluminum wire, the need to separate it gently from the other wire that had to be cut. It was glued and nearly impossible to do. Just getting the device in front of him defused would take all his time. There was no way he'd be able to help Lillian with hers.

"Okay, I see it." She muttered a curse. "I really don't like whoever put this damn thing together."

"You found the adhesive, I see. Forty-five seconds."

"Yep, damn it. Wanna race?"

Jace couldn't keep from chuckling. Lily. God, if he had to go out, there was no one else he'd rather go with.

Guy inside was wailing now.

Jace carefully eased his blade through the tiny wire, using the utmost caution not to cut the aluminum wire around it. He took in a breath to focus and then made the final cut.

"Clear," he breathed.

He looked over at Lillian. They had less than fifteen seconds. Jace stayed where he was. The best thing he could do now was let her do her job. Trust her to do it. And he did, he realized. She was crouched there, small flashlight now in her mouth pointing down at the device, completely focused on the task at hand.

That was the Lillian he'd always known. Able to handle anything.

C'mon, Tiger Lily. Save our lives.

He'd no more than finished the thought when she looked up, grabbed the flashlight out of her mouth and grinned.

"Clear."

Chapter 13

"Canceling the LESS Summit is not an option," Congresswoman Christina Glasneck said an hour later, since she had decided to attend the SWAT debriefing to provide her own input. Colorado was her state and LESS was her baby.

And she wasn't happy.

"Omega Sector is supposed to be made up of the best agents the country has available for service. So, can you handle this or not?"

Lillian would've told the woman off, but Derek remained unflappable. "Yes, ma'am. We can handle it."

Congresswoman Glasneck tapped a heeled foot as she leaned back against the conference-room chair. "So we had a break-in at city hall last night and a bombing scare today. Are the two incidents related?"

Lillian was glad she'd worn a high-necked dry-fit

shirt under her gear. The bruising around her neck was extensive. And although Derek had let the team know she had thwarted some sort of break-in at the City and County Building, he hadn't provided many details.

Although someone—probably someone sitting inside this very room—knew many more details about last night than they were letting on.

"It's too early to ascertain with any certainty," Derek responded to Glasneck. "But as of right now, we have nothing to suggest the two events are related."

Lillian glanced over at Jace. His face was stoic, as were the faces of the entire team. The congresswoman had requested everyone be here for this meeting, which wasn't normal protocol and was a waste of time. There was a crap ton of more useful things the team could be doing than sitting here listening to a lecture from someone who wanted to feel like she had a finger on the pulse of law enforcement.

It gave Lillian a new respect for Derek, who had to sit through these types of meetings all the time.

"As you know," Congresswoman Glasneck continued, "LESS has been my project from the beginning. I pushed it through Congress to get the necessary funding." She looked over at Philip Carnell. "Mr. Carnell, you've been instrumental in the setup of the system, and I know a number of other members of Omega Sector have worked tirelessly across the country to make sure this system happens. I think you helped, too, didn't you, Mr. Poniard?"

Saul nodded. But Carnell, true to form, barely even acknowledged the congresswoman's words. He sat with his arms crossed over his chest.

Derek nodded. "We all understand the importance of

LESS, Congresswoman. And of protecting the summit. None of us want it to be canceled, but we do need to decide on a final location. Right now it seems the primary and secondary locations have been compromised."

The congresswoman's lips thinned. "I agree that this federal building is out. After the elevator incident today, I'm sure no one wants to place a large group of VIPs here. But I disagree about city hall. That's one of the oldest buildings in Denver. Iconic."

Again, Lillian wanted to jump in and argue why the outer appearance of a building should be the last thing they were concerned about. This was why Derek had told the entire team to just keep quiet unless they were asked a direct question.

"It is a beautiful building," Derek conceded. "But the fact is, it was compromised. We had eyes on someone infiltrating the building, but that person got away."

"I'm not trying to tell you how to do your job, Agent Waterman, but isn't it true that we have no credible intel on what the person who slipped into that window was doing? We don't know if the perpetrator had anything to do with today's bomb scare, nor do we have intel suggesting it was someone with nefarious purposes aimed at the LESS Summit. As a matter of fact, a broken cash box in the café on the first floor suggests it might have been a burglary. Perhaps even a juvenile."

Lillian had had enough. "Like hell. That was no kid I fought last night—"

Derek held out a hand and Lillian quieted.

"Agent Muir is one of our top team members, Congresswoman Glasneck. I trust her implicitly. If she says it was an adult she fought, even though the perpetrator was wearing a mask, I believe her."

Glasneck glanced over at Lillian and gave her a slight nod. "I appreciate any woman who works and fights in the midst of what is primarily a man's world. I know a little about that. So I'm honestly not trying to be disrespectful when I say that I'm sorry the perpetrator was able to get the best of you in a fight."

"Guy had the help of a Taser," Jace said.

"That's just about the only way someone would get a jump on Lillian otherwise," Saul insisted. Everyone else nodded.

At least Lillian knew her team felt she was fully capable of taking care of herself in a situation. Derek hadn't provided any details about what had happened after the guy had Tasered her. Lillian didn't know if Congresswoman Glasneck knew, either.

Not that it mattered. The long and short of it was, Lillian had gotten her ass handed to her. And almost died because of it.

"I'm sure that's true," Glasneck said. "But the point is, Agent Muir wasn't in any shape to ascertain the perpetrator's true intent. It quite possibly could've been a burglar she stumbled in on."

"The facts of the situation let us know that it was definitely not a simple break-in," Derek said.

Lillian knew he was trying to keep the details about the "suicide" note confidential.

"Suffice it to say we have definite cause to believe the person who broke in was someone who knew Lillian. Was probably a terrorist named Damien Freihof that has been plaguing Omega Sector for months."

The older woman huffed out a breath. "But you have no proof of that."

Derek remained steady. "No, no proof. But we also know, based on evidence left at the scene, it was someone acquainted with Agent Muir. So although it may not have been Damien Freihof, it also means it wasn't a simple break-in."

Derek definitely wasn't mentioning the mole was probably sitting somewhere inside this room. That would not instill confidence.

"Okay, it wasn't a burglar." The congresswoman held out her hands in front of her. "But you can agree that maybe it was someone with a vendetta against Agent Muir. And that it had nothing to do with the summit itself."

Derek nodded shortly. "Yes. That is possible. But I can tell you that hosting the summit at the Denver City and County Building, no matter how picturesque, is a mistake. Someone wanting to attack the summit has had too much time to prepare. Moving to an unknown secondary location will put any potential attacker back at square one."

"Also puts us back at square one," Carnell muttered. "Finding a suitable replacement, getting all the plans, figuring out the details…that's going to take time we don't have, considering the summit is tomorrow."

A lot of that work would fall on Carnell because of his computer skills, so Lillian couldn't blame him for his frustration. Neither option—sticking with the building they were familiar with, but so was their enemy, or moving to an entirely unknown place—was very good.

"Agent Waterman, we have dozens of important people from all over the country coming to witness the initialization of the LESS system. And that doesn't include the thousands of other government officials and law-enforcement officers who will be watching from their stations as LESS goes live."

"We're all aware of the VIPs, Congresswoman. You're one of them."

"I'm least of them," the woman said, and laughed. "But thank you. I don't want this summit to take place in some back room across town just because of what might be a potential threat, but might not be. The very purpose of LESS is to show terrorists and criminals that law enforcement will not cower. We will face terror and crime head-on, standing together."

It was a rousing speech, one the woman obviously already had planned before this debrief had started. But Lillian could see her point. Looking around, she saw it was obvious the rest of the team could, too.

"Yeah, boss," Saul said. "Let's prove what we can do. What law enforcement can do. We don't cower."

Lillian almost had to roll her eyes again, but she couldn't fault the newbie's enthusiasm. Evidently, neither could Derek.

"All right, Congresswoman, since we don't have conclusive evidence of any upcoming attack, we'll keep the summit at city hall. But you have to understand that if intel changes, so will security plans. I won't put people at undue risk just for some photo ops."

Glasneck nodded. "Agreed. And I wouldn't expect you to. Now, I'm sure your team has better things to do than sit around and talk to me. I'll let you get to your business and I'll handle mine." The woman nodded, then left, her aides and Secret Service agent, on special loan for the summit, following behind.

Derek turned to the team, who was mostly lined up across the wall. "Okay, people, you heard the lady, we're back at the City and County Building. We will be resweeping it from top to bottom. I know it's nobody's favorite job, but we'll be doing it anyway. We'll be checking every damn nook and cranny until we know it's secure."

Saul was already nodding enthusiastically, like he couldn't wait to get to it. That would pass. It was something Saul didn't understand and it might be part of the reason why he'd never been chosen for a permanent part of the team. He wanted action all the time. But a lot of SWAT work was boring. Routine. Knowing how to handle the boredom was just as important as knowing how to handle the action. Maybe even more so because there wasn't any outlet for the boredom.

You either figured out how to handle it or got another job.

And now they had a lot of hours of tedious work in front of them. Made even more difficult since they didn't know if the mole was someone on the team. It was the other reason why Derek hadn't pushed harder against Congresswoman Glasneck for a new location for the summit. Because if one of their inner team members was the mole, changing locations wasn't going to protect them against an attack.

Nothing would.

Lillian stood to join the rest of the team as they began to exit the conference room. Dizziness assailed her and she grabbed the back of a nearby chair to steady herself.

Jace was immediately next to her. "You okay?" He said it softly enough that no one else could hear and blocked the rest of the room from being able to see her. He was protecting her in the way he knew would mean the most to her.

Just like he'd trusted her to get the bomb defused earlier. If he hadn't, if he'd tried to rush in and take over for her, they'd both be dead. Them and that poor sexist bastard who'd been hyperventilating in the elevator.

Jace was strong enough not to feel threatened by her strength. He also knew her well enough to know she wouldn't want him fawning over her in this moment. That the best way he could help was by being a human shield to keep others from seeing her in a moment of weakness.

How could this man still be so perfect for her after so many years?

Lillian couldn't help it, she breathed in his scent as he stood so close to her. Sweat. Male.

Jace.

They were both still in full tactical gear from the elevator incident, so being too close wasn't even possible. But he was still the sexiest thing she'd ever seen.

"Lil?" he asked again when she didn't answer. "You okay?"

"Yeah." She nodded, clearing her voice when the word came out hoarse from the earlier trauma. "Just stood up too fast. Plus, it's already been a long day and it's about to get longer."

"You need a break?"

She felt his hand on her elbow.

"Maybe we shouldn't have used all your downtime for…other activities this morning."

Lillian smiled. She couldn't help it. She couldn't even pretend that what had happened in the hotel room between them was anything short of spectacular. "I liked the *other activities*."

Jace winked at her and she felt heat zip through her. "Good. Because I'm hoping to show you some variations on those *other activities* later."

More steady now, she turned with Jace and followed the others out of the room. Derek joined them, shooting off assignments as he went. Denver PD would be sending backup to help with the initial securing of the building, but someone from Omega Sector would be double-checking every floor. And then a different person from the Omega team would check it again.

To an outsider it would look like diligence, having two separate team members looking for security leaks. And maybe it was diligence. But it was also to try to protect themselves from the mole.

As they walked back over to the City and County Building from the federal building, the crowds of people were steadily getting bigger. Lillian noticed Philip Carnell was walking alone. Not unusual—most people didn't want to converse with Carnell unless they had to.

But Lillian noticed he was walking stiffly, as if he was in pain. A few moments later he moved the material of his long-sleeve shirt—and she saw a bruise on his forearm.

Right where bruises would've been if he'd blocked some kicks and punches in a fight.

Lillian tried to focus on the details of her fight with the masked man. Could it have been Carnell? She didn't think Carnell was physically capable of the fighting skill level of the man she'd gone up against.

But heaven knew Carnell was brilliant enough to have been faking his weaknesses. The guy had a mind like a computer—he could've figured out long ago that he needed to appear weak physically to the team to throw suspicion off himself.

The masked man she'd fought had been roughly the same height. She'd thought he was more muscular than Carnell, but he tended to wear such loose clothing at Omega Sector that Lillian couldn't say for certain what his actual physique was.

Was this the bastard who had attacked her, Tasered her, then strung her up in the hallway, leaving her to die?

"Carnell, wait up." She marched over to him as they reached the steps to city hall. He slowed slightly, looking at her with irritation.

"What do you want?"

The guy really was a jerk.

"Where'd you get that bruise on your arm?"

Carnell's eyes narrowed. "None of your damn business."

She grabbed his wrist. "Is it new? It's pretty purple. Hasn't turned green, so it must have happened in the last twenty-four hours."

Carnell snatched his arm back and pushed down his sleeve. "What do you want, Muir? I'm trying to work out the best way to split up the team to be most effective in securing the building. I don't have time for your little power play."

Before he could move farther away, Lillian had his left wrist in her hand. She twisted it, to bring his arm around his back, and pushed him against the metal banister of the stairway, her other hand reaching up and applying pressure at his throat. "Do I look like I'm playing anything, Carnell? Where the hell did you get the bruise on your forearm and why are you walking so stiffly? Do you have other bruises? Maybe take a kick to the ribs? A punch to the sternum?" All had been blows she'd delivered during her fight.

"Are you crazy?" Carnell yelled, eyes wide. "Let go of me!"

"Mind if I get in on the fun?"

Lillian heard Jace's voice just over her shoulder.

"He's got bruises on his forearm, Jace. Looks a lot like defensive wounds. And he's walking funny, like he got in a fight recently. Pretty suspicious, don't you think?"

"What the hell are you talking about?" Carnell spat out.

"Let him go, Lillian." This time it was Derek over her other shoulder.

"Derek—"

"I understand your concerns," Derek continued. "But let him go so he can talk."

Reluctantly Lillian took her hand from Carnell's throat and released his wrist. She didn't lower her guard, ready to move quickly if he went to draw a weapon or run.

Carnell looked over at Derek. "Did you see that? She attacked me for no reason. She's emotionally unstable."

Derek turned to the rest of the team. "Everyone else inside. You know your initial assignments, so get to them."

The rest of the team dispersed, although they looked like they wanted to stay.

"Where are the bruises from, Philip?" Derek asked once everyone was gone.

"I don't have to tell you," Carnell sputtered. "It's none of your damn business."

Lillian felt the heat of Jace's body directly behind her shoulder. "It is when it seems like some of your bruises match some of the hits taken by the guy who attacked Lillian late last night."

"Know anything about that, Carnell?" Lillian asked.

"What? No. I wouldn't attack you, Muir. Why the hell would I want to fight you? Everybody knows you could kick my ass. Everybody on the team could kick my ass, that's why I'm not an official SWAT member, remember?"

She narrowed her eyes at him. "Maybe you've just been acting like you couldn't fight. Throw suspicion off yourself."

"Suspicion of what? Me being the mole?"

"You know anything about that?" Derek asked.

He rolled his eyes. "You said there was no proof, but we all know there's a mole somewhere inside Omega. Somebody's helping Damien Freihof. But it's not me."

"Where'd you get the bruises, Carnell?" Lillian asked again. He certainly had the know-how and the smarts to be the mole. She didn't like to think that he'd beaten her in a fight, but it was possible.

"It's none of your damn business, but if you must know, I got a little roughed up by a couple of guys outside a bar last night."

Derek's eyebrows shot up. "What the hell were you doing at a bar when we're all on duty?"

Carnell snorted loudly. "I wasn't actually at the bar. I don't need a lot of sleep, so I was walking around town. I passed a bar as a couple of guys were coming out and I may have made a disparaging remark about the team on their sports jerseys. They didn't like it and I took a few punches."

Lillian looked over at Jace and then at Derek—they both wore matching bemused looks. None of them had a problem imagining Carnell getting beat on because he ran his mouth to the wrong people.

"I blocked one punch," he continued, "but still took a couple to the midsection. Luckily some other people came out of the bar, and I left while they were distracted."

Was he telling the truth? It seemed like it, but Lillian didn't know the younger man well enough to know. And she had to admit after everything that had happened in the last twelve hours—attacked, almost killed, earth-shattering lovemaking, almost killed again by a bomb this time—she was not at her sharpest.

"Can anybody vouch for you?" Derek asked. "Your whereabouts?"

"I'm sure if I could track down the jerks who jumped me they'd be glad to try to finish the job. But no, other than them I wasn't really socializing. Why the hell do you guys care anyway? I'm sick of being everyone's punching bag. First strangers and now my so-called teammates. Don't we have enough bad guys to concentrate on?"

"Go on in the building and get set up, Philip," Derek said. "We'll be inside in just a minute."

Carnell was still muttering to himself as he left and walked into the building. Lillian wiped a hand across her face as she turned to look at Jace and Derek.

"That very well could be our mole," Jace said, taking a step closer to her. "God knows he's smart enough to be."

"The guy you fought knew what he was doing, right, Lillian?" Derek asked.

"Yes. If it wasn't for Carnell's bruises, I would never have suspected he could've been the guy that got the jump on me."

Jace shook his head. "It could've been a second person. You don't know."

"Following Carnell stealthily, trying to see what he was up to without his knowledge, probably would've been the better plan than a hostile confrontation."

Derek's tone was completely neutral, but Lillian knew she'd made a huge tactical error in what she'd just done. "I'm sorry, Derek. I screwed up."

"You're tired, in pain and your judgment is being affected."

Again neutral. But Lillian still felt like she might vomit. "I—"

Derek held out a hand to stop her. "You'll go back to the hotel and rest for twelve hours before coming back on duty."

What? "You need me here. You need every man you can get."

"I'll need you more over the next two days as the summit swings into full gear. So get the downtime you need so you can come back in top shape." Derek put his hand on her shoulder. "Lillian, if anyone else had been through what you had yesterday and today, you would encourage me to give them the time they needed to regroup. This is not a reflection on your ability. This is about keeping the team running as efficiently as possible."

She knew Derek was right, but it still sucked. She felt like she'd let him down. Let the team down.

"We're going to be on rotating shifts from now until

the summit is completed," Derek continued. "You're just taking the first down shift."

"Okay." Damn it.

Derek looked over at Jace. "You two are on my very short list of people I know I can trust. I'm going to need you firing on all cylinders." Derek squeezed her shoulder, then turned and walked into city hall.

She looked at Jace. "I guess I'm grounded and am going to take a nap."

He smiled. "I guess I shouldn't have kept you up this morning."

She rubbed her eyes. "Then we can agree that me acting like a complete moron and losing us the upper hand with the potential mole is all your fault."

"You reacted. It happens."

Lillian rubbed her eyes again. "Derek's right. I'm tired. My judgment is impaired."

He pulled her closer by her tactical vest. "Then do what the man says and get some rest."

She grabbed her extra hotel card key out of a Velcro pocket, held it up to Jace and told him her room number. "Join me later if your downtime happens to coincide with mine?"

She didn't want to think too hard about the butterflies she got inside her chest when he nodded and smiled. He kissed her on the tip of her nose, turned and jogged into the building. She couldn't tear her eyes off him.

She was in so much trouble.

Chapter 14

It had been a long-ass day. Jace had worked with the others, helping to confirm the security of the Denver City and County Building. Derek had used Jace mostly to double-check particularly vulnerable places, since he knew Jace couldn't be the mole. There were definitely no unsecured windows or doors in this building now.

For the moment. Jace and Derek both knew the mole could come back and change that situation.

Jace had left a few markers—invisible to anyone but him—in areas he thought would be potential targets for Freihof or the mole. These markers, generally made of pretty innocuous items like tape and string, would let him know if windows or doors had been opened or tampered with when he went back and checked them. Derek was doing the same, trying to keep the LESS Summit secure and catch the mole at the same time.

They both knew fighting a war on two fronts was the surest way to lose. But right now it was their only option, especially with someone potentially working against them.

Was it Carnell? The bruises were suspicious. Even in the short time Jace had been around he'd noticed the man was always angry. Always talking about elitist problems in Omega Sector and the lack of pedigree in law enforcement in general. Definitely corresponded with some of the "Manifesto of Change" document Ren McClement had shown Jace back in his office in DC.

But Lillian had said the man she'd followed in the window had put up a pretty good fight before she'd been Tasered. Jace had difficulty believing she couldn't drop Carnell in under five seconds flat.

Hell, she could drop Jace in under ten if he didn't use every skill he had.

So neither he nor Derek thought Carnell was the man who'd fought and strung up Lillian last night.

Speaking of, that damn key card had been burning a hole in his pocket for the past seven hours. Jace had purposely forced himself not to think about Lillian, to focus on the task at hand as he worked. The job required his focus, and Lillian needed time to rest.

Seeing how upset she'd been with herself over how she'd handled Carnell had been painful. Derek had been right to give her the first down shift. Everybody had their limits. Lillian's body and mind had evidently reached hers.

Jace damn well hoped she'd spent the last few hours sleeping. Now that Derek had told him to break, Jace planned to wake her up in the most pleasurable way possible, then hopefully talk her back into another nap afterward. In his arms. Both of them naked.

Full-on grin covering his face, Jace found himself all but jogging back to the hotel. It was already dark again. He should be exhausted, but as he peeled away his tactical gear and showered, all he could think about was getting to Lillian.

She'd given him her room key. And while that wasn't exactly an engagement ring, Jace recognized it for what it was: a statement of trust.

Nothing about Lillian then or now suggested she gave her trust easily.

He used the key to enter her room. It was dark inside except for the light on in the bathroom with the door cracked. Evidently Lillian didn't like the dark.

"Lil, you awake?" he said softly, looking at her small form huddled in the bed. She'd kicked part of the blankets off, showing off one leg. She was dressed in just an oversize T-shirt and her underwear.

It was possibly the sexiest thing Jace had seen in his whole life.

"Lil?" he said again, moving closer.

"Hey," she said sleepily, turning toward him. "What took you so long?"

It was all the invitation Jace needed. He stripped his shirt over his head, pulled off his sweats and climbed into the bed with her. God, he had been purposely *not* thinking about this all day, knowing he'd never be able to focus on the task at hand if he did.

Bracing his elbows on either side of her head, he lowered his weight on her. "Hey, sexy."

He brought his lips to hers, easing them open. She shifted beneath him, a soft sigh escaping her. He grabbed her under one of her knees and hooked her leg up over his hips, bringing their bodies closer together. He couldn't stop the moan that escaped him. Didn't even try.

He ran one hand up and down the outer part of her thigh on the leg wrapped around his hip. His other gripped her hair, tilting her head back so he could kiss her more fully. He felt her fingernails grip into his shoulders and groaned again.

His lips moved down her jaw to her throat, to that place right under her ear that he knew was so sensitive. He nipped at it. "You have no idea how good it feels to be here with you. It was difficult convincing myself that national security mattered when I knew I had that key in my pocket."

He waited for a sarcastic comment, but none came. She hadn't said or done anything since he first climbed on top of her. He hiked her leg up a little higher, rubbing their bodies together more fully. Maybe she just needed a little bit more time to wake up.

He brushed his lips back down her throat, the bruises still noticeable even in the semidarkness. She was hurt, a little fragile, he needed to remember that.

"You okay, sweetheart?" He moved the edge of her shirt aside with his lips, kissing across her collarbone. She still didn't answer.

He leaned up on his elbows so he could look down at her more clearly. Her brown eyes stared directly at him. "This can wait, you know." He smiled and trailed a finger across her cheek. He brushed her lips against his and her mouth seemed to automatically open for him. He kissed her again softly. "We can just sleep if you want. Believe it or not, I can convince certain parts of my body to simmer down when needed."

Again, no smart-aleck remark. He didn't even think Lillian was capable of that.

"You're going pretty easy on me tonight," he said. "Are you sure you didn't get some sort of head injury?" He kissed her again. Her lips opened as soon as his touched hers, but then she didn't respond.

As a matter of fact, her hands were still on his shoulders, and hadn't moved. Her leg was still around his hips, where he'd placed it.

As soon as he removed his lips from hers, her mouth closed. Jace bent down to kiss her again and they opened.

But then did nothing.

What the hell was going on?

"Lillian?" He eased his weight off her farther. Her hands remained on his shoulders, her eyes open and looking right at him.

"Lillian." He shook her a little. "Lily? What's going on? Talk to me, sweetheart."

Did she have some sort of head injury he hadn't been aware of? She'd been fine earlier. Maybe a little off her game, stressed, but she certainly hadn't been blanking out when she handled that bomb scare today.

He rolled his weight completely off her. Her arms dropped to her side on the mattress. Her eyes still had that blank stare. Like the body lying here was just an empty shell of the strong, vibrant woman she usually was.

Jace had seen this sort of blank stare before…a checking out of reality. But it had been men in the army suffering from PTSD.

And always, if the person was in no danger of hurting himself or others, the best thing was to leave his subconscious to work through it in his own way.

"Come back to me, Lil. Whatever it is, whatever you're going through, we can work through it."

Tears streamed out of her open eyes and down the sides of her face, but she didn't move, didn't blink, didn't talk.

She was trapped in some hell in her mind and there was nothing Jace could do.

It was only a little over twenty minutes before Lillian came back to him, but it was one of the longest passages of time that he'd ever lived through.

He was still sitting next to her on the bed, holding her hand, when she finally started blinking. Tension rolled through her body and she began breathing more heavily.

"Lily? It's Jace. You're safe."

She snatched her hand out of his before scooting over to the far side of the bed, pulling the comforter up to her chin. Her eyes darted around the room like she was looking for danger. Like she couldn't figure out where she was.

"You're safe, Lillian. You're at a hotel in Denver."

She got out of the bed now, back to the wall, obviously ready to fight.

Jace kept his voice even and his body still, not wanting to send her into a full panic. And he sure as hell didn't want her reaching for the sidearm that sat on the bedside table while she was in this condition. "We're on a mission with the SWAT team to protect the LESS Summit. You...fell asleep. You're disoriented."

It took her a few more moments of him repeating the same words before they began sinking in. And while she didn't relax, at least she didn't look like she was about to fight off an entire army.

"Jace?"

Thank God. "Yeah, sweetheart. It's me. You scared me there for a bit. We were in the middle of making out and I lost you."

To his utter dismay, big tears filled her eyes and rolled down her cheeks. Not counting the tears that had seemed to leak out of her eyes of their own accord a little while ago, this was the first time Jace could remember seeing Lillian cry. The sight of them gutted him.

"Lily—"

She took a step back. "I'm sorry, Jace. Please don't look at me like that. It's not you, it just happens sometimes."

His eyes narrowed. "What happens?"

She squeezed her eyes closed, one hand pulling the blanket more tightly around her, the other gesturing toward the bed. "I blank out during sex. But I promise it's not your fault. It's me. Please don't take it personally. It wasn't you."

Jace could feel bile pooling in his stomach as he took in the ramifications of her words.

This wasn't the first time this had happened to her.

The blackouts didn't have anything to do with combat. This was centered around sex. Steve Drackett had been right back in Ren's office.

Lillian was recovering from some sort of sexual assault.

He forced himself to ignore the way his heart seemed to be shattering around him. He had to understand exactly what she was dealing with. "This happens to you a lot?"

She kept her eyes tightly closed. Almost like a child who believed the monsters would go away if she didn't face them. "I don't want to talk about it. I just didn't want you to think it was your fault. That it was something you did."

He eased a little closer on the bed. "Did it happen this morning when we were together?"

Now her eyes opened. "No! No, this morning was… great. I was there. *Completely* there. The whole time. But this morning was the exception, not the norm."

"But…it happens to you a lot?"

Her tiny nod told him everything he needed to know. The thought of this happening to her when she was with someone else. Someone who wouldn't notice, or worse, take advantage. Jace struggled to tamp down the rage. "*How* often?"

"Until this morning? Pretty much always."

"For how long?" Maybe the trauma was recent. That, while still being horrible, was at least understandable.

She shook her head, obviously not wanting to answer the question. Keeping his hands out in front of him, palms up in a gesture of nonaggression, he eased closer again.

"It's behind me," she whispered. "That's all you need to know."

"It's obviously not behind you, based on the fact that thirty minutes ago when we were kissing, your eyes were open and your hands were on my shoulders, but your conscious mind was miles from that bed. It had hidden itself away to protect your psyche."

She opened her mouth to respond, but no words came out. Finally, she just shook her head.

"You were raped." God, he hated to even say that word to her. It was bitter, unbearable in his mouth.

She nodded, her brown eyes not leaving his.

He thought his heart had already been shattered, but he'd been wrong. Watching that small move of her head confirmed everything he'd feared, but hadn't wanted to believe… The pain nearly doubled him over. "How long ago?"

She shook her head adamantly.

Why would she not want to answer that question? Was it so recent that she couldn't bear to think about it at all?

"Lily, I need you to tell me. I want to be careful not to do or say anything that will trigger you in any way." He got out of the bed and took a step closer, now just a few feet from her, relieved when she didn't flinch away. "What we had this morning was special. It can be again. But I need you to trust me enough to tell me what happened to you so we can navigate this together. Please, baby."

"I can't, Jace," she whispered, those big brown eyes begging him to let it go. "I'm sorry."

He didn't want to push. Didn't want to ask her to give more than she could. But he also couldn't risk doing something that would have her retreating into that shell again.

"Okay, you don't have to talk to me." He pushed down the hurt. This wasn't about him. "But I'm going to go. I don't want to stay here with you and take a chance on triggering you again."

"Jace…"

The pain in her voice tore at him.

"I'm not mad, Tiger Lily." He took a chance and stepped closer. When she didn't move away, he slipped a hand in her hair at the nape of her neck. He pulled her forward until his lips met her forehead. "I understand you don't want to talk about it. But I can't stay here and take a chance on hurting you further. Doing damage because I'm not sure of how to navigate your emotional terrain."

He backed away, giving her the best smile he could. His Lillian was broken, and she didn't trust him enough to try to help her put herself back together. He really wasn't mad about that—she needed to work through this however was best for her. He would be her friend if she wanted it. But he would not take a chance on hurting her further. Of using her the way she'd obviously been used by other men.

"We'll talk more when you're ready. Maybe after this op is over." Pulling away was like a knife ripping him in the gut. But what else could he do? "I just don't want to hurt you more."

He gave her a gentle nod, then turned and walked toward the door. He was almost to it, hand on the knob, when he heard her words. He'd thought nothing she could say would've been worse than the initial knowledge that she'd been raped.

He was so, so wrong.

Her words changed everything he'd always held true.

"Twelve. I was raped twelve years ago."

Chapter 15

What was she doing? Was she really going to tell Jace the truth? The truth about her? About Daryl? About what had really happened?

She'd only ever spoken about it to Grace Parker. And even then she'd left out details. Jace was not going to let her leave out details.

He turned from the door and moved back into the main section of the room. She could see his blue eyes staring out at her. Not in disbelief—she'd never for one second thought he wouldn't believe her—but in full tactical mode.

He was trying to put together the pieces.

"Lil, you have to just tell me. Because I swear nothing you could say would be any worse than what I'm imagining in my mind."

Wanna bet?

She didn't say the words but knew the truth was worse than whatever Jace was thinking. Was almost more than she could bear to think about. She didn't want to hurt him unnecessarily. Daryl was his brother. They'd never gotten along, and Jace had joined the army to get out from Daryl's thumb as soon as possible, but Daryl had been his brother.

No one would want to believe their own flesh and blood was capable of what his brother had done.

"Oh, God, it was Daryl, wasn't it?"

The anguish in Jace's voice made her want to rush to him, to hold him. To erase the agony in his eyes as she nodded.

He seemed to age right before her eyes. "Tell me."

"It was after my eighteenth birthday. The day before we were supposed to leave. After you and I…" She nodded and shrugged.

Jace knew what she meant. After they'd had sex. She'd wanted to have sex with him for months before her birthday, but he'd refused everything but making out. Had said they'd have a lifetime together to make love. They could at least wait until they were both legal.

God, she'd loved him for that. It had made her feel so special, cherished. That she was worth waiting for.

"I got a text from you saying to meet you at the warehouse," she continued. Daryl's warehouse, where a lot of his illegal activities had taken place. "I knew you didn't like me to go there alone, but I thought you'd gotten home from your job for Daryl early. The last job. I can't even remember what it was anymore." Not surprising, given all that had happened afterward.

"I was supposed to deliver an order of pharmaceutical drugs," Jace whispered. "To a place clear on the other side of the state. The dealer I was supposed to deliver them to never even showed up."

They looked at each other, realizing now it had all been a setup.

Lillian moved back over to the window, needing some distance, unable to face the blueness of Jace's eyes for this next part. "I got to the warehouse and Daryl was waiting for me. Said he had found out we were leaving to join the army. Said there was no way he was going to let two of his best and most loyal runners leave at the same time."

God, she'd been so naive. Had thought there was nothing Daryl could do to stop them. Had laughed at Daryl and told him that. Now that she was eighteen she could go wherever she wanted. And Jace had already been twenty. He would've left earlier if it hadn't been for her. If he hadn't wanted to be able to leave with her legally.

She wished they'd just run away from the very beginning.

"I told him he couldn't stop us, we were leaving the next day." She pressed her head against the cold glass. "He hit me in the stomach over and over. Dislocated my shoulder. Kicked me in the legs. It was before I knew how to fight. How to protect myself."

The muscles and bones in question still twinged in horrific memory.

"He didn't hit you in the face."

She could hear the coarse tightness in Jace's voice.

She shook her head against the glass. "No," she whispered.

"Because he didn't want there to be any bruises I could see. He knew that if I thought he'd forced you in any way, I would fight him. Kill him."

She heard Jace pacing.

"Or die trying to get you out."

"He—he raped me. Then locked me in the tiny janitor's closet and left me in there all night. I knew you'd be looking for me. That all I had to do was survive until you found me." That whole day was a blur of pain and trauma, but *that* she could remember. The knowledge that Jace would come for her. Would make her world all right again.

"Lillian…"

The pain in his voice was too much. She continued faster. She wasn't helping either of them by dragging it out like this. She took a second to distance herself from the story mentally. "Daryl came back and got me the next morning. I was in pretty bad shape from the beating. He raped me again, then threw clean clothes at me to put on. Told me to get dressed, that you were coming over."

She heard Jace's strangled sound behind her. She continued. "Daryl told me there was no way both of us were leaving. He told me he had one of the guys in the rafters of the warehouse, with a rifle on you. Told me that if I didn't just sit there and shut up, he would have you shot. And that while you were bleeding out he would rape me again right in front of you before you died."

Jace's curse was vile.

She finally turned from the window. "Looking back on it now, I think he was bluffing. You were his *brother*. I don't think he would've killed you. He might have killed me to keep you from leaving, but he wasn't going to kill you."

"Lily…" He took a step toward her, but she held out a hand to ward him off. He could not touch her right now. Not at this very second.

"Daryl overplayed his hand. I think he thought you would come back. That you would fight him for me or something. I'm not sure. I don't think either of us thought you would just believe his lies so easily. Believe that I just jumped into his bed straight from yours."

Jace shook his head, no color left in his face. "Daryl came to see me a couple hours before I came by there. Told me you had come to him. That you had said I was moving too fast, that you didn't want to leave. That you didn't know how to tell me you weren't coming with me to join the army. That you wanted his protection and were even willing to sleep with him if that was what it cost."

She hadn't known any of that. "You believed him?"

"No, although I had to admit it was not outside the realm of possibility. I was talking forever and marriage and you were barely eighteen, for crying out loud. Thinking I was pushing too hard was my button. And Daryl didn't just push it, he *stomped* on it."

"It was always his talent."

"When I got to the warehouse and saw you there, saw you clinging to him… I thought for once in his miserable life my brother was telling the truth. That I had pushed you too hard."

She nodded. "He manipulated us both."

"I'm so sorry, Lily. I should've gotten you alone. Talked to you."

She shook her head. "I wouldn't have told you. I really thought he would kill you."

"Why didn't you come find me afterward? Once I was in the army Daryl couldn't hurt me."

She'd told him this much. She had to tell it all. "He kept me locked up. In that closet. He knew I would run, would tell you if I got the chance. He kept me there in the dark and only let me out when he…when he…"

She didn't finish, but she didn't have to. Jace knew what she meant. Daryl let her out when he raped her. Those days, those weeks, were all a blur of agony and darkness to her. When Daryl had gotten tired of her, he'd given her to a couple of his best men as a reward.

By then her brain had learned to check out every time a man touched her. So she didn't remember that at all.

"He had other girls there, Jace. Daryl did. I think it's part of the reason both of us were feeling the itch to get out. It was one thing to run drugs or weapons every once in a while…"

"Quite another to find out human trafficking is involved," he said, finishing for her, and nodding. "I had my suspicions things might be heading that way before I left, but didn't have any proof. And then Daryl died and everything he'd put together disbanded, so there wasn't much point in trying to prove it one way or another."

She had to tell him all of it, Lillian knew that. Would he hate her for it? It didn't matter, because even if he did, she didn't regret her actions. "I killed him, Jace."

He didn't even blink. "Good."

"I'm serious. I was…with him when the fire started. He ran over to see what was happening and I hit him over the head with a bottle of tequila he had lying around. The whole building was going up in flames and I ran."

"Good," Jace said again.

"You don't understand, I could've told someone Daryl was still in there. There probably would've been time to get him out."

"No, you don't understand, Lily. I'm glad you killed him. That saves me the trouble of committing cold-blooded murder now. Because that's exactly what would be happening if my bastard brother was still alive."

Relief coursed through Lillian.

"You look surprised." He shook his head. "Did you really think I would be okay with what Daryl did to you?"

She shrugged. "He was your brother."

"He stopped being my brother twelve years ago, the second he touched you. Don't have any doubt about that." He scrubbed his hands across his face, looking older. Pained. "I can never make up for what happened to you. But I am so sorry."

"It wasn't your fault."

She flinched as Jace slammed the back of his fist against the wall. "It damn well was my fault. At least part of it. I knew Daryl was edging from risky ventures into downright dangerous ones. Knew he was crossing lines that no one would think was okay."

"That's why you wanted out."

He took a step toward her. "That's why I wanted *both* of us out. Because he was becoming unstable. It was just a matter of time before everything blew up in his face—which it did, literally—and I didn't want us caught in the flames."

They stared at each other for long minutes.

"Why did you believe him, Jace?" Why hadn't he been able to see the truth?

"It's like you said, Daryl was the master manipulator. He'd played on my deepest fear, that I really was rushing you. You were so young. Hadn't had any life experiences. That I was forcing you into a life you didn't really want, taking away your choices."

"I wanted to go," she whispered. More than anything in the world she'd wanted to leave with Jace.

"I was a fool. Blinded to the truth by my own insecurities. That you might want someone like Daryl. More powerful. Stronger. He hinted that it was true and I bought it like a sale at Christmas."

Her heart broke as she watched his eyes fill up with tears.

"I'll never forgive myself, Lily."

"You didn't know."

"I should've reconfirmed. I should've made sure you were okay. Hell, even if you really did want him, I should've barged in and tried to convince you otherwise. The first thing we learn in the army is that you never leave someone behind. I left you behind, Lil. You were tortured, for God's sake."

She wanted to disagree with him but knew words wouldn't pacify him. And he was right. She had been tortured. Physically, mentally, emotionally.

She couldn't take his pain away, but she could help him understand what had come from it. The phoenix that had risen from the ashes. "But I grew stronger,

Jace. Yeah, I may still be a bit of a mess when it comes to sex." He flinched, but she continued. "But I'm also a kick-ass warrior because of what Daryl did to me. I became determined never to be a victim again. And have spent my life trying to keep other people from being victims also."

"You *are* a warrior, Lil. A formidable one."

She felt something ease in her heart. "I am. I know that. And because of it—knowing the lives I've saved in the years since I've joined Omega—I can't fully regret what happened to me."

"The blackouts…"

Now it was her turn to rub a hand across her face. "The blackouts are problematic. And part of it was because I refused to get emotionally attached to anyone before having sex with him. I was working with a psychiatrist about that before she…died. But I didn't have a blackout with you this morning, Jace. I was with you. Completely focused on the moment. And it was the best thing that has happened to me in a dozen years. My body remembers you, I think. Or my mind knows that you would never hurt me."

He took a step toward her. "I would never hurt you, Lil. Never."

She smiled. "I know. I've always known. And even with my blackouts… I'm not afraid. I'm confident of my ability to fight my way out of any situation if needed. But it's like my brain doesn't know how to process the old and the new information together. I feel a man's weight on me and my brain just shuts down."

"And when you come back?"

"I have no memory of what has happened. My brain is still trying to protect me from trauma even all these years later. Even though I don't want it to. Grace—my psychiatrist before that bastard Damien Freihof killed her—said it was because those men meant nothing to me. That eventually when I had sex with someone who I truly cared about, my brain wouldn't shut down."

"Like this morning." The ghost of a smile crossed his lips but then disappeared. "How can you ever forgive me? How can you even bear to be in the same room as me? I failed you so completely."

She walked over to him, more confidence filling her with every step. Grace had been right. Her brain had been shutting down because she was making bad choices, not because of fear. Now that she had the chance to be with someone she knew cared about her, she wasn't going to shut down.

"Jace, you would never have left me there if you'd known." She cupped his cheeks. "I always knew that. You would've died trying to get me out. We both made mistakes. We both paid a price. But I refuse to give Daryl any more of my history. He's dead. He can stay dead."

"You blanked on me tonight."

She shrugged. "I'm always going to have triggers. Maybe just make sure I'm always fully awake before starting anything."

"Deal. As long as you promise to tell me if anything I do or say starts to frighten you in any way."

She breathed a silent sigh of relief when he wrapped his arms around her. She listened to the reassuring beat of his heart for long minutes. "I was afraid you wouldn't want me once you knew."

"Not wanting you is never even going to be an option, Tiger Lily."

"Good, because I'd like to give tonight another try. I hate to think I'd missed out on all the fun."

"Are you sure? We can just sleep. We don't have to—"

She kissed him. She knew he was feeling guilty. But if there was one thing her training had taught her, it was that facing problems head-on as soon as they came along meant that they didn't grow into something insurmountable the next day.

Like she said, she refused to give up any more ground to Daryl Eakin. He'd taken too much. Now he could stay in his grave, where he belonged.

The brother she was always supposed to be with was here in her arms. She pressed herself closer to him, deepening the kiss. When she heard him groan, she knew she had him.

And this time she wasn't sure she was ever going to be able to let him go.

Chapter 16

Four hours later, Jace was out for a run, pushing himself much harder than he should have, given the parameters of the mission and what would be required of him over the next two days. Lillian had reported back for her shift about thirty minutes ago.

He turned down Oak, a deserted street, glad the temperature was at least a little over freezing even though it was February, and he didn't have to worry about ice. He knew enough about Denver to know he was on the rougher side of town, but he wished— Jace literally looked up at a star in the night sky and *wished*—some asshole would mess with him right now.

Jace wanted to fight. To feel the bones of some predator breaking under his hands. To throw his head back and howl in agony.

But mostly he wanted to go back in time and change what had happened to Lillian.

Daryl.

Jace wasn't kidding when he said it was a good thing his brother was dead. Otherwise Jace couldn't promise he wouldn't be about to turn his back on everything he'd ever held important and true—law, order, justice—and be on his way to kill his brother right at this second.

He was glad Lillian had left the bastard there in that fire. Had saved herself.

Jace had been in boot camp when Daryl died. The body had already been identified by one of Daryl's friends and put in a closed casket by the time Jace arrived, so Jace didn't know if Daryl had suffered, had burned. He'd hoped not, at the time. But now that had changed.

He took a turn down another deserted street, relishing the feel of the colder wind as it blew between buildings, the ache of his muscles as he pushed them further, the tightness of his lungs as he tried to draw in air.

Jace wasn't sure he was ever going to be able to draw in a full breath again for the rest of his life without it hurting.

He had failed Lillian in the worst way someone could fail another. The thought of her helpless in Daryl's clutches for two weeks burned like acid in his gut. She'd been so young, maybe not exactly helpless, but nowhere near the warrior she was now.

She'd been raped and abused so many times that her mind had shut down almost every time she'd tried to have sex since then.

And Jace…well, he'd just happily lived with his self-proclaimed righteous anger for a dozen years, believing *he'd* been the one who'd been wronged.

It would be downright laughable if it wasn't so pathetic.

The miracle of it all was that Lily didn't hate him. He'd watched her as she'd slept after their lovemaking tonight.

Lovemaking that had taken on an entirely new tenor. Now that Jace knew how close he'd come to losing her—physically, emotionally, in every way possible—all he could do was cherish her. Worship her with his body.

She hadn't let him treat her like she was fragile. And he did understand that. Lillian wasn't fragile.

But damn if he wouldn't treat her like the treasure she was. The treasure he would've had next to him, healthy and whole, for the past twelve years if he hadn't been so blinded by his own insecurities and tricked by a psychopath's words.

So many mistakes.

Watching Lily as she slept, he'd tried to process everything. Tried to wrap his head around the enormity of it all. He'd refused to let rage consume him at that moment. All he wanted to do was be there for her. Hold her if she needed it. Pull her back if she began to slip away again.

But she hadn't. She'd stayed there with him—with them—the entire time. No scary blank stares and waking up not knowing where she was. He'd counted every single second with her as a treasure.

When she'd gotten up and dressed to head in for her SWAT shift, he'd just watched her. Leaned back in the bed with his arm tucked behind his head, and stared at her as if he didn't have anywhere else in the world he'd rather be.

Which was damn near the truth.

"Pretty sexy, huh?" She'd gestured to her cargo pants and tactical boots.

"Damn right, more sexy on you than me."

She grinned at him, waggling her eyebrows. "I'm not so sure about that."

In that moment, grinning at each other, just enjoying each other's company the way they always had, it was impossible to reconcile that this woman—so in control, capable, strong—had been damaged in such a way.

He'd fought to not let his smile slip. Refused to look at her with concern or sympathy in his eyes. That wasn't what Lillian needed. The phoenix had risen from the ashes on her own. He would not drag her back down as he came to grips.

But now as he was out running, away from her, the rage coursed through him. Jace let it. Let his muscles take the punishment as his mind struggled to comprehend everything. By the time he made it back to the hotel, he was dripping with sweat, despite the cold. He wiped himself down with his sweatshirt before entering the lobby. Even though it wasn't time for his shift, he'd grab breakfast and head back to city hall.

Because sleep was not in the cards for Jace any time soon. It would be a long time before he could close his eyes and not picture an eighteen-year-old Lillian hurt, terrified, hoping he was going to rescue her from the darkness.

A rescue that had never occurred.

Rage pooled through him again.

"Eakin, are we not giving you enough to do that you need to spend your downtime doing extra workouts?" Derek was getting a cup of coffee from the small breakfast section of the hotel.

Jace couldn't even smile at the other man. "Just needed to work off some steam. Trust me, this will help me be more focused."

"You look like you'd like to go ten rounds with someone in the ring. This have anything to do with a petite brunette we both know?"

"She's not the one I want to fight, believe it or not. Although I'm sure she'd give me a run for my money anyway."

Derek offered Jace a glass of water from his table while he continued to sip his coffee. Jace thanked him with a tip of his head while he drank it down. The two of them studied each other in silence for a long moment.

"Is this where you warn me not to hurt her? To keep away from her?" Jace knew his tone was combative. Left over from his own frustrations.

Derek, unflappable as ever, just smiled and shook his head. "Lillian can take care of herself. If you hurt her, she'll be the one to kick your ass. I won't have to do it. To be honest, I'm just glad she's letting someone close enough to even be in the realm of possibility of hurting her."

"Maybe she has her reasons for not letting people close."

"Maybe." Derek held his hands out in a motion of surrender. "I'm not trying to fight with you, Jace. I've been her team leader, and *friend*, long enough to know that Lillian has some scars. And I'm human enough to know that not all scars are visible."

All the frustration just flowed out of Jace, despair taking its place. "Scars I could've prevented."

Derek pushed out the chair across from him with his foot and gestured for Jace to sit in it. "My wife is a forensic scientist. Works part-time for Omega now that we have a baby at home. Molly is quite possibly the most opposite of Lillian possible."

"How so?"

"Molly is shy, quiet, insecure outside the lab. She couldn't do a pull-up to save her life, and despite my best effort to teach her otherwise, still punches with her thumb resting against the side of her fist."

That caused the slightest of smiles to break out on his face. "Like a girl."

Derek's smile was much bigger. "Exactly."

"Lillian doesn't punch like a girl."

"No, she very definitely does not. Molly is soft. And I mean that in the very best way that word can be used. And we both know that Lillian is not soft. And I mean that also in the very best way."

Jace knew Derek had a point, so he took a sip of water while he waited for him to continue.

"A couple of years ago a psychopath kidnapped my Molly." All hint of a smile gone from Derek now. "Drugged and tortured her. Got her a second time and began breaking her fingers one by one while he was on the phone with me."

Jace sat up straighter. "Damn."

"What would Lillian do if someone did that to her?"

"I don't know. Probably work out a dozen different moves so that it would never happen again."

"Exactly. That's *exactly* what Lillian would do. Because Lillian needs to know that she can take care of herself physically in whatever situation she finds herself in. That under normal circumstances—Tasers being the exception—no one will ever get the drop on her again. Something she learned the hardest of ways before I ever met her."

Jace could only nod.

"Lillian and Molly are different because I've tried to teach Molly some self-defense moves, and while she'll learn them to humor me, generally after twenty minutes of practice she leans over and whispers that she'll just trust me to come rescue her if she ever gets back in another dangerous situation." Derek grinned. "Then distracts me into activities not having anything to do with self-defense."

"Somehow I can't imagine Lillian ever doing that."

"Of course not. But mostly because Lillian is never going to need you to come rescue her from a dangerous situation."

"Because in almost all situations she can rescue herself." Jace leaned back in his chair. "It's not that I don't appreciate it, but I'm not sure I'm getting the main point of your little pep talk."

"My point is, I never mistake Molly's softness for weakness. And her trust that I will get to her no matter what if she needs me is a vow I take very seriously. I will save her or die trying. But the fact is, Molly also saved me. Her strength—her emotional fortitude—is what dragged me out of the darkness when I couldn't find the way myself."

Jace nodded.

"Now, my wife is brilliant," Derek continued after another sip from his cup of coffee. "So she never asked me if I needed any emotional self-defense lessons.

Not that she had to be brilliant to figure out that I'm too stubborn to admit I might need help in that department. But the fact of the matter is this—the same way she trusts that I'll get her out if she's in trouble physically, I know she'll get me out if I'm in trouble emotionally."

"And you think that's what Lillian needs."

"I think she can take care of herself physically, but emotionally is a different story. She won't ever ask for help. Hell, I don't even know if she knows *how* to ask for it. I sure as hell didn't with Molly."

Derek was right. Probably about all of it.

"And believe it or not, helping her in that way— helping her discover and meet her emotional needs— is going to help you just as much as it helps her. I'm going to assume that whatever has you running like the hounds of hell are chasing you in the middle of a February night has to do with Lillian's scars."

"Maybe."

"Well, running or fighting or smashing your fist against a wall may help you feel better temporarily, but ultimately it's going to be helping Lillian heal in the way she needs most that's going to make this rage pass."

"Derek, I'm not sure this rage is ever going to pass."

"Maybe not. But she doesn't need your rage. Lillian's got enough of that herself. She doesn't need you to fight her physical battles for her, but she needs you to stand with her emotionally. Of course, if you're just around temporarily, then maybe you shouldn't even try to get close to her."

"That's not the issue. I've owned a ranch outside Colorado Springs for a number of years now. Have plans to raise animals."

"Like what you were talking about with that bridge jumper?"

"Exactly. Someplace people could go who have PTSD, who just need to get away."

"It's interesting that the two of you lost touch with each other so long ago and then ultimately ended up settling within fifty miles of each other."

That fact had not escaped Jace's attention, either. He nodded. But he also knew that physical proximity wasn't enough. "I just hope she'll give me the chance." Because despite the great sex and friendly banter between them, Jace wasn't sure Lillian would be able to ever truly give herself to a man again.

Especially not him.

Chapter 17

Dawn on the day of the summit found the streets of Denver packed with people of every type: angry, happy, scared.

And they were all loud and carrying signs.

The cold front that had settled over Denver this morning hadn't seemed to deter people. Nobody had expected this many this early, and while the Denver PD were in charge of crowd control, and so far doing a good job of it, Lillian had found she had to fight her way just to get from the hotel back to the City and County Building.

It was going to be a long day. The entire team would be on high alert as the politicians, police chiefs and other high-profile shareholders in the LESS program from all over the country arrived. The official debut and demonstration was scheduled for six hours from now.

Jace was already on-site, the rest of the team either already there or, like Lillian, on their way. She and Jace hadn't had much more time off together, but just having him near, knowing the truth was finally out between them, had eased a heaviness in Lillian that, along with the weight of everything else, she hadn't even known she'd been carrying.

Jace had never stopped looking with anything less than respect in his eyes. No pity. No sideways glances to make sure she wasn't about to fall apart. Just respect.

And lust. She'd take both.

But not right now. Today there was no room for anything else but the LESS Summit.

Derek was coordinating with the transportation security team of the summit members. Once they were released from the vehicles in the underground parking garage and escorted into the building, the summit members would officially be Omega Sector's responsibility.

As Lillian elbowed her way past another set of protestors, she couldn't shake the feeling in her gut.

Trouble. The air was all but saturated with it.

Lillian wasn't prone to superstition or gut feelings. She liked to make informed decisions based on facts and preparation.

But she couldn't get the hairs on the back of her neck to settle down. Someone was here with death on their mind.

It didn't take a genius to guess that person was Damien Freihof. This was a perfect stage for him to continue his sick play. But they had spent the last day and a half making sure security was as tight as it possibly could be inside city hall.

She ducked as a protestor haphazardly thrust a sign in her direction, her feeling of dread increasing. What if Freihof's plan wasn't to destroy the summit itself, but to attack the people out here? Nobody was guarding them.

Freihof had never gone after innocent people. He'd focused his attacks over the past few months on people attached to Omega Sector. Their loved ones. But that didn't mean he wouldn't change his MO. And ultimately they couldn't protect everyone in the world from him. But they would damn well make sure city hall and the summit were secure.

Lillian finally forced her way through the crowd and into the building. She identified herself to the security officers. She was about to head to the third floor—to the auditorium where the summit would be held—when she caught sight of someone slipping through the door leading down to the basement. The same one where she'd almost died.

And if she wasn't mistaken, it was Philip Carnell heading down there. Philip, who should be up in the control room right now, finalizing details. Lillian could think of a number of reasons why Carnell might be heading down to the basement level, and none of them were good.

She'd stayed away from Carnell over the last day, since she'd accused him of being the mole. Both Jace and Derek had been watching him and assured her they didn't think Carnell was the traitor. That he hadn't made any suspicious moves.

This was damn well suspicious.

She reached for her comm unit, then cursed when she remembered she hadn't checked in yet, so she didn't have it. She jogged over to the corner door Carnell had disappeared through. She didn't want to go barreling in, accusing him once again of malicious intent—that was probably the surest way to get herself on administrative leave. But she wasn't going to just let him get away with whatever he was doing. If Carnell was moving to assist Freihof in some way, she was going to stop him. And she'd text Jace or Derek once she knew what was going on.

She opened the stairwell door quietly, closing it behind her gently so it didn't make a click. The sub-basement was three floors below the lobby level and she could hear Carnell's steps as he moved quickly down the stairs.

Lillian followed silently, listening for the door she knew would lead to the basement. When the sound didn't come she moved more quickly, trying to figure out what was going on. When she got to the door, she stopped, staring at it.

It was closed. Locked with a bolt and padlock Omega had put there to keep this entire basement floor unavailable for the summit. There was no way Carnell just opened this door and went through it without her hearing. She spun around, but Carnell was nowhere to be found and there was nowhere to hide. The only other room was a small closet at the end of the hall. She'd seen it herself yesterday while double-checking the security of this level.

If Carnell was in there, he was hiding, because there was nowhere else to go.

Maybe waiting with his handy Taser? Not this time, rat bastard.

She pulled out her extendable sentry baton from its holder at the back of her belt. With a flick of her wrist it was open to its full length of over eighteen inches. A Taser wasn't going to help Carnell this time.

Deciding the element of surprise was her best bet, Lillian threw open the closet door, then jumped back, expecting to see Carnell pounce toward her. When nothing happened, she grabbed her flashlight and shined it into the closet, baton still raised.

Empty. Cleaning supplies, shelves, but no Carnell. What the hell?

There was nowhere else he could've gone. She'd come through the lobby level, and the subbasement level was still locked. So where the hell had Carnell gone?

She was turning to backtrack, to see what she'd missed, when she felt it. Just the slightest of breezes. But it was coming from the closet behind her, not the hallway.

How could a breeze be coming from a closet?

Lillian spun her flashlight back around, looking more carefully at the walls of the closet. One of the shelving units was ajar, not flush against the wall. Putting her baton back in the holder, she stepped closer and aimed her flashlight more fully at the gap between the wall and shelf.

It was an opening of some kind.

Knowing Carnell could already be into the deadly stages of whatever he had planned, Lillian didn't hesitate. She flipped off her light and slid the shelf just the smallest amount needed for her to fit through.

She stayed low and alert, allowing her eyes to adjust to the darkened space, expecting another basement room. It was more. A series of rooms, interconnected with a number of doors.

What was this place? The damp, darkened cinder blocks suggested this had been built decades ago, if not longer. Definitely not recently.

But these rooms should've been in the building plans. Even if the rooms weren't being used, the information about them should've been made available.

She had to call this in. There was no way in hell Carnell could accuse her of acting unreasonably now by following and accusing him of misconduct. City hall was not secure.

Her phone was in her hand when she saw Carnell come running out of one room—a look of frustration and concern clear on his face—before turning and opening another door. What the hell was he doing?

She couldn't lose him now. Lillian slipped her phone back in the pocket of her tactical vest and, keeping to the edge of the wall and shadows as much as possible, moved toward the door Carnell had just entered.

She opened the door and found Carnell with his back to her, kneeling on the floor.

Facing the largest explosive device she'd ever seen. That thing would bring down the entire building and everyone in it.

Lillian pulled her weapon out. "Step away from the device, Carnell. Do it right now. Get your hands up."

"Muir, listen…"

"Right damn now, Carnell." Lillian took another step closer.

Carnell raised his hands. "It's not what you think."

She let out a curse with her laugh. "Really? Because what I think is that I am looking at you messing with a big-ass bomb. Is that not the case?"

Lillian felt the movement behind her just a second too late. A gun was resting at her temple before she could make a move.

"I think what dear Philip is trying to tell you is that it's not *his* big-ass bomb, isn't that right, Phil?"

Saul Poniard.

"What the hell are you doing, Saul? Are you guys working together?"

Saul gave her that friendly smile she now realized had always been completely fake. "Nah. Not working together. Phil must've stumbled onto my contribution to the LESS Summit." He pressed the gun deeper against her temple. "Gun on the floor, Muir."

Lillian gritted her teeth and placed her Glock on the floor. She would be able to take him in a fight, but there was no way she could stop him from shooting her with his gun at point-blank range. He immediately kicked it away.

"Did you position yourself on my weak side on purpose, Saul, or did you just get lucky?"

Saul shot her a grin. "What can I say, Lily? You taught me well."

"I also taught you not to call me Lily."

"Eakin gets to, so why can't I?"

"Maybe because Jace isn't a lying, traitorous psychopath who plans to blow up a bunch of innocent people."

Saul actually chuckled. "Don't be so shortsighted, *Lily*. I plan to do much more than just blow up the people here."

"Oh, my God, those things are real?" Philip, still standing over by the explosive device, sounded like he was going to vomit.

"Shut up, Phil. It's not quite time to reveal the whole plan. Get down on your knees, hands behind your head."

He gave Lillian a shove toward the floor. Reining in her temper, she dropped to her knees. A time to fight was coming, but she needed to wait until she had some sort of a chance. If Jace was here, he'd do something to distract Saul long enough for her to be able to move on him.

Philip Carnell just looked like he might pee his pants. No help was coming from him.

And if she tried anything on her own right now, she'd just get a bullet in the brain for her troubles. But when Saul secured her wrists behind her back with a zip tie, she wished she had tried.

"Saul," she said, "you have to know that Derek's going to notice that we're missing. Maybe you not being around would've been overlooked, but all three of us not being at our proper places? They'll never hold the summit here. They'll cancel it outright."

"That's why you're going to call your boyfriend and tell him you found proof that Phil is the mole, that you've got him in custody and you'll be reporting soon. I'm sure in all the chaos and relief that they finally caught the person giving information to Freihof, they won't even notice I'm missing."

Lillian just shook her head at him. "You know I won't do it, Poniard. You can go to hell."

The friendly surfer facade disappeared from his face. Saul grabbed her by the hair and snatched her head back. He pointed the gun at her temple again. "I think you will."

"You're going to kill me anyway. We both know that. So why would I help you blow up a building full of innocent people? Not to mention all the protestors outside that would also get hurt in the panic."

He gripped her hair harder and jerked her head to the side, pulling out a knife from his own SWAT vest. "I think you will, Muir."

Lillian didn't even try to stop the laugh that bubbled out of her. "You think you can torture me into helping you? You're the one on the clock, Saul. Every second we spend down here is another second the team continues to wonder where we are. Just a matter of time before they empty the building. I daresay I can withstand any torture you want to dish out until they do that."

Damn it, she didn't want to die. Not now...right when she was beginning to find herself again. And Jace. Not when there was the possibility of a wonderful new beginning.

But she would. She would take whatever Saul thought he could do to her to get her to lie to the team.

She saw his fist flying toward her face but couldn't brace herself with her hands tied behind her back. She fell to the floor hard, but forced herself to sit back up immediately.

She spat blood to the side of Saul's feet. "You're going to have to do better than that."

She expected his fist again, or a kick. But instead Saul just laughed. "Actually, you're right. Nobody could ever break you physically in that short amount of time. But I don't have to break you." He turned to Philip. "I'll break *him*."

Saul began walking toward Philip, who had stayed silent during their exchange. Before she could say anything to stop him, Saul did a one-two combination move, punching Philip in the abdomen, followed by a roundhouse kick to the jaw.

Philip fell to the floor, groaning.

Saul turned and actually winked at Lillian. How had she ever found him likable? "You helped me perfect that move. Thanks."

She watched in horror as he turned back to Philip and stabbed him in the shoulder, ripped out the blade, then brought it back down and sliced through Philip's arm. Philip's anguished cry tore at her heart.

"Damn it, Saul…"

"One call, Lillian. Just two sentences."

Philip shook his head back and forth. "No, Lillian, you can't."

Saul sliced at Philip again. Saul was trained in combat. Philip's fighting ability was minimal at best, and without a weapon, he was a sitting duck.

"Enough, Poniard," Lillian yelled. She had to get Saul's attention back on her.

"I don't have time for this. So you either make the call or the next stab is into a vital organ of Phil's. Then, if you still won't do it, I'm going outside, grabbing the first mom and kid I find and bringing them down here. We'll see how long they can withstand torture."

"Lillian…" Philip's words came out between jagged breaths. "He's bluffing. Don't…"

Saul brought the knife back up and she knew he meant what he'd said.

And knew what she had to do.

"Stop!" she yelled. "I'll do it."

Saul snickered at her but at least walked away from Philip, who was still lying on the floor groaning, blood spilling from his wounds.

Saul got right into Lillian's face. The temptation to head-butt him was overwhelming, but she knew it wouldn't accomplish anything.

"You know what your problem is, Lily? Lack of follow-through. You can't stand to see others get hurt, even when it's necessary for change. Surely you can see that we've reached a point where change is necessary in modern law enforcement?"

"The only thing necessary for me is for you to stop monologuing. Give me the damn phone."

He pulled out her phone, along with his Glock, and after punching Jace's contact button, put the gun to one of her ears and the phone to the other. "Talk to the boyfriend and tell him you've got Philip in custody and have proof he's the mole. That you'll be back as soon as you can." He tapped the side of her head with the gun. "You try to tell him what's really going on and I will make sure you see innocent people die right in front of you as horrifically as possible. They'll die screaming."

Lillian pursed her lips. "All right, simmer down there, Hulk-Smash. Give me the goddamn phone."

Saul hit the send button for Jace.

"Hey, you."

Just hearing his deep voice helped settle her. Like it always had.

"Hey." Her own voice came out husky.

"Where are you? Derek was expecting you nearly thirty minutes ago."

Saul narrowed his eyes at her and brought his knife up in Philip's direction.

"Jace, tell Derek it's going to be a while before I make it in. Don't be mad, but I caught Carnell sneaking into the marked-off basement and I followed him. I caught him, Jace. Have him in custody. I'll explain later, but Carnell is definitely the mole."

"You're sure?"

She had to find a way to warn Jace. She hoped this worked. "One-hundred-percent. I swear on my brother's life I'm telling the truth."

Jace laughed. "You don't have a brother."

Lillian gave the most lighthearted chuckle she was capable of. "Fine. Then I swear on your brother's life that I'm telling the truth. You know how much I love your dear brother."

"Yeah, a lot of love." The slightest change in Jace's tone clued her in. He knew there was something up. She had his attention now. "You need help bringing in Philip? There's nothing going on around here until the bigwigs arrive."

Saul shook his head in warning.

"Nah. I can definitely handle Carnell. You stay where you are. He won't get the drop on me down here again."

Would Jace understand? It was all so vague.

"You sure?"

"If Philip keeps running his mouth, he's going to end up just like that perp Daryl. You remember me telling you about what I did to Daryl?" She chuckled again to try to throw Saul off. "Carnell is going to end up just like him if he keeps talking trash to me."

"Hey, you be good," Jace finally said. "And be careful. Don't want you to get in any trouble for roughing up a suspect."

"I'll see you in a bit."

Saul hit the disconnect button as soon as the last word was out of her mouth. She could only pray Jace understood what she was trying to tell him.

"Who the hell is Daryl?" Saul hissed. "Why'd you bring him up?"

"He's just some guy I fought with once. And I brought him up because if I treat Jace like we're nothing more than professional colleagues, he's going to know something's up, okay? You got what you wanted, Saul, you damn coward, so just shut the hell up."

She saw his face turn red with rage, as his arm flew toward her. The world spun to black as he cracked her in the back of the head with the butt of his gun.

Chapter 18

The second Lillian's call disconnected, Jace was running out into the hallway to find Derek.

"We need to evacuate the building right now."

Derek immediately put away the papers he was looking at. "Why? What happened?"

"I just talked to Lillian. She's in trouble. And there's a bomb in the building, probably in the basement."

"She told you that? Why didn't she radio it in? Call the bomb squad?"

"She was talking to me under duress, trying to get me a message. She was talking about my brother, Daryl."

Derek looked confused. "Your brother, Daryl, planted a bomb?"

"No, my brother, Daryl, is dead. But he died in an

explosion. Lillian was trying to get that across to me by mentioning him."

Derek shook his head. "No offense, Eakin, but are you sure? Maybe she was just bringing him up as part of a conversation."

Jace stepped farther into Derek's personal space. They didn't have time to waste. "She told me she had proof that Philip Carnell was the mole. That she caught him. That she would swear on her brother's life that it was him."

"I didn't know Lillian had a brother."

"She doesn't. When I brought up that point, she said she would swear on *my* brother's life that Carnell was the mole."

"Okay, weird. But what makes you think she's under duress?"

Without providing details about Daryl that Lillian might not want to share, Jace explained what she had said about Daryl and what she was trying to explain to them.

Jace knew without a shadow of a doubt that Lillian had risked her life to get him that message. He wasn't going to waste what she'd done, regardless of whether Derek agreed or not. He didn't want to have to go over Derek's head, but he would if he had to.

Jace trusted Lillian. Trusted what she was trying to tell him. He couldn't even allow himself to think about the fact that she had now served her purpose for whoever had forced her to make that call and might already be dead. Because that damn well wasn't going to happen.

"Derek, I'm right. You know Lillian would've handled this differently if Carnell really was in custody. She wouldn't just leave us in the middle of an important lockdown when every person on the team is needed. Not to mention, she would've died before calling and leading us astray unless she had a plan to try to warn us. *Mentioning Daryl was that plan.*"

"All right, I trust you. And moreover, I trust Lillian. Let's get this building cleared now. But calmly."

Within seconds Derek was on the comm units with the rest of the Omega team and the added security personnel. Thankfully, because of the LESS Summit, half the people who would normally be working here had been given the day off. Within minutes everyone with security clearance was helping to escort people quickly out of the building.

All Jace wanted to do was find Lillian and make sure she wasn't harmed. But he knew she would want to make sure the building was secure first. That innocent people were safe. And while Jace didn't like that, he would respect her wishes. He had no doubt she'd paid a price to get that info to him. He wouldn't let it be wasted.

As they were escorting the last of the people from the building, he could hear Derek explaining on the phone what was happening to an obviously livid Congresswoman Glasneck.

"Glasneck refuses to cancel, so we're going to the emergency third location." Frustration was etched on Derek's face.

"I didn't even know there was a third location." And to be honest, he didn't care about the LESS Summit anymore. All Jace's attention was focused on getting to Lillian.

"The Clarke Building. An ordinary office building about three blocks away." Derek provided the address. "Small, unimpressive, nondescript. A conference room with no windows on the second floor. Opposite of what Glasneck wanted."

"I'm not coming, Derek. I've got to find Lily. She's in trouble." Jace respected the man but didn't care. What could Derek do, fire him? Even if this was his real job, Jace wouldn't care.

But Derek just nodded. "Find her. LESS is now going to be bare-bones anyway. The ceremony and pomp will have to be done some other way. This is just going to be Congresswoman Glasneck and a couple other key people flipping a switch." He provided a few more details about where they would be.

Jace was already taking off toward the lobby. "I'll report in as soon as I know something about Lillian. And we'll get to you if we can."

He prayed they'd be able to.

The last of the civilians were being led out the main entrance and police were clearing all the protesters in the vicinity of city hall. Jace had already tried calling Lillian's phone a dozen times. Each time the call went straight to voice mail.

"Jace."

He turned to find Saul behind him. "Is your sector clear?"

Saul hesitated a second before nodding. "When last I checked."

"Okay, I think the building's clear, then."

Saul didn't give his usual grin, just nodded. "Good. I'm glad you figured out that there was a threat."

"It was all Lillian, she clued me in, even though I'm almost positive she was under duress. Have you seen her? Or Carnell?"

"Um, yeah, a while ago, before we started the evac.

I think she was just getting here. Said something about having proof about Carnell."

"Yeah, that's what she told me, too. I'm sure Derek can use your help securing the new LESS location. The Clarke Building, two blocks east of here. It's bare-bones, most of the VIPs won't be a part of it now, but LESS is still going live."

Saul's lips thinned. "Okay, I'll head over there right now. I've just got one thing to do first."

Jace didn't know what could be more important than getting directly over to the summit, but he honestly didn't care. Protecting the summit was Derek's concern now. This building was clear and Jace was damn well going to find Lillian.

"Eakin!" Saul called as Jace ran toward the stairs. "When I saw her as she came in, Lillian mentioned something about the roof. I don't know if that's where she is, but maybe."

Jace gave a wave of acknowledgment but didn't slow down. As he turned the corner bringing him to the main stairwell, he had to make a decision. Up or down. If Saul was right and she was on the roof, Jace didn't want to waste time looking in the basement section.

He won't get the drop on me down here again.

Those had been Lillian's words. *Down here.*

Maybe she'd been heading toward the roof when Poniard saw her earlier, but she wasn't there now. Or at least hadn't been when she called him to get the people out of the building. He headed down the stairs, memories of finding Lily's swinging form haunting him from the last time he'd taken these stairs. He prayed he wouldn't find something worse.

A few minutes of storming through rooms—even the ones behind the padlocked door—had Jace worried he'd made the wrong decision. Maybe she was up on the roof. He was about to make his way up there when he heard a sound coming from the supply closet—like a call for help.

But Jace knew before he even opened the door that couldn't be right, the sound was from too far away to be coming from the supply closet.

He reached for the handle and found it locked. That was strange. It hadn't been locked as they were securing the building the past two days.

He heard the sound again—a muffled male yell—and stepped back to kick in the door. The door flew from its hinges when his foot hit it and opened.

Nothing. Nobody bound and gagged, like he expected.

He wiped a hand over his eyes. Wishful thinking. The stress was getting to him. Obviously the sound couldn't be from here. He would check the roof, since he'd already checked every possible room in the basement.

But as he was closing the door he heard it again. Jace's head jerked up. That damn well hadn't been wishful thinking or stress. That had been a yell for help. And it had been coming from right in front of him. Right through the wall. A wall that should lead nowhere, according to the building plans he'd studied extensively.

Jace immediately began knocking against the far wall, more frantically, when he heard the yell again.

"Who's there? Keep yelling," Jace yelled back. When he moved a shelving unit he saw the hole. Doubling his efforts, he threw the shelf to the side and crawled through the hole.

What the hell?

"Help. Please."

The voice was becoming weaker.

"I'm here. Keep yelling."

"Eakin? We're here. Help us. Hurry."

"Carnell?" What the hell was going on? Jace moved farther into the large room. What was this? "Where are you?"

"Here. God, hurry, Eakin. There's a bomb."

Jace ran toward Carnell's voice and found him tied up in an adjoining room. Bleeding heavily.

Lillian was tied up and gagged next to him. Very much alive. She was not only alive, but had also somehow gotten her pocketknife out and, with her own wrists secured behind her back, was attempting to cut through Carnell's tied hands. She'd already gotten his gag out, and would've had them both untied before too long.

Jace glanced at the explosive device. But maybe not fast enough.

"You're hurt," Jace said to Philip before diving down to help Lillian.

"I'll be fine. Thank God you're here," Philip said as Jace cut through Lillian's bonds first then did the same to Philip's. "We've got to get everyone out of here. That bomb is set to go off in less than twenty minutes."

"We've already evacuated the building."

As soon as her hands were free, Lillian reached up and pulled the gag out of her mouth. "You understood. Thank God."

Jace reached over and cupped the back of her neck, pulling her forehead against his. "Mentioning Daryl was smart. Clued me in immediately."

"It was my only option," she whispered. "Poniard was torturing Philip. Threatening to grab a mom and kid—"

"Poniard? Poniard is the mole?" Jace let out a blistering curse. "I just saw him. He was acting a little weird, but everything was already crazy with the evacuation."

"Thank God you stopped the summit," Philip said as Jace got Lillian to her feet and helped him stand. "I didn't even get to the part that sent me down here in the first place. The much worse part."

Phillip looked from Lillian to Jace.

"What?" they both demanded at the same time.

"You know how Saul has been traveling to police stations all over the country for the last eight months to help with the setup of the LESS system? What he conveniently failed to mention was that he also rigged those stations with biological weapons. If LESS had gone live today, Saul had rigged it so the connecting systems all over the country would've released the biological hazard. The death toll would've been in the thousands, maybe tens of thousands. All law enforcement."

Lillian's ugly curse was the exact sentiment Jace was feeling. And she didn't even know the half of it.

"That's a pretty big problem," Jace said. "Because we got this building clear, but the summit is still on at a different location. And I just told Poniard where it's being held."

Chapter 19

Jace was reaching for his cell phone before he finished his sentence. He immediately cursed before putting it away.

"No signal. Poniard had to figure I would eventually end up down here. He probably set up some sort of jammer."

Jace and Lillian both ran over to the bomb. "We've got to get this thing disarmed," she said. "If the building comes down, there's no way there won't be complete panic outside."

"I'll take care of the bomb. You guys have to get over to the summit and stop Poniard." Jace told them where the summit had been moved to, then began studying the explosive device more closely.

Lillian's gut clenched. "Jace, there's no way for you

to call for backup. For you to get the bomb squad in here. You'll be completely on your own."

Jace stood, wrapped his hands on either side of her face and brought her in for a hard, quick kiss. "There's no time for them to get here even if I could get a call out. Law enforcement is maxed out outside. We're on our own."

Lillian grabbed his wrists and kissed him again. They both had jobs to do. He was trusting her to do hers, and she had to trust him to do his. "Then I'll see you soon. You damn well better make it out of this."

His grin sent heat to her core. Almost enough to melt the ice of fear surrounding her for him. "Bet on it."

He let her go and turned back to the explosive device. Lillian studied Philip. "We're going to have to move fast. Can you make it?"

"I have to. I'm the only one who can get LESS shut down in time to stop it from killing thousands of people."

They were through the passageway, out of the building and running into the Denver streets as fast as the crowds would let them. Backing people away from the City and County Building had just made the other areas more crowded. The sounds of chants and jeers were nearly deafening.

Lillian cleared a path for Philip, who was looking more and more pale. But he was right, they didn't have any choice: he had to make it. She had a new respect for the determination in his eyes.

They finally made it to the small, almost unnoticeable building between two much taller ones. This was everything Congresswoman Glasneck *hadn't* wanted for the LESS Summit.

Not knowing the building specifics put Lillian at a tactical disadvantage, but Saul hadn't known about this backup location, either, so he couldn't have left them many surprises.

"We've got less than fifteen minutes," Philip said as they made it inside. "And we can't just go barging in. Saul has had this set up for months. He's only waited for the LESS Summit because he wanted to have these law-enforcement offices and stations around the country to be as crowded as possible. All he has to do is flip the switch to make LESS live, then start the computer program that opens the containers. He's probably already got it saved to a single keystroke. That's what I would do."

Lillian let out a string of curses. "So you're saying if we knock the door down and shoot him, he still might have a chance to put the program in motion and release the biological weapons."

"Exactly. I'll bet you any amount of money he's walking around with either a keyboard or a phone. Either can be used as his trigger. All he needs is a second to end the lives of thousands of people."

"Okay, then I'll knock the phone or keyboard out of his hand."

Philip shook his head. "That buys you time, but not much. He has a timing device as a backup plan. That's how I stumbled onto this whole thing to begin with, the countdown. Once LESS goes live, one minute afterward the canisters will release."

This just kept getting worse. "Can you stop it?"

"Yes. If I can access Poniard's digital trigger, whether it's a phone or a computer, I can stop it. I'll have to work the system backward, but I can do it."

"In under a minute?" Lillian tried to keep the incredulity out of her voice, but failed.

"You have your gifts, Muir. I have mine."

Lillian nodded at him. "I owe you an apology." For more than just accusing him of being the mole. For the way she'd treated him—like he wasn't good enough to truly be on the team. Now he was standing in a puddle of his own blood, ready to fight in the best way he knew how. It was all anyone could ask.

Maybe Philip wasn't such a jackass after all.

"Later, Muir. I don't have time for female hysterics or teary heartfelt hugs."

Or maybe he was.

Lillian notified the extra security guards of the problem and set them up outside the conference room door, ready to breach on her mark. She quickly explained the danger of rushing in too soon.

Since the summit had been downscaled, the only security out here was private sector and Denver local PD. Any Secret Service agents who'd been assigned here were in the closed conference room with Congresswoman Glasneck. Derek was in there, too. All of them could be counted on to take out Saul, but not if they didn't know Saul was the traitor.

And Saul would be waiting for someone to come through this door. Would be ready for that.

"Lillian, we've got less than ten minutes until LESS is scheduled to go live."

"Turn on your comm unit," she told him. "Be ready to burst in with the security team. I'll get the trigger away from Poniard, and then you'll work your magic."

"This is the only door. There's no windows. How are you going to get into the room?"

"You have your gifts, I have mine, Carnell. And right now mine includes my size."

Less than a minute later one of the security guards was giving her a boost up to the industrial-size air-conditioning vent. Lillian belly-crawled as quickly as she could through the small ductwork without making noise.

Arriving at the square grate over the room took longer than she wanted, and then she cursed when she found the situation to be even worse than she'd thought. Things had already escalated.

A Secret Service agent, most probably dead by the amount of blood lost from the bullet wound in his neck, was lying slumped over in the corner. Lillian shifted to be able to see the other side of the room better, and her breath caught in her throat. Derek had been shot also, perhaps multiple times. A man in a suit was holding a balled-up shirt against Derek's thigh, and blood was running unchecked from his shoulder.

Saul Poniard was pacing back and forth. "The current state of law enforcement is a laughingstock. Surely you can see that by resetting the baseline I am doing this country a great favor. Something that is needed."

"By killing innocent people?" Congresswoman Glasneck asked. She was over against the south wall, huddled with half a dozen other people.

"The price of liberty is sometimes death itself. Plus, these people are not innocent, they are part of the problem."

"And us, Saul?" Glasneck asked again. "I've been working with you for months. Are you going to kill everyone in this room also?"

"I will not be deterred from what I am meant to do.

It is my destiny. Individual lives are not what matter. Change is what matters."

Lillian looked at her watch. Four minutes. Four minutes until LESS was scheduled to go live and the bomb at the City and County Building was set to detonate. She couldn't even allow herself to think about Jace. She trusted him to be able to do what he needed to do.

"They'll know it's you." An older, heavyset man next to the congresswoman glared at Saul. "Do you think you're going to get away with this? That no one is going to notice a room full of dead people, including a congresswoman?"

"I think there's going to be enough chaos in just a few minutes to leave everyone in utter confusion. The lives of half a dozen will be of very little consequence in the bigger picture. And out of the confusion, I will rise up and lead. Lead law enforcement to the greatness it can be. To reset the path of this country the way it needs to be reset."

Saul's voice was rising with his passion. Lillian used the noise to speak into the comm unit.

"Philip," she whispered. "Poniard's got a phone in his hand, like you said. Gun in the other one. He's ready for an ambush through the door, so make sure everyone stands down."

"Roger that. But we're out of time, Lillian. Less than three minutes."

Saul was still yelling at the people huddled against the wall. "And never again will someone like me—someone with vision, focus and purpose—be denied the chance to serve in whatever capacity they see fit. To be a part of the most elite. Never again will I be rejected. For years, Omega Sector thought I wasn't capable of being on their precious SWAT team. Unfortunately, they'll all be dead, so I won't be able to gloat in their faces that I'm smarter than them."

Spittle flew across the room as he said it. Lillian barely refrained from rolling her eyes. This was all about Saul being jealous because he didn't make the SWAT team?

"Lil, once LESS goes live, the one-minute countdown is on, no matter what," Philip reminded her in her ear. "You've got to take him."

Philip was right. Lillian was treating this like a normal hostage situation, where she could just wait out the perp. Eventually he'd tire himself out and lower his weapon or become complacent.

They didn't have that kind of time now.

As Saul continued his rant, Lillian silently moved the grate that covered the vent opening, progressing slowly but with purpose.

"Thirty seconds until LESS goes live."

Lillian said a quick prayer that Jace had gotten the bomb disabled. They'd know for sure in just a few seconds. Saul would, too, and once he did, he wouldn't hesitate to immediately release the biological weapons all over the country.

Lillian waited until he crossed under her again, then forgot all about quiet and yanked the grate up and dove out of the opening, headfirst, landing on top of Saul.

Her training said to get the gun out of his right hand, but she pried the phone from his left hand instead. Keeping him from triggering the canisters was most important.

She was able to get the phone out of Saul's hand. She was too close for him to shoot, but she grunted when he hit her with his gun, barely missing her head and grazing her shoulder. Damn it, this bastard had hit her with that gun enough times for one day.

Keeping the phone out of his reach, she used her momentum to roll both of them forward, bringing her elbow up to catch him in the jaw. She jumped to her feet and grabbed Saul by the shirt, pulling his back off the floor. She slammed her fist into his nose, hearing the crack as it broke under her force.

"It just went live, Lillian. LESS just went live!" Philip's voice shouted into her ear.

One minute. That was all the time they had left.

"Breach! I've got Saul's phone." She heard the door burst open behind her and turned to toss Philip the phone. The security force trained their weapons on Saul.

Still held up by her fist on his clothing, Saul began to laugh. "You're too late. That bomb in the City and County Building is nothing compared to what's coming."

Lillian glanced over. "Philip?"

Philip didn't look up as his fingers typed rapidly on Saul's phone. "Working voodoo now. Do not disturb."

She brought Saul closer to her face. "Philip found out about your canisters and knows how to stop them."

Saul's face mottled in fury. "Don't do it, Carnell. Omega Sector is just using you. You know how elitist they are. We can be a part of something new. Better."

"New and better by killing tens of thousands of people?" She brought her fist into his jaw again. "Shut up."

Saul spat blood. "Philip. You know I'm telling the truth. Omega's best-of-the-best crap? According to who? The wrong people are making the decisions. It's time for a change."

Philip walked over to them. "You know what? You're right, Saul, it *is* time for a change."

"Philip." Damn it. Philip couldn't let Saul get into his head now. There were only seconds left. "Don't let him…"

Philip dropped the phone on the floor next to Saul. "But not your way. Law enforcement, Omega Sector included, needs to take a good long look at itself. Make the needed changes. I want to be a part of that. But not your way." Philip turned to Lillian. "I did it. The connection to the canisters has been severed. It's safe."

Saul jerked away from Lillian and made a tackle for Philip, but Philip was ready. It was his fist that hit Saul this time. Saul fell to the floor, moaning.

Lillian nodded at Philip as the guards handcuffed Saul and led him away. One was already on a radio, calling in an ambulance for Derek. Lillian rushed over to him where he was propped against the wall. Congresswoman Glasneck joined her at his side.

"Derek?" His normally tan skin was devoid of all color. He was so still, Lillian reached up to take his pulse. "Wake up."

"I'm awake," Derek muttered. "You did good, Lily."

"Excuse me, but you're not allowed to call me that." Only Jace was. "Don't think that just because you've successfully gotten yourself shot twice, I'm going to let you call me anything short of my full name."

She said it jokingly as she removed the shirt covering the wound on Derek's thigh to glance at it.

"How bad?" he muttered, eyes closed.

He knew she wouldn't lie. "Not life-threatening." Unless he kept bleeding. "But bad enough that you need to be taken straight to the hospital."

Derek nodded, then leaned farther back against the wall.

"I have to go check on Jace. We had to leave him with the explosive device in city hall. Poniard had set it up so the explosion would happen the same time the canisters were released. Maximum chaos and damage. There hasn't been an explosion, so I'm assuming he took care of it." Thank God.

Congresswoman Glasneck stood when Lillian did. "Thank you. I had no idea Saul Poniard was capable of such treachery."

Lillian gave a half shrug. "He was convinced of the rightness of his own actions. I hope the LESS system can still be utilized."

Glasneck shook her head sadly. "Maybe one day, but not right now. If there's anything I've become convinced of in the last hour, it's that although connecting all law-enforcement systems may help fight crime, it also allows for law enforcement as a whole to be attacked rather easily. You bring down LESS, and it can do countrywide damage."

Lillian gave the congresswoman a nod and then turned to jog out the door. She gave Philip—who was now sitting on the floor looking exhausted—a nod and continued past him when he gave her a small salute. Saul was loudly explaining his intentions and proclaiming his innocence to the guards who had taken him into custody. Lillian ignored him completely. She'd heard more than enough out of him today.

Outside, the local police were still clearing the area, keeping demonstrators back from the buildings. She saw her teammate Ashton Fitzgerald helping with crowd control and made her way over to him. She explained what had happened with Saul and Derek.

"Do I need to get in there to help Derek?" Ashton had to shout to be heard over the roar of the crowd.

"No, just make sure the paramedics can get to him. You're needed out here. Have you seen Jace?"

"No. Cell-phone coverage is still down, and honestly we can't do anything until we clear this crowd out."

Lillian nodded. "I'm going to check on him and then I'll be back." She had to see with her own eyes to make sure Jace was okay.

Ashton nodded. "Okay. Comms aren't worth a damn out here, either, with the noise level. So just find me when you're back."

Lillian sprinted for the City and County Building. They needed as much help with crowd control as they could get. She entered the building and ran down the stairs toward the opening in the supply closet.

"Jace?" Nothing. "Eakin, you okay?"

She scurried through the hole, into the opening. "Jace! I just wanted to make sure you're okay."

She heard some sort of scuffle from farther back in a room, past where the explosive device had been placed. "Jace?"

Something was definitely not right. Had Jace hurt himself somehow after defusing the explosive device? Was someone else down here? Lillian pulled her sidearm, keeping it close to her chest.

The muffled sound came again and Lillian rushed into the far room. At the other end, near some sort of second entrance, stood Damien Freihof, a gagged-and-bound Jace in front of him.

He had a gun pointed directly at Jace's temple.

"Agent Muir," Freihof said, his smile large and wide. "I was wondering how long it would take before you came to look for Mr. Eakin."

Lillian's weapon was immediately pointed directly at Freihof. She didn't have a shot right now with Jace in front of him like a shield, but Jace wouldn't be anyone's human shield for long, particularly not Freihof's. Jace didn't seem to be hurt. When he made his move, Lillian would be ready.

She glanced at Jace's face, ready to read whatever it was he would want her to do.

The sheer agony she saw in his eyes caught her off guard.

"What the hell did you do, Freihof?" she whispered. Had he hurt Jace? There had to be some sort of terrible wound she couldn't see that was putting that look on his face.

"No need to be angry. As a matter of fact, everyone should be thanking me." Freihof's voice rang with childlike excitement. "I haven't done anything bad. As a matter of fact, all I did was stage a reunion between brothers!"

A reunion between bro—

"You remember Jace's brother, Daryl, don't you, Lillian?"

For the first time in her professional career, Lillian's weapon faltered as her own personal nightmare stepped out from the shadows beside her. Her hand began to shake as shock flooded her whole body. The Glock shook so greatly in her hand she could hardly keep hold of it.

"Hi, Lillian, baby. I've been looking for you for a long time." Daryl trailed a finger down her cheek. All she could do was stare at him.

His fist crashed into her face and Lillian let the blessed blackness consume her.

Chapter 20

As soon as Daryl's fist flew toward Lillian, Jace dove at them. Freihof was expecting it and just laughed, grabbed Jace and pulled him away. He watched, helpless, as Lillian fell to the floor.

"Brother dearest seems pretty excited to see your girlfriend," Freihof whispered in his ear. "He told me a little about what happened between them. Don't you just love a classic romance?"

Jace dove toward them again as Daryl crouched down to stroke Lily's face. She was already regaining consciousness. Freihof grabbed Jace and threw him to his knees, clocking him against the back of his neck with the gun. Jace ignored the pain, yelling at Daryl through the tape.

"I think your brother wants to talk to you, Daryl." Freihof ripped the tape off Jace's mouth.

"Don't you touch her, Daryl. Keep your damn hands off her."

Lillian was moaning on the floor, still having not quite woken up. It wasn't because Daryl had hit her that hard. Lily could take a punch. It was because her brain didn't want her to wake up. Didn't want to force her into trauma she wasn't ready for.

Daryl now looked as evil on the outside as he was on the inside. Burns covered over half his face and trailed down his neck before they were cut off by his T-shirt.

"I can't believe you would choose her over your own flesh and blood, *brother*," Daryl spat out. "She left me in that warehouse to die."

"We both know why. What you did to her." If Jace could reach his brother right now, he would rip him apart limb by limb.

"I had that warehouse ready to blow up," Daryl scoffed. "I knew the cops were closing in. I had been stupid to move into trafficking. Even had a body that looked sort of like mine. Some dealer from across the border who happened to be the same height and weight as me."

Jace sucked in a breath as Daryl stood. He pushed Lillian with the toe of his boot but didn't do anything further. "Lillian was the one who was supposed to be in that fire, not me. Fortunately one of my guys came in and dragged me out after she clocked me over the head with that bottle. The rest of our scheme went as planned. He identified my 'body' to the police. Then we took off."

Lillian gave a pitiful moan, her head tossing back and forth. She'd be waking up soon. Waking up to a nightmare.

Daryl nudged her again with his foot. "I looked for her. All over Tulsa, then even farther. Never dreamed she'd join law enforcement, as pathetic as she was. But she won't be any good to anyone—especially law enforcement—once I'm through with her."

Lillian's eyes opened at that moment. Bile rose in Jace's throat as a look of terror blanketed her features. Almost immediately she was shaking again, her brown eyes darting all around.

"Lillian, look at me, baby," he whispered, trying to eliminate the desperation from his tone. Her eyes continued to dart from place to place, her rapid, shallow breathing causing her to shake further.

"Tiger Lily." He kept his tone firm. Calm. Banished every bit of fear and panic threatening to bubble up from inside him. "It's Jace. I'm here with you. I'm here with you, and you're going to be okay."

Her eyes finally rested on him. "Jace?"

He would give every cent he owned to never see this look of terror and helplessness cross Lillian's face ever again. "I'm here, sweetheart. With you. I'm here."

"You're here." Her words were weak, but her breathing slowed just enough that he stopped worrying that she would pass out again. He nodded at her, keeping their eyes locked.

A roar erupted from him as Daryl reached down and snatched her up by her hair, yanking her face back. "Guess what, I'm here, too, bitch!" Daryl backhanded her and she fell hard to the floor.

This time, she didn't pass out. This time her small hand tightened into a fist.

That's right, sweetheart. Find your fight.

Daryl was weak, pudgy. Lillian was capable of taking him down in under ten seconds. Her mind just had to believe that she could. She sat back up, her eyes finding Jace's again. They were still laced with fear, but her breathing was more under control. If Daryl kept pushing, he was eventually going to find that Lillian could now push back.

Much, much harder.

"That's right, Tiger Lily. You just take a minute and remember who you are. What you can do."

"Stop talking to her!" Daryl screamed, shoving her again.

Her other hand was clenching into a fist now, too. Jace tensed his muscles, trying to balance himself more fully, ready to throw himself backward at Freihof when Lillian completely woke up and made her move. It wouldn't be long.

But then Daryl stopped yelling. Stopped the violence. He dropped behind Lillian, wrapping his arm around her shoulder, pulling her back up against his chest.

Eyes so much like Jace's own looked back at him as Daryl trailed his fingers up and down Lillian's throat and cheek from behind. "You two were so inseparable when you were kids. Like she was your family instead of me. Like I hadn't raised you and given you everything."

"You raised me in a gang and had me performing illegal activities before I was a teenager."

"You got to go to school. Got to eat three square meals a day. Had clothes and money when you needed it. And then you met Lillian and everything changed. Everything became about her. All I wanted was my brother back."

Lillian was frozen in Daryl's embrace.

"Let her go, Daryl. You can have me back. We can do whatever you want, we'll make it work."

Daryl snuggled in closer to Lillian's neck, breathing in her scent. "Did I ever tell you how sweetly she begged? Begged me to spare your life? Begged me not to put her back in the closet where I kept her. Begged me not to hurt her. She was so good at it."

Daryl nuzzled her neck, then forced her head back and kissed her.

Jace prayed she would come out swinging, that she would use one of the hundreds of ways she knew to break out of Daryl's embrace.

But as soon as Daryl moved away from her, Jace recognized that blank stare. Pain and violence had scared her but kept her present. She would eventually have fought back.

But not from this. Just like the other night, Lillian had completely shut down. Her brain had disassociated, was keeping her conscious mind at a distance.

She wasn't feeling any fear, but this Lillian was helpless. Not able to fight, not able to provide any tactical assistance to help get them out of here. There was no way Jace could fight both Daryl with his knife and Freihof with his gun, especially bound like he was.

"I think I'd like to hear you beg again." Daryl leaned away from her, pushing at her, obviously expecting hysteria and fear like before. But Lillian just looked at him with wide eyes, almost like she was a child.

No fear. No pain. But also no fight.

Daryl didn't have the insight to realize what was going on with Lillian, but Freihof did. "Interesting," he said quietly from behind Jace. "Disassociation."

"What are you looking at?" Daryl finally said when Lillian just continued to stare at him blankly. He slapped her, and her head fell to the side. She blinked but then looked back up at Daryl like she was waiting for him to tell her what to do.

Jace began to struggle more frantically against the duct tape that bound his hands behind his back. Lillian frightened and shaking had been nauseating to watch.

Lillian utterly defenseless was beyond terrifying.

Daryl stood and yanked her up by her tactical vest. At her continued blank stare he pulled her right up to his face. "Not scared anymore?"

His mouth covered hers in what would've technically been described as a kiss, but was really meant to be a device of pain and dominance. On any other given day, under other circumstances, Lillian would've kicked him on his ass.

Now her hands just came up and weakly rested on Daryl's shoulders. Just like they had on Jace's in bed when she blanked out. She wasn't kissing him, but she wasn't pushing Daryl away, either.

"Lily! Come on, baby. Come back to me," Jace called out.

Daryl stepped back, smirking at Jace, keeping an arm wrapped around her limp shoulders. "I've been waiting a lot of years to find sweet Lillian here. To remind her whom she belongs to. When Damien found me a few days ago and told me he knew where she was—where both of you were—I knew I couldn't miss the chance. To get her back. To make her pay for this." He gestured to the scars that ravaged most of his face.

Jace ignored him. "Lillian, come on, sweetheart…" She just continued to stare blankly ahead.

"I'll admit I thought it would be a little harder. Thought I might have to kill you both outright." Daryl pulled out a knife. "But now it looks like I'll just take

Lillian with me. I'll find a nice cage to put her back in and take her out when I want to play with her."

Daryl held the knife right in front of Lillian's face like it was a toy. "That okay with you, little pet? Ready to be my dog?"

Jace lunged for Daryl again as he took the knife and made a shallow cut along the side of Lillian's neck. Freihof grabbed him and pulled him back, but Jace immediately lunged again as Daryl made another small cut and Lillian didn't move.

Freihof's pistol came down on the base of Jace's skull again, making him sink to the floor. Through the haze he heard Freihof chuckling. "I realize this might be the pot calling the kettle black, but your brother is pretty sick. I never knew I'd be getting such entertainment when I brought him here."

Jace looked up, fighting back blackness, to look at Lillian again. "C'mon, baby. Fight for me, Tiger Lily. I love you." Her blank brown eyes stared out at him.

Daryl moved away from her and walked over to stand in front of him. "She'll be coming with me. But you, baby brother, you're just a loose end that needs to be tied up. I guess I'll finally need to finish what I threatened to start twelve years ago."

No emotion crossed Daryl's face as he stabbed the knife through Jace's shoulder. The force threw him back, but Daryl grabbed him by the hair and twisted the knife. Agony flooded through Jace.

"That's for the fact that you would've chosen her over your own flesh and blood all those years ago." He pulled out the knife and brought it to Jace's throat. "And this is for the fact that you would still choose her today. Even as broken as she obviously is."

Chapter 21

The fog was soft and cloudlike all around her. Gentle, yet permeating. Time moved differently here. More slowly. She didn't have to worry about all the things waiting for her on the outside. She could just stay here, where no one could hurt her. Where there would be nothing left to remember when the fog finally lifted. Just blessed numbness.

But even as she clung to the fog—the only darkness she'd ever known that wouldn't hurt her—something beat against her mind. The knowledge that something was different.

Lily.

The voice penetrated the fog. A good voice. Strong. A voice that would never hurt her. But she pushed it away. That voice didn't belong here. Nothing belonged here but the emptiness. The numbness.

Come back to me.

Lillian tried to melt further into the fog. Why wouldn't this voice leave her alone? There were things outside the fog that would hurt her. If she followed the voice she knew pain waited at the other end.

Agony. Terror.

Fight for me.

She didn't want to go. Didn't want to face what was out there. Knew that the devil waited just beyond the fog. That if she faced him now, the fog would never protect her again.

She couldn't do it.

She felt the prick of pain in her neck at a distance. It didn't really hurt, not much. But she shouldn't feel it at all. The fog had never let anything in before. When the prick at her neck came again, Lillian tried to pull herself back more fully into the blessed darkness.

"Tiger Lily."

Jace. That voice was Jace's.

She didn't move. Didn't blink. Didn't breathe.

But the fog began to sink away in layers.

Jace. Jace was here.

"I love you."

More of the fog slid away and she could see as well as hear.

Oh, God, it was Daryl. Daryl was here. He was alive. Her mind demanded that she go back into the fog. That if she stayed in the light, if she left the fog, she might never be whole again.

She couldn't risk it.

The fog fell back around her as Daryl turned away and walked over to stand in front of Jace. He said

She heard the weak call from Jace on the other side of the room, then felt something hit her foot. He'd kicked Freihof's gun over to her.

Daryl swung his arm around with the gun in hand as she dropped and grabbed the weapon Jace had provided. She heard a gun fire, felt the recoil of her own. She waited for pain but felt none.

Daryl groaned as he fell back, his weapon falling from his hand. She'd gotten off the shot. Hit him in the chest.

She ran over, kicking the gun away, but she needn't have bothered.

Daryl was dead. For good this time. Checking his pulse confirmed it.

Lillian brought her weapon back around to train it on Freihof. He was just as deadly. But he was no longer where she'd been fighting him, over by Jace. Instead he was at a back entrance to the room.

"I reset the bomb. Hope that's okay." He gave her a small salute. "Another time, Agent Muir. Give my regards to your colleagues."

He slipped out the door.

There was nothing Lillian wanted to do more than go after Freihof, but she couldn't.

Lillian ran over to Jace. He had lost a lot of blood from his shoulder wound. She grabbed the knife and cut through the tape binding his hands. "You're bleeding bad, Jace."

He nodded. "I know. But we've got to stop that bomb. Get me over there. I stopped it once, I can do it again."

Jace was shaky on his feet. She put his good arm around her shoulder and, taking as much of his weight as she could, led him back over to the explosive device.

She held him upright, and with shaky hands he once again dismantled the bomb, with just seconds to spare.

"There," he said to the bomb when he was finished. "Stay dead this time."

"Exactly my feelings about Daryl." She kissed his shoulder as they both slid to the floor. "You got that gun to me just in time."

Jace gave her a smile, bringing his hand to her cheek. "You came back from where you were just in time."

"Because you called me back. It was you who got through the fog."

"I'll always call you back, Tiger Lily. Just like you do for me."

Lillian reached up to kiss him, but before she could, he collapsed to the floor.

Chapter 22

It was touch-and-go for three days. The shoulder wound was bad enough, but it was the internal hemorrhaging from being clocked on the head that actually put Jace's life in danger. The surgeon had to drill an emergency hole in his skull to allow release of the pressure. Then he had to be kept in a medically induced coma to give his brain every opportunity to heal.

The time between Jace collapsing in her arms and when those blue eyes opened to look at her again were the longest three days of Lillian's life.

She hadn't left his side. Teammates had brought her clean clothes and food and necessities. Lillian wasn't leaving Jace alone.

Because she knew if the roles were reversed, he wouldn't leave her alone, either. She trusted that— trusted *Jace*—with every fiber of her being.

On the third day of Jace's coma, the day they began waking him up, she sat holding his hand, staring at his face. Willing him with every bit of energy she had to open those blue eyes. The doctor had explained that it took each person a different amount of time to wake up. To find his or her way back to consciousness.

But, the doctor also had to warn, on rare occasions they never found their way back.

Jace would. He would find his way out of the fog. She would lead him, the way he'd led her.

She reached over and planted a kiss on his unmoving lips. "I'm here, Eakin. Find your way back to me."

A few hours later Jace still wasn't awake. The doctor had come by twice outside his usual rounds, and although she hadn't said anything negative, Lillian knew she was concerned.

Jace would find his way back to her. He had to.

Molly Humphries-Waterman wheeled her husband through the door in a wheelchair an hour later. Derek was still recovering from his gunshot wounds, but the prognosis was good. It was going to take physical therapy, but Derek would eventually be back to full speed.

But it was yet another member of the Omega Sector team down, thanks to Damien Freihof.

"How's he doing?" Derek asked as Molly went to get them coffee.

"Nothing yet." Lillian had Jace's hand in hers. "The doc says it takes different people different amounts of time to wake up."

"It won't be long. Eakin is strong. And even more, he has someone here waiting who is the most important thing in the world to him."

She reached over and brushed a small lock of hair off Jace's forehead, willing him to open his eyes.

"So you heard Saul Poniard made a full confession?"

She looked over at Derek. "No. I've pretty much just been here. I don't know what's going on."

"I'm sure Steve Drackett will be providing an update to you soon. But yeah, Poniard gave up his whole Manifesto of Change, parts of which had been discovered within the Omega system a couple of weeks ago. Saul had nicknamed himself Guy Fawkes."

"As in the guy who tried to blow up the British parliament?"

"The very same."

Lillian rolled her eyes. "I have to admit, I never saw it. Never really looked past his surfer-boy grin."

"Poniard was setting you up for the fall, Lillian. Making it look like you set up both the explosive device in the City and County Building and the biological weapon canisters that would've gone live with LESS."

"I never dreamed Poniard hated me that much."

Derek shrugged. "Honestly, I don't think he did. I think you were an easy target. No family, no close friends. A loner."

"Someone easy to set up."

Derek smiled. "Not as easy as he and Freihof thought."

"Freihof got away." Frustration still ate at her. She'd been so close to taking him down.

"But with Saul out of the picture we've crippled Freihof in a lot of ways, including the broken nose you gave him. Plus, Ren McClement says there's been some new developments. We'll be hearing more about that soon, I'm sure."

"Good."

"And Daryl Eakin is dead. I know you know that."

Lillian hadn't told Derek many specifics about what had happened in the past with Daryl, but Derek knew it hadn't been good.

She nodded. "I got a second chance to fight my own personal monster, and this time I won. Not everybody gets that sort of second chance."

Derek pointed at Jace. "That man loves you. He would fight your monsters for you."

"I know, but—"

She stopped her sentence as Jace's voice interrupted her from the bed, husky and low. "No. I wouldn't fight your monsters. You can do that yourself. But I'll stand with you as you fight them. Every single time."

Lillian leaped over to him, cupping his cheeks. "That's even better." She smiled, kissing him as she stared into those blue eyes. "Hi. You found your way back to me."

"I always will. No matter how long it takes, I always will."

They would always find their way back to each other.

Lillian slept in the hospital bed with Jace that night.

Maybe he'd been slow to initially come out of the coma, but once he started Jace made much faster progress than was expected. Within a few hours he was sitting up with no dizziness and not long afterward was even taking steps by himself.

Different members of Omega Sector had come by all day to check on them and Derek. To shake Jace's hand and hug Lillian tight. To thank them for a job well done. Even Philip came by, finally stitched up from the wounds Saul had given him. He even smiled and spoke without making anyone mad.

The traitor who had resided inside their family was now gone. Freihof would fall next.

The last visitor was someone Lillian hadn't ever talked to directly in person, but knew about. Ren McClement. Omega's most revered and somewhat notorious agent. In his midforties with brown hair and dark eyes that looked like they never missed a thing.

Rumors were that McClement's specialty was undercover ops. Long-term assignments. The ones no one with family or friends would take. McClement answered to very few people and always got his man, no matter what the cost.

The only thing that people agreed on about Ren McClement was that no one really knew him.

Except Jace. Evidently Jace knew him, given how the two embraced with a strong hug before Ren ruffled Jace's hair.

"Nearly dead wasn't what I was expecting when I brought you on for this mission, Eakin," Ren said as he sat down in the chair on the other side of Jace's bed from Lillian and nodded at her. "Agent Muir."

"Lillian, please."

She enjoyed watching the two men banter with each other for the next couple of hours. Despite insults thrown on both sides, the respect the men had for each other all but permeated the air. Both of them made a point to draw her into the conversation as much as possible.

"I'm glad you two are okay," Ren said. "Your dead brother showing up was…unexpected."

Jace's eyes met hers. "Yeah, for all of us." He turned to Ren. "I'm sorry Freihof got away."

"Well, speaking of dead people being alive, we've had a pretty big development when it comes to Freihof."

"How so?" Lillian asked. She wanted Freihof behind bars so badly she could taste it.

"Evidently Natalie Freihof, Damien's beloved wife whose death is the very reason he's been taking his revenge on Omega Sector, is actually alive."

"What?" Jace and Lillian both said it at the same time.

"Yep. We're not sure if she's working with Freihof or not, but we're going to find out. I *personally* am going to find out."

Ren's dark eyes were so cold Lillian felt a little sympathy for the woman she'd never met.

"Whether she's working with him or not, his obsession with her is the key to drawing him out and trapping him. One way or another she'll help us bring Freihof down. I'll see to it."

Collateral damage sometimes happened in battles like this. But Freihof had to be stopped. If this dead wife could help, Lillian wouldn't argue against it.

"But this is all on me now," Ren said. "You two are just supposed to heal. Jace, I'm sure Steve Drackett's going to be in here any minute now asking you to join the Omega team permanently."

Jace smiled. "Nope, not for me. All I want is to get to my ranch and get it started. I'm out of this game for good."

Ren smiled. "Since your ranch just happens to be forty miles from Omega HQ, I'm sure Steve may still call on your services from time to time."

"I'm thankful for many reasons that my ranch is only forty miles from Omega." Jace turned to Lillian, heat clear in his eyes. "But none of them have a damn thing to do with Steve Drackett."

In the evening after everyone was gone, Lillian settled down in the uncomfortable lounge chair next to Jace, ready to try to get some rest.

She heard the bed shift and the next minute Jace's arms were scooping under her and tucking her in beside him. He lifted her as if he hadn't been stabbed and in a medically induced coma just a few hours earlier.

"Pretty sure heavy lifting isn't a good plan, Eakin," she said, but snuggled into his chest.

"First, not even under the most absurd of circumstance could you be considered heavy lifting. Second, you sleep next to me. Every night from here on out."

She didn't try to move away. There wasn't anywhere she wanted to be besides right next to him. But she couldn't just let his words slide. She had to make sure he knew what he was in for.

"I'm still broken," she whispered. "I know I made it back from the darkness and fought Daryl, but that doesn't end the nightmare for me. There are parts of me that…might never work correctly again. I'm permanently broken, Jace."

She felt his hand slide over her hair. "I've worked with the most elite soldiers in the world and can say that you are stronger and more capable than anybody I've ever known."

"Daryl almost won. I didn't even fight. If you hadn't found a way to call me back…"

His lips rested against her temple. "But you did fight. You fought your way out of the darkness and then you fought Daryl and won. You kept Freihof from killing me and thousands of innocent people."

"My PTSD can get pretty bad. I just want to make sure you know what you're getting into. Before you start saying things like *forever*."

"Then I'm glad I'm about to have a ranch full of animals specifically for people like you."

"I thought you were supposed to be helping soldiers."

"It's for people who need time to put themselves back together. That includes you."

She wrapped her arm around his waist and threw a leg over his hips. "I can't promise I'm ever going to be normal. That I'll ever be like other women."

His thumb reached down and tilted her chin up so he could kiss her. "Thank God. I wouldn't want you any other way than what you are."

"Then you better hurry up and heal so I can get you home and back into a real bed."

"I don't care what bed we're in as long as every day that I wake up, you're in it with me. We have twelve years to make up for. And everything else we'll work through."

"I can't leave my job with Omega."

He laughed. "I wouldn't dare even try to suggest it. It's more than just your job. They're your family."

"You are, too. You always have been."

"And I always will be."

* * * * *

HARLEQUIN

Heartfelt or thrilling, passionate or uplifting—Harlequin is more than just happily-ever-after.

With twelve different series to choose from and new books available every month, you are sure to find stories that will move you, uplift you, inspire and delight you.

Love Harlequin romance?

DISCOVER.

Be the first to find out about promotions,
news and exclusive content!

Facebook.com/HarlequinBooks

Twitter.com/HarlequinBooks

Instagram.com/HarlequinBooks

Pinterest.com/HarlequinBooks

YouTube.com/HarlequinBooks

ReaderService.com

EXPLORE.

Sign up for the Harlequin e-newsletter and
download a free book from any series at
TryHarlequin.com

CONNECT.

Join our Harlequin community to
share your thoughts and connect
with other romance readers!
Facebook.com/groups/HarlequinConnection

Get 4 FREE REWARDS!

We'll send you 2 FREE Books plus 2 FREE Mystery Gifts.

Harlequin Intrigue books are action-packed stories that will keep you on the edge of your seat. Solve the crime and deliver justice at all costs.

FREE
Value Over
$20

YES! Please send me 2 FREE Harlequin Intrigue novels and my 2 FREE gifts (gifts are worth about $10 retail). After receiving them, if I don't wish to receive any more books, I can return the shipping statement marked "cancel." If I don't cancel, I will receive 6 brand-new novels every month and be billed just $4.99 each for the regular-print edition or $5.99 each for the larger-print edition in the U.S., or $5.74 each for the regular-print edition or $6.49 each for the larger-print edition in Canada. That's a savings of at least 12% off the cover price! It's quite a bargain! Shipping and handling is just 50¢ per book in the U.S. and $1.25 per book in Canada.* I understand that accepting the 2 free books and gifts places me under no obligation to buy anything. I can always return a shipment and cancel at any time. The free books and gifts are mine to keep no matter what I decide.

Choose one: ☐ **Harlequin Intrigue Regular-Print** (182/382 HDN GNXC)   ☐ **Harlequin Intrigue Larger-Print** (199/399 HDN GNXC)

Name (please print)

Address   Apt. #

City   State/Province   Zip/Postal Code

Email: Please check this box ☐ if you would like to receive newsletters and promotional emails from Harlequin Enterprises ULC and its affiliates. You can unsubscribe anytime.

Mail to the Reader Service:
IN U.S.A.: P.O. Box 1341, Buffalo, NY 14240-8531
IN CANADA: P.O. Box 603, Fort Erie, Ontario L2A 5X3

Want to try 2 free books from another series? Call 1-800-873-8635 or visit www.ReaderService.com.

---

*Terms and prices subject to change without notice. Prices do not include sales taxes, which will be charged (if applicable) based on your state or country of residence. Canadian residents will be charged applicable taxes. Offer not valid in Quebec. This offer is limited to one order per household. Books received may not be as shown. Not valid for current subscribers to Harlequin Intrigue books. All orders subject to approval. Credit or debit balances in a customer's account(s) may be offset by any other outstanding balance owed by or to the customer. Offer available while quantities last.

Your Privacy—Your information is being collected by Harlequin Enterprises ULC, operating as Reader Service. For a complete summary of the information we collect, how we use this information and to whom it is disclosed, please visit our privacy notice located at corporate.harlequin.com/privacy-notice. From time to time we may also exchange your personal information with reputable third parties. If you wish to opt out of this sharing of your personal information, please visit readerservice.com/consumerschoice or call 1-800-873-8635. **Notice to California Residents**—Under California law, you have specific rights to control and access your data. For more information on these rights and how to exercise them, visit corporate.harlequin.com/california-privacy.

HI20R2